A Terrible Unrest

A Terrible Unrest

Philip Duke

TOP HAT BOOKS

Winchester, UK
Washington, USA

First published by Top Hat Books, 2014
Top Hat Books is an imprint of John Hunt Publishing Ltd., Laurel House, Station Approach,
Alresford, Hants, SO24 9JH, UK
office1@jhpbooks.net
www.johnhuntpublishing.com

For distributor details and how to order please visit the 'Ordering' section on our website.

ISBN: 978 1 78279 437 0

A CIP catalogue record for this book is available from the British Library.

Design: Stuart Davies

Printed and bound by CPI Group (UK) Ltd, Croydon, CR0 4YY

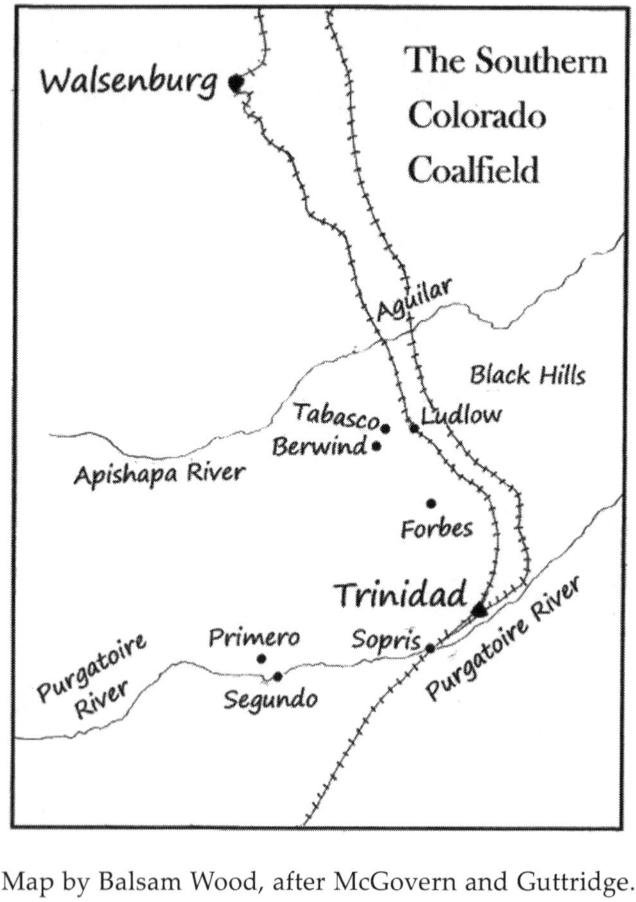

Map by Balsam Wood, after McGovern and Guttridge.

Prologue

Southern Colorado

"The place is so peaceful now," the old lady said, mostly to herself. It was a fine June day but still she pulled her coat tight, as if trying to guard against something unseen. "It's all so peaceful now, even I find it hard to imagine it took place on this very spot."

The teenage girl at her side looked at her grandmother. "What happened, Gran? Tell me. You've been acting kinda' strange since you got up this morning."

Her grandmother smiled and took her hand. "Oh, honey, it happened all so long ago when I was a little girl just a bit younger than you."

"Gran, I know it's something to do with when you were a little girl. Daddy told me last month that's why we were coming here, because of what happened to you, and your mom and dad. He wouldn't tell me anything more, said that was up to you. But, Gran, it's gotta' be important for us to come all the way here."

"Well, your dad is right. It is important. You know, don't you, that my mom and dad were from Crete. You know, in Greece. I've shown you pictures of the villages they came from. Remember?" The little girl nodded. "Let's go for a walk, honey, and maybe that'll make it easier for me to tell you." Her grandmother smiled again, a smile that let you know that all was right in your world.

The girl slipped her arm though her grandmother's and together they walked into the Colorado prairie. Apart from the muted noise of the traffic on the highway a mile away and the occasional chirrup of a bluebird, all was quiet. Even the wind seemed in thrall to the place and held its tongue. The flat grasslands stretched away endlessly. Only to the west was the landscape different, for there, dissected by small valleys and canyons, lay the foothills, a prelude to the high Rockies a few miles beyond.

As they picked their way among the gopher holes and mounds that dotted the field, and tried their best to avoid the cow pats, baked hard and crusty by the wind and sun, the two of them came across old broken bottles and bits of rusted tin cans, a fragment of a broken plate or the handle of a china cup. The old lady would sometimes stop and look around her. She was seeing something else in the prairie field, something that nobody else could see, something that, by the look in her eyes, was ineffably sad.

They stopped again. The older of the two looked first west and then east, as though trying to orient herself to some unknown point. "Yes, I think this is where our tent was." The girl pursed her brow. Then, the old lady nodded slightly to the south. "Yes," she whispered to herself, "that's where Sally and Frank's tent must have been. Sally was my best friend you know, I played with her every day. And Frank was such a fun little boy, he used to tease his little sister no end, sometimes make her cry until his mom laid down the law and he had to stop. But even though he teased her, you know it was Frank who was always there to help her when she got into trouble; it was Frank who…"

She stopped in mid-sentence and could no longer stop the tears welling in her eyes. She began to take short labored breaths, and her granddaughter became a little frightened, because Gran had had problems with her breathing for the last few years. Although the granddaughter was barely in her teens, still she held her grandmother's waist as though her own body might just for a while bear the burden her grandmother felt so heavily.

"Are you okay, Gran? We can go back to the car anytime. Daddy can have you back in the hotel in twenty minutes."

"Don't worry, sweetie, just the ghosts of yesterday saying hello to me." She crossed herself, and continued on across the flat expressionless landscape.

They came to a steep arroyo. It was about fifty feet deep and its edge was covered with the debris that they'd seen all across the prairie field – broken crockery, metal and smashed glass. Here it was so thick on the ground it looked like a garbage dump. The old lady looked into the arroyo's depths and shuddered.

A little further on they came to the remains of a large concrete-lined water cistern dug into the ground. It had filled in over the years and wild prairie grasses now grew where fresh water had once been stored. The cistern was about ten yards from the railroad line that still carried freight up and down the Front Range of the Rockies. In the distance, as it made its way down from Denver, they heard a train's horn, the most mournful and lonely sound in the world. The old lady looked into the cistern and she crossed herself again.

Finally, they completed their circuit of the prairie field and came back to the car, where her son patiently waited.

"I think I can look at it now, Nik," she whispered.

Together with her son and granddaughter she walked from the make-shift parking lot, through an iron gate and into a small fenced paddock. It contained a granite memorial bearing a list of names, and two statues, one of a man, the other of a woman holding a child. On the ground nearby, lay a large metal panel hinged to a concrete flange. The son lifted the panel to reveal a set of steps going down about six feet into a concrete-lined cellar.

"This was the Death Pit." Her voice became almost inaudible. "Or at least that's what it's called now. Of course, it wasn't like this years ago. I suppose the union wanted to make sure it was never filled in."

Nik embraced his mother, held her tight, and finally her tears came and wouldn't stop, as memories flooded back into the old woman's mind. Sob after sob wracked her body, and the granddaughter clung to her, afraid of what her grandma, brave and strong, had become.

Finally, the tears slowed. She looked at her granddaughter.

"Maria, this place is called Ludlow and the day after tomorrow there is going to be a memorial service for what happened here years ago. Men died here, and innocent women and children, too, some of them younger than you. Murdered, if the truth be known. They didn't want to be rich, just to have a decent place to live and work."

She took her granddaughter in her arms and gently held her. "I'm fine now, sweetheart. Let's go back to the car, your dad can drive us back to Trinidad and I'll have a cup of tea before dinner. And then I'll try and tell you what happened here all those years ago."

Back at the hotel, the old lady was true to her word, and over two cups of tea that stretched for the better part of an hour, she told Maria and Nik what had happened on that prairie field all those years ago.

"Gran," Maria yelled, "you should write this down."

The old lady chuckled. "That's exactly what granpa always said, too. But, you know I never really had time, what with helping in the business and bringing up your dad. He was quite the handful, you know."

Nik smiled. He'd heard this complaint before. "Ma, she's right, you know. That's a heck of a story."

The old lady smiled again. "Well, as it happens, I haven't been completely idle these past few years. And one of the reasons I wanted to come back here after all this time was to see what the place looked like, to see if my memory was pretty close to what it was really like.

"Look, I want to be around a lot longer, so don't go all sad on me, but I'm no spring chicken and when I do join Granpa, God rest his soul, you'll find a little parcel waiting for you, little Maria, at my lawyer's. Don't worry, he knows all about it. You can do with it what you want."

And with that, the old lady stood up and declared firmly that all this talking had made her ravenous and she was going to the restaurant even if they weren't.

Part One
Crete 1900

1

The shotgun blasts rolled through the valley. The men lowered their guns and looked at each other expectantly. In the distance they heard the chapel bell toll midnight, and then all the villagers in unison shouted *"Christos Anesti,"* Christ is Risen. *"Alithos Anesti,"* Truly He is Risen. Their voices filled the small village square in a paean of hope. As the villagers yelled the timeless litany, young men lit a bonfire that quickly turned the darkness of the night into day, and everybody watched the flames hungrily devour the life-size Judas effigy perched atop the pyre. The men broke out their raki flasks and toasted the resurrection of the Lord, their God. *Truly he is Risen.* And truly this year, they prayed, things would be better.

The smell of lamb and goats baking in the village ovens made everybody hungry and they nibbled on kaltsounia, delicious cheese pies. Eagerly they anticipated the feast that awaited them, for at least tonight and tomorrow nobody in the village would go hungry.

At the edge of the square a small man stood alone. He called out, "Spiro, drink with me."

Spiro Andrakis dutifully obeyed his father. In one gulp, Spiro tossed down a tumbler of the clear liquid and felt its fire burn its way to his stomach. As the bonfire crackled and threw huge sparks into the night sky, Spiro looked at his father and smiled wistfully. He remembered his father as a strong and vibrant farmer; how he would lift him onto his shoulders as they walked out of the village to tend to their olive groves or to make sure the flock was safe for the night. Those were the memories that Spiro wanted to etch into his mind forever. But now all Spiro saw was a broken husk of a man. His father was only in his early forties, but his back was bent and his face creased with the lines of a lifetime of worry and hunger. Spiro knew that if he stayed on

Crete his father's fate awaited him.

Spiro was almost twenty-one and still retained the strength and vigor of youth. He was not a tall man, few Cretans were, but his shoulders were broad. His round face was not yet lined by the cares of living, and his smile was still genuine. He was popular around the village and not a few girls had dreamt longingly of him, but he had remained unattached.

"Drink with me, son, for I do not know when we will drink again." Spiro tossed back another tumbler and saw that his father's eyes were wet with tears.

"Don't say that, Papa, you know I'll only be in America long enough to make my fortune and then I'll return. I promised you and Mama, and I will keep that vow."

"No, Spiro, don't make promises you may not be able to keep."

Spiro held his silence and simply looked away.

At that moment, Manoli, Spiro's best friend from childhood, came over, carrying a glass of raki that he kept sloshing onto the ground, try as he might to keep it all in the glass. "Ah, there you are," Manoli slurred his words, at the same time inadvertently spraying his drink all over Spiro's father. "Ah, there you are. Why don't we fill our glasses and drink to this glorious day. For He is risen, Spiro, He is risen."

Spiro's father walked over to a group of older villagers who were standing at the door of the church. He shook their hands and said his farewells. Spiro deliberately turned his head away, but out of the corner of his eye he could see his father look back at him and wipe his eyes. Not for the first time, Spiro wondered if he was doing the right thing, leaving when his family needed him. But Spiro also knew that there was little future for him on the island; it was well-nigh impossible to make a living, and leaving, hard though it was, was for the best.

Spiro issued a command. "Manoli, get me drunk. Make me forget what I'm supposed to do tomorrow. Please."

Manoli hugged his friend. "I won't do that. I've seen you drunk. First you get sad, and then you get mad, and then all hell breaks loose. No thank you, not tonight." He laughed. "Come on. Let's see where the others are."

Spiro allowed himself to be led away from the crowd of villagers in search of their friends. The two of them walked up the narrow lane past Spiro's house. It was attached to the village's wine and olive press, and in better years the Andrakis family had been relatively wealthy. But hard times had hit the island again. Now, although the family still pressed the harvest, prices were so low as to make it not worth their while. Only the duty of tradition kept them at it year after year after year.

Manoli and Spiro came into a small square at the southern end of the village where they met three of their friends coming to celebrate around the bonfire. They were carrying shotguns and laughing at the noise they had made through the valley right before the church bell began to peal. Despite his wish fifteen minutes earlier, Spiro chose to stay sober. He knew that he always became maudlin when he drank too much, and sometimes, Manoli was right, he became violent. This, together with what lay in store for him tomorrow, did not make the party the one his friends had planned for him. Within an hour, Spiro made his farewells, promising he would see them all before he set off tomorrow. Alone and sad beyond a depth he had ever felt before, he made his way home.

He walked up the alley, lit by the lanterns the family had set out earlier that evening. They were still up when he arrived home, all awaiting his return. His mother was sitting in front of the fire stirring a pot of boiled lamb; his father was next to her, cleaning his shotgun; and his young sister, Anastasia, was busy laying out sweet biscuits.

The walk home in the crisp spring air had cleared Spiro's head of the little liquor he had drunk, but he couldn't shake his sadness. He noticed his mother had been crying, for her eyes were red. She put on a smile when Spiro came through the threshold.

He kissed her gently on her forehead. He long ago realized that like her husband, his mother had been beaten into submission by life on the island. Her every day was an unceasing struggle to keep her family fed and clothed.

"Christos Anesti, Mama."

"Alithos anesti, pethi mou," his mother replied. Truly he is risen, my child.

"I'm glad you've come back so soon," she whispered. "When Papa said you'd gone off with Manoli, we didn't know if we'd ever see you again." She tried to smile, but it was too difficult for her. Anastasia offered her family a plate of sweets, and Spiro took one even though he was not hungry.

The four of them sat in silence in front of the little fireplace, its flames throwing their shadows onto the walls like so many ghosts in a macabre dance of death.

Spiro woke before dawn and lay there for a few moments. He could hear nothing but his father's snores from the other end of the house, and through the thin curtain separating his bed from Anastasia's he heard only the gentle murmuring of his little sister as she slept peacefully on.

He remembered how as a child he would curl up in this very bed with the sheets pulled up over his head, hoping against hope that he could stay there forever, safe in its warmth. He looked up at the stone arch that ran the whole length of the house, thinking of how he would count the stones until he fell asleep. But the pain of that childhood memory was too sweet to bear, and so slowly, taking care not to make any noise, he got up. He dressed quickly and silently, his clothes and the few personal possessions he was taking with him wrapped in a thick cloth at the side of his bed. While he had promised his family that he would wake them before he left, he knew that it would all be too painful and that his family felt the same way.

Spiro looked around. How many generations of Andrakises had walked this floor? He drew out a small envelope from his pocket and placed it on the small table by the fireplace. In the envelope was a letter explaining why he had left the way he had. "Until I come back," the letter ended. "Please pray for me as I will pray for you." The village priest had helped Spiro write the letter and would be able to read it to his parents. As the words *mama* and *papa* formed in his brain, Spiro choked with sadness. He feared deep in his heart that his letter was a lie meant to ease his family's pain. That he would never see them again. That he would never again tend sheep with his father. That he would never again hear his mother scolding him for stealing a piece of stew before she had put the pot on the table. And that never again would he lift little Anastasia onto his broad shoulders and carry her down the village street to the church on a Sunday morning, or tickle her nose with a blade of grass as they lay under an olive tree in the hot summer sun.

Quietly he picked up his cloth bag and opened the door. He turned around and one last time surveyed the living room. He slowly took the picture in as though he wanted to keep it fresh in his memory forever. The olive wood glowed in the fireplace. A small photograph of his grandfather taken just before his death a few years ago stared grimly at him, as though he disapproved of what he was doing. The lingering smell of lamb, sweet biscuits and olive oil filled his nostrils. Spiro Andrakis crossed himself, kissed the small icon to the Panagia, Mary Mother of God, which hung by the door, and stepped across the threshold.

At the other end of the house, in bed behind a curtain, his mother had lain awake most of the night, dreading this moment, and she heard the click of the door as Spiro gently closed it. She rolled over onto her side and sobbed quietly to herself. Her only son had gone.

Spiro had the village to himself. He managed a half-smile as he heard the neighbor's cock crow. He remembered how the villagers would laugh that if the damned thing ever crowed when it was supposed to they'd all be dead, because a miracle had happened and the Second Coming of The Lord was on them.

Spiro didn't have to meet the agent of the shipping company until six that evening, in the port of Chania, about twenty miles to the west. He wanted his last trip on his homeland to be a special one, one that would allow him one final look. So, instead of walking north and then skirting the coast, Spiro immediately cut west from his village and crossed the low lying hills that ran to the sea. He had figured that the journey would take most of the day, as he intended to take his time. The young Cretan could just make out ahead of him the silhouette of the Turkish fort on the headland for which he was making. After several hours of walking he began the final steep climb to the crest of the hill and he could feel the light around him getting stronger. He stopped and turned back. To the east the sun had risen fully over the hills and bathed the olive-grove plains below. Breathless from the exertion, Spiro sat down on a rock and lit a cigarette. Before him lay the Bay of Souda, the rising sun turning the sea a deep red color that reminded Spiro of the local wine his family had made for generations.

He let the nicotine seep deeply into his lungs, his eyes following a steamer that was making its way slowly out of the bay into the open Aegean. *Soon you'll be on a ship like that,* he told himself. *First Piraeus, then Patras, the priest said it is on the west coast of the mainland, and then New York.* Suddenly, he became excited by what lay before him. He, Spiro Andrakis, was off to America. And maybe he would make his fortune, and then after all maybe he could come back to his little village, marry a good girl, raise a huge family and keep everyone safe and warm for the rest of their lives. *You were sad last night,* he chided himself, *but that was last night. Papa was wrong. And you were, as well. You will come back one day and drink wine with him.*

Spiro jumped up, eager to be on his way. Almost as an afterthought, he looked back, bade his little valley farewell and began the descent to Chania.

While Spiro sat with his family that last night, in a village south of Chania another family was getting ready for sleep. The Easter celebrations had tired them, and Niko and Anastasia Petroulakis began their nightly ritual. Anastasia snuffed out the oil lamps and Niko made sure the fire in the hearth was properly damped down for the night. Their eighteen-year-old daughter, Maria, had felt a tension between them all through the Easter service, and she had gone to her room, as soon as they had arrived home. She was tired, too, and wanted all her energies for tomorrow.

After they had finished their nightly chores, Anastasia took a small oil lamp, lit it and placed it on the rough table that her father had made as part of her dowry. She sat down in front of the fire and looked at her husband. Her words were gentle but firm.

"Husband, let me tell you what you yourself said months ago. It was you who said that we could no longer get enough from our little piece of land to make ends meet. It was you who told us that Greece was never going to get any better. It was you who said America was our only chance."

Niko resignedly poked the fire in their small living room as though trying to find something to do other than respond. Finally he nodded. "I know, my dear, I know. And it's true. But my family has lived here forever, and…" He let the last sentence hang in the air, and the smoke from the dying fire snatched it and carried it up into the black sky above.

Anastasia knew what he was thinking, the way she'd known his every thought since they'd married twenty-five years ago. His thoughts were of their only son, Dimitri, who had died fighting the Turks just a few years earlier, and whose bones lay in the village graveyard along with those of countless other generations of their family.

"I know your mind, husband. But on his sainted grave, I believe that Dimitri, could he speak, would tell us we're doing the right thing. He would tell us that slowly dying of starvation is no life. We have little Maria to think of. Dimitri would tell us that, too."

Niko Petroulakis could only nod. He knew what they were doing was right, but that didn't make it any easier. His wife stood up and laid her hand on his shoulder. He forced a smile. "You are right, wife. Come on, let's go to bed. Tomorrow we go to America."

"Maria, Maria, Maria, come on, girl, we need to go," Anastasia scolded her daughter. "Don't you realize that big ships don't wait for anybody."

"Oh, hush, woman, leave her be." Her father jumped to the daughter's defense, but smiled at his wife nonetheless.

"I'm coming, Mama." Maria's young voice was enthusiastic and her infectious laugh cheered her mother and father. Gone were the uncertainties of yesterday evening. All three of them were ready to move to the New World.

An hour earlier, Niko's brother and his wife had joined them for they too were off to America, and Maria impatiently watched the two men load their small set of trunks onto the cart that their neighbor Thanasi had offered them for the journey to Chania. The three men tied the trunks down tight, for the road they were to take was bumpy and dangerous in places. Anastasia and Maria walked around their tiny home one last time. As they came out, wiping their eyes, Thanasi teased them. "No crying, ladies. I wish I was going with you. In two years' time, you'll be back here, rich Americans, and then you probably won't even speak to poor old Thanasi."

Maria rushed to him held the old man tight. "I'll never forget you. I mean it. I won't even when we're rich."

Now that the cart was loaded, there was no need any more for them to delay their departure. Thanasi would come with them to Chania, so that he could take the cart back home.

Niko had estimated that the trip would take them until late afternoon. The two families looked at the weather ahead of them. The clouds were moving in from the west, but at most they would have a little rain. Niko and Thanasi sat up front, and Maria, her mother and her aunt made themselves as comfortable as they could amongst the suitcases, while Maria's uncle walked alongside the cart. Thanasi slapped the donkey's rump, and the small company set off. The cart had no springs and the wheels were worn, so the three women felt every bump in the road. After an hour, Maria cried out, "Papa, I'm jumping out. I can't take it anymore." She laughed and with childish abandon leapt over the side of the cart. Even the light drizzle that had begun to fall did not dampen her spirits.

"That's better," she yelled. As the teenager skipped along the side of the road, she marveled again at what she and her family were about to do. *Go to America, can you believe it? America, where everybody is rich. Go on a huge ship. America. Meet Cousin Yanni there, get jobs in New York, and live like royalty.* At least that's what his last letter said. As she passed the time daydreaming, she picked some of the first spring flowers, beautiful purple and yellow on tall stalks. Maria knitted herself a small garland. "See, Mama, now I'm a real princess. Like I'll be in America."

2

The walk tired Spiro more than he had imagined. As he dropped to the coast he passed the new docks at Souda with huge naval vessels rocking at anchor, their guns pointing out menacingly like the porcupine he had once seen in a book the village priest had. Carrying on, he finally caught his first glimpse of the city walls. Entering the city gate he walked towards the harbor, then past the old arsenali where the Venetians had once stored their galleys. Spiro had only ever been to Chania once before and he was nervous at its size and strangeness. Although his stomach was growling he wanted to make sure everything for his trip was settled before he would allow himself the luxury of a meal, and so he steadfastly ignored the temptation of the numerous tavernas that fringed the small harbor.

When he had bought the ticket months ago, Spiro had been told to look for a large office, flying an American flag, by the harbor mosque. This was the office of the Greek-American Shipping Company, and it was here he would find the agent who would start him and the other immigrants on their long voyage to the New World. Spiro was dismayed when he couldn't see any office that fitted the description. Dismay turned to fear when he thought this might have been a big fraud and that even now some cheat in Chania was laughing at how those stupid Cretans had given him their money, thinking they were off to America. As he stood there, unsure what to do, a young boy of about ten came up to him. The urchin had no shoes, and his clothes were tattered beyond repair. Holding his hand out, he asked Spiro for an Easter alm, for something to eat. Spiro dug into his pocket, but at the last minute, before he flicked the drachma coin at the boy, he stopped and said, "Boy, you can eat, but only if you tell me where the Greek-American office is."

The boy blinked, as though he hadn't heard Spiro correctly.

"Office, are you joking? Office? How about that tent over there?" The boy pointed behind the mosque, and there Spiro saw a small, circular gray-colored tent. Its shape told him that it had once been used by the Army, but even the soldiers had apparently given up on it and sold it on. Spiro flipped the boy his coin and walked on over.

Spiro's heart sank. *Is this the office of the great Greek-American Shipping Company? Is this what's going to get me to the promised land?* As he got nearer, he noticed that something appeared to be hanging from the center pole of the tent. It was two flags, one Greek and one American. The breeze had wrapped the two of them around each other.

Spiro was wondering what to do next, when he heard someone shouting. He turned around to see a small, rather portly man, waving at him frantically, trying to run as best he could and shouting something. The hubbub of the harbor made it mostly unintelligible, but Spiro did hear the words, *American, wait, coming*. Now that he had Spiro's attention, the man slowed down.

"Welcome, my friend," the man panted at Spiro, as at last he made it to the tent. "Please, just a minute, let me get my breath. I am the agent for the Greek-American Shipping Company." The man's demeanor instilled as much confidence in Spiro as the tent had. He was in his fifties and continuously mopped his brow with a large red handkerchief. He wore a battered felt fez which had seen much better days. One half of his shirt front was hanging out of his trousers as the shirt did battle with the man's stomach to see who could stay in the longest, and his suspenders seemed about to give up the ghost at any minute as his trousers bobbed up and down on his waist at an alarming rate. Spiro couldn't help but chuckle. "Allow me to introduce myself. My name is George."

Spiro noticed that he used the American version of his name. That made Spiro feel a little better; perhaps the man had actually been to America.

"I take it, young man, you are sailing tonight?"

Spiro nodded. "Here is my ticket."

The man looked at it and then walked into the tent. He came out a few minutes later, with a large bundle of papers.

"Spiro, can I call you Spiro, these are the papers you need. Guard them with your life. There are three tickets, one from Chania to Athens, one to Patras, and then the last is to New York. Everything is in order. Also, there's some papers for the immigration people. Don't worry, everything is in order. Yes, everything is in order." Spiro didn't like the way George kept repeating that phrase; it was as if he was trying to convince himself as much as Spiro.

Spiro looked over the papers. They didn't mean much to him; he wasn't much good at reading, but the fancy picture at the top of the papers of a large boat, two flags and what he thought was the Statue of Liberty at least made the papers look official.

"Er, what do I do now?"

"Well, you wait, Spiro, you wait. See that boat over there?" He pointed to a small wooden caique anchored at the harbor mouth. It looked very small, thought Spiro. "That's our boat," the agent continued. "We can board at nine tonight. Should be in Athens in three or four days, good weather and God willing. Don't worry, everything is in order." There was that phrase again. "Until then, why don't you join the rest of our little party. Most of them are in one of the tavernas where you came in." Spiro didn't know what else to do, so he thanked the agent and went in search of food and drink.

After walking an hour, Maria and her family had left the valley and arrived at the wide fertile plain around Chania. It was full of olive trees, vineyards and smallholdings that looked much more prosperous than their own. Below lay the city. Maria made out the domes of the Orthodox churches and the Moslem minarets, as well as the huge mansions once owned by wealthy Venetians before the Ottomans had occupied the island. And beyond, where the sparkling Aegean began, she saw the majestic curve of the old harbor wall with the centuries-old lighthouse standing at its seaward end, their destination. Her feet were sore, and she wanted to get there as quickly as possible so that she could rest. But it took the party another two hours of walking before Maria could finally sit down.

"Maria, go sit over there while we see the man about the tickets." Maria's mother pointed to a small stone bench against a wall. Maria nodded and gratefully did as she was told, glad to take the pressure off her aching feet. As she rested she looked around her and took in the picture. The harbor was crammed with fishing vessels. The fishermen sat in the shade by their boats, mending nets or chatting as they got ready for their evening expeditions. Excitement overcoming her sore feet, Maria decided to take a closer look at a freshly painted caique. As she walked past a seedy-looking tavern she heard a voice.

"Hey, darlin', you look lost. Come over here, we'll help you." Five French sailors were sitting at a table outside the taverna, clearly enjoying themselves by the number of empty wine jugs on their table. Maria didn't understand what they were saying, but she knew from their looks that it wasn't good. Her face colored and she hurried on.

"Come on, honey, we'll look after you." One of them stood up and ran the ten paces to her. He grabbed her arm from behind and tried to pull her around to face him. "You need a drink, come over here."

Maria was terrified. Nobody had ever grabbed her like this before. She tried to pull away but the sailor's grip was too strong.

As the sailor began to drag her back to his friends, a hand clamped down on his arm. Maria heard someone firmly say in Greek, "Malaka, ghamisou. Jerk-off, fuck yourself. She's my sister."

Maria paled; she had heard Thanasi swear like that, but only once, when a tax collector had tried to get a bribe off him.

The sailor turned to face the intruder. Maria saw the Frenchman flinch. She looked at the stranger and saw why the sailor was afraid. The other man was small, but his barrel chest showed that he could be more than a handful in a fight. But worst was the stranger's eyes. They were inhuman, nothing in them but a cold, lifeless stare. Maria shivered and involuntarily crossed herself.

The Frenchman took the chance to escape. The other sailors stood up to help him but he waved them down. "Hey, sorry, didn't know." He let go of Maria's arm and hurried back to the group. He said something and laughed. The group laughed back, but whether at him or with him Maria couldn't tell.

Now that the crisis was over, Maria felt tears beginning to roll down her cheeks. *I must look quite pathetic,* she told herself. The man who had rescued her now started to walk away, as though embarrassed by what he'd done, but Maria called to him. "Thank you for what you did. I..." She wanted to say more, but she couldn't think of anything else.

The man stopped and turned back to her. "I'm sorry I swore, I don't normally, but, you know, if you were my sister, well..." He hesitated. "You look like you could do with a glass of water. Where are your parents? You shouldn't be here alone."

Maria started to explain, but it seemed it would take too long, so she simply said, "Oh, they'll be along soon."

"Well, that's good. Like I said, you shouldn't be here alone."

The stranger smiled at her, and Maria saw his eyes twinkle in a way that quite took her breath away, quite different from a minute ago. Although he was only a few years older than Maria, there was something about him that made her feel safe and, if she was honest with herself, different in ways that both excited and frightened her at the same time. And it just wasn't what he'd done to the sailor. No, it was something else, and she had no idea what it was.

Maria heard her father calling her name, and she turned to see him running towards the two of them. He took Maria's arm and was about to say something when Maria interjected. "Papa, it's fine, this man helped me. I was silly, he helped me." Niko looked doubtful but he nodded at the stranger nonetheless.

"Come on, child, I have our tickets." Niko saw the man's ticket sticking out of his jacket pocket. He gestured, "You off to America, too?"

The man nodded.

"Well, I suppose we'd better get to know each other. I am Niko Petroulakis. My daughter, Maria."

"My name is Spiro, Spiro Andrakis. I am pleased to meet you."

Part Two
Southern Colorado
June 1913

3

The two of them knew what they were doing. They were old hands at this. Practice makes perfect. They had chosen the victim two hours earlier and now it was time to act. Patiently they waited for him to leave the bar. He was about thirty-five years old; all they knew about him was that he was a miner, perhaps Italian. They didn't know his name, nor did they need to. They saw him stagger slightly, stop and then look around slowly as though trying to clear his head before proceeding. They watched him walk slowly up the main street of the town. They waited as he slipped into the shadows of a building. They saw him fumble with his fly buttons, take a satisfying piss, button his trousers back up, and then continue on his way. At the point where the road left the town and continued on into the canyon, his two followers quickened their pace.

Right on time, a third man stepped out of the shadows of the trees. He acted drunk. He fumbled for a cigarette and asked the miner for a match. The miner obliged and was about to say something when the man coldly and efficiently drove his fist into his stomach. As the miner doubled up in pain, he received a knee in his chin. He dropped to the ground.

The other two caught up with them and picked the miner up. They walked him back into the shadows and held him erect while the third man took out a bar of metal about an inch across from his pocket. It had been bent back double upon itself. He held it so that one half was in the palm of his right hand and the other curved over his knuckles. He nodded to his accomplices and then he began to punch the miner, slowly and systematically. He started on the chest and then went to the arms but he never touched the face. The miner started to scream but one of the men put his hand over his mouth. None of the three attackers had yet said a word.

The miner groaned, barely able to stand up. He had almost passed out but the three of them knew their job. They waited until he had regained some of his senses. And then they began again.

This time the man hit harder. He heard a rib crack, then a second. Almost time now to stop.

Two of them continued to hold the miner tight. He sagged forward from their grip. The man with the bar took the victim's hair, yanked his head back and looked straight into his face. The miner stared into his torturer's eyes. He felt fear like he had never known before, a fear that turned his testicles to liquid. He felt warm slimy shit sliding down the inside of his trousers and sour vomit rising up his gullet.

The man holding the miner's hair spoke the only words he would ever say to the victim. "We saw you leave that union meeting. If you go near the union again, you'll remember this as a picnic." The miner hesitated. "Fuckin' wop. Do you understand?" He spoke slowly as though talking to a child. The miner nodded. The man let go of his victim's hair and at the same time crashed a powerhouse punch straight into his face. He heard the cartilage and gristle snap as the nose splayed over the miner's cheek. Blood splattered his face. They let him fall to the ground. He didn't move.

The three of them looked at each other. "Come on," one of them said, "still time for a beer."

It was a long way from Crete to Colorado, but Spiro Andrakis and Maria Petroulakis had made it. The hardness of the Atlantic voyage, the disappointments of New York, whose streets they quickly discovered were not paved with gold, Spiro's long courtship before their marriage was allowed by her father, and then the long train journey to the coalfields of southern Colorado seemed several lifetimes away.

What once had been the pristine and harshly beautiful foothills of the Southern Rockies was now an industrial wasteland where lived and worked thousands of miners and their families, most of them recent immigrants from southern and Eastern Europe. The Colorado Fuel and Iron Company, a part of the Rockefeller financial empire, was the largest of the coal companies in southern Colorado and employed over 14,000 miners. The coalmines and their towns were strung along the eastward-running canyons that crossed the foothills. The mine entrances were dug into the canyon walls that rose up two hundred feet or more.

Together with Anna, their ten-year-old daughter, Spiro and Maria lived in the town of Berwind, situated right in the middle of the biggest coalmine in southern Colorado. Berwind was not really a town at all, just a collection of houses on the floor of the canyon, some built by the Colorado Fuel and Iron Company and rented out to the miners, others jerry built on company land. Besides the houses, there were mine offices, a schoolhouse, a jail and two general stores. And, of course, the mine workings: the ever-hungry tipples, their mouths always open for their daily feeding of coal, the mountains of waste slag and coal awaiting transportation to the ovens for processing into coke for the steel mills in Pueblo sixty miles to the north, overwhelming noise most of the time as trucks moved coal from one place to another, the trains ferrying materials up and down the canyon, the horses, donkeys and automobiles, their fumes adding to the pall of yellow smog that shrouded the whole valley. The small streams that cut through the canyon ran black with coal dust and, if the latrines backed up, with something much worse. Here lived seven hundred men, women and children.

Maria knew that Spiro hated mining, but it was the only job he could find with even the promise of decent pay, and she loved him for hardly ever complaining about his lot in life. Still, it was a letdown for both of them after the promises they had made each other on their voyage to America.

Mining was one of the most dangerous jobs in the world, and also one of the most physically demanding. The mineshafts and work rooms, where the miners pick-axed the coal from the seams, were rough cut, and standing and walking in the mine passages for hours on end meant that a miner's boots bore the brunt of that work. The soles could only be replaced so many times and once the uppers had worn thin the boots had to be thrown away. The constant physical demands of digging at the coal face destroyed boots and clothes even faster than it destroyed the men who wore them.

Spiro desperately needed new boots. He had saved up for them for months and now that he had enough money he marched down to the company store, family in tow. Maria could see the disappointment in his face as soon as the shopkeeper told him that they didn't have any boots in his size.

"Never mind, Maria, let's go to town. We'll go for the day and we can buy little Anna that pistachio ice cream she loves."

Although her birth name was Anastasia, Maria and Spiro always called her Anna. "We're all Americans now," they once grandly told her. "Citizens of the greatest country on earth, so we should act like Americans." So, Anna the little girl became. Not that she minded, for like her mama said, Anastasia was a mouthful for anybody, let alone a ten-year-old girl. Spiro and Maria's English was not very good and they spoke in Greek a lot of the time. But they always insisted that family talk be in English as much as possible, so that Anna could practice and perhaps sound not quite so foreign. In truth, Anna's English was far better than her parents' thanks to her schooling in Berwind. Consequently, conversations between the three were a combination of Greek and English; Anna precociously called it Greeklish. Anna still carried, even with her meager diet, the remains of her baby fat, but she was beginning to show the same beauty as her mother. Her face was developing the contours that would set her apart from other women for the rest of her life, and her hair was gaining a lustrous, blue-black sheen to it. Maria paid special attention to Anna's hair, washing it more than Anna liked and never failing to comb it for ten minutes every day.

"Anna," her mother more than once had chastised her, "I can't dress you in lovely clothes, but with this hair, you don't need them. So, hush, little girl, and let me finish."

Maria wasn't too keen on Spiro's plan to buy new boots. "Look, Spiro, it's not good to buy outside the camp. You know what the company thinks. Let's wait until they have your size."

'No, no," he quickly replied. "It's no problem now. We don't have to buy from them anymore, and I have real American dollars, not just the company scrip. I hate paying their prices anyway. They're always double the prices in town. Besides, Anna has her heart set on her ice cream, and we can't disappoint her now, can we?'

Anna looked at her mother and smiled.

"Oh, my sweet love," Maria smiled back, "you're just like your papa. How can I fight that?"

So the next day, a gloriously warm Saturday, she packed them a small picnic lunch of bread, cheese and apples, and in a wagon that Spiro had borrowed for the trip they set off for Trinidad, fifteen miles to the south. It was so beautiful a day that Spiro even allowed Anna to bring along her pet dog, Kali, who curled up in the back, her head resting on her mistress's lap. Anna had found the dog scavenging in the garbage dump a couple of months ago and had started playing with her. When Anna began to walk back home, the mangy pup had followed her. At first, Anna tried to shoo her away, knowing that a dog, however adorable, was still another mouth to feed. But the puppy was so thin and timid that Anna and Maria both took pity on her, and so despite her father's objections the little dog found a home. It was Anna who chose the little dog's name, the Greek word for good.

As they left Berwind and moved east down the canyon into the open grasslands that stretched hundreds of miles to the east, the sulfurous yellow clouds began to dissipate. Crossing the railroad that ran from Denver and on into New Mexico to the south they picked up the main road to Trinidad. Behind them they heard a horn as a train pulled into the nearby Ludlow rail depot.

The trip to Trinidad took over three hours but the Andrakises didn't mind. It was a beautiful day, and as Anna kept telling them, she had her beloved mama and papa and they were going to get pistachio ice cream, oh, and Papa's new boots. The prairie grasses waved in the wind as though God Himself was gently passing His hand through them, the cattle contentedly munched their fill and the birds sang. It was so different from the filth and grime of where they lived, so glorious a day that even Maria said she didn't miss her homeland quite so much.

The wagon wheels creaked ominously as the family made its way over the rickety bridges that spanned the deep gullies that filled with rushing water during the spring run-off.

"Mama, what is that funny name you and Papa call the gullies?"

Maria smiled. "Arroyos, little lady, arroyos."

"Well, I can't say that so I'm gonna call them gullies." She skipped off the wagon and ran alongside it, throwing bits of wood she picked up alongside the road for Kali to retrieve, impatient to get to Trinidad.

Trinidad, which straddled the Purgatoire River, was the Las Animas county seat and a market center for surrounding farms and ranches, one of many similar towns that had been founded in the last hundred years along the east flank of the Rockies. The town's wealth was enhanced by the coalfields and the three rail lines that intersected in its center. Trinidad boasted hotels, restaurants, churches, lots of different shops and all the goods that a person could want, not that most miners could afford to buy them.

Crossing the river, the Andrakises slowly rode down Main Street before stopping in front of one of the town's shoe stores. They tied the horse to a hitching post and stepped onto the boardwalk that fronted the shops. The boardwalk was dusty for it hadn't rained much in over a month, but Maria knew that the mid-summer rains would soon be upon them and then the streets would turn into rivers of mud. Many of the people, she saw with envy, were busy shopping, their arms loaded down with bags and packages. Others were simply enjoying a pleasant stroll. Husbands and wives walked arm in arm; children played ball or chased each other for the sheer fun of it. Automobiles jostled with horses, carts and wagons for space on the streets.

It took the three of them an hour, trudging through just about every shoe store in Trinidad, before Spiro came upon the right pair of boots, an hour that saw his wife and daughter getting more and more impatient.

"You really are worse than a woman, Spiro," Maria teased him, not altogether jokingly. Even Anna asked him when he'd be done, as maybe Mr. Cassano was going to run out of pistachio ice cream before they could get to his shop. All Spiro did was laugh along with them. "You know, Maria, sometimes even our life is good, yes?" Maria could see the pride in his eyes as he looked at her and their daughter.

The pair of boots he finally settled on was made of solid black leather with extra patches on the toes for protection. They had strong brass eyelets and stout cord laces. Spiro asked the price and when the shopkeeper told him his heart sank. He didn't have enough money.

Keeping some money in his pocket for Anna's pistachio ice cream, he held out everything else. "I know I'm a bit short, but not much. I really need those boots, sir." Spiro did not whine but his plaintive voice came close.

At that moment, Anna and Maria, who had been waiting impatiently outside, came into the store, Anna looking adorably cute, Maria looking radiant as the sun through the open door caught her hair. The shopkeeper smiled at the two of them, and nodded to Spiro. "Okay, you can have them." Spiro thanked him profusely, as did Maria. Anna just continued to smile angelically at him. The shopkeeper wrapped Spiro's new boots in brown paper and carefully tied the parcel together with string. Spiro took the parcel almost reverently and the three of them stepped out onto the street.

They passed a photographic studio, its window filled with wedding and family portraits. Maria stopped and looked at the photographs. "You know, Spiro, one day we should have our picture taken, too." As she spoke a young man came out the studio.

"Good morning, Ma'am, my name's Jimmy, and I'm sure Mr. Dold, he's my boss, would give you a great deal."

Maria looked at her husband, but she quickly realized that this was a luxury way beyond their means. She smiled at the young man and the three of them continued down the street.

"Ela, pethi mou," Spiro grinned at Anna. "Come, my child. How about your ice cream?" That was all she was waiting for, and she ran ahead of both of them to her favorite place in the whole world, Cassano's Ice Cream Parlor. Maria left them to check out some new skirt cloth she hoped she might be able to buy in the next month or so.

As Anna ran down the boardwalk, alternately playing hopscotch and jumping up to try to slap the signs hanging over each shop's entrance, she thought of all the different ice creams Mr. Cassano had. There was vanilla, chocolate, strawberry, pistachio; he seemed to make a new one every day, there were so many. But she didn't care. Her favorite was pistachio. She loved its creamy softness and the hard little bits of nuts that she always left to the end so she could nibble on them and feel them between her teeth hours after she had left the parlor.

Angelo Cassano's ice-cream parlor and soda fountain was cool after the heat outside. Down one side of the shop was a long counter with leather- and chrome-plated swivel seats. At the far end was a bank of ice creams, each flavor housed in large cardboard tubs. Spiro picked his daughter up and seated her on her favorite chair in the parlor. It was next to the cash register and she loved to talk to Mr. Cassano.

The Italian came over, a huge smile on his face. "Ah, beautiful Anna. How are you, my little dark-haired princess? If I was fifty years younger, I'd marry you, you know, and we'd go and live in a magical palace in a magical country called Italy." Without fail, he always said this to Anna whenever she came for ice cream. And Anna always giggled because Mr. Cassano was even older than Mama and Papa. Spiro smiled at how this wonderful man made his daughter's face light up with happiness.

"Now then, bambino, what would you like today?"

Anna pointed to the pistachio, and Mr. Cassano scooped out a huge dollop and carefully placed it on a cone. Lovingly, he handed it to Anna.

While Anna ate her ice cream, making it last as long as possible on that hot summer's day, Maria rejoined her family. The Italian told the adults that he'd heard the coal company was fed up with the union for always demanding more money and better working conditions, and whining to the governor if it didn't get its way. Spiro bristled, not sure of every word of his friend but catching enough to get angry.

"Hey, I'm just tellin' you what I hear, that's all," Angelo responded defensively.

Spiro shrugged. "Well, there's nothing we can do about it. Anyway, I'm not in the union. Last night a miner got beaten up real bad in Berwind for going to a union meeting. I guess I'll have to keep out of trouble, and hope it stays away from me."

Angelo wasn't sure. "All I'm saying, Spiro, is that I know the union got the company to agree to its demands, but now it's back with more, and the company is fed up. The company's been looking for a fight for years to finish the union off."

After Anna had finished her ice cream, making sure that she still had some nut bits wedged in her teeth for later, the family walked back to the wagon. On the other side of the street, outside one of Trinidad's many saloons, they saw a huddle of young men who, from their clothing, looked like miners. They kept glancing over their shoulders as if they were doing something wrong and didn't want to get caught. As Spiro untethered the horse, one of them called him over. Maria took hold of Spiro's sleeve to hold him back but the man was insistent. Spiro shouted across the street that he had to get back home but then they all began to tell him to join them. People on the street were beginning to see what all the shouting was about, so Spiro reluctantly gave in and walked across to them. After a few brief moments, he rejoined his family. Maria didn't know what they talked about, but it was clear from Spiro's face that he was boiling mad.

"What's wrong?" his wife asked him.

He didn't say anything at first, but after Maria asked him again, Anna for one of the few times in her young life saw her father angry at her mama. "It's none of your business, woman." He said it angrily, insultingly, demeaningly.

Maria was as shocked as Anna but she never said another word, and the three of them rode back home in silence. Even the little bits of nut Anna had stored just for the journey had lost their taste.

By the time they approached Berwind, Spiro had begun to soften a little. He and Maria talked about nothing in particular, but although Maria was still a little frightened of what had happened on the street in Trinidad, she at least had her husband back. Spiro didn't even get angry with Anna when she knocked a jug of water over the brown paper packet that held Spiro's brand new boots.

"Don't worry, Anna," Maria said consolingly. "It's okay." Maria liked to use American words like okay, and she didn't at all believe Spiro who insisted it came from *ola kala*, Greek for everything's good. No, okay was all American. Maria leant back and pulled the wet paper off the boots so they could dry out and be ready for him when he went to work.

As they got closer to Berwind, the land around them began to change. The familiar smell of burning coal was back in the air, and the grasses were flecked with coal dust. Even the few streams that still ran after the spring thaw were splotched black and brown with coal dust and sewage. Ahead of them, hanging over the canyons to the west were dark yellow clouds of soot from the hundreds of ovens that turned the coal into coke. They turned to the west and entered Berwind canyon. At its mouth they were forced to stop at the company guardhouse manned by armed guards. They were supposed to be there for the miners' protection, but everybody knew what they really were there for. Berwind was a closed town. The coal companies didn't own just the mines. They owned the stores and dictated what was sold and for how much. They ran the schools and wrote the curricula for the different grades. They even decided what religions could be openly practiced. As Spiro once told Maria after a particularly hard shift in the mine, "We're all just owned by the company, bought and got rid of when we've lost our use. That's all we're good for."

That afternoon, Dave Watson was on duty. Watson, a man in his early twenties, was related to Jeff Farr, the sheriff of Huerfano County just to the north. Farr was a company lackey who could be relied upon, along with his deputies, to harass the miners at every possible chance, and Watson took full advantage of his relative's status. Watson had a reputation for beating up miners simply for the fun of it, and, worse, for trying to bed their wives. The rumor was that he'd force the women to acquiesce by threatening to get their husbands fired if they refused. Watson stood at the entrance to the guards' hut, his carbine leaning up against the wall. In his right hand he held a long axe handle, which he smacked against the palm of his left hand. His jeans were tucked into the tops of his cowboy boots. He wasn't a big man but he had the menace of authority as he stared at Spiro.

The company guards hated the miners, but they detested the Greeks. Although Spiro and his countrymen made up only a small portion of the mining workforce they had an undeserved reputation as troublemakers and rabble-rousers, probably because most of them were single and, so the official thinking went, had less to lose if things became violent.

"Hey, Andrakis, where ya' bin?" Watson yelled nonchalantly.

Maria did not like the idea that Watson knew her husband's name, and from the way he bristled neither did Spiro. But thinking that a show of friendliness might work, the miner replied with a smile. "We've been to Trinidad, I'm not on the shift until tomorrow, so we had a family trip."

Watson didn't say anything at first. He continued to stare at Spiro and then looked for a long time at Maria. Despite childbirth and the harsh life of being a miner's wife, Maria Andrakis was still a striking woman. Now she wore her lustrous jet black hair untied. Even the rough dress that she had cut and sewn herself did not fully hide the curves of her body. Maria knew exactly what Watson was thinking. Out of the corner of her eye she saw Spiro clench his fists ever so slightly. Watson came close to winking at Maria, but still Spiro said nothing. Finally, as if he was bored with it all, Watson walked to the back of the wagon. Maria breathed a sigh of relief.

"Hey, Greek, what are these?" Watson held up Spiro's brand new boots.

"I bought them this afternoon in Trinidad, with my own money," Spiro replied, quietly because he knew where this conversation was going.

"Mr. Watson," Spiro continued, almost obsequiously despite the fact that Watson was the younger of the two and had clearly made advances to his wife. "There's nothing to stop me from shopping in a private store, I don't have to use the company shop anymore. And anyway, I checked at the company stores first, none of 'em had my size."

Still holding Spiro's brand new boots, Watson walked back to the porch. Looking back at Spiro over his shoulder, he laughed and said, "Well, Andrakis, now they do."

Maria knew Spiro had lost his brand new boots for good, and she knew also that her husband could do nothing about it. Seething inside, Spiro kept his own counsel on the ride up the canyon to their house, and when his wife tried to say something, his look silenced her immediately. Spiro left Maria and Anna at their home and returned the horse and wagon.

Maria and Anna put away their belongings. Their house, not much more than a cabin, had only two rooms, and the company charged them four dollars a month. They could barely afford it, but Spiro had insisted that they not share their home with anybody. And on an evening like this, when she and Spiro were at odds, she was glad of the privacy.

Spiro should have taken only about thirty minutes to rejoin his family, but it wasn't until after eight that evening, two hours later, as the sun was beginning to set behind the mountains that he finally showed up. His face was flushed red, and Maria was forced to ask him if he'd been drinking. He said nothing, just demanded his supper, and Maria sent Anna into the other room so she could not see her father. He sat down heavily at their kitchen table, a poorly built piece of furniture that he had repaired with bits of scavenged lumber from the mine workings. It creaked whenever anyone sat down at it, and this time Maria was afraid the thing would collapse entirely. She served his dinner in the large bowl that the family ate out of, for individual plates were reserved for special occasions, and slammed the bowl down on the table, furious with her husband, not so much because of the incident with Watson but because of how he was behaving. The meal was a chicken she had cooked a few days earlier. She had butchered the bird the way her mother had taught her, simply taking a large cleaver and chopping it into pieces small enough to fit into the pot along with some potatoes, onions and carrots. Spiro delicately separated the bone shards from the meat, as though unaware of his wife's stare.

She was unsure what to do next, so to keep herself from losing her temper, for she knew Anna was in the next room, she dusted their few pieces of furniture. It was a never-ending task, one to which she often summoned her daughter, for the wind seemed to blow constantly and despite Spiro's best efforts at chinking the walls, soil and coal dust were always finding a way in.

She finally couldn't control herself anymore. "Spiro, can I say some…?"

"No, you cannot, woman." Spiro harshly interrupted her. "You will speak when I tell you to." He went back to the chicken.

Maria had never heard him talk like this to her. Unable to speak, because she simply did not trust herself, she kept on dusting. She turned to the knick-knacks that in Greek fashion she had on virtually every horizontal surface. The ornaments sat on embroidered lace cloths, part of her meager dowry: icons of the Panagia and Saint Titos of Crete, cheap trinkets bought in Trinidad. She took extra care on the few family photos. Her favorite was of her father dressed in Cretan high boots, leather jerkin, cummerbund and black headscarf. Fabric knots fringed his scarf, reminders of the tears shed for freedom by so many of her countrymen and women over the years.

Finally, after what seemed to Maria an eternity of dusting, she heard her husband. With a poorly concealed belch, Spiro pushed his plate away from him. "Thank you, wife."

Maria ignored the flecks of chicken and bone that now lay on the floor underneath him. Encouraged by his belch, she decided to press the issue. "Spiro, there's nothing you can do about those boots."

He did not reply at first and Maria wondered if he was going to explode at her after all. But finally, as though speaking was almost too painful, Spiro said, "I know, Maria, but that doesn't make it easier. My great grandfather, God preserve his soul, died fighting the Turks, and I carry his name. And even though Andrakis means 'little man', I am proud of it because it was his. But today I am ashamed, and he is, too." Spiro looked as though he was about to cry.

Maria wrapped her arms around her husband's chest. She said nothing, nor did he. But she felt the wetness of his tears on her blouse and she cried with him.

Spiro took his chair outside as the warm evening turned chilly. Perhaps he thought the coldness that wrapped his soul could find companionship in the cool Colorado air. He smoked cigarette after cigarette, staring into space, as though scouring the sky for something important but elusive. Finally he got up and telling his wife that he was going for a short walk, he set off down the street.

When the streets of Berwind were empty of people and only the constant workings of the mine machinery and the muted roar of the coking ovens at Tabasco down the canyon could be heard, Spiro staggered home. Maria was waiting for him, quietly sitting in her chair in the dark of their living room. Spiro was drunk, no doubt about it this time. Alcohol always ended up making her husband maudlin, even on crazy, happy days like Easter Sunday when the wine flowed freely and all men were glad to be born Christians. Often she had to ask him to slow down, after one too many glasses had begun to work its effect. But now was no time for scolding. Her husband was in pain, and for once she was glad alcohol could be his friend. Spiro swayed into their bedroom and flopped down onto the bed. Carefully and lovingly Maria pulled his boots off, placed a blanket over him and lay down beside him to try to find what peace she could in a world that had spiraled out of control.

4

"I do love these summer days, darling," Cettie Rockefeller gushed, as she passed the silver sugar bowl across the table to her husband, John D. Rockefeller Sr., patriarch of the wealthiest family in America.

Every year at this time, the Rockefeller family spent a few pleasant weeks in Kykuit, one of the most audacious summer estates in the country. A short drive from New York City, the house had six stories, two of them underground, all connected by a labyrinth of corridors and tunnels. The estate's landscaping was planned by Frederick Olmsted, the architect responsible for Central Park. But, typically, Rockefeller had decided he could do better and for a while supervised the landscaping himself before turning to a different architect.

The weather at Kykuit was typical for the time of year, and as the day wore on the air had grown warmer and increasingly dense, harbinger of an evening thunderstorm. Rockefeller's light wool suit scarcely helped. The sweat trickled down the inside of his shirt, and the starched collar rubbed against his throat. Cettie was proud of how her husband always conducted himself on these occasions. He was a true Victorian; he had an important business meeting later that day and for that he must dress correctly, regardless of the setting or the weather.

The room was Cettie's favorite. It was decorated in a mixture of different styles but to her eyes they complemented each other perfectly. The crown molding was severely Classical, in harsh contrast to the exuberance of the marble-topped Baroque table. The Irish Chippendale furniture, her husband's favorite, gave the room a homeliness that belied their cost. The French windows opened to green lawns that commanded magnificent views of the Hudson River two miles away. Cettie set down her bone china tea cup and saucer and opened the doors to allow the breeze, almost imperceptible though it was, to help cool the room.

She returned to her chair, slowly sipped her tea and looked at her husband as he gazed out of the window, lost in thought. She remembered how, just a few years ago, a gutter-press newspaper had described him as a wheeling-dealing, Christian capitalist, Bible in one hand and ledger book in the other, who had ended up controlling virtually all of America's wealth and many of its politicians. They had laughed it off at the time, even complimenting the journalist's imagery, but Cettie was well aware that under the façade such criticisms confused and even rankled her husband. All she saw across the parlor table was what he himself thought he was; a seventy-four-year old God-fearing man, a good husband, a good father, a hard worker and an unceasing donor to numerous charities throughout the land. And she knew, too, that her husband did not feel smug about the vast wealth he had accumulated. Rather, he felt that it was all due to a benevolent God who looked down kindly on those of his creation who worked hard. "No," Rockefeller had once told her, "I have nothing to feel but gratitude to the Lord and a little pride in my own industry."

The Rockefellers had lunched privately, and later that afternoon they were to be joined by son and heir, John D. Rockefeller, Jr., whom everyone called Junior, together with the family's right hand man in Colorado, Lamont Montgomery Bowers. Precisely at three that afternoon, Junior arrived. He had come up from the city and he would stay with his parents that night. Cettie hoped that they might be joined by his three sisters but she never knew what their schedules were; with families of their own they were no longer totally under the Rockefeller control.

After ten minutes of catching up with news on his son's family, Cettie Rockefeller took her leave. She had never felt the need to be in the family's formal business meetings, although she prided herself on giving advice to her husband whenever he had asked for it. The woman's absence left a void in the room, especially for Junior who worshipped his mother. It was she, he told his friends, who had instilled in him the true meaning of duty, both Christian and filial. Cettie's departure and perhaps the heat of the afternoon disinclined the two men to much in the way of conversation.

Junior was slightly more portly than his father and of the same height, but he always seemed to recede in size in his father's presence. As a child, he had had little intimate contact with his father whom he respected but feared just as much. Having to come all the way here when he had pressing business at the family's headquarters in New York silently irritated him for he had grown, if not to dislike, then certainly not to care as much as he should for his family's business dealings. He was much more interested in developing the philanthropic interests that his father had started. However, as his father often reminded him, he couldn't be a philanthropist without the family's financial empire, so on this occasion Junior would dutifully attend – he was, after all, his father's son – and attempt to solve the problems plaguing their Colorado mine holdings.

Junior helped himself to another cup of tea, and not for the first time reflected on his father's business prowess, in particular those Colorado mine holdings. The family's company, Standard Oil, once held a virtual monopoly on that resource in America until Senior was forced in 1911 to break it up into smaller companies. But he had seen the writing on the wall years earlier and – brilliantly in Junior's eyes – began to diversify their assets. Senior had particularly liked the look of the coalfields in Colorado and through a series of machinations that he considered honest and his competitors considered deceptive if not downright illegal, he acquired a controlling interest in the Colorado Fuel and Iron Company. The previous owner, John C.

Osgood, may have been bested by the Rockefeller machine, but he still kept controlling shares of the hugely profitable Victor-American Mining Company and remained one of the important players in the southern Colorado mining industry, something which Junior kept in the forefront of his thoughts.

He was glad that Lamont Bowers would attend this meeting for he would be able to help them decide what needed to be done in Colorado. And he was glad his father was here too. Although officially retired, Senior still demanded consultation on all major issues that affected his empire, and Junior was honest enough to admit that he still needed his father's advice and approval.

Father and son began to feel uncomfortable with their silence as they waited for Bowers, and so they began to talk desultorily about the price of oil and the family's other business interests, as well as the collection of art and antiques that Senior was acquiring for the estate.

His son had noted that over the past several months more and more his father would lapse into reverie about how his fortune was due only to God's good graces and his own willingness to work hard. Today was no exception.

"Junior," his father intoned, "I cannot understand why people do not believe that if a man works hard then it is right and proper that good fortune and riches come his way. I still don't understand why they resent what God has given us. And those unions. I will not allow them in Colorado. I did not allow them here." Senior paused and drew breath. Junior knew that a few years ago his father had summarily fired all his estate workers for just attempting to form a union.

"Perhaps, Father, envy is…," but his sentence was interrupted by a butler who announced that Bowers had arrived. He had worked for the Rockefellers for years all over the country, serving their business interests – and his. So, when Bowers moved to Colorado because of his wife's ill health, it seemed natural to put him in charge of their business dealings there. A native of

Binghamton, New York, Bowers at the age of 66 still cut a trim figure, his moustache neatly trimmed, his collar starched, his suit well-tailored. Years ago, Rockefeller had told his son not to be deceived by the New Yorker's appearance. "Trust me, Junior," his father had warned him. "Bowers might look like a retired British army officer, but his mind is as sharp as a razor, and you know what razors can cut. It's not just beards." Junior had never forgotten the advice.

Without much exchange of pleasantries, the older Rockefeller asked Bowers to get to the gist of the crisis in the Colorado coalfields.

"Well, Mr. Rockefeller, you told me to maximize the company's profits come hook or by crook and I have endeavored hard to do just that. And I always will." Junior noticed that his father squirmed ever so slightly in his chair, as though uncomfortable with Bowers' sycophancy. Junior watched Bowers with interest. To him it seemed that Bowers clung to his father's good opinion like a schoolboy. Junior couldn't help but note that Bowers' behavior reminded him of little else but his own behavior on those occasions when he was allowed into the great man's presence.

"As you know," Bowers continued, "the Colorado fields have been plagued by union anarchists for a decade. But the other mine operators and I believe that the current labor unrest is caused by a small group of revolutionary Eastern Europeans. And the worst of these are the Greeks, in my opinion, though the Italians aren't much better. Most of them are single men with no responsibility but to themselves and their cause. They have no intention of becoming good Americans, by the way. Most of them will take our money and run back to their homeland with it as soon as they can. A lot of them already send most of their wages back to Europe as fast as they can earn it. If we can break their backs I do believe that the rest of the miners, good God-fearing folks if they would only be allowed to get on with their work, would immediately cease their unrest and get back down the mines where they belong.

"I must also point out that Colorado is in the West," Bowers added, almost disdainfully. "While it is true that I have moved my wife to the state because of her health, and we are most happy with the treatment she is receiving, nevertheless Colorado is a new state. I sometimes think," he smiled slightly, "that Colorado hasn't yet discovered the twentieth century and they think everything can be settled with a gun."

If you're being deliberately ironic, Junior smiled inwardly, *you're hiding it well, Bowers, considering that at this very moment you are in the process of hiring a private detective agency, one with a national reputation for violently breaking strikes.*

The senior Rockefeller pursed his lips thoughtfully as Bowers spoke. "I profess again, Mr. Bowers, that I remain mystified that the miners are unhappy. It is not as though they actually work for us, the way our cooks and gardeners do. No, they are independent contractors, free to stay or move of their own free will. And if some choose not to follow that path then surely we cannot be held responsible if their lot is not what they expected. Mr. Bowers, I remember on a holiday in France..." Rockefeller Junior and Bowers leaned forward although they had heard this story a dozen times before. Junior could not help but wonder why a man obsessive about economy – in work, in life, in everything – would repeat this particular story to people who'd heard it many times before. But perhaps his father was simply getting old.

"A young beggar boy asked me for some money, held his hand out. Well, I did not know what to do. As you can imagine, this little scene began to attract some of the villagers. Finally, a man in the crowd spoke to the boy and he ran away. I asked him what he had said. The man replied, 'I said, you should have some self-respect.' That was the right thing to say and I'm sorry I did not think of it first. Self-respect. That is all these miners need. But whether they will ever gain it, I very much have my doubts."

"A very good parable, indeed, sir. Self-respect – if only." Bowers began to speak in detail about the union leaders, but Rockefeller waved him down. Junior knew his father was not interested in the actual personalities of the people who worked for him and in this case caused him so much trouble.

For the first time, Junior spoke. "Where does the governor stand on all this, Mr. Bowers?"

"Mr. Rockefeller," Bowers responded, "I do not need to tell you that the election of President Wilson last year was not good for our interests or, for that matter, the country's. The Republican Party lost a lot of their support in southern Colorado, as well. I am sure you will agree with me that the Democrats might want to make hay of our, shall we say, relationship with local politicians and law-enforcement officials, not just in Colorado but elsewhere. Governor Ammons is new to the job, and I think for a while at least he will want to go along with public opinion."

"Do you have any specific suggestions for resolving the situation in the mines, Mr. Bowers?" Junior asked.

"Well, I intend," Bowers slyly replied, "to ask the other mine operators to join with us in posting notices in all our workings that each company is non-political and that each man is encouraged to vote however they wish, freely and without intimidation. At the same time, we are taking every legal step to ensure that our own point of view is also put forward." He emphasized the word legal, and all three of those earnest and upright gentlemen in that quiet summer room knew what great latitude came with that simple two-syllable adjective.

"As you know, and I thank Mr. Rockefeller for his help in this," Bowers continued, nodding to Junior, "we have kept most of our money in Colorado banks despite their lower interest rates. I am sure that our banking friends in Denver can be relied upon to offer the right type of advice to the new governor. After all, he is new to the job and we must help him all we can."

Rockefeller Senior pulled out his watch, and Bowers knew that the interview was over. He immediately rose from his chair. "Thank you and good day to you both. I will be returning to Denver in the next few days, I have some personal business to attend to on Wall Street."

"Thank you, Mr. Bowers. You will, of course, keep us informed," added Junior.

Bowers nodded to them both and left the room as quietly and as unobtrusively as he had entered exactly one hour earlier.

At about the same time Lamont Bowers was having tea with the Rockefellers, a discussion took place in the Miners' Union office in Trinidad, and had he been a fly on the wall, Bowers might not have been so convinced that only the Greeks were the problem in the Colorado coalfields. One of the two men in that discussion was John Lawson, a stocky, barrel-chested man, in his early forties. He had been sent to Las Animas County by the United Mine Workers of America at the beginning of the year to help unionize the miners and spread the unrest beyond the northern fields where the miners had already been striking for three years.

Lawson had a well-deserved reputation for being able to withstand the physical dangers of union organization. He had been thrown in prison, threatened and assaulted in broad daylight, and had even been shot and wounded, all in the cause of workers' rights. Eleven years earlier his house had even been dynamited. Lawson wanted only to be a law-abiding citizen but he had a strong sense of justice that superseded his innate caution, and he knew that if the miners were to be treated fairly, then ignoring the law might be their only recourse. But, he always reminded himself, all legal means had to be exhausted first.

As he waited for the second man to show up, Lawson rehearsed how he would approach the meeting. He was the first to admit that he did not understand the majority of the newly-landed immigrants who now made up the bulk of the mining population in southern Colorado. According to the latest estimates, twenty-four different languages were spoken in the mines and seventy percent of the miners spoke no or very little English. And it just wasn't their languages that baffled him. He also knew that within the miners themselves, there were racial, cultural and ethnic prejudices. The Europeans looked down on the African Americans and the increasing number of Mexican workers with almost as much as disgust as they heaped on the small number of Japanese working in the mines. And the European immigrants displayed long-standing national enmities towards each other. Lawson knew he would have a hard time organizing these people into anything approaching a solid united front.

He heard the door open. A man in his late twenties shyly walked in, almost on tiptoe as though he felt himself an interloper. He looked like any other miner but Lawson noticed that his clothes were newer and his black dress shoes smartly polished. Louis Tikas, for that was the man's name, was small, as most of the Greeks were; Lawson thought that a single gust of good prairie wind would blow him over.

Lawson motioned him to sit down. He watched Tikas very carefully roll up his cloth cap and set it almost delicately on the table before he took a chair.

Lawson began. "Louis, I'm glad we could meet. You've been in the coalfields up north, so you've got some general idea of what's been happening, and I know you've been here a couple of weeks now, but bear with me for a couple of minutes, so I can tell you exactly where we stand at this moment."

Tikas nodded in agreement. He helped himself to a cup of coffee and sipped it slowly as the union man got down to business, inspecting a chip in the rim of the cup as though he had never seen such a thing before.

"Louis, you know that things aren't going well for us. Yeah, the companies have given us a bit, but it's like they're throwin' a couple of bones to a pack of dogs.

"I could sit here for hours and list for you the shit the boys in the mines put up with every day, the injustices they suffer. And it's not just the big stuff, like the explosion at Primero. You know how many got killed, by the way? Seventy-nine. I'm also talking about the little things that all add up to a big fat zero. The company stores, the beatings, the cheating weighmen. And don't get me started about wages. It's pathetic to begin with, and then they're soaked for their houses, their blasting powder, their supplies, every little goddamned thing. I don't know how they survive, I honest to God don't. Yeah, okay, I'll shut up, you get the picture." Lawson had noted Tikas' wry smile.

"But just let me finish, okay? The companies pretty much own all the sheriffs and officials down here. And they rig all the elections in their favor. So, the chance of getting local help is zero."

"Our union is the now biggest one down here. Remember, a few years back up north, the Western Federation of Miners and the International Workers of the World joined with us to organize a strike. But it failed, as you know, mostly because of that bastard, Chase. I think he thought he was born to be an Indian killer, but we've run out of them, so I guess miners are the next best thing. I don't know if the other unions lost interest, but right now, down here, we're it and we want it to stay that way."

Tikas' face set hard. He would never forget how Chase, a Brigadier General in the Colorado National Guard, had arranged for mercenaries to be paid for by the coal companies and then to serve under him. He had locked up hundreds of the strikers in pens without the benefit of even a trial. "I can still see them, John, standing in wooden corrals like they were cattle."

"Anyhows," Lawson continued, "You know what happened. A lot of the miners gave up and left the state. A lot of the newcomers come from your neck of the woods, or at any rate your end of Europe. We need to get them into the union."

Tikas continued to gaze at the wall behind Lawson and sip his coffee. The Greek shook his head slowly, as if baffled that fate had placed him in such a position. Then he spoke at length for the first time. His English accent was heavy, but the grammar sound and intelligible. "You know, I come from a small village in northern Crete. Sometimes," Tikas said, as he stared at Lawson, "sometimes, my father would let me come with him to the port close to where we lived. It was only a couple of miles from our village but it was so different. Until I came to America I thought it was the biggest place in the whole world. How wrong can a man be?"

Tikas seemed to drift off to another world and he sat there in silence for several minutes, looking again at the chip on his coffee mug and slowly drinking his coffee while Lawson looked him over and reviewed what he knew of the Greek.

Union officials from the northern fields had told Lawson that Tikas was typical of thousands of other East European immigrants. He had left Greece because of its miserable economic conditions. *Okay,* thought Lawson, *but what of Tikas the individual?* He'd heard the Greek had come to America just a few years ago and had owned a coffee shop in Denver and had been some sort of community leader, but had walked away from it and started working the northern fields. And now he was working for the union and had even been shot at and wounded by company guards. *What on earth,* Lawson wondered, *turned a man from coffee-shop owner to militant activist willing to die for the cause in a few short years?* No one he had talked to had been able to give him a satisfactory answer. *Maybe,* Lawson surmised, *he'd just got restless to try something new. Maybe the Greeks just liked fighting.* But those questions were for later. Better to let the Greek take the conversation where he wanted to.

"What are you thinking of, Louis?" Lawson probed.

Tikas came back to the present. "Oh, just things," he

shrugged, but the tug of the past that morning seemed too strong. "You know," he continued, picking up the thread of earlier, "in Rethymno, that was the name of the port, my father would leave me to myself while he tried to sell his vegetables, his fruit, his olives, whatever he had and we couldn't eat. Sometimes he'd find a job for a day loading a boat or maybe some rich guy was building a house and needed help. I'd go down to the old Venetian harbor and sit by the lighthouse and look out to sea. It was all so beautiful. I'd sit there and eat the hard crusty bread he'd buy me. I thought what it must have looked like when the Venetians were there. Shopkeepers, traders, sailors, lords and ladies. Just like New York, huh?" Tikas cracked a feeble joke. "There was a stone fortress by the harbor, to my little eyes it was huge. But when the Turks came the fortress fell like cardboard and they killed all the Venetians. A dark cloud came to my island and the sun couldn't get through."

Tikas finished his coffee. "I'd have stayed if there'd been work. But there was nothing. So I came to America, thinking that here there'd be no clouds and I could feel the sun again. But I can't. The clouds are still here." Tikas stopped. His face reddened with embarrassment. "Sorry, I talk too much."

"It must have been rough for you, Louis. But let's forget the past. We can do good here, now and for the future."

Tikas' eyes narrowed. "No, my friend. There are some things you should never forget."

Lawson momentarily wondered if he had said the wrong thing.

"John Lawson," Tikas abruptly said, "let's get back to business. I'm here to help you if I can. Tell me what I can do."

Lawson knew he was getting a man who'd be passionate about the cause. He also had found a man with a gift for the blarney, an indispensable gift when you're trying to rally men to join a union.

"Okay, Louis, glad to have you on board. This is what I need."

Jeb Stevens had seen it all, or so he thought, in his eighteen years on the Colorado railroads. He'd even carried the bags for a certain William F. Cody. *What a character he was,* Stevens chuckled to himself, *even dressed the part. Big floppy Stetson, fancy fringed leather jacket, a silk bandana. And don't even think about those pearl-handled pistols, Jeb boy! He'd a' given the great Barnum himself a run for his money when it came to chutzpah!* But nothing prepared Mr. Jethro Stevens, late of North Carolina and Chicago and now a porter on the Denver/Trinidad run, for the sight that confronted him that July day.

A frail old lady dressed in widow's black handed her ticket to the guard. Her gray hair was pulled back in a bun and she wore an old-fashioned bonnet. She thanked him with the trace of an Irish burr and gave a slight smile when he told her the train would pull out of Denver in twenty minutes. Unobtrusively she made her way to her seat, but aware that her presence had caused a buzz around the carriage. Mary "Mother" Jones knew she was being watched and smiled to herself, knowing the confusion that her looks and her clothing caused. As if to complete the image, she pulled from her purse a ball of wool and two knitting needles and proceeded to work on a scarf. She knew that this persona, the fragile old woman whose own age she pretended never to remember, threw people off and this was an important weapon in her armory.

Mary Harris Jones, to give her full name, was a legend in union circles, and her fame was now spreading throughout Colorado as it followed the rumors that she was to arrive. Because if Mother Jones put her weight behind a strike, all hell was sure to break loose. Just a few years earlier, the West Virginia Attorney General had called her the most dangerous woman in America. Nobody was quite sure why Mother Jones had become such a political firebrand. As a child in her native Ireland she had witnessed firsthand the brutality of the English Army. After moving to America, she had lost her husband and young children to Yellow Fever in Tennessee, and then the Great Fire of Chicago had destroyed her home and her dressmaking business. She had suffered, but so had millions of others in late nineteenth century America, and very few of them became radical hell raisers.

Jones had worked in the cause of the United Mine Workers for years, but many of its leaders were ambivalent about her simply because she operated outside the existing hierarchy of the union. Some downright resented her because she didn't hold back in her criticisms if she thought the union was being too passive. However, even if she was sometimes hard to control, no one doubted her own physical courage or her ability to rally the strikers, and their wives and children. She had once confided to the wife of a miner back in West Virginia. "Honey," she told the woman, "always keep the men guessing. They ain't very bright, you know." Jones remembered that conversation as she looked at the furtive glances from the other passengers. *Yes, Mary dear, always keep them guessing,* she chuckled to herself.

Yet despite her radical politics, Mother Jones was a throwback to an earlier age for she had little sympathy with the Suffragette movement which was currently raising a stink in national politics. As she asked often in speeches, "Who needs the vote when you can give 'em hell?" She had advised the West Virginia woman, "Stay at home, dear, your children need you more than the union does."

The train click-clacked its way to Trinidad. About half way there, it stopped at Colorado Springs to take on water and Mother Jones took the opportunity to stretch her legs. Colorado Springs sat right next to the foothills of the Rockies, with the massive Pikes Peak looming over everything. The town was an important farming and supply center for the region. As Jones walked up and down the platform, she saw in the distance the buildings of Colorado College, a private college, the best in the state. *I wonder if they really know what's going on in their own state, all those rich little kids without a care in the world?* she asked herself. *Probably not, and if they do they don't give a hoot.* She knew that this particular college admitted female students. She did not approve. *No, Ma'am,* she said to herself, *women should stay at home where they belong.* That she didn't was an irony lost on her.

After a thirty minute stop, the train started up. Another hour and in the distance Jones saw the lights of Pueblo and the heavy orange glow of the steel mills, responsible for most of the steel production west of the Mississippi. These were the mills that gobbled up all the coke that Spiro and his co-workers could produce. The train finally rolled through Pueblo and passed the freight yards and mills, giving Jones a chance to look at them in detail. Rail lines crisscrossed the open yard in front of the mills; large metal pipes, several feet in diameter, snaked from one building to another; tall chimneys exhaled black, choking smoke. And all through the yards she could see men, miniscule and scurrying hard, against the backdrop of those huge steel contraptions that she could scarcely understand. They worked frenetically, as though afraid that any slacking would get them fired. Which, of course, she told herself, is exactly what would happen.

The train picked up speed now that it was through Pueblo, and Mother Jones again looked at open prairie fields. The contrast between Pueblo and this idyllic scenery was abrupt and startling to her eastern eyes. She saw small herds of cattle, but she also noted smallholdings of cultivated fields neatly arranged around modest houses and barns. Jones was not the first visitor to realize that Colorado was a strange place. In Denver, she could have imagined herself back east. The downtown buzzed with financial and mercantile activity; tall buildings were shooting up as Denver quickly became more than just a large cow town, on its way to being the most important city in the Mountain West. Waiting for her train, Jones had seen men in smart business suits sitting next to ranchers in pointed boots and wearing large felt Stetsons. She saw migrant workers from Mexico hanging out by the rail yards, looking for a day's work and their own piece of the American dream. But here on the prairies, nothing but grass and sagebrush, it was another world. Here there was still cattle rustling, train robberies, posses and even Indians, although they pretty much kept to their reservations. Cowboys still wandered the ranches looking for work, although a realist like Jones knew that they were just another form of labor, to be exploited and thrown aside when they'd outlived their usefulness. She'd read somewhere that most cowboys couldn't even afford their own horses.

To Jones, traveling through Colorado was like going back in time, to a romantic place she and her children used to read about in the penny magazines she'd buy for them. *Boy,* she smiled to herself, *I could keep them up all night if I'd wanted to, just reading those stories.* The thoughts of her children kindled in her a sad loneliness that she wanted to keep buried deep inside, and so, as though reaching for the drug that would take away her pain, she turned her thoughts back to what lay ahead.

As Jones looked through the window and out into the limitless grasslands ahead of her, she saw the evening sky began to take on an ominous red glow. Coal country proper was announcing its arrival. She consulted her map. There was only one other town between her and Trinidad, and that was Walsenburg, the seat of Huerfano County. It had a population of about 4,000 and marked the northern edge of the southern coalfields. After a stop there, she assured herself, it would finally be Trinidad, and hopefully a good meal, a bed, and tomorrow the start of another round in the ongoing fight against capitalism.

"She just left Union Station, Mr. Bowers. No mistake. It was her." Arthur Stubbs, an employee of the Baldwin-Felts detective agency, hung up the mouthpiece on the public phone just outside the station and nodded to his partner.

"Bastard doesn't say much," Stubbs grunted. "It was like it

was killin' him to speak to me."

"Probably was," Sam King, the second man snickered. "He's from New York, they're all shits in that state. C'mon, let's get a drink, I need one bad."

Bowers hung up and sat thoughtfully at his desk for a few moments. He began to compose the telegram he would send to John D. Rockefeller, Jr. Its contents were of little importance and would only take a few minutes. But still, he'd been told to call in any new developments and as always when he communicated in any way with the great family, he wanted to make sure his words were right. He adjusted his tie and stroked his moustache to make sure it was in place. Even a long-distance telegram made him nervous; he needed to make sure he looked as perfect as he could, even though he knew what he was doing was ridiculous. He finished the telegram and silently handed it to his assistant who immediately left for the Western Union office.

As the message winged its way east, John D. Rockefeller Jr. was doing what he did best and loved the most, spending his father's money on philanthropic causes. Neither of the Rockefellers seemed troubled by the inherent paradox of a philanthropy made possible by the sweat, blood and deaths of their Colorado mine employees.

Junior was in the middle of a minor disagreement with the Rockefeller Foundation's chief accountant. The two of them were in a capacious oak-paneled conference room at the family's New York office complex, and their voices echoed as they consulted papers strewn across the conference table.

"Sir," the bean counter ponderously intoned, "I assure you that we can get a slightly better rate of return if..."

Junior's hand stopped him in mid-sentence. A clerk had placed a small slip of paper in Junior's hands. He read it impatiently. Bowers, again.

This is the fifth message this week, Junior thought to himself. *I know we want him to keep us informed, but at this rate he'll be sending me his dinner choices every afternoon to make sure I approve.*

"I am sorry, Bellingham, but I must look at this. In the meantime, consider amortizing the loan over five, not ten, years."

The message was brief. "Mary Jones left Denver for Trinidad earlier today. Recommend we continue to have her followed and her contacts reported to me. Have also gained friends in the Italian camp."

Rockefeller thought for a few minutes. He called his assistant back. "Send this telegram," he ordered. "Just one word, 'Acknowledged'." The Rockefellers were nothing if not economical. He picked up the papers in front of him and went back to the discussion.

5

The summer wore on and the rural landscape of southern Colorado shifted. The white-capped peaks of the Rockies turned brown and then gray as the first snows of last winter melted away. The prairie streams ran dry, and the grasses flapped listlessly in the wind, as though too tired to do anything. In the afternoons, mile-high thunderclouds took shape, harbingers of the late summer rains, or monsoons as the locals called them, that would soon arrive. But the danger and drudgery of work underground continued. The mine workings disgorged their black riches, and in the canyon the yellow smoke belched from the coke ovens at Tabasco.

Daily life for Anna changed little too. School had long finished for the summer but her mornings were still full. At seven, the same time every day, she got out of her tiny bedroll on the floor. First thing, while she was still wiping the sleep from her eyes, her mama made her use the outhouse behind their home. It was a small earthen pit with a bench of rough timber and a hole cut in it. Over it Spiro had built a slouching planked shack. Now that it was summer, the latrine smelt and Anna held her hand over her mouth to keep from gagging.

The effluent supposedly filtered into the ground but often on rainy days it seeped out and ran into the streets and gullies that crisscrossed Berwind. Even the town's main sewage system was simply an open trench, and Anna, young though she was, could remember horrible outbreaks of typhoid and dysentery: the high fever, the heavy sweating, the rosy splotches on the skin, the unbearable cramps; the awful yellow liquid.

While her mother worked on their light breakfast of bread and butter, Anna fetched water. Throwing on a rough dress, she grabbed a metal bucket and set off down the street to one of the communal pumps located around the town. Whenever she went to the pump she could always count on meeting somebody, and the first person she met was Nora Davis. Nora was married to one of the Westerners, as the Eastern Europeans called them, still working the mines. She was well known to the women in Berwind, for she served as a midwife when the doctor was unable to help. She was, so Anna guessed, anywhere from twenty to a hundred years old. Anna thought that Nora liked her, but her jokes were hard to figure out, and sometimes she thought Nora was making fun of her. But her mama got on well with her and she once told Anna that she came from a place called Wales and the people there only teased you if they liked you.

"Hello, my lovely," Nora greeted her in a sing-song voice that Anna liked to listen to, except when she was being teased. "Out helping your ma'm, for once, I see."

There, she's doing it again, said Anna to herself. But Nora had a grin on her face, so Anna put it down to the strange ways of Nora's people.

"Hello, Mrs. Davis," Anna politely replied. She wasn't old enough to have a comeback for Nora just yet, but she often thought that one day, when she was older…

Anna didn't mind fetching water when the weather was good because this was where the women exchanged town gossip. Although Anna didn't understand a lot of what was said, simply by watching the faces of the women as they talked to each other she could tell if the general mood of the town was happy or sad, or, as happened a lot these days, frightened.

A small number of women were standing at the pump. They were all dressed in their working clothes, long brown skirts and rough blouses. Some of them were wearing thin woolen cardigans. Most of the women were only in their thirties but already the coal camps made them look older than they were. They wore their hair pulled back and that accentuated the worry lines on their cheeks and necks and around their eyes. But despite the hardship of their lives, they still managed to laugh and joke with each other that June morning.

Anna recognized some of them. There was Mary Petrucci, her tummy showing the bump that Maria had told Anna meant the Petrucci kids were going to get a new brother or sister. The woman with her was called Costa, or something like that, but Anna wasn't sure. Today, all the women seemed in a good mood, the feel of warm sun on skin rendering their miseries less so. Even the Serb woman, Jasna Lazovic, looked as though life was bearable. Her husband, Milan, was not a particularly bad man, but he was notorious for getting drunk, coming home and then beating her, for no other reason than he hated his life and Jasna was available. This morning, Jasna still bore a bruise around her left eye from last Saturday's homecoming. The beatings were never bad, or at least that's what Jasna always maintained. The other women had seen her in this state so often that they barely even raised an eyebrow as long ago they had realized that Jasna always blamed herself, as though she deserved what he did to her. Each of the wives knew of their own husband's frustration and anger, and perhaps that explained why so many of them had sympathy not just for her but for her husband as well.

Anna's face cracked into a huge smile when she saw Mrs. Hoffman and her daughter Sally, Anna's best friend. The Hoffman family had been in Colorado for many years but the mother had never lost her German-accented English. After Anna had helped her pour water into a large earthenware jug, Sally and Anna set about the serious business of playing. Sally was a precocious eight-year-old. Sally wasn't her real name, but that's what everybody called her, for reasons nobody in the family could ever remember. She had light brown hair that hung straight from a central part, its greasiness making it stick to her head, so it always looked like she was wearing a metal helmet. Today, she was showing off a new porcelain doll that her parents had given her as a birthday present and whom she called Greta. She loved to look at the doll's glass eyes. She told Anna that she wanted eyes that deep and dark, but Anna laughed.

'Sally, I want Greta's lips. Look at them, they are so red and her mouth is so tiny.'

Together the two of them washed Greta and then Sally rocked her to sleep.

They'd been playing for about ten minutes when Sally heard, "Come on, let's see what your brother and sisters are up to."

But Sally had to wait until her precious little Greta was completely dressed. "I don't know what you'd do if you ever lost your Greta."

"No, Mommy," Sally shot back. "I won't, she'll be with me forever."

After the two of them had gone home, Anna found herself alone again with the older women, so she finished off her chores. Although the pump supplied supposedly clean drinking water, it often ran short. Consequently, many of the miners' wives would take water from the creeks for washing clothes and crockery. The water was often filled with fragments of cinder, coal dust and occasionally the unspeakable if the latrines had backed up. Fortunately for the women, the water was clear as it came out of the pump. Still, Anna, like she had been told, sieved the water into her jug through a muslin cloth. At least this time, she didn't have to throw alum into the water to kill any bugs. It made the water taste horrible but it remained a sight better than the alternative.

As Anna was filling her bucket, she saw one of the town grumps, Mrs. Rogers, coming down to the pump. Her husband, Bill Rogers, was one of the oldest miners at Berwind and earned a regular hourly wage, unlike the other miners who only got paid for the coal they produced, not the time spent in digging it out and bringing it to the surface. His job was handling the explosives to blow open new coal faces, skilled and dangerous work. Mrs. Rogers never missed the opportunity to lord it over the other miners' wives, especially the ones who'd recently come from eastern and southern Europe. Anna's mood changed; she'd had tongue lashings off the woman before, for no reason as far as Anna could see, and she didn't want another one.

Mrs. Rogers looked at all of them and peremptorily told them to get back to the only work that was important, looking after their husbands. One of the Italians muttered something under her breath, and her compatriots giggled. Mrs. Rogers glared back at them and asked what they had said. Innocently and sweetly, Mary Petrucci told her, in Italian, that she had wished only that her grandchildren would bring shame and dishonor on her family. Anna could tell that Rogers knew she'd been insulted but also knew that she couldn't do anything about it. So, the woman haughtily turned away and left.

"Who the hell does she think she is, treating us like that?" one of the wives asked. "Just because her husband is a shot firer, she acts like she's married to one of the bosses, when all the time she's as bad off as the rest of us." She looked at Anna. "You stay away from her, little girl, she's bad for you."

Anna nodded, and picked up the bucket and began the walk home.

As Mrs. Rogers receded into the distance, the sun peeked back from behind the clouds. The group talked a little while longer, but knowing they had work to do, they gathered their things and picking their way as best they could through the lumps of dirty coal, horse and mule droppings, they went about their business.

Their daily chores done, Anna and Sally decided to take a walk in the hills west of Berwind. The girls thought it was the best way to spend a summer's afternoon. No mines, no dirt, no foul air, no noise. There wasn't a cloud in the sky, it was warm but not too hot, and the wind whispered through the canyon. They had brought along Kali, as they always did. After walking for an hour, the three of them were in true forest. The pines, which had replaced the scrub oak of the lower canyon, stretched into the sky and shaded the two little girls from the sun. They took off their shoes, and the grasses of the meadows felt rich and luxuriant on their feet. Higher they climbed and were able to catch glimpses of the world beyond the canyon. To the west lay fold upon fold of hills and in the distance the peaks of the high Rockies, austerely beautiful. The beauty and quiet, broken only by the wind blowing through the trees, rendered both girls mute. They felt as though they were in a church.

As they walked deeper into the woods, Anna suddenly gripped Sally's arm. They both stopped, and as Sally started to ask what was up, Anna put her finger to her lips.

"Shush," she whispered, and pointed up ahead. At the same time she held tight to the rope collar around Kali's neck. There, not twenty yards away, were three deer. Their heads were to the ground, and the girls were close enough to hear the deer as they pulled at the grass. Sally and Anna stood there, transfixed, never having seen anything so beautiful. The deer were a lustrous light brown, and their hooves shone black. Their huge ears pointed up to the sky, their white tails bobbing rhythmically with their heads. Slowly, one of the deer looked up. She saw the three of them, but her large, sad, brown eyes registered no fear, even when Kali pointed herself in the doe's direction. After a few moments, the deer turned her head away and went back to her bounty. Anna and Sally quietly backed away and left them in peace.

After walking a little while longer, they rested by a stream. The walk had made them hungry too, and they turned their attention to their picnic lunch, a couple of pieces of bread thick with jam and a jug of water. They ate ravenously, and even though there was not much, especially after Kali had had her portion, the setting made them feel like they'd banqueted. Afterwards, with full tummies, they dangled their legs in the stream, the crystal clear water eddying around and washing away the accumulated grime of the camps. As Anna was bending down to scrub her legs, Sally couldn't stop herself. She kicked the surface and drenched Anna square in the face.

"Right," squealed Anna, "I'll get you back."

She leant down and with both arms soaked Sally. Sally retaliated and soon the two of them were sopping wet, and laughing so hard that after a while they gave up and just lay on the bank, enjoying the warmth of the sun on their bodies. They felt perfectly at peace as only children can, as though in washing away the filth of the camp they might wash away its memory too. They laid their clothes out to dry and sat on the bank of the stream in their knickers.

"Anna," Sally spoke first as the two of them put their clothes back on. "Daddy says if you take a train for days and days and days you'll come to a huge sea. And there are big towns by that sea, much, much bigger than Berwind, even bigger than Trinidad. Can you believe that, Anna?"

"I think so, I mean why would your pa lie to you? Papa told me that Denver is a thousand times bigger than Trinidad, so maybe those cities are as big as Denver, maybe even bigger. In school, they showed us a picture of New York and that was huge, the buildings seemed to go on up forever. And Mama and Papa lived there and they said all the buildings were like that."

"Anyway," Sally continued, "I'm going there. If I have to walk by myself, I'll do it. I'm not staying here all my life. Come with me, Anna, please come with me."

Anna looked at her friend in surprise. "What would we do there?"

"Anything," Sally replied, "anything we want. Promise you'll come with me."

"But what about Mama and Papa? And what about your family?"

"Silly, we'll both be beautiful and we'll grow up and marry princes, I'm sure they have princes in the big cities, and we'll be rich and we can send for them and they'll live like lords and ladies. I'll even let Frank come." Sally giggled as she said this, and Anna joined in. Sally's enthusiasm was infectious and soon the two of them were describing the house they'd live in, what their princes would look like, and what they'd do every day.

"Can you think of not working anymore, Sally? No more running to the pump for water, no more guards with guns, no more dirt in our hair?"

For a brief while they were silent as each of them dreamt of a life beyond the camps, and slowly the two of them fell asleep, two little girls in a meadow beside a mountain brook. Two little girls with their whole lives still ahead of them, and little else but dreams of princes and the memory of three deer to keep them warm.

It was late in the afternoon when the two girls woke up and started for home. The walk back downhill was much easier, but they were still looking forward to their beds. As they came to the outskirts of Berwind they passed one of the town bars. A group of miners was standing outside. One of them whistled and looked leeringly at Anna, raising his right arm at the elbow while placing his left hand just above the joint. She had seen some men do it to her mother, who always had hurried on as though frightened of what might happen. Sally gripped Anna's arm, and the two little girls quickened their pace. Another of the men said something as they ran down the street and the rest laughed with him, but the danger had passed.

Anna and Sally made it to the main street where they mingled with the rest of the townspeople and tried to forget what had just happened. As the two of them said goodbye, Anna asked Sally not to tell anybody what had just happened.

"Please, Sally," her friend pleaded, "if Papa finds out he'll kill them."

At first Sally thought Anna was joking, but the look on her face told her otherwise. Sally promised to keep silent and the two of them went their separate ways.

Late that afternoon, Spiro was sitting in front of his cabin. He was not on the shift until tomorrow and he knew that he had a grueling day ahead. He rocked quietly on the back legs of his chair, rolled and smoked a couple of cigarettes, and enjoyed a few moments of escape. Anna sidled up him and sat on the floor at his feet.

"Papa," she quietly asked. "Can I grow up to be anybody I like, like they tell us in school?"

Spiro looked at his daughter. He cocked his head at her, as though he didn't really understand her question.

"Well, Papa, you know today, well, Sally and me talked about what we'll be when we grow up. And the teacher in school says we're Americans, so we can be anything we want. Is that true, Papa?"

Maria had heard the conversation and quietly came out to join her family. She didn't say anything.

"Well, little Anna…" Spiro hesitated.

"Anna," he finally spoke. "We won't be here forever, you know. Mama and me have plans to move on. We'll go west, and then you'll be in a proper school, in a proper house, and, yeah, then you can be anything you want."

Maria looked at her husband, her eyes full of love for his simple lie to keep their daughter contented.

"Come here, little girl," Spiro gently commanded her. Anna climbed on her papa's lap, smelt the familiar odor of coal dust and tobacco, felt the warmth and comfort of his body, his arms wrapped around her, and knew she was completely, totally and utterly safe. Spiro gently rocked the two of them and Anna fell asleep as the long shadows of July crept down the canyon.

6

The afternoon cuddle with his daughter played fondly in Spiro's memory as he grabbed the small bucket of food Maria had left for him. At six in the morning, the canyon was shrouded in shadow and there was a chill in the air, so Spiro was glad of the jacket he had thrown on. As he walked down the main street he was joined by his pit partner, Alberto Scarpelli. They didn't say much to each other. Spiro's English was fairly good, better at least than most of the other Greek miners, but far better than Alberto's. The two of them had been paired by a pit boss who had been instructed along with all the other bosses to make sure that men of different nationalities were paired with each other. That way talk, especially about the union, could be kept to a minimum. That was the theory popular with management anyway, but the ploy hadn't stopped the union from growing. Like Alberto said to Spiro one day in his halting English, "Do they think we're stupid?" They had worked together for six months and were comfortable with the silence. They trusted each other when they were down the mines, and that counted for everything.

They trudged up the hillside to the mine entrance, a large wooden door framed in concrete with a number painted on its lintel. The slope beneath the door was littered with loose rocks and boulders. Once across the threshold there was a long passageway that led to the mine workings proper. The two miners hung their brass medallions onto a board nailed to the side of the entrance, a marker of who was in the mine should things go wrong and the owners had to inform their next of kin. Like the other miners, Spiro and Alberto had no doubts that their bodies would be entombed in the shaft if it cost too much to drag them out.

Just inside the entrance the pit boss sat at a small rough desk. He was in charge of making sure all the work went smoothly and was responsible for assigning the miners their particular work area, or room as it was called. Spiro and Alberto knew this particular boss of old, so to make sure they were treated well, Spiro bade him an obsequious good morning, and for good measure Alberto threw some coins into his cap, which lay conveniently on the corner of the table. Both knew from experience that a pit boss could reassign them without recourse to a wet room, where the ever-seeping water made work miserable, or worse, to a room they'd never worked before. In that instance, all the effort of digging and shoring up a particular room, for which they were never paid, would have been in vain. So, as much as they resented it, every miner bribed the pit bosses to look after them.

The pit boss was small and gruff, aged about forty. He had once worked on the coal face, his former occupation marked by the black dust permanently etched into his face. His left arm was shriveled and hung uselessly from its shoulder. Regardless that he had once been like them, he had no sympathy for the miners. The little sliver of power that the owners had thrown him had, in his eyes at least, now raised him above these common diggers. He looked at a chart, glanced at his cap to see there was something in it, and assigned their room. "Thank God," Spiro whispered to himself, realizing they would still be in the room they'd been working for a week.

As Spiro and Alberto walked the fifty yards down the passageway, they heard the dull, clanging chorus of dozens of shovels grinding into coal, the hammers pounding bits into a new face, the grunts and groans of men, the old-fashioned clopping of the mules that pulled the individual coal cars to the electric trolleys that pulled the coal to the surface for weighing. The two men's electric lamps were all that broke the utter blackness of the tunnel. When Spiro had first started working the mines, his partner, an old miner from England, had deliberately turned off their lamps. He wanted Spiro to know the complete, soul-chilling blackness of a mine without light.

"Get used to it, Spiro," he told him. "Don't be afraid. Feel your way around. Don't be afraid."

Spiro had been afraid, deathly afraid, and he had almost panicked. But the reassuring words of the miner had soothed him. He realized that the darkness brought nothing new but fear, and that could be dealt with, if only for a time. The lights bounced off their glistening, sweat-covered bodies and the black rock all around them. That rock had once been living plants until the pressure of millions of years had turned them, miraculously, into an object of men's desire. For this they risked their lives and that of their families.

In their room, the air was turning foul, and Spiro and Alberto knew that they'd have to abandon it soon but they didn't want to do this just yet as they had made good money, even if a ton of coal only brought them about 50 cents. At the far end of the room they had wedged wooden props between the wall and the ceiling. Here the coal was loose and for more than four hours they ferreted away with pick and shovel to clear the remainder of the coal from the exposed face. Earlier, the two men had laid down rail lines they had taken from abandoned rooms. They filled cars with the loose coal and pushed them away from the face so that ultimately mules could pull them to the main rail lines. Now it was time to loosen more coal so they could dig it out. Alberto took his hammer and rasped it on the edge of the room's ceiling to make sure it was still solid. He inspected the pillars of coal that they left as support for the roof.

"Sounds good, friend."

Spiro nodded. Hoping that the vein continued well beyond the edge of the room, Spiro and Alberto hand-drilled long narrow holes around all four edges of the coal face. This is where the explosives would go. They looked at each other and, from years of practice, crouched silently in the room with ears cocked. They were listening for methane gas escaping into the room. They heard nothing and their safety lamp burned cleanly. Many a miner had died because they had forgotten these simple precautions. Everything looked and sounded safe.

They placed the charges, and then Spiro fetched the shot firer, the specially trained man who would ignite the charges that the miners had laid. Normally, big explosions were only fired at night when fewer men were working. But because the charge would be so small, the firer agreed to the detonation, helped along by a little something in his cap from both of them. He checked their charges. Too little would have no effect, and the expensive charges would have been wasted; too much and the ceiling could come crashing down with disastrous consequences. The three of them walked away from the coal face as the firer paid out the cable.

"Fire in the hole," he shouted. A muffled boom reverberated through the room and a blast of coal dust erupted from the wall. After a few minutes the dust had settled enough to see that they had done their jobs well. The far end of the room was a jumbled mass of coal. Now the digging could begin again, but first Spiro and Alberto needed food. They unwrapped their sandwiches and devoured the rough bread and cheese, ignoring the fine layer of coal dust that covered everything. A few gulps of water from their canteen, by now warm and musty-tasting and they were ready. The two of them loaded up more cars and Spiro waited while Alberto went to the surface to bring down a mule. They had now been underground six hours. Six hours with only their lamps to show them where they were or what they were doing; six hours of listening – always – for the sound of cracking timbers, collapsing ceilings, the slow hiss of gas; six hours of hard unremitting toil; six hours of salty sweat pouring into their eyes despite the bandanas around their foreheads; six hours of breathing foul air laced with dust particle; six hours of hell. And it was not over.

Tired now. Really tired. Too tired to talk. Too tired to think. Too tired to worry about the aching of your body; it's as though the whole earth is crushing down directly onto you, and you alone are all that's holding up those tons of grey and black rock. Too tired to stop the black sweat running into your eyes. Too tired to think of the cuts and bruises all over your body. Act like machines. Pull the coal from the coal face and load into the car – again and again. Don't stop or you'll never start back up. Don't stop. Too tired to think of anything.

How many times that shift had Spiro backed the mule onto a car so it could begin its ascent into the world above? Six, seven, ten? He had lost count. How many times in his young lifetime had he done that? He and Alberto joked they could do it in their sleep. And today that's what they were doing.

In his first week in the mines, Spiro had been told to watch out for the mules, they were just too cantankerous, especially when they were tired. Spiro could still remember the old English miner's words. "Don't stand anywhere near their asses, Greek, otherwise you'll get gelded, and then where will your missus be, huh?" And he had always followed his advice. Until today.

Maybe he was just too beat, or maybe he was already thinking of how much money the haul would make him and Alberto. It didn't matter. Without thinking, Spiro walked behind the mule to grab its harness and walk it to the front of the car. At that moment a piece of rock, no bigger than a man's fist, fell from the roof and caught the mule a glancing blow on its rump. The animal reacted by kicking out. The hoof caught Spiro just below the side of the left knee. *Thank God,* Spiro thought later, *it didn't hit my leg full on.* But the iron-shod hoof still packed a punch and it did damage, serious damage. Spiro went down. Alberto immediately ran over and pulled Spiro from behind the mule, just in case it wanted a second round. He'd been in the mining business long enough to know that he had to get Spiro out of the mule's line of fire.

"Jesus Christ, man, my leg. Watch it," Spiro cried out. The mule looked at them as though nothing had happened, likely content for a moment's rest. Alberto took out his knife and carefully cut away Spiro's trousers. There was a thick gash on the side of Spiro's leg. Blood ran from it, splattering onto the ground to form a sticky black mud. A large blue-red bruise was already creeping over the rest of the limb.

"Spiro," Alberto spoke gently, "this is gonna' hurt like hell, but I've gotta' do it."

"Okay, I know." Spiro could hardly speak.

Waves of pain were crashing through Spiro's body, but they were nothing to the tidal flood when Alberto wrapped his bandana around the wound and pulled on it as hard as he could. Spiro dug his hands into Alberto's shoulders.

"Oh, fuck, that is so fucking bad."

Alberto tied the bandana tight. "Look. I've gotta get you out of here. I've gotta get help."

Even though he was now talking Italian, Spiro nodded in understanding. Spiro didn't know how bad it was, but he knew he couldn't walk. "Go, Alberto, but be quick."

His partner nodded and ran as fast as he could.

Spiro lay there, unable and unwilling to move. Slowly calming down, he felt the pain begin to subside. The bandana cut into his leg, but at least the blood flow was less. Spiro was beginning to feel as though he was going to survive.

He heard voices. Alberto had brought back two miners and a makeshift stretcher made of two pieces of lumber threaded into a couple of old sacks. But any hopes that the worst of the pain was over for Spiro were dashed as they picked him up and put him on the stretcher. The miners had done this many times before, had had it done to them, so they were as gentle as they could be. But nothing they did could make Spiro escape the agony. Now there was just one permanent throb of pain, as though his leg was bursting and exploding through the rest of his body. At some point in the journey back to the surface he blacked out.

As they came out into the sunlight, they were met by a small group of miners, curious as to who had been injured this time and how badly. "He's okay," Alberto shouted to them. "Just out with the pain. Damn mule kicked him."

As they loaded Spiro onto a wagon to get him to the camp hospital, their pit boss came up to them. "Any damage?' He looked at Alberto.

"Well, like I said, boss, I think he's okay but…"

The pit boss interrupted him. "Not the Greek, you prick. The mule. How's the mule? Expensive animals those, hard to replace."

Alberto and the other miners looked at each other. They didn't know if he was joking or not.

While Spiro and Alberto sweated underground, Anna and her mother had not been idle. That morning, the two of them walked from their home to the company store, five minutes away. It hadn't rained hard in a few weeks so they were able to make their way quickly through the wheel ruts that etched the street and over the horse shit that hadn't yet been picked up for garden manure. Anna told her mother again about her picnic in the hills. Maria was a little concerned because her daughter was rapidly coming to that age when men were beginning to look at her, and she didn't like her daughter to roam so far from home. But Anna seemed so happy, and it was such a good morning even for Berwind, warm and cloudless, that Maria decided not to spoil their day with a lecture that was becoming all too frequent.

The companies had finally allowed a private store to open in Berwind but the owner was unable to extend much credit to his customers, and so Maria was forced to use the company store. But that came at a price, literally, for the virtual monopoly they had in each of the mining towns meant they could, and did, charge considerably higher prices than the private stores. The official line was that the higher prices paid for the transport costs from Trinidad but everybody knew that this was, to use one of

Alberto's favorite English phrases, "a load of shit." They charged what they liked because the miners and their families had virtually no choice but to shop there.

The storekeeper had loaded his front window with enticing displays of canned goods, coffee, sugar, molasses, candies and clothing. Even the flies and wasps lying dead on the inside window sill hardly detracted from the allure of the display. Maria stopped to look and there, in the corner, were Spiro's boots. She tried to get into the store as quickly as she could, but Anna had already seen them.

"Mama, aren't they…"

Maria gently hushed her, embarrassed that her daughter had remembered the incident. But even a ten-year-old knows when her parents have been humiliated. Anna said no more as her mother hurried them inside.

As they shopped, Maria played in her head what had undoubtedly happened. Watson had sold the boots to the storekeeper, and the shopkeeper had then put them up for sale at a price much higher than what Spiro had originally paid for them. So, Watson got to make money, the shopkeeper got to make money, and only Spiro, who had paid for them in the first place, would lose anything. *All in all,* Maria thought glumly, *a neat little parable of what happened every day in these cursed coalfields.*

The shop smelled of musty vegetables still with the earth on them, soap and coffee, and all the other items that a general store in an isolated Colorado town had to carry. Sun beams lanced through the shop window catching the dust in the air. Anna made a beeline for the corner of the store to stare at the array of candies on display in a glass-doored cabinet.

Maria had made out a shopping list and now she took this out of her purse. The shopkeeper gave her the creeps. His trouble was that he was almost too nice to her. She didn't see him fawning over most of the other wives like he did with her, and this made Maria think that he might have something else on his mind. *Oh well,* she thought, almost amused by the thought, *He's not the first, and probably not the last.*

But still it did not fully ease her discomfort. The shopping that day was made even more difficult because of Spiro's boots. She wanted to say something to the little man, but she kept silent. Like every other family in Berwind, the Andrakises had a long line of credit with the shop and she knew that her family would be in a deep hole if he cut that line off. She had to be nice to him.

Spiro had made some decent money in the last two weeks, and so Maria took the opportunity to buy some extra treats. Along with the canned goods, she brought fresh vegetables, extra cut tobacco for Spiro and a candy cane for Anna. The shopkeeper chattered on as he helped load the goods into her bags. Although he was as little educated as his customers, once he had acquired the running of the store, he had decided that he had to adopt the air of a man about business. And so he spoke in a manner that he thought was a good imitation of rich people.

"It is a wonderful day, is it not, Mrs. Andrakis?"

Maria could do nothing but agree, because indeed it was.

"And if I may say so, you are looking particularly lovely this morning. How is your husband, by the way? Well? I hope so, indeed I do." And so he prattled on until Maria took out her purse and he shifted back to business.

After he had totaled up her purchases and been paid, he took out a black, red-spined ledger book from under the counter. This was his customers' credit book, and one of the most important objects he owned. Turning to the Andrakis' entry he realized that it was about time they brought the figure down.

He coughed slightly as though embarrassed, and pointed out to Maria, "I'm a good man, you know, I understand how difficult it is for all of us in these troubled times," (*for some more than others,* thought Maria), "but I am sure you will understand that if you could pay this down a little, I would be eternally grateful."

This was not a request but an order, but Maria knew that deep down the shopkeeper was a good man, and at least he was polite. So, she gave some coins as a down payment on the credit line. The shopkeeper counted it out and looked at her as though it was not enough, but Maria, who knew how to use her charms when she had to, demurely looked up at him through her long eyelashes and asked ever so kindly if that amount would do.

"Mrs. Andrakis, I respect you and your husband. But please, do try to pay down the rest of the credit as soon as you can."

"Of course, I will. And thank you for helping us. You are a good Christian."

Maria called Anna to help her with the groceries and left for home, satisfied with a good day of business.

As the two walked back home, they passed an alleyway between two of the mine offices. It was narrow, and even at noon little of the sun penetrated. Crossing over to the other side, Maria heard moans and the sound of scuffling. Intrigued, she told Anna to stay on the boardwalk, and very quietly and carefully she walked the few yards into the darkness of the alley. She saw a man on the ground, hunched up in agony as two others stood over him, kicking him without pause. The man was trying to crawl to safety but there was nowhere to go. One of the men, she was horrified to see, had a sheriff's badge on his coat lapel. His accomplice had his back to Maria.

She couldn't hear everything they were saying through their breathless grunts, but she picked out a handful of words: *union, go home, bastard.* She screamed at both of them to stop it but they acted like they didn't give a damn. Without even acknowledging her presence they sauntered back down the alley and onto the street, but not before giving their victim one last kick each for good measure. The two attackers passed Anna who was still standing on the boardwalk, and one of them, the bigger of the two, leered at her and bending down so that his face was almost in hers shouted 'boo' loudly. Anna could smell the liquor on his breath. She started to cry, but the two of them just laughed at her and continued on down the street as though nothing had happened.

Anna ran into the alleyway to see Maria trying to lift the man into a sitting position. He was holding his ribs and Maria guessed they'd been broken. Both of his lips were split and there was a gash across his forehead. The blood was pouring over his face, so Maria took out a cloth from her bag and held it against the wound. She didn't recognize the man, but knew from his coal-stained clothing that he was a miner. He was finally able to thank her, although his lips were now doubled in size.

"Why?" she asked.

"Because they can. I did nothing, but they dragged me down here off the street and, well, you saw what they did. I'm just glad you came along."

Just then Maria saw Anna, still and silent, transfixed by the scene, tears running down her cheeks.

"Oh, my God, are you okay?" Maria rushed over to her daughter. Anna didn't say anything. "Did they hurt you?" Maria asked, almost hysterical by now. Anna shook her head.

"Look, mister, I've gotta' get her home. Are you goin' to be okay?"

He nodded. "And lady, thanks again."

As Maria got to the end of the alleyway she looked back at the man who was following her out. He was clutching his ribs and was limping, but at least the blood seemed to be under control.

"Who were they, do you know?" she called back to him.

"Oh, yeah, I know them. Met their kind back East years ago. You a miner's wife?"

Maria nodded.

"Well, tell your hubby that Baldwin-Felts are here. He'll have heard of them. And if he hasn't, he soon will."

It was late afternoon. Spiro lay in bed in the company hospital, a wooden, two-room structure with twenty beds. Along with the schoolhouse and some of the company offices, it was one of the few buildings in Berwind with fresh running water. Apart from Spiro, four of the cots were occupied by miners, like him suffering from work-related accidents. There was also a case of food poisoning – a six-year-old who didn't know he couldn't eat every berry he found up in the hills – and one miner who'd come second best in a bar fight.

He opened his eyes slowly, trying to remember what had happened and why he was in a hospital bed, when he heard Maria.

"Oh, my God, tell me you're not hurt," she wailed in fear as she saw he had regained consciousness. "Alberto wouldn't tell me anything, except you were too hurt."

Spiro tried to smile, but the leg was throbbing like hell. "Hey, come on now, of course I'm hurt, look at me, but I'm okay." He looked at Alberto, standing next to Maria, who smiled back at him as if to say, *women*.

Maria crossed herself, almost retching as she saw the blood-drenched bandage around her husband's knee.

A stern but kind voice at the door made all three of them look around as the nurse strode into the room. "Come on, let's see what all the fuss is about. You men, I don't know what you'll get up to next."

She wore a gray dress and a pinafore that probably had once been white many years ago, but the dress was clean and the pinafore starched. A pair of scissors hung from one of the pinafore's straps. She had the gentle surliness of all nurses, as though the simple act of believing the patient would pull through was three quarters of the battle.

"As soon as I'm done here, I'll get the doc in. He'll set you to rights."

She hummed to herself as she worked on cleaning the battered leg. She gave Spiro a sip of something strong and he involuntarily choked on its harshness. Spiro thought it tasted of nothing but uncut alcohol, but at least it helped with the pain. He winced as she dabbed a moist cloth on the dried blood to expose the wound. He held tight onto Maria's hand; when the nurse dug deep with the swab, Alberto had to pin his leg down with both hands as Spiro tried to move it away. Finally the nurse was done. Spiro dared himself to look down at his leg, but Maria, sensing what he was about to do, quickly took hold of his face in her hands and kissed it, as a mother would.

"Does Anna know?"

Maria shook her head. "No, she's playing with some of the other kids. Time enough to see you when we know how bad it is."

As she spoke, the doctor came in. He was in his early fifties and wore a black suit, in keeping with his elevated professional status. Nobody knew if he really was a trained physician, but he had a reputation among the miners for competence, and right now that was good enough for Spiro and Maria. The doctor looked at the wound and played thoughtfully with his moustache, heavily stained from nicotine. Finally, he began to probe the area around the cut. Spiro held firm as pain burnt his whole leg.

"I'm sorry, young man, but I have to do this." The doctor sounded sincere, and Spiro held on.

After what seemed an eternity to Spiro but probably took only a few seconds, the doctor declared himself satisfied.

"You're a lucky man, damned lucky," he intoned. "The cut is pretty deep, right to the bone actually. The bone itself is bruised but it is not broken. Don't worry about the bruising on the surface of your leg. It looks worse than it is. But still you'll need a few weeks off work. No walking on that leg for a few days. I'll keep you here overnight, there's room."

He turned to Maria. "I'm afraid that you'll have to fetch and carry for him when he comes home, at least for a little while."

Maria managed a smile. "So, Doc, what are you telling me that's new? I'm always fetching and carrying for him."

The man smiled briefly and quickly moved onto his next patient.

"Alberto." Spiro managed a hoarse sentence. "Alberto, I don't know what to say, how to thank you."

Alberto took his friend's hand. "Hush, man. You, Maria, Anna, you're my family. You know I do anything for you. I checked on Anna, made sure she's okay. Don't worry. The doc, he says it's gonna be fine. Maria, I tell Spiro, I kick his butt if he stays in bed too long." He smiled and Maria smiled, too.

"Alberto, thank you," she quietly added, as Alberto left the ward.

Maria tried to feed her husband some bread that Alberto had fetched but Spiro couldn't find any appetite. The constant throbbing of his leg made it hard to think of anything, let alone do anything. Sometimes he dozed, but just as he was about to drop off into blessed sleep the pain would suddenly flare up again. He tried to find a more comfortable position, but that only made the pain worse. Maria wiped his forehead, held his hands, and prayed. About nine, as the shadows began to darken the hospital ward, Spiro finally slipped into a deep sleep. The nurse looked in on him and said that it was time for Maria to go.

"Goodnight, Spiro, my love," she whispered softly. "Tomorrow, we'll come and get you. Don't worry about anything. I will look after you like you have always looked after me." She kissed him gently on his forehead.

During the hours she sat at his bedside Maria had time to think of the consequences of the accident. She had always hated Berwind. It was a dirty and dangerous place for adults, let alone a ten-year-old girl.

But what happens if the doctor is wrong and Spiro can't work in the mines anymore, she wondered to herself. *Worse, what happens if he ends up a cripple. He can't do anything else but hard labor. We're not able to do anything else.*

For the first time since they had moved to Berwind, she became frightened at the thought of having to leave it. She became angry at herself. *My God,* Maria thought, *is this the best an Andrakis, a Petroulakis can do? Berwind. How pathetic I've become. We'd all still be back on Crete if I'd been like this then.* She realized, not for the first time, that responsibility to others was a horrible burden for anyone to carry, especially if you loved them with every fiber of your being, every speck of your soul. She had to carry on; now more than ever, she had to be strong.

Five minutes later, Maria was knocking on the Hoffmans' door, and Anna flung it open it even before Maria's hand was back at her side.

"How's Papa, Mama, he's going to be okay, isn't he? I mean he's fine, isn't he? Please tell me, Mama, please. Alberto said papa had an accident."

Maria whisked her daughter into her arms.

"Of course, he is, my love. He's fine, just a bit sore that's all. Tomorrow we'll bring him home and in a few weeks, he'll be back to normal." Anna hugged her mother even more tightly.

Maria looked over her daughter's shoulder at Elsie Hoffman. The look between them said that things were not going to be that simple. Even if Spiro's wounds healed totally, Maria knew that an accident like this, and the loss of wages, made a man angry, and that could lead to trouble.

Elsie picked up Anna's cardigan and placed it around her shoulders. She kissed the two of them goodnight, and Maria and Anna walked in silence back to their little home.

Despite the anxiety of the day, Anna was tired. She had just enough strength to feed Kali, but as soon as the dog had settled down for the night, the little girl followed suit. Maria had told Anna she could sleep with her, and the little girl snuggled down into the comfort of her parents' bed. Maria, too, was tired, too tired even to eat, and she quickly cuddled up next to her daughter. But sleep would not come easily as the anxieties of the future played over and over in her head.

Right now, she told herself, *all that matters is getting Spiro on the mend. We've got some money put by but that won't last long.* She realized that whether Spiro liked it or not, she was going to have to find some paid work. *He'll just have to get over his Cretan pride,* she defiantly told herself. Other wives, she knew, helped their husbands' meager pay by taking in washing or doing housework for the bachelors in the town. However, that is as far as she would go to fulfill their wishes; laundry and cleaning. *Unlike some women I could name,* she chuckled to herself.

As sleep finally began to capture her, she sat bolt upright in bed, as though she had been hit by an electric current. *Of course, of course, of course. I know. I can go to the Eriksens. They'll give me work. Why didn't I think of it earlier?* As she lay in bed, now wide awake, she reflected warmly on how she had met them.

About a year ago, while they were shopping in Trinidad, Anna had run around a corner without looking and slammed hard into Ingrid Eriksen's stomach. Ingrid was a large woman with what the midwives called 'child-bearing hips'. Her gray-blond hair was pulled back in a bun, and her face, especially around the eyes, was creased from years of squinting in the prairie sun. Her age was anywhere from forty to sixty. Anna ended up on her backside, winded, but instead of yelling at her like most others would have done, Ingrid picked the little girl up and dusted her off. Maria was full of apologies, but Ingrid waved her down.

"Oh, like you and me never did that sort of thing when we were her age?" The Eriksens had been in America long enough to have very little trace of their Norwegian accent.

"Still, Anna, say you are sorry to the nice lady."

Anna did as she was told, looking quite sheepish, but all Ingrid did was smile and then actually invite the two of them to coffee and soda in a nearby ice-cream parlor. As they drank the coffee, Maria thanked her again for her kindness.

"I don't mind, Maria, my grandpa was a miner in the old country, so I know it's tough for you people out there. And we're doing just fine, the good Lord willing."

As they parted ways, and Ingrid refused for the tenth time to allow Maria to pay for her coffee and Anna's soda – refusals that Maria was mighty glad of if she was truthful to herself – Ingrid asked if Maria and Anna would like sometime to visit her little farm.

"It's out towards Aguilar," Ingrid explained. "Where are you from, honey?"

Maria told her Berwind, and her new friend grinned back. "Heck, I guess we're neighbors then. Okay, you know that water pump just after you cross the creek on the way to Aguilar?" she asked.

Maria nodded.

"Well, that's ours. One of us is always home, mostly me. Come by on a Sunday, that way you'll find us both there."

Maria smiled at how that lucky meeting had turned into such a friendship. Now that she had a plan, she felt stronger and, for the first time since she'd been told of Spiro's accident, a little less afraid.

Alberto was already at Spiro's bedside when Maria arrived the next morning. Talking to Spiro, bent low over the bed, was another man whom Maria did not recognize. From his build, he looked like he was a laborer, although he wasn't wearing the rough and tattered clothes that the miners habitually wore. As soon as he saw Maria walk in, the stranger moved away and sat down in the corner of the ward, saying nothing more, just watching. Maria put on a brave smile as she walked to the bed, and leant over to kiss her husband, who feebly smiled back. He still looked weak but, to Maria's optimistic mind, a little more like himself. Still, Maria reminded herself, he had a long way to go.

As Maria fluffed Spiro's pillow, Alberto told them the good

news.

"After I leave you, I go back to the pit. We got full money. They don't cheat us. It's okay." Alberto continued in his halting English. "They're not gonna' steal when he's around. He check it for us." He nodded in the direction of the stranger in the corner of the room. The man then stood up and walked over to join the three of them. Maria could not help but notice that he walked with a limp and that his face was bruised.

"Maria," Alberto said, "This is Mike Livoda."

Livoda shook Maria's hand and then retreated to the corner. Maria had heard of the Croatian, knew he'd come to the coalfields to work for the union. She had heard too that he'd been harassed by Sheriff Jeff Farr in the obligatory rite of passage for a new union organizer and that about a month ago, in an incident bad even by Colorado standards, he had been beaten up by a deputy sheriff and a couple of cronies. Yes, Maria knew all about Mr. Livoda, and his presence at her husband's bed frightened her. But Maria's immediate concern was to get her husband home, so she turned her attention to Spiro.

"Hi, babe," Spiro managed a new Americanism loudly and cheerfully. "Look at me, would you, ready to go."

Maria and Alberto looked at Spiro and did a double take. They could hardly recognize the man they had just seen two minutes ago, let alone the patient who only a day before had been writhing in agony. Spiro sat up in bed. He held out his hand for Alberto to shake and even waved at Livoda.

Maria was confused by her husband's apparently miraculous recovery. "Okay, let's get you home."

Spiro beamed and as Maria stooped down to help him off the bed, he gave her a huge kiss on the cheek.

"Spiro, what are you doing, we're in public."

"Sorry, babe, couldn't help it." Maria knew that this wasn't normal, but gradually she realized that Spiro's enthusiasm was forced. *But why*, she asked herself.

In the room at the end of the ward, through the window that the nurse used to check on the patients during the night, somebody was talking to the doctor and pointing towards Spiro. Alberto whispered to Maria that it was the pit boss who'd made the joke about the mule being more valuable than the miner. He was checking up on Spiro, the Italian continued, to see if his wound was too bad for him to go on working. To see, in other words, if Spiro needed to be fired. And what Spiro was doing was putting on a show, to let the bosses know that he was okay and would be up and back to work in no time. Alberto took Maria's elbows and moved her aside. He and Livoda grasped Spiro on either side and began to lift. Spiro buried his face in Alberto's chest. "Christ, man, it hurts. Take it easy."

"I'll say one thing," Livoda whispered to Spiro and gestured with his eyes in the direction of the pit boss, "they don't waste time around here."

"Okay, boss," Alberto whispered. "Keep your head down." Gently, they lowered Spiro onto the stretcher. Spiro lay on the stretcher panting, as they got ready to carry him out of the ward. But just before they took the strain, they heard a call from the end of the room.

"Hey, Andrakis, before ya' go." It was the pit boss, and he was coming towards them. "Just wanna make sure you're okay."

"Hell, boss," Spiro joked, "I've had worse off the old lady on a Saturday night. Doc says I'll be good in a week." The three miners laughed, hoping they sounded sincere, and even Maria forced a smile for she too had cottoned on.

"Good to hear it, boy. You know, I like you, so I'll check up on you. No problem. You know, see how you're doin'," the pit boss smirked back. And nonchalantly, as though in a gesture of good will, he squeezed Spiro's bad leg just above the knee. Agonizing pain shot though Spiro's whole body. Maria saw the color drain immediately from his face. How Spiro didn't scream out in agony was something she never fathomed out for the rest of her life. But he kept silent. The pit boss took his hand off Spiro's leg and watched his face.

The pit boss nodded to Alberto and Livoda, conspicuously ignoring Maria, and as quickly as they could, they got Spiro out of the hospital. As soon as they couldn't be seen from the hospital, Spiro asked them to stop.

"Are we clear of the hospital?" Spiro whispered.

Alberto nodded, and without more ado, as the tension flooded out of him, Spiro leaned over the edge of the stretcher and threw up violently. Then he lay down, thoroughly beaten, and croaked through vomit-spattered lips, "Get me home, Maria. Get me home."

As they expected, Anna was at the front door when the four of them arrived, and Maria had to stop her daughter from throwing herself all over her papa's body and making him feel even worse than he already was. "Hey, I thought you loved me," he said, trying to sound better than he felt.

"Anna," Maria ordered, "get out of the way," and the little girl retreated into the corner, her feelings hurt.

Alberto and Mike laid the stretcher down, trying to figure out where exactly was the best place to hold the invalid so they could put him to bed. The trick, they discovered, was to have Maria support his injured leg either side of the wound to take pressure off it. Alberto took Spiro around his torso, while Mike got the bottom of his legs.

"Okay, Maria?" Alberto whispered as he and Mike positioned themselves.

"Yes," she nervously replied.

Together the three of them lifted Spiro and as quickly as they could, lowered him onto the bed.

"Not too bad," Spiro said, "any more of this and you'll get it right." His weak grin still couldn't hide the fact that even that short movement was terribly painful. But at least now Spiro was home and in his own bed. Slowly his breaths became deeper and slower and gradually, as they stood there in the bedroom, he drifted into sleep. Maria quietly motioned for everybody to leave and she closed the bedroom door behind them.

Maria was nervous around Livoda, but she had to acknowledge he had been a big help. The tall young man blushed slightly at her gratitude; it was no big deal, he assured her, and if she needed any more help, Alberto knew how to find him. Livoda left, leaving Maria and Anna with Alberto.

Speaking softly Maria asked Alberto if he would look after Spiro until she got back from some errands. "It may take a few hours," she added.

"No problem, Maria, take all day. Me and Spiro are just fine. Anyways, he's sleeping right now. You go ahead."

"There's food in the box, Alberto, help yourself, and I think a beer outside, too. Come, Anna," she said quietly to her daughter. "Let's go."

It was only when they got outside that Maria told her daughter they were off to the Eriksen's farm. Although she was sure Spiro was asleep, she didn't want him to know where she was going in case he suspected her reason. For Maria was going in search of work, and Spiro would not have liked that at all.

Maria and Anna had an hour's walk ahead of them. Leaving Berwind and heading east to the open prairie, they passed the huge coking ovens at Tabasco belching out thick acrid fumes. The two of them coughed incessantly and held cloths over their mouths. Sometimes, like today, when there was little wind, it seemed that you could cut the air with a knife. But they'd done this so often that the two of them barely noticed it. At the east end of the canyon where it opened onto the prairie, the pair turned north towards the Ludlow rail depot and then walked along the railroad tracks for about a mile before crossing a stretch of grassland, all the while looking out for rattlesnakes. Finally they picked up a cart track that cut northwest towards the small town of Aguilar, and which would take them past the Eriksen's small farm.

It never ceased to amaze Maria how quickly the country could change. Although the sky was still yellow from the mine and coke workings, they were in another world. Grasslands still with cattle on them, gophers poking their heads up from their tunnels and shrieking at the interlopers, hawks holding steady in the light breeze as they searched for prey. This was the Colorado described to her all those years ago in New York when she had stepped off the immigrant boat. Here, as the man handing out brochures had told her, was a country fit for an American, where you could raise a family in peace and prosperity. If only she had known, Maria thought grimly, before she and Spiro had turned their backs on New York.

Maria came back to reality. "Don't look at them, little girl," she ordered Anna.

Ahead of them were three ranch hands repairing a section of barbed wire. As Maria and Anna approached, one of them nudged his partner. They both stopped work and the other joined them.

Maria never knew how the local farming community would react to the miners and their families. Some of them, like the Eriksens, were good Christian souls. But others, for some reason Maria could never fully figure out, resented their presence. She didn't know if it was the mines they hated or the people in them, or maybe it was just being East Europeans, because she'd noticed, or maybe just imagined, that the Western miners didn't seem to get the same treatment. As they passed she saw them whispering to each other and then smirking. But they said nothing she could hear. All the time Maria had kept up a conversation with Anna.

"I think Papa will be back to work next week, Anna. Look at that beautiful blue flower up ahead. Let's go and look at it." On and on, until she felt they were safely out of harm's way, and she could begin to let her guard down.

Finally they spied the Eriksen's farm. The Norwegian couple had got the house and the small piece of land along the Apishapa River when Peder's parents, the original homesteaders, had died. Peder and Ingrid had been in their thirties and since then had continued to grow and raise as many different plants and animals as they could: potatoes, corn, beans and alfalfa for winter forage, sheep, rabbits, and chickens, even a few goats. They even had a very small cattle herd, but nothing like the great herds that once roamed the state, now long gone in the face of competition from the Midwestern beef industry. They could have existed on this, barely, but Peder also worked as a pipefitter in the mines and together the two of them were able to keep their financial heads well above water.

As Maria and Anna walked through the gate and into the front yard of the small ranch house, Ingrid came out to meet them. Her smile was met with Maria's worried look; she looked pale and very tired. Ingrid sensed that something was not right, that Maria needed to talk.

"Just in time, Anna, the chickens need feeding." Ingrid took control. "But first, why don't you bring your ma and yourself a glass of lemonade. You know where the jug is."

As soon as she was gone, Ingrid asked if Maria was feeling well. At first, Ingrid thought she might be pregnant but as she was about to ask, Anna came back with the drinks. Anna sloshed hers down thirstily and then went to the coop behind the house and began to strew food from the bin among the chickens.

"What's up, Maria? I don't see you like this often," Ingrid said.

Maria flopped onto the swinging chair, looking so pathetic that Ingrid sat down beside her, and for a few minutes she just held her tightly. Slowly she began to ask Maria questions and gradually she learnt of what had happened.

"Maria, you know you're like a daughter to me. Right now, what with Peder just having to lay out for that new truck transmission, we can't do much."

"Ingrid, no, I wasn't looking for a handout." Maria looked hurt, as though Ingrid thought so little of her.

"Don't take no offense, girl, I meant no insult."

Maria smiled, ashamed that she had thought ill of such a good friend.

"This is what we'll do, Maria. Can you get out here a couple, three times a week, with Anna if you like, that'd be great?"

Maria nodded.

"Okay," Ingrid continued. "In that case, you help me around the kitchen and the garden, these old bones ain't what they used to be. I can't pay you much. But you can start your own garden if you like. Peder's always got seeds and cuttings he don't know what to do with. You can keep or sell what you grow. And you can use my canning jars any time you like. Deal?"

"Deal," said Maria and even managed a weak smile at her friend's kindness.

7

The trip to the Eriksens had invigorated Maria, giving her a sense of purpose and resolve to deal with Spiro's accident. But still, in the days that followed, Maria realized that probably for the first time in their marriage she could cheerfully have strangled her husband. Men are not, or so the saying goes, good patients, and Spiro did his level best to prove the saying true. The first three or four days he behaved himself. He lay on the bed and only asked Maria and Anna four or five times an hour to get him something. Sometimes it was an extra cup of coffee, sometimes a cigarette, and sometimes he just wanted someone to scratch his leg for him.

At the end of the fourth day even Anna was getting fed up. "Mama, when will Papa be able to go to work?" she innocently asked after Spiro had made her run to the store for a bag of tobacco. She had got caught in a sudden late afternoon rainstorm, and was drenched through by the time she came back.

As she toweled Anna down, Maria felt herself losing her patience. She turned to her husband. "For God's sake, Spiro, your leg's busted and now you're trying to drown our only child. Look at her, Spiro, she's soaked to the bone."

"Ach, woman, a little rain never hurt anybody. I remember back home when..."

But Maria had already turned her back to him to get dry clothes for Anna.

The next morning, as Maria was removing the overnight bandage, he took her hand. "Yeah, I know I was bad the last few days, but you pulled me through. And, you know, it's time I got moving again."

"Are you sure, Spiro?" Maria had hoped for this moment but still she thought it was too soon. "Look, forget about yesterday, Anna and me were tired, that's all. Take a few more days."

"No, Maria, let's look at the wound."

The nurse had told them that they had to check for blood poisoning and gangrene. She said that if they saw red lines running along the leg or if the wound smelled bad, Maria had to get Spiro back in right away. Maria changed the dressing and as they always did, the two of them looked and sniffed. The wound still looked ugly but it was clean and there was no odor. Spiro motioned for Maria to help him up. With her arm around his waist, Spiro gingerly stood up. They'd done this a lot since he'd come home, mostly just to get him outside for a pee or a dump, always with Maria supporting him. But this time Spiro wanted to try a few steps unaided. Anna came back into the house as he stood there, but Maria grabbed her arm as she looked like she was about to rush over to him. Maria gave him the small straight tree branch that Alberto had fashioned into a walking stick.

"Be careful, Papa," Anna squealed, holding her arms up ready to catch him. Maria stood there, too, but Spiro looked straight ahead and slowly, ever so slowly, put some weight on his injured limb.

"Okay so far," he whispered through gritted teeth. Still leaning heavily on the stick he moved his good leg forward and then slowly brought up the trailing leg. Maria went toward him, but he shooed her away. "Right, do it again, Spiro," he said out loud. And he did. It took him almost five minutes to make it outside, but finally he was there. "My God, Maria, a pee never felt so good." He grinned at her like a little boy.

But getting back alone was too much. He called for Maria, and the two of them staggered back to the bed. He sat down on it, breathing heavily. "I'm gonna' be okay, Maria, okay." For the first time since the accident, Spiro smiled broadly. Maria had her husband back, almost. After that, Spiro improved rapidly. Rest and exercise did their work, although he still couldn't go down the mines again just yet.

The weeks since Spiro's accident had been hard on Maria,

perhaps harder than on Spiro, for on top of all her regular chores like cooking, cleaning house, shopping and tending to Anna, she had an invalid to mend. Friends dropped by, but no one had helped more than Nora Davis, one of the few Westerners to give her even the time of day. Nora's husband was paid by the hour because of his skill as a winch operator, so they had a little more money than most. Still, that didn't mean she had to regularly bring the Andrakis family tinned meat, peaches, bread and whatever else she could afford. Nor did she have to stay to read with Anna while Maria tended her husband's leg or went out on errands. And now that Nora herself was ill, it was simple Christian charity to help her out in return.

Most of the mining families lived in Berwind itself, but some with a little more money had been able to rent houses away from the town proper. Nora and her husband lived in a four-roomed house up a small side canyon where there was more privacy and some protection from the winds that gusted down the main canyon. Maria knew, even before she left home, that she shouldn't be going to Nora's; it was late in the day and would soon be dark. But if she could not return Nora's favor, what sort of a friend was she, Maria asked herself.

"Hi, Nora, I hope you're feeling better," Maria said as she knocked on the door, at the same time opening it and walking through.

"Hah, it'll take a lot more than filthy water to put this old hen down," Nora cackled back. Still, Maria couldn't help but notice the gray rings around her friend's eyes. "Come in, come in, and take a weight off your feet."

As Maria made herself comfortable, she looked around, a little envious of what she saw. The Davis' home was twice the size of Maria's, with two bedrooms, a separate kitchen with a range and a living room. Nora had picked up a used three-piece living room set in Walsenburg. It had a heavy chintz design and Nora had covered the worn arms of each chair with embroidered cotton throwdowns. Against the wall there was a heavy Welsh dresser that contained a fine set of china crockery. Each plate and cup had the same design and Maria guessed that it must have been a wedding present. It looked as if it had hardly been used.

Nora looked a lot better than she had just a few days ago. Like all the other inhabitants of the mining towns, the Davises regularly boiled any water before they drank or cooked with it, but this time it hadn't been enough, and Nora had been hit with stomach poisoning. She and Maria knew that the only cure was rest. If it was simple food poisoning or even dysentery then a few days of bed would be sufficient. If it was typhoid, then only God could tell what would happen.

Maria had brought a pot of vegetable stew, made from produce from her own little garden and from some she'd got working for the Eriksens. She held the cup in front of Nora's mouth and allowed her to take a few small sips from a small spoon. Nora smiled in appreciation. Maria then broke a small piece of rough bread, soaked it in the liquid and gave it to Nora who gently placed it in her mouth as though she was afraid to risk upsetting her stomach again. As Nora chewed she appeared to get a little better. Maria thought she even saw some color come back to her friend's cheeks.

"Maria, I heard that the bosses said Spiro's accident was his fault."

Maria nodded. "I wasn't surprised, Nora. Right after the accident that man, Mike Livoda, told me he was sure they'd blame Spiro. And they did. So, until he can get back to work..." She let the sentence linger, as she thought of how difficult the next few weeks would be, even with the Eriksen's pin money to help them.

"Well then, my lovely, how is that daughter of yours?" Nora asked, changing the subject. "You know, when I saw her the other day, I said to myself, she's turning into quite the young lady. You know you're always jokin' about that baseball bat Spiro has? Well, I'd be telling Spiro to get it ready. You never know when he's going to need it." Nora saw a cloud momentarily cross her friend's face and she cursed herself for her clumsiness, but Maria's face then brightened and the two of them entertained themselves with scenes of Spiro running, or hobbling, as Maria put it, up and down Berwind looking for some suitor to protect little Anna from.

"Seriously, though," warned Nora, for she couldn't keep her concern unspoken, "keep an eye open for her. You know what some of them are like. They don't care if she's ten or twenty."

Maria knew that Anna was indeed striking, and she knew that before long she would turn the heads of more than a few young bucks.

It was dusk before Maria had gathered up her bowls and spoons. Nora was able to see Maria to the front door. Already the side canyon was dark, but the setting sun was still casting long shadows down the main canyon and gave Berwind a golden glow. The last words Maria heard as she set off home was Nora's sing-song voice wishing her *Nosdda,* that lovely little Welsh word that meant *Goodnight,* followed by Nora's warning to be careful. In her innocence Maria thought that stumbling in the dark was all she had to be careful about.

The time spent with Nora had put Maria in a good frame of mind. The evening was beautiful and even Nora's words of warning about Anna seemed exaggerated. She gave herself over to enjoying her evening stroll. Here, in the side canyon, the noise of the workings seemed distant, and even the odors that normally stuck in her nose and throat did not seem so bad. At times Maria almost forgot where she was. So lost in thought was she, that she did not notice that someone was in front of her. But then she heard what she thought was the scuffle of a shoe on the rough stones of the path. She peered ahead but the long shadows of the canyon walls made it difficult for her to see anything. At first, she thought she had imagined it. Almost immediately she heard a human cough, deep and guttural, the one sound in nature that cannot be taken for something else, and she knew for certain that she was no longer alone.

A man stood in the shadows, and his dark clothing made it difficult for Maria to see who it was. For some reason she noticed that his trousers were tucked into his boots.

"Well, ain't we lucky? Meetin' here, all alone."

She immediately recognized the voice. It was Dave Watson's and she knew for sure what he wanted. Watson stepped up to her, grabbed her by the wrist and forced her close to him. Maria tried to pull away but he was too strong for her. She could smell the alcohol on his breath, the stale tobacco smoke on his clothes.

"You little Greek bitch, I've seen how you look at me. Ain't it time you had a man, not that chicken-shit husband of yours? Hell, he can't even walk straight, the little cripp." Maria had dreaded that this would happen to her. She knew rapes happened in the camps but no woman had ever come out and made an open accusation. *Why bother*? the victims had always asked themselves. *Nobody would believe me, and if I complain my husband loses his job. And I'd still have been raped, so why bother. Just take it, shut up and try to get on with your life.* Maria had always told herself that's what she would do, but now that she was confronted with this horror her first instinct was to fight.

She didn't really know what she was doing, but managed to swing one fist wildly. It glanced off Watson's cheek and this enraged him all the more.

"So you wanna' play." Still holding her wrist, he stepped back and slashed the back of his hand hard across her cheek. His hand was calloused and its harshness brought tears to Maria's eyes and blood to her cheek, but still she fought. She struggled and tried to twist her wrist out of his iron grip, but it was hopeless. He got her in a bearhug and began to force his legs between hers. He tried to knee her but her skirt took most of the force.

Watson lost patience and punched her in the mouth. She felt

one of her teeth give and tasted the salt of her own blood. As her body strength ebbed, Watson threw her onto her back under an oak bush. He slapped her again and pinned her down with his own body weight. The ground under Maria was rough and sharp, and the stones dug through the dead leaves into her back and thighs. The rustling of the leaves sounded huge in her ears; surely, Maria prayed, someone would hear and rescue her.

Watson fumbled with his trouser belt and then expertly hitched up Maria's long skirt. He forced Maria's legs apart, pulling down her bloomers as he did so. He thrust himself inside her roughly and began to move up and down. His beer breath was hot on her face; his belt buckle dug into the top of her thigh. She tried to wriggle from under him, so he punched her again in the face. Finally her strength began to ebb. She stopped struggling and became numb to everything being done to her. She counted the leaves on the tree above her; she thought of Anna and Spiro; she thought of walking the hills of her homeland. At one point she imagined she was floating above it all, watching him assault her, his lips slobbering spittle over her face, his hands groping and twisting her breasts. Finally, and thankfully, Maria Andrakis lost consciousness.

She had no idea how long she had lain there before she came to. The canyon was dark, and below her only the lights of Berwind gave her any inkling of where she was. Maria did not want to believe that the unspeakable had happened, but she felt the blood in her mouth, her blouse and slip ripped open to her breasts and her bloomers still wound pathetically round her right ankle. She lay there for a few minutes more, trying to take stock of what to do. Ultimately, she steeled herself, nobody must know what happened. She re-arranged her clothes and spat out as much of the dried blood as she could. She felt dirty. She *was* dirty. Dirtier than she had ever been in her life.

As Maria staggered back home she hoped that nobody would see her and prayed to God, whom she had believed in all her life but for the first time doubted, that Spiro would be asleep by the time she arrived. A small part of her wanted Spiro to know what had happened so that Watson would get what was rightfully his. But the other, stronger, part of her knew that if that happened Spiro would be convicted of murder and hanged in Trinidad by the end of the week.

As she saw her house ahead, Maria's worst fear was realized. The light was on; someone was home and awake. Maria hesitated, as though she hoped that the delay would make everything change: that she had not been violated and that everything in her world was as it had been that afternoon. She knew she had to go on, but still she couldn't place one foot in front of the other. She pulled her shawl tighter around her shoulders. She felt his rough denim shirt rubbing against her, felt those calloused hands exploring her, forcing her apart, felt…

Maria knew she had no choice. Straightening her clothes as best she could, she walked down the street to her house and stepped through the door. The house was quiet and against all hope she dared to believe that neither Anna nor Spiro was home. For once, she would forgive whoever had forgotten to turn off the oil lamp. Perhaps Anna was still over at the Hoffmans, perhaps Spiro was at the men's club with Alberto and the other miners. Giving thanks to God for this one small mercy, she began to undress, but as she threw off her shawl, she heard Anna stirring in the bedroom.

Now it starts, she thought to herself. Anna came out of the room but without really looking at her mother began to tell her about the fun time she'd had with Sally, and she looked at her mother to see if she was listening. Her expression changed instantaneously.

"Mama," she cried, "what happened? Your face, it's bloody, your lip is cut. Mama."

Maria knew she had to brazen it out. "It's nothing, my child. I was stupid. I left Nora's house too late, it was dark, I slipped, I fell, I hurt myself, it's nothing."

She knew she was beginning to babble, that the hysteria was taking control, but she held on. She took a deep breath. *Act normal,* she told herself. Act normal, even though every nerve in her body wanted to explode.

"Anna, tell me again about Sally and you."

"Oh Mama, it was so funny." Anna began to involve herself in the story, and Maria breathed a little more easily as Anna told her how Sally had this really cute doll, Greta, but Frank said the doll's lips were way too small and it made her look like she'd sucked on a lemon. "Mama, Sally was so mad, she tried to hit Frank but he's too quick you know, and he just ran away, round the kitchen table they went. I laughed so hard my belly ached."

Anna's voice became louder and louder as she told the story and Maria looked fearfully at the bedroom door.

"Sshh, little girl, you'll wake Papa."

"Mama," Anna whispered, "Papa's fast asleep. Uncle Al came by earlier and he had some drink for them both. Papa's fast asleep." She gave her mother a disapproving look, and Maria almost managed a smile. Maria gently opened the bedroom door and confirmed that her husband was indeed lost to the world, at least for the next few hours.

Relieved, now she knew Spiro wouldn't disturb her, Maria forced herself to fix a cold plate for Anna. She took out a piece of chicken from the cold box and cut two slices of bread which she slathered in butter, smelling slightly rancid in the heat. Anna never noticed the taste, however, and she consumed the meal hungrily. Maria could barely stand the sight of the food let alone think of eating it.

Finally, Maria told Anna that she was going to clean herself up. Thankfully, Anna was too young to suspect anything and after she had washed her bowl, the little girl went back to the corner of the room to play with her dolls. Maria went to the corner of the room that served as a kitchen and from the shelf took a washing bowl, a towel and a block of carbolic soap. She went outside to the back of the house. Kali was tied to a stake with a short piece of rope and the dog jumped up expectantly when Maria approached, but this time Maria shooed the dog away, and in the shadows behind the house she poured water into the bowl. Taking the towel, she soaked it and began ever so gently to clean her private parts, hoping that the soap and water would flush out as much of him as possible, but knowing that it was too late. He was inside her and she could only pray that nothing would come of it. Then she washed herself. But she did not just wash. She was trying to scrub every last smell, every last fiber, every last everything of that man off her body. The block of soap was hard and coarse and it did not lather easily. Maria did not care; the pain acted as a penance for what she insanely thought was her fault. She scrubbed herself so hard that her skin became red raw. She scrubbed her thighs the hardest, even though they were beginning to turn blue with the bruising and were already painful. She felt so tired, too tired to go on. She had to sit down. Maria slumped onto the stony patch of ground that passed for a garden and lethargically stroked Kali's neck. The dog licked her face. It was then that she began to cry. Quietly, and without stopping, the tears came, as the shame and horror overtook her.

At last, the tears ended for there was none left to cry. She stood up and went back into the house. Anna had gone to bed. Maria went to the cabinet and from it took the bottle of whiskey that Spiro kept for special occasions like Easter and the family's name-days.

Well, Maria thought wryly, *if this isn't a special occasion, I don't know what is.* She poured herself a stiff shot, and drank it down in one gulp. The whiskey hit her hard, and she choked on it, hoping that Anna would not hear her. Wearily, she dragged herself to the bedroom, undressed and pulled on her nightgown. She looked at little Anna, asleep and innocent in the corner of the room. She had never looked so beautiful. A pain wracked Maria's heart and took her breath away. Ever so carefully she lay down next to Spiro, who slept on, mercifully unaware of his wife's anguish. Just one night ago the bed had been a refuge of love, safety and comfort for Maria. Now it felt defiled, like everything else in her life. She lay there unmoving until the sun rose the next day, wishing for a sleep that never came.

The weeks that followed the rape were almost too painful for Maria to bear. Walks through town were nightmares. Everywhere she went she expected to see Watson. She would start to tremble if she saw someone who even looked like him. Only once did she actually see her rapist. He was at the other end of the street and did not notice her before he walked into the mine office. But just the sight of him, and wearing the very shirt he had worn that night, sent cold sweat pouring down her body. She had to stop and lean against a hitching post, to catch her breath. She turned around and headed back home, the shopping forgotten. All she wanted to do was crawl into her bed, pull the sheets over her and pray that the Lord would put her out of her misery.

Worse than the days were the nights. Maria would lie awake in bed, reliving the rape over and over in her mind. Sometimes she was convinced that Watson was in the room coming to take her again. She could almost smell him as he rushed at her, laughing and sneering. Sleep would finally take her as the first rays of dawn began to work their way over the canyon. In the morning as she awoke from another night's fitful sleep, for one blessed moment Maria had forgotten what had happened to her. But then the memories would flood though her again, jolting her all the harder because briefly her mind had expunged the horror.

Worst was the repulsion she felt at the man who lay next to her. Maria asked God's forgiveness for feeling almost happy for Spiro's injury because it provided the excuse to avoid lovemaking. Maria loved her husband with all her heart, and she had even got to like what he did to her, even though her own mama had told her that what men did to women in bed was simply so they could have children, God's greatest gift and joy. But now it was different. Every time Spiro came close to her, she recalled that night when Watson had taken her. If she felt Spiro's breath on her cheek during the night, she smelt Watson's beer. Even a gentle touch from her husband as he positioned his leg more comfortably brought back her living nightmare.

For the past days, a terrible fear had been growing in Maria, for she had not bled for over a month. Normally that didn't worry her as her periods were never regular. But in the middle of one night, when fears can overtake even the strongest minds, she was aghast to realize that her lateness this time might mean something. *What if,* she asked herself, *I am carrying a child, his child.* Someone had told her, years ago, that if a man attacked you, you couldn't get pregnant unless you had a thrill, an orgasm. *But what if I had had one and didn't know it,* she punished herself mercilessly. *That would mean I secretly enjoyed him.* Sleep would not come to her the night of that realization. She tossed and turned wondering what to do. Her stomach knotted, and she was forced to slip quietly outside and throw up.

Lying back down next to Spiro, who slept peacefully on, she remembered that some miners' wives would go to an old woman in Trinidad if they wanted to get rid of an unborn baby. It cost them money, but to them it was better than the alternative. She had heard that some women even did it to themselves and that sometimes the women and the babies didn't survive. But she knew she could never do that. If she was pregnant she could not destroy an innocent child. *No,* she decided, *the only thing I can do is to make sure that Spiro never suspects anything.* And she knew finally, as the rays of dawn peaked over the prairie horizon, how she had to do it.

It was an irony not lost on Maria Andrakis that the following day was special to her and her church, for the fifteenth of August was not only her name day, a far more important date to a Greek than a birthday, but also the day of the Feast of the Dormition, when the spirit of Mary, mother of Jesus, was taken into Heaven, to be followed three days later by her body. Arising early, for she knew she could not sleep, Maria left a tama, a small votive offering, in front of the icon that stood on their little chest-of-drawers, and then prayed, as she always did, for a better life and eternal protection. But she doubted what she was doing, questioned whether God even existed. *What,* she asked herself as much as the Panagia, *did I do to deserve this?* The little icon glittered in the morning summer sun, but this time it offered no crumb of comfort. Nothing came back to her from the benevolent face of her saint. Maria stood up, crossed herself and left the room, tears rolling down her cheeks. She was alone; even her saint had deserted her.

Late that afternoon, Maria and Anna were baking sweet cakes in celebration of her name day. Anna helped her mother put them on a plate and asked if she could be the first to try them. "Anna, you know better. You can't ask for them. You have to wait."

But Maria managed a smile as she chastised her daughter, and within a few moments both Anna and Spiro were helping themselves to the little delicacies. They were mostly flour and water with sugar icing, but still to Anna they tasted wonderful.

After dinner, as she and Anna cleaned their plates and dishes and Spiro went for a walk to exercise his leg, Maria realized that now was the time to put her plan into action. The very thought of it filled her with nausea, and she prayed for a forgiveness of which she was not certain. But she could think of no alternative. A westerly breeze was sweeping through the canyon, removing most of the yellow clouds that hung over the mine workings. The evening sun cast long shadows over the canyon and mellowed its ugliness

Maria put on a smile. "Anna, why don't we enjoy this beautiful day and visit Sally?"

Anna didn't need a second invitation. She ran to the back and grabbed Kali, who greeted her as though she hadn't seen her mistress in years.

At the Hoffmans' house Anna immediately thrust Kali's lead into her mother's hand and ran off to find Sally. Elsie came out to see what all the commotion was about. "I'm surprised to see you, Maria, but very glad. I've missed you the last few weeks."

Maria paused. "Elsie, I haven't felt good and what with Spiro's injury, I haven't had much time to myself. Elsie, could you do me a favor and look after Anna for the night?"

She looked surprised, but when Maria smiled slyly, she cottoned on. "Well, I think we can do that for you. You just leave her here and enjoy yourselves."

When she heard the last words of the sentence, Maria shuddered. *I just hope I can,* she silently prayed. She walked to the back of the house where Anna and Sally were playing with Greta, Sally's doll. The other Hoffman kids were there, too, including Frank, Sally's nemesis. But he was involved in whittling a piece of wood, trying to look too grown up to bother with silly little girls.

"Anna, would you like a special treat? You can stay here tonight and play with Sally. Mrs. Hoffman says it's okay."

"Love to. See you tomorrow. Oh, can you take Kali back?" Anna barely looked up at her mother.

"Elsie, thanks, this means a lot to me." As she walked back home with Kali, Maria told herself that that had been the easy part. The worst was to come and she steeled herself to do it properly. As she tied Kali up, she heard Spiro inside. Reluctantly she walked inside.

"Where's Anna?" Spiro asked perfunctorily.

"Oh, I thought you and I could enjoy a night alone. She's over with Sally. It is my special day, remember." Maria gave her best attempt at a smile. Spiro smiled back.

"Are you sure you're okay?" Maria asked him.

Spiro simply nodded, speechless with surprise at the change in his wife. Since the accident he had convinced himself that she was using his wound as an excuse to avoid making love. The evening sun had dropped behind the hills and the house now lay in dark shadows. Slowly, because his leg still hurt, he walked across and kissed her gently. He took her hand and led her to the bedroom. Drawing the curtain, he removed his clothes and climbed into bed. Maria did the same.

The lovemaking did not last long. As she felt him about to explode in her, she quickly took his erect penis and deftly, for this was how they'd practiced birth control for most of their married life, pulled her body away from him. But this time, she deliberately took too long and she felt his penis pulsating as semen flooded into her. Finally, Spiro was done and he carefully rolled over to his side of the bed, breathless. He looked at his wife.

"Thank you. It was like I remembered it. Wonderful. But we weren't quick enough, we're we?"

His wife smiled back at him. "Well, my love, what happens is always the will of God." Now that it was over, Maria felt relieved. She had done this out of fear, and a part of her, the biggest part, still loathed herself for deceiving Spiro. But it was good to have Spiro inside her again. And with that thought, she kissed her dozing husband and snuggled her body around his to try to find some needed sleep.

8

Frank Hayes, vice-president of the United Mine Workers of America, scratched his chin and looked at the three men on the other side of the table in the dingy union office. John Lawson, Ed Doyle and John McLennan virtually ran the union in Colorado. There was no small talk. Hayes began. "You know it's bad if they've sent me to Denver to handle this personally. I'll give it to you straight. At headquarters they're really frightened the union's becoming irrelevant. Working conditions aren't getting any better and the last we heard we're just not getting enough miners to sign up. We need something to shake people out of their apathy. I've got the go-ahead from headquarters to call a strike if the owners try to stop us from recruiting members or fail to recognize us as the miners' representatives. I know. A strike does nobody any good. We'll lose money, sure, but so will they. But, I have to say, I don't think we're at that point yet. Right now, regardless of anything else we might try, we have to keep on talking to the companies."

The three looked at him in puzzlement, and Lawson quickly asked, "Frank, you're not saying we just do nothing are you? Look where that's got us."

Hayes smiled thinly. "No, John, quite the opposite. But don't you see, if the public knows that we kept on trying to talk to the companies until it was useless, then public opinion swings towards us. We've got to make them make the first move. So, guys, you're in charge of operations down there. How's it going?"

"Okay. I agree that the membership drive has kinda' stalled." Lawson replied. "But we're trying a new plan, and we think it's working. We've got about forty of our people down there, working in pairs. One of the two acts like he's the recruiter, the front man. He's the one that takes the heat from Farr and Reno and the other company thugs. The other man works underground as it were." Lawson smiled at his little joke, although their blank faces showed the others didn't get it. "He's the one who actually makes contact with the miners and gets them to join up."

"Yeah," added McLennan, "and he's the one who licks the bosses' boots and then fingers the scabs as union organizers. In a couple of cases we've had them kicked out the mines. It's kinda' clever, if you ask me. Oh, and we've got the Greek guy, Tikas. You'll know him from the Northern fields. He's pretty useful to us. John recruited him. He's great at getting the Greeks to join."

"Right," Hayes moved on, "tell me about Governor Ammons."

It was Doyle who answered. "I dunno', I honestly don't. If you look at his record, I'd say he was sympathetic, and his Labor Commissioner, Brake is, I'm pretty sure, well I think he's in our corner, but they're both cagey about it. I think Ammons is getting jerked around by some of his advisors, and I'm sure he's getting pressure from Bowers, Osgood and the other owners."

"Bottom line, John?" Hayes asked, looking directly at Lawson.

"Right now, we have to go it alone. I think Ammons wants a deal that'll make everybody happy. He's pretty naïve, if you ask me. And I can't see him coming out for us publicly whatever he might think in private." The other two nodded in agreement.

"Right then." Hayes wrapped up the meeting. "Oh, one other thing, all of you. Like I said. It's real important we keep the public on our side. So, you're gonna' have to be careful about keeping your hotheads under control. I know some of them'd like nothing better for this all to turn violent. But if it does, it can't be us who started it. Understood?"

The three bobbed their heads in agreement.

"All right, I'm done. Next meeting we'll talk about the convention later this month, it's coming up fast. We need to figure out who's speaking and when." He added, "I'm as dry as dust. Is it too early for a beer?" The others smiled and headed to the door and downstairs onto the busy Denver streets.

As they were walking down the stairs, Hayes pulled Lawson back. Standing alone on the landing, as the other two continued down, Hayes asked Lawson point blank, "What's this I'm hearing about you and Lewis?"

Lawson grimaced; he knew this was going to come up at one point. Tom Lewis had been union president but after being kicked out of the position two years earlier had gone over to the other side.

"Frank, he showed up last week. He seems real concerned about what the strike would do to the union financially; we're not exactly loaded." Lawson kept calm. He was tired of this accusation, especially after all he'd done for the union, and he didn't like being lectured to by a much younger man. But he knew he had screwed up and had it coming.

Hayes' face reddened. "Come on, Lawson, Lewis is a traitor, you know that, he doesn't give a toss about us. He's one of them. Goddamn it, John, since we kicked him out of the presidency…" Hayes' anger stopped him from finishing his sentence. Instead, he said, "Hell, he even publishes magazines that take their side, says how good they are to their workers. What I'm hearing is he's persuaded you to tell people we'll give up on union recognition by the owners, so long as they give us a few more concessions."

"That's not how it is, Frank, you know me better than that. I was just fishing, seeing what else was on the table, you know, seeing what he was really up to."

"Look, John, a lot of people don't trust you. They still think you're Lewis's stoolie. This crap you've just pulled doesn't exactly help your cause, does it?"

Lawson was taken aback by Hayes' anger. "No, you're right," he conceded.

The union vice-president calmed down a little, as he realized he had to handle this diplomatically. "Okay, John, I guess we need you down there too much. But no more, okay, no fuckin' more. I'm issuing a statement to the press tomorrow. It'll say that all of us union leaders are as one in our opposition to Lewis interfering in our business. And don't be surprised if your name comes up."

Lawson felt the color drain from his face. "Okay, Frank, you can count on me."

"John, as far as I'm concerned, it's over. Let's join the others. I'm really thirsty now. By the way, I got your joke, you know, 'underground.' Very good."

Lawson managed a thin smile, but that was all.

Denver was suffering through another late summer's afternoon. The heat was oppressive, there was no wind, and ceiling fans just served to stir the cloying air. Only the bursting of the monsoon clouds in the next hour or so would bring the temperature down. But despite their discomfort, the heads of the three major Colorado coal companies still met for their regular strategy conferences: Jesse Welborn and Montgomery Bowers of the Colorado Fuel and Iron, David Brown, representing the Rocky Mountain Fuel Company, and John Osgood of the Victor-American. They settled down to the meeting, stirring their iced teas, trying to stay cool in a room that offered no respite while chatting about the current baseball season. Bowers, a native of New York, was convinced that the Giants would run away with the World Series. "Not so fast," twitted Welborn with a forced jocularity. "I remember you saying the exact same thing two years ago. And look what happened. Philly took the series."

Bowers smiled. "Welborn, you know lightning never strikes the same place twice. This time it's ours. I guarantee it." Everybody laughed at this. Bowers could guarantee most things, but a baseball series?

Osgood finally brought them down to earth. He pulled at his collar to allow the sweat to trickle off his neck. Even his moustache held drops of perspiration. "Gentlemen," he began, "I think you would agree that the baseball season should, if this were a just world, be far more important than what's going on in our mines, but unfortunately, as my father always said, 'John, whoever told you life was fair was full of it.' I don't think this meeting will take long. I'm sure we're all on the same page." The men smiled at Osgood's homespun ways.

"As you know," Osgood continued, "agents working for Baldwin-Felts are convinced that the union has decided to strike; they're just waiting for the right time. I understand that they have increased their attempts to enroll miners…"

"And now that evil woman, Mother Jones, is down there," Bowers interrupted. "I agree, John, they're going to strike." Bowers was not a regular at these meetings, but this time he had some interesting news for them. He continued, "Our lawyers in Washington have persuaded the federal government to stay out of this disagreement. It's a local affair completely, we told them. And they apparently agreed."

Osgood did not like being interrupted by Bowers, who as far as he was concerned was simply a Rockefeller lackey. In fact he hated even being in the same room for he still smarted from losing the Colorado Fuel and Iron, and hearing Bowers let it drop that it was the Rockefellers who were the ones talking to Washington simply rubbed salt in his wounds. But he kept his silence as the room digested the fact that this would give them almost total independence in handling whatever was to happen.

"What amazes me," Brown finally said, "is how the union can contemplate a strike after all we've conceded. You know, we've got rid of scrip. We've given them the eight-hour day. Hell, even a ten percent raise last year."

What amazes me, thought Osgood as he looked at Brown with apparent interest, *is how you can continue to state the obvious, meeting after meeting.* But sensibly he kept the thought to himself, something he did a lot at these meetings. Now was not the time to rock the boat.

Before he'd lost control of the Colorado Fuel and Iron, Osgood reflected as Brown droned on, he had shown what he thought was unparalleled paternalism, going so far as to establish a sociological department that would tend to the miners' needs (including free kindergarten, organized camp picnics and religious meetings) and even a weekly magazine that would extol the virtues of life in the camps. But that wasn't enough and like little children the miners had flung a temper tantrum. *So be it,* he concluded. *They started it, but we'll finish it.*

The group now turned to other matters. Osgood raised the problem of handling the press. Bowers admitted that some reporters were saying that the union was not dead set on striking, at least not right away. They still want Ammons to step in.

"But it seems to me," Bowers said, pressing the issue, "that if the union wants Ammons to mediate then they're simply buying time until they've built up their funds and planned the strike in detail. You know, they got hit pretty hard over the past few years, what with all the strikes they've called. If they let Ammons mediate, it'll be weeks, maybe months, before anything is resolved. You know what he's like. And that's exactly what they want. But, gentlemen, they'll strike. Trust me."

"I don't care in this instance what the press says," Osgood jumped in, "but Bowers is right. I'm convinced that the union's prepared to strike. It's just a matter of when. And we'd be crazy if we let them set the timetable. Personally speaking, I'd like to see them strike as soon as possible. That way we can break them quick and have as little interruption to the winter coal supply as possible. Perhaps we need to turn the heat up on the union again."

Welborn hadn't said much; he never did when Bowers was present, and when he did venture a comment, Osgood had long ago realized, it nearly always agreed with Bowers' position. This wasn't sycophancy, but simply due to the fact that the two of them were cut from the same cloth when it came to dealing with workers and their unions. Yet, despite their shared business philosophy, the relationship between the two was complicated. Welborn had been president of the Colorado Fuel and Iron for six years. Bowers was only a vice-president, chairman of the company's executive committee and also its treasurer. But most importantly, Bowers spoke directly for the Rockefellers; he was their man in Colorado; he was the Colorado Fuel and Iron. And so Welborn deferred to his supposed subordinate.

But now Welborn finally did speak. "Look, we've conceded a lot, and like the rest of you, normally I don't worry too much about the press. But I think it's crucial we keep public opinion on our side. If the only thing we won't give the miners is union recognition, and they strike, then I don't think they'll get much sympathy, especially if coal and coke prices go up. All we have to do is hold on tight, and see them off like we've done before. I think we'll come out of this stronger, both politically and economically."

The owners murmured their agreement and rose from their chairs.

David Brown raised one final item. "Gentlemen, I wonder if you and your wives might be interested in joining me and my party for a charitable social evening. It's not until next month, but I know how busy you are, so I thought I'd get to you early."

"What's it for?" Welborn asked.

"Well, as you may know, my cousin is on the Board of Trustees for the Museum of Natural History. They're bringing in an exhibit from the Field Museum in Chicago. It depicts the different arts and crafts of the aboriginals. Before reservation life, of course. There'll be totem poles from Canada and pottery from Arizona, that sort of thing. They had it in Washington, and it was very popular."

"Sounds interesting," Welborn added.

Brown continued. "Carolyn thinks it's important that we

show how, well, quite advanced some of the tribes were. I wouldn't go as far as civilized, of course, but quite advanced."

Osgood was the first to agree to purchase the tickets. He was a member of the so-called Sacred Thirty-Six, Denver's ultra-elite set, and felt he should take the lead.

"Well, I'm not sure if both of us will be able to come, of course," Bowers followed, "but it sounds like a good cause. So, put me down."

Welborn followed suit. As they left, they felt pleased with themselves at how charitable they were, when the cause was just.

In his nondescript brown suit, Elias Milton Ammons looked like just another anonymous run-of-the-mill businessman, rather than the governor of the state of Colorado. His face was thin but not gaunt, and his nose was what could charitably be called aquiline. His receding brown hair gave him a high forehead. He stared out of his office window, never tiring of the wonder of the Rockies a few miles to the west. In the height of summer, the thin morning air made the high peaks crystal clear against the washed out blue of the sky. He could see traces of snow on the highest peaks, although even with his new glasses, he wasn't sure. *How different,* Ammons thought, *from the so-called mountains of his native North Carolina.* August there would be oppressively humid, shirts would be soaking wet within minutes of putting them on, and any attempt at work would seem doomed and not worth the effort of beginning. Even the evening breezes failed to cool anything off. But here in Colorado everything was clean, bright and pure. Ammons laughed to himself. *Pure? With what's going on in Trinidad? If only it were.*

Ammons had become governor just a few months earlier and though he had served in the Legislature and knew his way around the capitol, he was finding that being governor brought with it a whole new set of constituencies who preferred to lurk under the rocks and only show themselves when necessary. What made his position worse was that he had once been a Republican but had changed parties. That was almost twenty years ago, but the party, and more importantly the Denver business establishment, had never forgiven him.

His reveries were interrupted by his secretary announcing that Edwin Brake, his labor commissioner, had arrived. Ammons adjusted his tie to stop the stiff collar chafing his neck and resignedly nodded his permission for Brake to come in. He was not looking forward to this meeting at all.

Even before he was comfortable in his chair, Brake started. "Governor, the companies are intent on forcing the situation in the Southern coalfields by refusing any more concessions to the union, no matter how minor. Plus, the union isn't exactly accommodating. Their only chant is union recognition, union recognition. It's like a broken phonograph. Governor, all in all we're at a stand-off. I think both sides want the fight. I know that you've tried to act as a hidden mediator, and that's good, but I think it's time you came out and told the public the harm being done to them."

"Edwin, I know all this and I realize it cannot continue, but you must understand the position I am in politically. The national party wants me to make a stand against Republican interests. And I am not, as you know, unsympathetic to the union's demands." After a short silence, ominously the governor added, "But there are other interests in this state that I must consider. I cannot be seen to kowtow to the unions."

Brake's eyes opened wide. "Do you mean Republican interests or company interests, sir? You know better than I that the Republicans think they own the southern part of the state. But they don't. Sure they take the graft money, but the companies own the Republicans. They're the ones who own southern Colorado. It's the companies we have to deal with. By the way, governor, did you know, talking of Republicans and money, that down in Trinidad, they make the prostitutes pay them a fee to practice their trade?"

Ammons, surprisingly, smiled at this revelation. "Well, I suppose that in politics we're all selling or buying something. Shame we didn't think of it first."

Brake didn't know if he was joking. He stared at the governor who had gone back to looking out of the window, trying to see something he had missed.

"Edwin, I have to tell you that I feel like a punchbag." Ammons smiled thinly at the analogy. "I met with the union the other day, and they reiterated that I needed to support them publicly. Well, guess what, that little meeting which was supposedly private was leaked to Osgood, who then stormed into my office the same day and told me on no account could I recognize the union. It must be serious if Osgood's still in Denver; he hates the heat here. I swear to God, they know more about these private meetings than I do, and I'm in them."

Ammons continued. "I know you're pessimistic about stopping this strike, and privately I agree with you, but we've got to exhaust every possibility. I need you to go to Trinidad, meet with the union representatives down there, try to make them see reason. Tell them they've got a friend in the state house but I can't be seen to side publicly with them. Try to buy me some time. Okay?"

"I'll do it, Governor, of course I will. But you know where I stand. I think it's too late. The big sticking point is union recognition, everything else is peripheral, and the two sides won't budge on that one. Look, I'll get down there to Trinidad this weekend. As you know, the State Federation of Labor is meeting down there on Monday. All the union bosses'll be there."

As he walked back to his office, not for the first time, Brake was confused by the Governor's attitude of conciliation. *He can't be frightened of the fight, surely.* Ammons had had a checkered but successful life, variously working as a cattleman, a laborer and a journalist. And Colorado politics was no place for a Sunday school teacher. Ammons had to have been mentally tough to leave the Republican Party and then get elected as a Democratic governor. And since taking office, Ammons had continued the progressive legislation he'd started as a state representative. He'd forced through the licensing of automobiles, established a system of state recreational parks, and he'd even legalized the eight-hour working day and clarified existing mining labor laws. But why didn't he fight for more mine reforms like he had fought for the others? Something held Ammons back. Was it simply, Brake wondered, that Ammons realized he was in over his head and couldn't make decisions of the magnitude required by events?

There were still many uncertainties but Brake was convinced that when all was said and done there was going to be a strike, and like everything to do with the coalmines, it would be ugly and dirty.

9

John McLennan was right; Louis Tikas was great at getting the Greeks to join the union. Tikas himself didn't know exactly why. It may have been because he'd run a Denver coffeehouse and had become a man to be sought after for advice. Maybe as a Cretan he subtly reminded his countrymen of their heritage of resisting oppression. Maybe, in his unassuming way, he was able to convince them that this was a fight worth having. Maybe it was simply because they knew he'd represent them honestly and to the best of his ability. Whatever the exact reason, when Tikas spoke, the Greeks listened and more often than not did what he asked.

This Wednesday morning, Tikas was calling on a miner who he thought would have a special reason to commit to the cause. After he had heard of Spiro's accident, Tikas had placed his name on a list for a meeting in the very near future. He knew that Spiro had always kept to himself, not joining the union, believing the best way to protect his family was to go unnoticed, hoping that hard work alone would lead to safety and security. Tikas intended to find out if he had changed his mind. As he made his way down Berwind's main street to the Andrakis' house, he reflected how strange the turns of life were. Here, in a mountain canyon thousands of miles from their Greek island home, two Cretans would meet for the first time, not to raise a glass of raki in simple friendship, but to talk, or so Tikas fervently hoped, of the struggle for freedom and dignity. Tikas managed a chuckle to himself. *Perhaps this isn't so strange after all, two Cretans meeting to fight against a common enemy.*

When he got to Spiro's house, he saw a table and two chairs sitting just outside the front door. On the table were two glasses and a small bottle of clear liquid, also a plate of cookies. The scene reminded him poignantly of the little stone balcony outside his family home on Crete, where his father would drink coffee with the other men of the village.

That's odd, Tikas thought, *Andrakis knew I was coming but I hadn't told him.* But then he smiled to himself, remembering, of course, that the Greek miners had a secret network of gossip that would put the Pinkerton Detective Agency to shame. Spiro would have known of the visit within an hour of Tikas telling the other organizers whom he intended to see. The little Cretan stood quietly outside the house enjoying the warm summer sun. A fly buzzed around his head and he shooed it away. Then he heard movement inside the house. Trying not to look, Tikas heard a whispered conversation, and then Spiro emerged. His leg was still heavily bandaged, but Tikas noticed that he did not need a stick, at least not for moving around his home.

"Kyrie Tikas, please sit down, I've been expecting you."

"Good morning, Kyrie Andrakis. Thank you for allowing me to see you."

Spiro greeted him politely, but still looked warily around him. The two of them sat down and Tikas allowed Spiro to pour him a small glass of the colorless liquid. The fiery drink burnt its way down Tikas's throat.

"Not raki, I am afraid," said Spiro, conversing in their native Greek, "but something similar. At least it looks like raki. I apologize also, kyrie, for my wife. Normally, she would serve our guests, but today she is not," he hesitated, groping for the right words, "Today, the last week, she has not been well. I know you will understand."

Tikas politely expressed his hope that he had not inconvenienced her. Spiro waved him away. So far the conversation had followed exactly what Tikas expected: formal hospitality from one Greek to another, no more, no less. As Tikas nibbled on the cookies, an obligatory offering from Spiro to a guest in his home for no Greek would offer a drink without food, he looked his fellow countryman over. Tikas had seen a thousand miners just like him. The rough clothes darned and repaired almost beyond reason, the heavy boots scuffed raw and black with coal dust. But for Tikas, their clothes only told part of their story. These miners had once been strong in body and mind, but both had been sapped by the dangers of their profession. Spiro's body bore the scars of numerous accidents, the cuts on his hand, the scar over his right eye when a pit prop had snapped unexpectedly and a splinter flew into his forehead; the bandaged knee. But worst of all was Spiro's face.

The man is old beyond his years, but he can't be much older than me, Tikas thought. Creases of worry were etched around Spiro's eyes. His moustache was prematurely graying. And Spiro's eyes were tired, as they seemed to stare ahead inevitably to a future that carried nothing for him and even less for his family.

He's frightened; he sees no point in doing anything. But Tikas kept these thoughts to himself. *If this man was to be brought on board, he would have to be handled carefully.* Tikas knew that a wife and child could easily change a man's approach to the world, make him softer, more compliant. But Tikas had also seen accidents far lighter than Spiro's tip a miner over the edge, as the callousness of the company became a personal insult.

Tikas made his move carefully. "Can I call you Spiro if you call me Louis?" He stopped, because Spiro was grinning. Tikas gave him a puzzled look, and then cottoned on. "Oh, Louis, I see. Well, blame it on the idiot at Ellis Island. Couldn't even spell Ilias. God knows what he'd have done with Spantidakis. So, Louis Tikas I became and I guess it just stuck. Spiro, thanks for the drink and food. It looks like your leg's healing. Is it okay? By the way, I'm sorry that the company wouldn't give you any money. There's a surprise."

"Well, our friends help us and it won't be long before I'm down the mine again," Spiro grimaced as the words came out.

Tikas picked up on Spiro's attitude. "I know you're tired, so let me begin. You know, Spiro, how many miners died last year in the mines? "

Spiro shook his head.

"Over a hundred. And you know how many widows got money?"

"No, but I can guess," Spiro replied. "Not one."

"Exactly right," Tikas scowled. "But what can we expect from those bastards? By God, one day a miner will have an accident and it won't be his fault. But then I don't expect to see pigs fly over Berwind any time soon." Spiro looked puzzled at this strange phrase, but smiled nonetheless.

Spiro absently looked down at his leg as though it was not attached to him, but belonged to somebody else. "Thanks, by the way, it is getting better."

Spiro said no more, just kept looking down at his leg and Tikas began to think that perhaps Spiro was too far gone to be of any help. But he persevered.

"If there's anything I can do…" Tikas let the sentence hang unfinished.

Spiro's eyes suddenly came alight. "Don't worry about me or my family. My leg won't be like this forever. Those bastards won't cheat me ever again. No compensation, they were more worried about their goddamned mule. Did you hear about that, Louis? Asked about the mule, nothing about me. And then there were the boots."

Tikas saw the change in Spiro immediately, and almost recoiled in shock. Spiro's face flushed red with anger and as he spoke he even banged his fist on the table. Tikas breathed a sigh of relief, his misgivings over, although he had no idea why Spiro was talking about boots. Still, if it got him angry, so much the better.

Tikas now changed the subject; he wanted to control this conversation, not Spiro. He talked of his life on Crete, of the oranges that fell from the trees without picking, of the olive harvests, of preparing the ground in spring for the crops. He talked of wandering the hillsides with his family, searching for the succulent greens that would make up the bulk of their meals, and picking the snails off the damp grass to add meat to their diet. He talked of the back-breaking and soul-destroying poverty that had forced them to come so far from home. And Spiro sat there, mute, as Tikas wove his web of words.

"Where are you from, Spiro?" Tikas asked gently.

Spiro took a small sip of his drink. "A small hill village in the west of the island. Nothing important ever happened in my village, I don't think anything ever will."

Tikas grinned. "I lived in the exact same village south of Rethymno."

Spiro continued. "My grandfather told me that the Turks once massacred hundreds of Greeks close to where we lived. Said he'd seen the stakes they'd stuck the leaders on. They'd been giving themselves up, but I guess that wasn't good enough for the Turks. Bastards."

This is going well, thought Tikas. He took the plunge and began to turn the conversation to how their fathers and grandfathers had fought the Turks and finally won. Tikas reminded Spiro that Crete had finally become part of Greece; all their struggles, all their pain, all their deaths had finally paid off.

"They were good men, weren't they?" Spiro added. "Good men and brave. We honor them." He raised a glass and Tikas joined him in the toast.

Now Tikas was ready to start setting the hook. "You know, I wonder," Tikas spoke, almost absent-mindedly, "I wonder how our fathers and grandfathers would act if they were here, in this place today."

Spiro looked at Tikas and smiled slyly. "Kyrie Tikas. I believe you're genuinely concerned about me and my family. I thank you. But I also know that you didn't come just to offer me comfort. I'm not stupid. I know why you are here. Yeah, I'll help you however I can."

Tikas nodded to his new-found ally. "Thank you, my friend. I will let you know when I need you. Are you in the union?"

Spiro nodded. "Mike Livoda signed me up just after the accident."

Tikas nodded his approval; he hadn't known until that moment how far ahead of him Spiro was. He stood up, shook Spiro's hand, thanked him again for his hospitality, and without more ado, left. Tikas could not believe that Spiro had joined the cause so easily, and he was realist enough to know that he had had to do nothing.

Two weeks after their meeting, Spiro sat beside Tikas in his beat-up Ford, Alberto behind them. The leather seats were cracked and the springs groaned in unison with the rattles of the running boards as they drove over the rutted country road. Every so often the gear stick popped out and Tikas would have to grind about until the cogs re-engaged. They talked about nothing in particular, for each of them was apprehensive for different reasons about the meeting they were headed to and was reluctant to bring it up. Fortunately, as Spiro was learning, Tikas had the knack for knowing when to be serious and when just to talk about the weather, the baseball season or even the cost of food in the company store.

Aguilar, their destination, was a small town, a fifteen minutes ride away from Berwind. It had started life as a trading post but when the railroad came through it had grown into a small regional center for local farmers. On its unpaved streets were shops, a jail and a large number of bars, frequented by the miners working the nearby Empire mine. One of the bars was nicknamed the '29th of July,' commemorating the day in 1900 when the Italian king was assassinated by anarchists. It was a place where men could dream fancifully of The Revolution over a cold beer; and where informers could get the dirt on union activists. The bar was also the headquarters of an Italian anarchist group. These men were used to going their own way, but Tikas knew that he somehow had to get them working with the union for they were a powerful force.

Tikas had never been to the bar, because if you weren't Italian you needed an invitation, and he was impressed that Spiro, on his first job, had got Alberto to invite both of them. The idea had been Lawson's, who argued that their shared Mediterranean background would break the ice between the two Greeks and the Italians, a source of great amusement to them as they bounced along the road.

"See, friends," laughed Alberto, "we eat olives and drink wine. So, no problem."

"Hell, Alberto, Spiro and me are from Crete. We're even different from the other Greeks. God knows where the Westerners get their ideas from. No offense, but I ain't no Italian, and you're sure as hell no Greek."

"Yeah," added Spiro with a huge grin on his face, "but we all look alike, don't we? So, like Alberto said, no problem."

As they approached Aguilar the importance of what they were about to do sobered them up. Parking the Ford on the main street, they walked into the bar and were hit by a wall of blue tobacco smoke, hanging thick and translucent. Pushing their way inside, Spiro's bad leg slipped on some beer and he ended up accidentally kicking over a spittoon. The brown globs of tobacco and mucous swilled across the floor. The barman didn't say a word, just took a mop and bucket of water and diluted the muck enough to make it unrecognizable. The miners were forced to lift their feet out of the little brown waves that washed around them. The bar went quiet and the Italian miners all stared at Spiro. Without thinking, he tried to apologize in Greek, but Alberto hushed him. One of the Italians muttered "Fuckin' Greek," but mostly to himself. The Italians returned to their huddled drinking, smoking and talking.

"Three beers, per favore." Alberto put the orders in. While the beers were being poured, Spiro looked about him. The ceiling and walls had once been cream but hadn't seen a paintbrush in years. The walls were covered with pictures of the Italian countryside pulled from magazines. Behind the bar was a large color picture of St. Peter's Square, a sepia photograph of the current Pope and a picture of the Virgin Mary by some unknown Italian artist, or so Spiro guessed, he wasn't really sure.

The beers came and the three took themselves to a small table in the corner. Alberto drew on his beer and looked around as though trying to spot somebody.

"Okay, boys," he declared, "I'll go get him."

He walked over to a small group in the corner of the bar. Alberto conversed with one of them briefly and then the two of them returned to the table. The stranger was a tall man in his early forties. He had recently shaved but even so his face was almost blue from the dark stubble just underneath the surface. For someone supposed to be a miner, his hands were smooth and clean.

Perhaps his talents lay elsewhere, Spiro speculated. But then he realized that he was staring at the man and quickly moved his eyes away.

"This is Paolo Rossi," Alberto introduced them and couldn't stop himself from preening that he knew such an important man. "And this is Louis Tikas. You have much in common." Rossi nodded in Tikas' direction but ignored Spiro completely.

Tikas offered him a seat, and Rossi sat down and lit a cigarette.

"Mr. Rossi," Tikas began, "as you know, the union's always looking for more members. We think it is the only way we can get the companies to agree to our terms, if we stand together, united."

Rossi sat silently, the cigarette smoke trickling up from his nostrils and forming a haze over the Italian's face.

"I think," Tikas continued, "that you agree with what the

union is trying to do." At that, Rossi nodded almost imperceptibly. "We'd like you to join us in this fight." Rossi said nothing. Spiro could see that Tikas wasn't getting through to him. "Mr. Rossi. I know you think we're stupid, trying to deal with the companies. I respect that, even if I think you're wrong. But nothing is gonna' change for the better, for my men or yours, if we don't stand together, if only this once. Don't you see that? The companies like it when we don't talk to each other."

Finally, Rossi spoke. "Tikas, I checked you out. Friends of mine talked to Lawson and that other guy, the one who's always looking for a fight, that German guy, Germer. They say I can trust you. But I heard you were once a scab, Tikas. I can't forget that. But I guess something changed you, don't know what, don't care, either. And like I said, they say you're on the level. So for now, I'll listen to what you have to say. You know what me and my men want."

Spiro could not follow all the words, but he could get the gist, as Tikas and Rossi quietly talked politics in halting but understandable English. Spiro learnt that Rossi was an anarchist. He chuckled to himself. He knew the origin of the word, it came from the Greek; how could there be an anarchist organization? Surely the two words contradicted each other? But he sensibly kept these thoughts to himself. Rossi was way too big a man to take liberties with.

Rossi spoke up so Spiro and Alberto could finally hear the conversation. "I don't think you're a communist or even a socialist, Tikas. I think you just want a better deal for your men. That's okay. No problem with that. I tell you what, Tikas. I won't tell my men to join your union. But I won't stop them either. You're free to talk to them. But if the union does things we don't like, we'll pull our members out and we're done with you for good. Okay?"

Rossi stood up, grunted at the three of them and walked to the other end of the bar. He pulled long and hard on a beer, wiped the back of his hand across his mouth and burped.

10

The balmy August air felt good to Angelo Cassano and his wife Claudia as they took an evening stroll and felt the stress of the day evaporate. They had left their son, Giuseppe, in charge of the ice-cream parlor for a few brief hours, but he had been well-trained and would keep the till drawer opening and closing, just the way Angelo liked it. Men and women, and children enjoying a special night out with their parents, sauntered up and down Trinidad's main street, chatting with their friends or listening to The Salvation Army band. The bandmaster liked "Onward Christian Soldiers" the best, selecting it every three or four hymns. If the players objected to the droning repetition of their concert, they kept it to themselves, and certainly the crowd didn't seem to mind at all, as they sang along with the music. Angelo walked over to a stall and treated his wife to a bag of cotton candy. She pulled at the pink gauze, feeling the stickiness between her fingers and on her lips and she luxuriantly savored one of her favorite treats. Cotton candy was still a relatively new sweet and it irked Angelo that she liked this American glue, as he liked to describe it, over his own home-made ice cream. He teased her about it.

"Hey, Mama, I know why you like this pinky stuff. It's because with my ice cream you get the best every day. Just like me, eh, the most perfectest, handsomest man in the whole wide world. So it's good you get to see what ordinary candy's like. "

He laughed so hard, bystanders stared at him; he laughed as though this was the first time he'd ever told the joke. And as though she'd heard it for the first time too, Claudia burst into laughter herself. She snuggled up to him, and lovingly whispered that no man, nobody, could match her Angelo. And so the two of them, arm-in-arm like a young courting couple, listened to the band play "Onward Christian Soldiers" again, each of them thanking the Lord for allowing them to find each other all those years ago.

Mingling with the crowd that Saturday evening were Baldwin-Felts' men, trying to pick up any conversations about what the union might be planning. They knew it was well-nigh impossible because by this time the union leaders had become canny about whom they told their plans to; knew their own ranks had more than their fair share of informers. But the detectives still moved through the crowd just in case they got lucky. Even though they prided themselves on being inconspicuous, most of the detectives stood out like sore thumbs. Some of them carried revolvers on their belts in open holsters. Nearly all of them had a swagger, a bearing that sent out the unmistakable message that they were a cut above the rest. And as the detectives would move closer to a suspicious group of men who might be talking about the weather, the latest baseball scores, the price of gasoline or, if they were really lucky, the union, so that group would turn in on themselves and hunker down and by their body language tell the interlopers that they knew who they were.

Two of the detectives on duty that night were Sam King and Arthur Stubbs. They were dog tired after a full day's work, and now they had been ordered to wait at the rail station to identify any union organizers arriving for the state labor convention. Their wait had been rewarded when the evening train from Denver opened its doors and out stepped Gerald Lippiatt, of Italian descent despite his name.

As Lippiatt waited to leave the station with the other passengers, Stubbs sidled up to the Italian. Very quietly he whispered in Lippiatt's ear. "Listen, you fuckin' Dago Wop, we know who you are and why you're here."

"Yeah," chimed in King just as quietly. "Remember, we know how to deal with you Commies. By the way, Italian boy, why the fancy name? Or did your mammy not know who your daddy was, too busy on her back was she to keep a list?"

King tapped the holster at his side to let Lippiatt know he meant business but Lippiatt had been too long in the union business to be intimidated. Arrogantly ignoring them, he walked past the two of them and headed out of the station, down Commercial Street and into town.

Now that the train crowd had dispersed, Stubbs and King felt less constrained. They ran after him.

Stubbs exploded. "You fuckin' son of a bitch," he called at Lippiatt's back. Stubbs moved his hand towards his gun but King held him back.

"Later," he said to his partner. "Later, when nobody's looking."

Lippiatt's first stop was the union headquarters in the Packer Building. He walked up the grimy flight of stairs expecting to see some activity, but nobody seemed to be around that late on a Saturday night. The door to the office was open, so he walked in and casually flipped through a stack of papers on one of the desks. But as he was about to leave, Lippiatt heard a chair leg scraping on the floor in the next room. More than a little nervous, he stepped across the threshold. Sitting in the corner, his face still bruised, was a man he recognized from Denver.

"Ah, you finally made it. Was wondering when you'd show up." It was Mike Livoda. He gestured to the coffee pot. Lippiatt poured two cups. He asked the Croatian about his beating, but Livoda just shrugged. Lippiatt saw a few carbines leaning against the wall in a corner of the room. Next to them was a cabinet, its top covered with cigarette burns and yellow stains left by years of beer glasses and coffee mugs. One of the cabinet drawers was half open. He could see a couple of open cartridge cases and the butts of two heavy-duty revolvers.

"Look," Livoda spoke quietly, noticing Lippiatt's glance at the guns. "You know the score, don't piss them off unless you have to. And don't cause trouble. They do that enough without our help."

Lippiatt nodded in agreement, but he balled his hands into fists. "Don't worry, Mike," Lippiatt assured him, "I'm too damned tired to do anything right now. I'll see ya' tomorrow. I'm off to my bed." As he made his way out of the building, hoping his bed would be as soft as he imagined it to be, he met Stubbs and King again. The two detectives didn't seem at all surprised to run into him; they had found exactly what they were looking for.

"Hey," King asked, "we still wanna' know who your daddy was. Any ideas, Eyetie?"

Lippiatt was tired and sweaty, his back ached from hours of sitting in a hard train bench, and he badly needed a beer to set the world to rights. He glared at them and immediately went back into the building.

King sneered. "Fuckin' foreigners; they got no balls."

But Lippiatt came back out just a few minutes later. Only this time he was carrying a .45. "Say again what you just said about my ma, assholes," Lippiatt roared.

Suddenly, almost without any conscious thought on their parts, all three pulled their guns on each other. Lippiatt fired first, hitting Stubbs in the thigh. As Stubbs stumbled, he fired at Lippiatt and King followed suit. The .45 each of them carried was a heavy gun, difficult to aim. But at that range it didn't matter. Six low-velocity slugs ripped into Lippiatt's chest and stomach. Blood and mangled bits of body followed the bullets as they exited his body. Gerald Lippiatt was dead before he hit the ground.

The gunfire rippled across the dusty streets of Trinidad. At first the crowd thought it was fireworks, but very soon the word spread that there'd been a shooting. Angelo and Claudia were swept along with the crowd towards the sound of the guns. The ice-cream maker saw Lippiatt's body lying on the ground in a rapidly spreading pool of blood and he quickly stood in front of his wife to block her view. Stubbs lay on the boardwalk clutching his leg. King stood calmly over Lippiatt.

As the crowd became silent, stunned by the awful sight, the sheriff's deputies appeared out of nowhere and unceremoniously picked up Lippiatt's body and threw it into the back of a wagon. Stubbs was thrown in the back of the wagon as well, a lot more gingerly because his wound hurt like hell even though he was still in shock. One of the deputies held up his arms and told the crowd to go about their business. "Everything is okay, folks, we'll look after everything."

The Las Animas County Coroner called an inquest into the death of Gerald Lippiatt at 11.30 am the following Monday in the county courthouse. It was formally attended by the Sheriff of Las Animas County, James Grisham, the District Attorney, John Hendricks, and a jury of six Trinidad businessmen. The union was represented by John Lawson and Mike Livoda. Sam King and five other Baldwin-Felts detectives were also there. No other members of the public were present, with one notable exception. Edwin Brake, Ammons's labor commissioner, who had arrived on the same train as Lippiatt, couldn't help himself. He had heard the shooting as he was putting away his clothes in his room on the second floor of the Toltec Hotel. The desk clerk told him there'd been a shooting by the union office. Realizing the location of the shooting was not coincidental, Brake had decided there and then to attend the inquest to see what justice was like in the southern part of his state. Waiting until the proceedings were about to start, Brake, as quietly and as surreptitiously as possible, sidled into the back of the courthouse and sat down, reasonably certain that, with the possible exception of John Lawson, nobody would recognize him. Brake checked his fob watch; 11.30 on the dot. *At least they're punctual down here,* he grimaced.

"In the matter of the death of Gerald Lippiatt, miner of no fixed address. Age thirty-two." The clerk of the court could barely stifle his yawn. The men stood up dutifully as the coroner, a small balding man, walked into the room. He stood behind a large raised bench in front of a huge Stars and Stripes, which made him look very small indeed. He sat down, the room followed him, and proceedings began.

The coroner started by reading out his findings regarding the death of Lippiatt. That the deceased had been killed by multiple gunshots, the coroner concluded, was not in doubt. At that range, as indicated by the severity of the entrance and exit wounds and the caliber of the gun, a Colt .45, death would have been instantaneous.

He continued. "It would appear, gentlemen, that the only issue revolves around whether the death of Gerald Lippiatt was an accident or an act of justifiable homicide, or whether it was done out of malice, either pre-meditated or, shall we say, in the heat of the moment. If any doubt exists as to the motive for this death, I shall have no recourse but to ask the District Attorney to convene a Grand Jury."

Brake hoped for exactly that because he knew the D.A., Hendricks, was sympathetic to the union. The coroner adjusted the papers on his desk. Apart from the occasional scraping of a chair leg on the wooden floor or the striking of a match as a cigarette was lit, all was quiet. The blue smoke hung motionless in the still August air. Brake knew that they were coming to the nub of the proceedings.

"Are there any witnesses to the incident?" The coroner looked at the dozen or so faces in front of him. Slowly, Sam King stood up.

"If it please, Your Honor, I believe that I can shed light on the incident."

The coroner ordered him to the witness stand, where the clerk perfunctorily administered the oath.

"...So help me, God," King concluded.

"Sir, please provide this court with your name, address and

present occupation."

"My name is Samuel King. I currently am a resident of the Toltec Inn, in Trinidad, employed by a private detective company providing assistance and consultation to a number of local employers, some of whom have national, indeed international interests." *Nicely done,* Brake thought. *Without mentioning any names, King has just told the coroner exactly who he works for and who in fact has the power in these parts. He must have been coached,* Brake concluded, *he's speaking too quickly and smoothly.*

"Well then, Mr. King," the coroner took over, "perhaps you can shed light on this matter?"

"Well, sir, my partner Arthur Stubbs and I were enjoying an evening constitutional Saturday night. It was a beautiful evening, as I'm sure you were aware, and we had had a full day's work. So, what better way to enjoy God's good bounty than a walk with a friend?"

Don't over-egg the pudding, my friend, Brake said to himself, *you'd do best to keep it simple.*

The coroner interrupted. "Mr. King, just keep to the facts, please."

King apologized and continued. "Sir, as Mr. Stubbs and I were returning to our hotel, we were stopped by the deceased. He had clearly been drinking, sir. His words were slurred and he had a hard job standing up. Mr. Stubbs tried to get out of his way, but the deceased stumbled against him. At that he turned on us and swore at us something shocking.

"We tried to ignore him, but he wouldn't leave us in peace. Well, Your Honor, Arthur, that's Mr. Stubbs, said something to the effect that Lippiatt needed to go home and sleep it off. At that he gave us a murderous look and he ran into the building we were outside of. He came down with a gun. He said we were done for and he fired at us. Sir, Mr. Stubbs was shot in the leg, and we felt we had no other recourse but to return fire. Which we did. We regret that this man had to die but we had no choice."

He's definitely been coached, thought Brake. *Evening constitutional, leave us in peace, a murderous look, no other recourse but…they're not the phrases of an ill-educated thug like King.*

The clerk was writing all this down as quickly as he could. There was silence while he caught up. Finally he nodded to the coroner, who continued with his questioning.

"I see, Mr. King. And you are certain that the deceased was intoxicated when you met him." *For God's sake,* thought Brake, *why don't you just tell him what to say and be done with it?*

"I'm positive, sir. And Mr. Stubbs will swear the exact same thing."

"Thank you, Mr. King. You have been most helpful. You may stand down."

As King returned to his seat, the coroner asked if there were any other eye witnesses to the shooting. Nobody in the room raised a voice.

"Is there anybody else who might wish to cast light on this matter before I turn the matter over to the jury?" The coroner again scanned the room and looked rather surprised when Mike Livoda stood up.

"Sir, if I may?"

The coroner stared at the miner and drummed his fingers on the desk. After a minute, he formally asked Livoda to come to the stand, state his name, address and occupation and take the oath. Livoda walked slowly to the witness stand. He still hadn't totally recovered from the beating of a few months ago. After he had been sworn in, the coroner asked him to proceed.

"Well, sir, I was with the deceased not five minutes before his death. And I can say that he was not drunk. He had not been drinking any alcohol. He had come off the train from Denver, and came straight to the office where I was. We had a coffee. He was as sober as you or me, sir."

"Did you witness his death, Mr. Livoda?" the coroner spat back.

"No, sir, I did not, but as God is my witness, he was not drunk." Livoda's voice was becoming high-pitched.

"Let me ask you, again, sir, did you see the incident that caused the deceased's death?"

"No, sir, I did not, but…"

"Well, then, Mr. Livoda, I thank you for your interest. You may stand down." The coroner began to write something.

Livoda looked as though he was going to shout something back at him but Lawson motioned him to stay quiet. The Croat angrily strode back and crashed down into his chair next to Lawson.

Turning to the jury, the coroner cleared his throat and instructed it to place the appropriate weight on the two statements, one from an eyewitness and the other from a person who had not been a witness. "In any event, gentlemen, the degree of sobriety is not, strictly speaking, relevant to this case. You may now start your deliberations."

The jury left the courtroom, but was back before anybody had had time even to stretch their legs. The foreman handed the coroner a slip of paper. He nodded in acknowledgment, read it and spoke:

"Gentlemen, in the case of the death of Gerald Lippiatt, it is the conclusion of this court of inquest that the deceased was killed in self-defense by Arthur Stubbs and Samuel King. A verdict of justifiable homicide is declared. No blame is attached to the two aforementioned gentlemen in any way, and this court of inquest is now adjourned. I thank the members of the jury for their time."

Brake looked at his watch. *Twenty-two minutes from start to finish. Not bad, not bad at all. They must have had a lot of practice.*

He slipped out of the courthouse before anyone noticed him. As he walked back to the Toltec Hotel he reflected on what he had just seen. It was a glorious Colorado morning, but its beauty was made bitter by how he had seen everything that he thought

America stood for trashed in exactly twenty-two minutes. He entered the hotel and sought out a table in the dining room where he could think undisturbed. It was still only late morning, so he was able to find a corner table.

His waitress came over to him as soon as he had sat down, overly solicitous because the hotel owner had told her that he was an important man from Denver. She fussed over the place setting, tried to move him to another table where the sun wasn't quite so strong, even asked him if he was enjoying his stay.

"Just coffee, Miss, no, no milk or sugar, just black," Brake curtly ordered, frustrated at the girl's stupidity. *Just leave me alone, why don't you.* Finally, she curtsied and left Brake to compose his thoughts.

The labor secretary traced his index finger along the red gingham check of the table cloth, deep in thought. He had already concluded, even before he had stepped off the train in Trinidad, that the point of no return had been reached. The union's demands and the company's recalcitrance were simply and irrevocably at odds. But Brake still refused to give up, still wanted to try one last roll of the dice. He bolted down the rest of his coffee and, too depressed from the legal farce he had just witnessed even to walk to the telegraph office, entered the hotel lobby. Next to the reception desk were two payphones. Each had its own booth. Brake knew that Ammons would already have heard about the shooting and would want to know his prognosis. Brake entered one of the booths and asked for a call to be placed. He gave the operator the number, Ammons' private phone number. The phone rang only three times before it was answered.

"Give me the bad news, Mr. Brake."

"Sir, you obviously know about the shooting death of this fellow, Lippiatt, Saturday night." A grunt from the end of the line told him to continue. "I believe that he was murdered, or at least he was not killed in self-defense, which was the coroner's verdict. The whole thing stinks, and the inquest just threw whitewash over it. They concluded the inquest just an hour ago."

"I know I told you to talk to the union, but forget that for now. Get back to Denver, Mr. Brake, I need to figure out where we go from here."

"I'll be happy to, sir, southern Colorado is a keg waiting to blow. But just to give you something to think on, my recommendation is simple: Get rid of all the guns down here. I don't care how you do it. Just disarm the whole damned bunch of them, union, company, everybody. Declare martial law if you have to. And whatever you do, get rid of Baldwin-Felts, they're just a bunch of thugs as far as I can tell. Sir, let me stress. There is a terrible unrest here, a terrible unrest."

Brake waited, wondering if he'd pushed the governor too far too quickly. "Just get back to Denver. Then we can discuss this matter further." The formality of Ammons' response told Brake all he needed to know; the governor had decided that sitting on a fence was the only thing to do. And as Brake walked back to his hotel the phrase 'a terrible unrest' kept reverberating in his brain.

As news of Lippiatt's murder spread, incensed miners streamed out of the workings. Some wanted to burn down everything owned by the companies, in the hope that a full scale fight would finally break out, but wiser heads prevailed.

Frank Hayes called a special meeting of Lawson, Doyle and McLennan to decide on action, both immediate and long-term. The meeting didn't take long. For months the union had kicked around a number of demands for the companies, waiting for the right moment to present them. Hayes was not alone in thinking that maybe they were wrong to have waited so long; perhaps Lippiatt might still be alive if they'd acted sooner. But as he had realized as soon as he heard the result of the inquest, Lippiatt's death had not been completely in vain for it had finally given the union a reason to act. He took out a piece of paper from an inside jacket pocket and carefully unfolded it. In a monotone he read out the list:

"One, recognition that UMWA is our official representative in all negotiations. Two, an increase by ten percent of our wages and tonnage rates. Three, an eight-hour day for all miners and oven workers. Four, all dead work should be paid for. Five, we freely elect all weighmen. Six, the right to trade in any store, to choose where we live and which doctor we use. Seven, existing mining laws to be enforced and the system of camp guards abolished.

"Are we agreed that the time is now to present these demands?" Hayes asked. All the faces at the table nodded in agreement. "Therefore, I propose that tomorrow we present these demands to the brotherhood and seek their permission to carry them to the companies." Again, the faces nodded their assent. "Then, tomorrow, we meet. And let us have the strength and determination to stay united, to the end, whatever it takes."

Hayes, who loved the melodrama of political action, couldn't help but end on a flourish. Standing up, he cried, "Union Forever!"

On the twentieth of August, hundreds of miners and their wives packed themselves into a nondescript theater in Trinidad, and those who couldn't get in spilled out onto the street outside. The stage lights were turned on and caught the dust motes moving lazily in the hot, sweaty air. Cigarette smoke drifted up to the rafters, curling and licking around the dry wooden beams like blue dragons' tongues.

By the time Maria and Spiro had arrived, all the chairs in the theater were taken, but they were able to cram into the back of the hall. The couple found a small space against the wall, and Spiro gratefully leaned back to take the weight off his leg. This was the largest gathering of miners they'd seen and that alone made the two of them realize that something big was going to happen. There was a buzz of expectation in the air as the reality of the situation began to envelop everybody. The miners knew that previous strikes in Colorado had been broken, viciously and violently. They knew that not only the state but also much of the local population were unsympathetic to their cause. But they also knew that if they let Lippiatt's death go unavenged, the companies would walk all over them.

"Maria, you know, don't you, that the union's already decided to strike? All they need from us is our support."

Maria nodded glumly. "I know, Spiro, I know. I thought it wouldn't come to this, but once that man was killed, well, so much for that fantasy. "

She looked tired and lines of worry creased her face and neck and she looked older than she was. Watson's assault consumed her, and her guilt at not being able to tell Spiro, and then deceiving him so wickedly in their bed, oppressed her more each day. And like all the other women, she knew that they'd have to bear the daily brunt of the strike. Although the men would confront the companies and their paid killers, it was the women who'd have to make sure there was enough food for the family, it was they who'd have to keep their homes clean and tidy, it was the women who'd have to act in front of their children as though everything was still fine. It was the women who'd have to tend to their men if they were wounded. And it was the women who'd have to support their families if, God forbid, they lost their husbands.

As the miners waited for the meeting to begin, their anger became more palpable. But they were frightened, too, and it was fear that drove them to the hysteria that was fast taking over the room. The delay, planned by Hayes, moved the crowd to even higher levels of emotion. Hundreds of heavy work boots crashed on the floor, and the theater shook as though the walls themselves would soon come crashing down. Some miners screamed, "Murderers." Others chanted "Kill them all", "Burn their camps." Spiro was one of the loudest. Maria looked at him as though he was stranger, afraid of what her husband was becoming.

At last, Frank Hayes, John Lawson, Ed Doyle and John McLennan trooped into the hall and took their places at a long wooden table on which sat a single pitcher of water and five glasses. And behind them, waving and smiling at the faces in front of her as though they were her own dear family, came Mother Jones. As the miners saw them a hush fell over the hall. Hayes and the others waited, clearly nervous, for they knew what was about to be unleashed not just on the miners and their families but on southern Colorado itself, and like a mineshaft full of methane, the results would be deadly.

Hayes began. "Comrades, Brother and Sisters, the Special Convention of District 15 of the United Mineworkers of America is officially open."

The crowd roared its approval. They were impatient to hear confirmation of what they all knew was coming. "Brothers and sisters, I now call upon John Lawson."

Lawson polished his glasses like a professor about to begin a lecture, and poured himself a glass of water, which he did not drink. He loosened his tie, cleared his throat and began. Lawson's face, pale and rigid, told the audience of the gravity of what was about to happen. He did not emote or raise his voice, and spoke slowly so that the translators throughout the hall could pass on his words.

"Brothers and sisters, we have been fighting for ten years. It's been hard for me, it's been harder for you. You know better than me how the companies still treat you. All we've ever wanted is peace in our coalfields, but they would not give it to us. We have wanted to be treated as human beings, with dignity and respect. But they refused. I don't think we're asking too much, do you?"

"No," the miners yelled back.

"To them," Lawson went on, "we are less valuable than the mules that carry their coal to the surface."

Lawson continued with the litany of charges against the mine companies. The miners and their wives murmured their assent.

"And now, brothers and sisters, they have taken the final act of villainy by killing one of our own simply because he belonged to our union. We know that justice for this act will not come by trusting the men in power. We have tried that before and it has failed. So, now, in this room, we make a solemn promise to make them give us the justice we deserve and to treat us with the dignity we have earned with our labor. Brothers and sisters, we must do whatever it takes."

The hall broke into wild applause. "I have here," Lawson continued, waving with his hands for calm, "seven demands." Slowly and carefully, he read them out. "If these demands are not met in full, then we'll see how long their mines stay open without us to work them." He sat down, and the hall again broke out into rapturous cheering. It continued for five minutes until Lawson stood up and with his hands again gestured for quiet.

The crowd knew who was to speak next. Mother Jones, the frail old woman dressed in her widow's black, who had stood back to back with workers all over the country, rose from her chair. She was famous for her flamboyant speaking style, which combined fiery Celtic passion with humorous asides and jokes. She stood in silence until the crowd settled down in expectation.

"Brothers and sisters, all my life I have struggled for the labor of workers to be honored in this country. I have stood with you in Pennsylvania. I have stood with you in West Virginia. I have stood with you in New York. And now I stand with you here, in Colorado. Our union has tried to make the mine owners listen to us, but they listen to nothing but the clink of money going into their pockets. Money earned with your sweat and blood. But hear me, boys, liberty ain't dead, she's just resting. I'm going to tell Ammons that I'm staying here with you, and by God we will win. And if any of you boys are too chicken to fight, then there's enough women here to come and beat the hell out of you.

"Brothers and sisters of the UMW, the time for talking is over.

We know what we face. I was in West Virginia and I saw those Baldwin-Felts thugs. They beat women to death, including pregnant women. We know what we have to do. I want you to pledge yourselves in this convention to stand as one solid army against the foes of human labor. For the sake of yourselves, your families and for workers in this country and all over the world, let us unite. The world is watching us."

She lowered herself slowly back into her chair. The miners tore the red union bandanas off their necks and waved them frantically over their heads, crashing their boots down in unison. Someone in the hall yelled "Union Forever, Union Forever." The miners and their wives joined in and the chant carried outside where the rest of the crowd took it up. It reverberated up and down Main Street, Trinidad. Passersby stopped. Shopkeepers came out of their stores. All of them stood stock still and listened to the chant, as thousands of men and women declared their solidarity to the world.

Finally, Hayes was able to calm the hall enough to be heard. Trying to hold to the formalities of public debate, he asked that a motion be put on the floor to strike and to present the coal companies with the seven demands. Lawson proposed the motion and Doyle seconded it. By unanimous acclamation the motion passed.

The fervor of the meeting had dispelled Maria's troubles, if only for the moment. It had taken her and her husband a long and arduous journey to reach this point, but like everybody else they realized that they had no choice.

"Maria, this won't be easy, you know that, don't you," a nervous Spiro whispered to her.

Maria nodded. Like Spiro, she realized that if their demands were not met, and neither of them expected that to happen, they and all the other mining families in all the coal camps from Walsenburg to Trinidad would be evicted from their homes. Then they would have to hope that the union would have enough money to support them as long as the strike continued.

Maria took a deep breath. "Spiro, when you married me, you promised to love and care for me forever. You've done that. And I promised to do the same. We're a family. We've got to do this for ourselves, and for Anna, too. I don't want her to be poor anymore. I don't want her to know the gut pains of hunger and the fear they'll never go away. Come on, husband, let's go home. We've got a daughter to see to."

Frank Hayes caught the train to Denver the next day to hand the demands to Bowers in person. The train seemed to take forever as it steamed northward but this gave him time to think through the implications of the strike. *First off,* he thought, *would be to confirm the arrangements to get the strikers to the field camps.* All through the summer, Lawson had set up a series of dummy companies in Denver and secretly leased twelve pieces of land at the mouths of the major coal canyons where the union would establish tent camps, knowing that when the miners struck they would be immediately evicted from the towns. The union would have to move thousands of miners, their families and their possessions. *Then I have to make sure that the tents coming from West Virginia will make it to Colorado in time. And then I have to make sure that there's enough ammunition and guns when things get ugly. And then...*but by that time Hayes' eyes had closed and he found some blessed relief in a deep sleep uninterrupted until the ticket collector announced they were coming into Denver.

That night he booked himself into a small hotel a few hundred yards from the state capitol. He was tired beyond what he thought possible and his whole body ached. Months of working with union officials, weeks of negotiating with company representatives, and then the debate on how to react to Lippiatt's death had all caught up with him. He flopped wearily onto his bed and with barely enough energy to pull off his shoes, he lay down.

The next morning Hayes dragged himself from his bed and hastily shaved. He put on his one good suit, and tried – unsuccessfully – to polish his shoes by rubbing them up and down on the back of his trousers' leg. At some point he decided he didn't care what he looked like, so he took his hat and walked downstairs to the lobby and out onto the street. His walk to Bowers' office suite took fifteen minutes. It was fifteen minutes that Hayes needed to prepare for the meeting that he knew would be polite on his part and peremptory on Bowers'. He took deep breaths as though the clean mountain air could rinse away the anger and sadness he felt. On that fine August morning surrounded by Denverites shopping or going about their business as though they had not a care in the world, it was hard for Hayes to reconcile what he saw with what was happening at the other end of the state. *Would the shoppers and businessmen be so carefree,* he wondered, *if they knew how their fellow citizens were being treated? Or would they simply shrug and put it all down to the laziness and ingratitude of people who came from the wrong end of Europe, people who didn't deserve to be in God's greatest country?* Hayes knew almost without conscious thought what the answer to that question was.

He arrived at Bowers' suite on the third floor of the office block. It commanded a magnificent view of the Rockies a few short miles to the west. *Why,* he asked himself, *did all this beauty have to be spoilt by greed?* Not for the first time, Hayes asked himself how many millions of dollars a man needed before he was satisfied with his lot in life.

Bowers' personal assistant, a small, bespectacled man with the recognizable air of the perennially put upon, received him formally, and even a little cordially. "Yes, Mr. Hayes, Mr. Bowers was expecting you, but unfortunately he has been called away. You understand, I'm sure. Would you like to wait?"

Hayes had been pulled into this trap early on in his negotiating days and was not about to go there again. The longer you had to wait for someone, he had discovered, the more indebted to him you became when he did finally show up. And already, even before the meeting began, you were at a disadvantage. You would always tell yourself that it wouldn't happen, that the wait would have no effect, but Hayes always found that it did, or at least he found himself inwardly arguing that it didn't, so he couldn't fully concentrate on what was happening in the meeting. Either way, Hayes would find himself behind on points even before the game had started.

Matching the assistant's demeanor, Hayes told him that he too was a busy man, and asked the secretary if he would care to give a letter to Mr. Bowers for his perusal at his convenience. Hayes liked to use formal phrases like "for his perusal." He got tired of the press continually portraying the union as a load of uneducated anarchists. The anarchist part he didn't mind so much. But the uneducated jibe really got under his skin. The assistant took the letter and Hayes went back to his hotel. Now all he could do was to wait.

Bowers had been in his office all the time. As soon as he heard Hayes close the door behind him, he walked into the anteroom, snatched the letter from his assistant's hands and quickly read through it. His response was typically laconic. "Damn them all."

On the phone for the rest of that day with the other mine owners, he persuaded them to accept all the union's demands with the exception of union recognition and the demand for a wage increase. Bowers, as he patiently explained to his colleagues, knew that all they would be doing was giving the union concessions already granted under Colorado law. All the mine companies had to do was to enforce those laws. Bowers figured that "giving away" so much would help public opinion turn against the miners, and public opinion right now was one of the most powerful tools in his arsenal. If the union still refused to cooperate it would be much easier for Bowers to persuade the

Colorado governor to support the companies with manpower and other resources. That way, the companies could break the union and finally finish it once and for all. And the state of Colorado would end up paying for all of it; simply an added bonus, as far as Bowers was concerned. He felt smugly optimistic. And Mr. Rockefeller Sr. would be pleased for hadn't the great man told him months ago to do anything, so long as he kept the profits flowing? The other mine owners, as he expected, went along with his scheme. And on the most important of the union's demands, they promised each other to stand firm, whatever the consequences. Collective bargaining was a much more powerful weapon for workers than individual negotiation. The companies refused to recognize the union.

"So far, so good." Frank Hayes gestured towards John Lawson and Ed Doyle sitting with him in their Trinidad headquarters. "Just a week since we struck, and I betcha' we've got almost a hundred percent support. We keep this up and we'll close down every mine."

Lawson agreed that the walk-out was big enough to put real pressure on the companies but he wasn't as sanguine as the other two about the ultimate result. He stood up from the table and walked over to the coffee pot. It had been sitting on the stove for hours and the coffee was bitter and sludgy, but he needed time to think out how to respond. He poured out half a cup, spooned in two large sugars and stirred slowly.

Hayes, Lawson knew, believed as an article of faith that socialism was on the rise and the collapse of capitalism was inevitable. Doyle seemed a typically irascible Irishman, a good man to have in a fight but prone to let optimism outweigh reason. Not for the first time, Lawson found himself in the unenviable position of having to tell the other union men not what they wanted to hear but what they needed to.

Lawson finally spoke. "I just hope we can hold out long

enough. They've got the banks on their side, and who knows where Ammons stands now. Personally, I think he'll come out for the companies despite the noises he's made in the past that he's on our side. And the mine owners can pay their guards over three bucks a day. A day. I'm frightened that they'll outlast us. I'm just being practical." He looked pointedly at Hayes, who rolled his eyes at Doyle. Lawson was well aware that Hayes still hadn't fully forgiven him for the colossal tactical error of trying to bring in Lewis last August. Plus, Lawson knew that what to him was realism was, all too often, to Hayes' and Doyle's ears, pessimism. *Sometimes,* Lawson cursed to himself, *I spend more time fighting my so-called colleagues than I do the companies.*

Hayes was about to say something in response to Lawson, but Doyle interrupted to head off an argument. "Listen, this is the final rate. Three dollars for each miner, a dollar for his wife, fifty cents per kid. Per week. I know, it's pitiful, but the men knew what they were getting into before they walked. And despite John's assessment, I think we've got the upper hand. The men are angry and they're ready to take this strike all the way. The companies'll break before we do. I'm convinced."

Looking straight at Lawson, Hayes commanded, "Let's move on."

Lawson brought up the next agenda item. "I've talked with Adolph Germer up in Walsenburg and he's buying as many rifles, shotguns and pistols as he can, at night away from company eyes. Good ones, Winchesters and Remingtons. The storeowners might not like the union but they sure like our money. Funny that. And there's a guy over in Pueblo who'll sell us all the guns he can get his hands on. We've got stashes of weapons and ammo, too, but I want to keep adding to them. We'll lose a lot of them; the companies have got spies just like us."

Doyle nodded in agreement. "Look, I think it's only a matter of time before Ammons sends in the National Guard. They're gonna' win again unless we're able to fight back, but this..."

Hayes finished his sentence. "But this time we're ready for 'em, not like ten years ago. This time it'll be different. Okay, John, anything else?"

Lawson sat down at the table. "Mother Jones." He paused and let the two words sink in. "Mother Jones. She's great for morale, we all know that, but she's charging all over the county giving speeches and riling everybody up. And the companies are using her and what she's saying to sway the public; you know, we're just a bunch of hooligans hell bent on anarchy."

Doyle laughed, trying to ease the tension in the room. "I like that word, John, hooligan. Do you know where it comes from? There was a mad Irish thief in London, Patrick Hoolihan or something like that. Always causing trouble for the polis, God bless 'im." Doyle had momentarily slipped back into a heavy Irish brogue. "Sorry, don't know what made me think of that. Carry on."

Lawson continued. "You know we've never really been able to control her, she's a law unto herself. I guess we'll just to have to hope she doesn't put her foot in her mouth too often. I'm more concerned with the East Europeans." Doyle and Hayes both nodded.

"Are they really that bad?" Hayes pressed Lawson.

"Tikas has the Greeks pretty much under control right now, and they're the worst of the lot, but it won't take much for them to go off the cliff. I've also got Rossi and the Italians to deal with. They think I'm..." Lawson quickly corrected himself, "They think *we're* too cautious." The other two didn't contradict him.

Hayes summed up. "So, let's get this right. We've got a virtual complete walkout, but probably not enough money to keep it up for any length of time. Ma Jones and the Greeks are threatening to blow up all of southern Colorado, the Italians are led by an anarchist, and the companies have got all the banks and the government on their side."

"That's about, it, Frank." Lawson agreed.

"And for good measure, Ammons is gonna' send in the National Guard, sure as eggs is eggs," Doyle quietly added.

The three of them sipped their coffee in silence, each of them unsure of what the future would bring.

Part Three
September 1913

11

Spiro pulled on his clothes quickly for it was cold, really cold, not like it should have been for a fall morning. Yesterday had been a regular September day, warm during the hours of daylight but turning cool as soon as the sun fell behind the hills and the shadows engulfed the canyon. Flipping his suspenders over his shoulders, he looked out of the window and had to rub his eyes to make sure he was seeing correctly.

"I don't believe this," was all he could say, as much to himself as anybody. Maria was still in bed and she picked the sleep out of her eyes. "I don't believe this," he repeated, this time to his wife who had joined him at the small window. It was September 23rd, but it looked like the middle of winter. The wind funneled down Berwind Canyon and whipped large wet globules of snow around and around in circles. The snow clung to the bushes and weeds, melted as it hit the ground, turning the roads into a glutinous mess. "Do you believe this, Maria?"

Her parents' talk roused Anna, and yawning she sat up to see what the commotion was all about it. Looking up through the small gap on the window pane where Spiro had rubbed off the condensation, all Anna could see was a white blur. She cuddled back up in her bed.

"Come on, Anna," her mother gently spoke to her, reluctant to take Anna from her haven. "It's that day, you know." The day to leave what little comfort and safety there was in Berwind, the day to go onto the prairies and start a new life.

It was nearly as cold in the house as it was outside. Spiro was drinking a cup of coffee, holding it in two hands to let its warmth seep into him. He pulled the front door slightly ajar so that he could look outside at a remarkable spectacle. The whole of Berwind's main street was clogged by a slow-moving procession of hundreds of miners and their families, some of them pulling or pushing the carts; others carrying suitcases. A few trucks crawled at walking pace. Women carried babies in their arms, bundled up as best they could against the wind. Small children, too heavy to carry, walked alongside their mothers, clinging to their skirts in hopes of some protection. The melting snow had turned their coats sodden, and it dripped off their hats and their faces. The marchers panted heavily with the exertion, the balloons of steamy breath instantly whisked away by the wind. The wheels of the vehicles and the tramping of hundreds of feet had turned the streets into rivers of mud and everybody kept slipping as they fought to keep their footing. Sometimes Spiro heard a loud slap as one or another miner fell face first into the mud as a cart got away from him. The miner would curse, pick himself up, then wipe the mud from his eyes and start anew. If not for the circumstances, it would almost have been comical. But what brought Spiro up with a start was their near total silence as men, women and children trudged onto the prairie, a silence broken only by curses or the occasional brief and labored conversation. And now it was time for him and his family to join the rest of them.

As Spiro looked out at the scene in front of him, Alberto arrived. They had decided to move all their possessions together and the night before the two men had loaded up the handcart the union had provided. "I don't believe it, Spiro, I don't believe it. Fuckin' weather." Alberto tried a grin.

"It'll be a bitch in this weather, my friend." Spiro grunted. "And my leg don't help."

"You're an old woman, Spiro, always moanin!"

They loaded the bed, Anna's bedroll – she had finally and reluctantly got up – onto the cart where it joined a small kitchen table and chairs, a chest-of-drawers and a few boxes that contained all their clothes and Maria's treasured trinkets. Maria had lovingly wrapped each of the ornaments the night before and made Spiro promise that nothing would happen to them.

But even with Alberto's two battered suitcases, the cart seemed pitifully empty.

"Are you sure that's all you're taking?" Spiro pointed at Alberto's suitcases.

"Spiro, if anybody steals the junk I left in my shack, they are a lot worse off than me. They deserve it. "

While Spiro checked that the cart was securely tied down, Alberto went inside for a cup of coffee. He watched Maria put Anna's coat on, tie a large scarf tightly around her neck and force an old wool cap onto her head. Anna began to cry, ever so gently, frightened to leave her home. Maria knelt down and held her daughter tightly in her arms. She tried to stay strong, but she too felt the pull of the familiar and had to choke back her tears.

"Sweetheart, please don't cry. It's going to be okay. I promise you. Do you think Papa would let anything happen to us? Everything will be fine. The snow will go away, the sun'll come back, and I bet in a few days' time, we'll be back here laughing about what a fun time we had camping."

Anna tried to smile. "I know, Mama, we'll be okay. And we've got Uncle Al, too." Alberto heard his name and came over. He gently squeezed Anna's shoulder to reassure her that everything would be fine.

Just then, Spiro came back inside and told them it was time to be off. He saw how frightened Anna looked and quickly moved to her. He picked her up in his arms and gently wiped her cheeks. "My child, we'll have a fun time, I promise. Remember what Mama and I said about the camp. Everybody will be there, Anna, we'll have tents and you and Sally will have lots of new places to play in. It'll be better than this old dusty place, I promise you."

Anna smiled. She walked into the back garden and untied Kali. The five of them, three adults, a little girl and a mongrel dog, stepped into the unknown.

Lawson had ordered Tikas to take control of the Ludlow tent

camp, named after the nearby rail depot. It was the largest of the twelve camps, or colonies as Lawson liked to call them, that the union had set up, and Tikas threw himself wholeheartedly into the task. At the south end of the camp by the main gate, he had set up the camp's headquarters tent, a nurses' and doctors' station, and a bandstand, and it was from the raised platform that he and his crew now looked over the flat expanse of prairie land to survey their handiwork. The camp looked barely big enough to hold the twelve hundred souls he'd estimated would be staying. The southern edge of the Ludlow tent colony was formed by the county road, and its western edge was the Denver-Trinidad rail line. Beyond the camp to the north was a deep, steep sided arroyo that stretched towards the Black Hills three miles to the east. Along the eastern boundary Tikas' crew had thrown up a wire fence. They also had staked out roads that crisscrossed the camp. All in all, Ludlow looked like a military encampment, and as he and the others watched the company agents driving up and down the surrounding county roads to check out what was going on, it increasingly felt like one to them, as well.

"Right, boys," Tikas said, looking around at their handiwork, "it looks like we're all set." He started to laugh and the crew joined in, for the tent colony had everything a tent colony could possibly need, apart from one item. Ludlow tent colony had no tents.

After a few moments, Tikas explained. "Lawson figures they've cleared Denver, so at least they're in the state. He said the union in West Virginia couldn't get them out because some of the rail companies kept losin' them. You know what that means.

"Anyway," he continued, "this weather should clear out in the next day or two, so we should be okay. But look, don't make a big deal of it when our folks show up. Act like it's no big deal, you know, that it don't matter. And the other camps don't have tents either, so it's not like we're being picked on." The other miners looked at him as though he was crazy, acting like no tents in a snowstorm was no big deal, but Tikas was in charge, so they went along with him.

The first of the miners, their families and the carts were now leaving the canyon and approaching the railroad track before turning north to the tent camp. As they got close, Tikas and his crew stopped their joking. For the whirling snow made the huddled figures look like wraiths, and some of the men on the dais crossed themselves as though trying to ward off an unseen evil. As the head of the line neared the camp, a small band struck up " Onward, Christian Soldiers" and marching tunes by Sousa, and then switched to the "Star-Spangled Banner" to greet the first families entering the through the camp gate. Mary Thomas, a red-headed Welsh woman, led the singing, and her clear voice carried the national anthem down the line, cheering the children especially as they hurried to get out of the snow.

Spiro and the others were way down the line of families that trudged slowly into Ludlow, but even from that distance they could see that the camp was a hubbub of activity. Through the whirling snow, Maria spotted the camp entrance and a large tent that the front of the line was snaking past. It all looked very efficient. But something was missing. Finally, it dawned on her and she looked incredulously at her husband. "Spiro, I don't want to act spoilt or anything, but shouldn't there be tents?" Alberto stifled a laugh as Maria gave him an icy glare. The move had exhausted her physically, and the constant backbeat of the rape mercilessly nagged her. She was at the end of her patience.

"Spiro, you've been working with Tikas. Didn't he say anything to you?"

"Er, no, Maria, not a word." Spiro was lying, because he'd harbored a horrible suspicion that if he'd told Maria yesterday there were still no tents she'd have thought long and hard about leaving Berwind at all.

"Damn it, Spiro, this is stupid. How the hell are we supposed to survive? This is stupid. You're all stupid. No, we're all stupid for agreeing to this." The stridency of her voice shocked Spiro more than what she had actually said, for Maria normally was able to take most things in her stride.

Fortunately for Spiro, at that moment Anna shouted, "Listen, they're playing that nice tune again." The band had started playing one of Anna's favorites, a hymn that she loved to sing at Sunday school. Maria got temporarily distracted and Spiro took the chance to kick up a new conversation with Alberto who had retreated from the family in case he was Maria's next victim.

"That was close, Spiro, she almost had you."

Spiro grinned back. "Thank God for little children, eh!"

Now that they were getting close to the entrance, they saw a long trestle table under a canvas awning. Two men were sitting at the table and were giving a slip of paper out to each family as it came in. As the family and Alberto waited in line, Maria went off for some of the hot milk and coffee Lawson had provided. Alberto nodded in the direction of the foothills where the clouds were a little higher and a bit thinner. "See, Anna, didn't Uncle Alberto get it right? Another hour, we'll have sun."

"I hope so, Uncle Al. Kali's really cold. Look at her." The melted snow was dripping off the dog's coat, her breath was steamy and her nose ran continually.

"It's okay, little girl," Alberto reassured Anna. "Them dogs is made for water. This is like a picnic for her. She looks bad but she's fine. Would Uncle Al lie to you?" As if knowing what Alberto had just said, Kali managed a short wave of her tail. Anna's face brightened and she went over and tickled Kali's ears.

Spiro had finally made it to the table. He gave his name to one of the men and received a slip of paper in return. It was the number of the tent they were to have, and its location. "Hey, Alberto, where are you?" Alberto, who had been next in line after Spiro, looked at his number, scratched his head and then gave the slip to his friend.

"You're in that section at the far end of the camp, with the other bachelors," Spiro explained, pointing off to the north end of the camp. "It looks like we're in the center. I see they put us with the other families and not with the Greeks." Alberto looked puzzled. "Tikas told me that of all the Greek men I'm the only one married. Did you know that? Anyway they want to be by themselves, so Tikas put them at the other end of the camp, away from you lot. Maybe he was worried we'd all get to drinkin' and fightin'."

Alberto shrugged his shoulders. "Spiro, I'll help you unload, and then I'll take off to my tent. Good joke, no!" Although there were no tents anywhere in the field, the Andrakises and Alberto still dutifully followed the lanes that had been marked out as though they were the only way to get to where they were going. It was slow going to walk even a short distance through a field already ground up by the countless feet zigzagging across the camp because every twenty yards or so they had to stop to remove the mud and grass that clung to their feet. And pushing a heavily laden cart made the walk almost impossible.

All around them, they could see other families setting up encampments, one of which, Anna was thrilled to see, was the Hoffmans. Anna drank the hot chocolate Maria had come back with. "Mama, are we close to Sally?" she squealed in excitement.

"Child, I have no idea. What do you think I am? Papa never tells me anything." Spiro looked back sharply at his wife, but sensibly said nothing. He had learnt when to pick his fights and this was not one of those times. Anna ran ahead to where Sally was helping her family settle in.

Spiro and Alberto were having a hard time pushing their cart though the thick mud, and were grateful when Sally's father came over to help them make the last thirty yards. "I was lucky," Hoffman puffed, his breath blowing in thin wisps ahead of him. "We got here early, it was bad coming down even then, must have been real bad for you guys." Spiro could only nod; he was more tired than he'd expected.

Finally, the Andrakises made it to their plot. There was a wooden peg in the ground to which was attached a piece of paper with writing on it. The ink had run but Spiro could just about see that the numbers matched those on his paper. This was their new home. Maria walked over to the stake and saw a canvas ground sheet that was lying next to it. "Spiro, let's wait to see if the ground dries out a bit before we unroll it."

"Good idea." Spiro hastily agreed with her, picking up on Maria's attempt to shake off her anger of a few moments ago. He looked towards the foothills and was encouraged to see blue skies spreading towards them. "Maybe the worst of the storm is over, huh?"

"Hey, Spiro," Alberto interjected. "I'm gonna' go to my place, but I'll be back to help."

For some reason Spiro couldn't fathom, Alberto's departure made him feel more alone than he had all day, even though he was surrounded by hundreds of men, women and children. He walked over to where his wife was standing by the stake in the middle of their tiny patch of mud. He placed his arms around her shoulders and hugged her tightly. "We won't be here long, I know it. Nobody wants this to go on long. We'll be back in Berwind soon, I just know it."

"You're right, husband. And I am sorry for before." Looking out to make sure that Anna and Kali were still with the Hoffmans, she turned to the wagon and helped her husband unload their belongings.

The weather cleared that evening, but the ground was still sodden from the melting snow, and the canvas ground sheets each family had been given didn't keep out the damp. Even lying under the wagon gave Spiro and his family little shelter from the wind. The night was chilly, and Spiro for once was really glad that Anna had Kali as he watched his little girl cuddle up to her pet for warmth. As Spiro lay there in the open field, trying to ignore the damp permeating his clothes and watching the clouds slowly move east, he wondered if this had been the right move. *Should I have stayed on at the mines like some miners have done,* he asked himself, *or should I have taken the chance to get away from the mines for good?* He remembered that California was the American dream. *Of course,* he bitterly told himself, *that's what they'd said about New York and Colorado.* As he rolled over and wrapped himself tightly against Maria's back, he realized that he had no choice but to stay. He and his family had been kicked around enough in their young lives; it was time to make a stand, and here, he concluded before sleep took him, was as good a place as any.

By the next day the storm had passed through and the blue skies of Colorado had returned. The three Andrakises walked over to the community tent and grabbed some bread and a cup of hot coffee. They even made Anna drink a cup, even though she had not yet acquired a taste for the bitter brown liquid that the adults couldn't seem to do without. Over a meager breakfast of bread and jam, Maria and Spiro chatted with some of the other families. Like the Andrakises, they were scared but glad that the strike had been called and that the time for waiting was over.

Buoyed by the conversation, Spiro decided to take Maria and Anna on a tour of their new home. "Anna, remember where our home is," he ordered his daughter. "Our tent number is seventy-nine. I'm gonna' paint it on in big letters. But if you can't find it, go to that big tent there." Spiro pointed to one of the two tents that had already been pitched. "Anna, that's where the nurse's gonna' be. She'll look after you if you get lost. Her name is Pearl, Pearl Jolly. She's a real nice lady, pretty, too."

Maria gave Spiro a withering look. Both of them had heard rumors that the twenty-year-old was a little too friendly with some of the men, although she was married. "Though not as pretty as Mama," he added in an effort to pull his boots out of his mouth. Maria's cold stare told him he had not been successful.

Spiro took his daughter's hand and together with Maria and Kali, they walked to the center of the camp. Lawson and Tikas had set up a wooden platform and there was a billboard for camp notices. Standing on the platform, Spiro pointed out the camp's landmarks. "See, Anna, all the streets have different names, Front, Main, North Main, Second and Third. It's a lot better than Berwind, isn't it?" Spiro pointed to the north end of the camp. "See there, that's where we can dump the garbage and I think that's where they'll set up the toilets. And over there is a well. That's where you'll get our water, Anna. And by the well there's piles of coal. That's for if it gets cold, but I don't think we'll be here that long. And see they've even got exercise bars, and I hear they're gonna' get swings for you kids."

Spiro kept to himself the fear that the camp looked very permanent for the short stay everybody was wishing for. But looking on the bright side, he noticed that there was a sense of community that Berwind had never achieved. People who wouldn't have given each other the time of day were now working together and sharing what little they had. Despite their lack of household goods and the fear of the unknown, the families seemed to be enjoying their new freedom and there was a buzz of contentment. Yet Spiro knew those feelings would not last if they faced the prospect of having to endure a Colorado winter under canvas.

Walking back to their plot, Maria commented that she was surprised that the streets in the camp were not parallel to the county road or the train tracks. "Yeah, I noticed that, too, so I asked Tikas. He told me that once the tents get set up, it'll be harder for someone to look straight down the streets from outside. So, it's a bit more private. Does that make sense?" Maria was about to respond but stopped when she heard a murmur that grew slowly until they realized that the whole camp was cheering and yelling in a Babel of different tongues. The three of them looked to the south end of the camp, which is where most of the noise was coming from, and saw a long convoy of trucks on the county road. The trucks were loaded with the long-awaited tents, beds and stoves.

"Finally," Spiro yelled at the top of his voice. "I knew the union would get them."

"Anna, go back to our plot and stay there with Kali. We won't be long," Maria shouted at her daughter in excitement. Without waiting for their daughter's reply, the two of them ran to the headquarters tent and joined the crowd that was forming as news of the shipment spread. Standing on the back of a truck, Louis Tikas was barking out orders through a megaphone. Maria hardly recognized the man who had come to their house just weeks ago, for more and more he looked a natural-born leader of men, that the weight of his personality alone would command men to his bidding.

"Listen, everybody." Tikas' heavily accented English cut through the cheer of the large group that was gathering in front of him. "This is only the first shipment. We've sent other stuff over to Forbes and the other camps. They need it too. But I promise you the rest is on its way. And I'm told by John Lawson that tomorrow the rest will come by train and they'll stop here."

Some of the crowd began to move towards the line of trucks, but out of nowhere a group of miners, clearly under Tikas' direction, formed themselves into a barrier. "Look," he explained. "You'll all get what you need, but for now we're giving this stuff out to families of four or more. And that's it. The rest of you will have to wait until tomorrow. I'm sorry, but that's how it is."

Maria looked at Spiro and attempted a joke. "I guess Kali doesn't count, does she?"

Spiro grinned back at her. "Well, I suppose it makes sense, Maria. We can last another night, can't we? But tomorrow, it'll be better, I know it."

That evening, Lawson had arranged for a magic lantern slide show to entertain the families, and after a cold dinner of bread and cheese the three of them walked over to the large community tent for the showing. Anna had expected a real movie like she had seen in Trinidad and she sulked when the lights went dim and all she saw were still pictures of New York City and Washington D.C.

"I know it's not real movies, Anna, but it's better than nothing," her father tried to cheer her up. Maria, too, was disappointed, but she figured that one child per family was enough so she bit her tongue. Anna ended up liking the slides, especially the ones of the Statue of Liberty. Spiro and Maria told her they'd seen it in person, from the ship when they came to America and that it was a lot bigger in real life. But as the slides of the statue continued to flash onto the screen, Maria and Spiro became more and more quiet. Over the head of Anna, who was sandwiched between them, Spiro gave Maria a look that was part confusion, part sadness: confusion over why they were in the middle of nowhere, doing what they were doing; sadness that the promise of Ellis Island, a promise that had kept them going through many hardships, had been broken beyond repair. The slide show had been spoilt for both of them, and they were glad when Anna yawned and asked if she could go home. Spiro picked her up and the three of them walked back to their little patch of land for another night under the stars.

12

"Please, Elizabeth, hold still for the photographer."

"I won't, Mommy, I'm bored. And I'm hot." The struggle between the mother and the eight-year-old had been going on for almost twenty minutes. The heavy lights made the portrait studio hot and clammy, and the eight-year-old was winning the battle of the wills and knew it. The photographer was losing his patience.

"Elizabeth, please, just a little more and then we're done." Lou Dold normally didn't mind photographing kids, but this one had really got up his nose. For just as everybody thought she was ready, the little brat would squirm and Dold would have to wait until she stopped her fidgeting. Dold was convinced that Elizabeth would be a lot better behaved if her mother had actually scolded her once or twice in her young life, but all the woman did was continually make excuses for the little girl's behavior. Clearly, Dold concluded, she was one of those mothers blessed with a perfect child, and it was the world's fault if something wasn't right, never her little angel's. *However,* as he had told himself at least five times since the two of them had come into his shop, *be patient, they're your bread and butter.*

Elizabeth was decked out in her best Sunday-school clothes; pink and white gingham dress, white ankle socks and polished brown leather sandals. Her blond hair was plaited into tight curls, and she was holding a stuffed toy bear that had become all the rage a few years earlier, thanks to a hunting incident involving President Teddy Roosevelt. The little girl was sitting on a three-legged stool in front of a large canvas painting of the Rockies.

"I feel stupid, Mommy. Why do we have to do this? It's too hot. Why can't we do it outside?" Lou Dold thought she was actually making a good point. *Why not come back after the storm's blown through, then go outside, and use the real Rockies as a natural backdrop,* he thought to himself. But he'd quickly learnt that although the painted canvas cost more, his customers, perversely to his way of thinking, liked to spend the extra money, just to show they could, he supposed. So, here they would stay and try to deal with darling little Elizabeth.

Lou looked over at his assistant, Jimmy Dingle, and surreptitiously winked. Jimmy was a local boy, a recent graduate of Trinidad High School whom Dold had reluctantly hired as a favor to his father, a family friend, but over the months, Jimmy had shown promise, Dold had been forced to conclude. He was developing a good eye for portraits, but what he had not yet developed was a businessman's tolerance of his customers, regardless of how irritating they might be. While Dold played with the precise angle for his shot and darling Elizabeth decided if she was going to cooperate or not, Jimmy walked over to the eight-year-old, who was still fidgeting on the stool and raking its legs with the back of her shoes, and gently took the teddy bear, making sure that he was between the girl and her mother. He then leaned over and whispered something in her ear. Finally, he placed the stuffed bear, just as carefully, back into the little girl's lap. The girl stared at him, her eyes wide open. Jimmy smiled and nodded, and suddenly, as though galvanized, the eight-year-old sat bolt upright, smiled sweetly at everybody and said, "I'm sorry, Mommy, I'm okay now."

The mother looked over at Dold suspiciously, but Lou simply returned the gaze and shrugged, as if to say "Little girls."

"I think she's okay now, Mrs. Black, sometimes it just takes a while for them to get used to it all."

The mother smiled insipidly but said nothing.

"Elizabeth, are you ready?" Dold asked the question for the umpteenth time. The little girl nodded, all the time sneaking glances at Jimmy. Jimmy grinned back at her, looking for all the world like the deferential assistant.

But just as Dold was about to start shooting, the mother stood up. "Elizabeth, dear, your front curl just needs to be moved a tad. Fine, yes, that's it, I think. We want you to look pretty for Daddy, don't we, darling?" Dold sighed quietly to himself, while the mother took two minutes to move the lock of hair about a quarter of an inch. Finally, the mother moved away.

"Look at the birdie, Elizabeth, and smile," he cajoled the young girl. Elizabeth stared intently at the lens with a fixed grin, as finally Dold was able to complete his business.

As Lou was preparing Mrs. Black's receipt, she chatted away. "You know those horrible miners have struck, don't you?" Lou nodded, acting as though he wasn't really listening, and continued to fill out the paperwork.

"I just don't understand them, I really don't," the woman continued. "We let them into our country, and this is how they treat us. They should go home." Lou remembered a similar conversation a few years back, although that time the conversation had made a lot more sense to him. But then, of course, he reminded himself, the "they" had been himself and all the other Europeans who'd come to America, and the speaker had been a Ute Indian. *Now they really have something to complain about with foreigners,* he wanted to say. Dold glanced at the woman and saw personified the bigotry and hate that ran through southern Colorado like poison in the blood. But she was his customer and her money was good, so he just smiled and bade her good day as she and her daughter finally left.

Now that they were alone again, Lou looked over at Jimmy, who'd kept in the background, cleaning up the studio and unloading the plates for developing. Jimmy tried to act like he was too busy to talk, but the photographer was nobody's fool and very quietly asked him what he'd said to Elizabeth.

"Well, Mr. Dold, I could see you was getting tired of waitin', and she was getting all hot as well, the sweet little thing, so I just thought I'd move things along. You know, I wanted to help her. "

"Jimmy, what did you say?"

"Oh, just that we was all hot and wouldn't some ice cream be good when all this was done."

"Jimmy, her mother had already used that. It didn't work. So, what did you say?"

"Well, truth be known, and I can't lie to you, Mr. Dold." A half-smile formed on Jimmy's face. "I told her that if she didn't stop actin' up, I was gonna' take that little teddy bear of hers outside, rip its goddamned head off and feed it to the dogs. An' if she blabbed to her ma, she'd be next. Sorry, Mr. Dold, shouldn't have done that, but like I said…"

"Jesus, Jimmy, you can't do that," Dold shouted at his young assistant. "What if the mother comes back? What if the husband comes, too? You wanna' call her daughter a liar? Jimmy, don't ever do that again. If I hadn't promised your dad I'd take you in, well, I don't know what I'd do to you. Don't do it again. Now get back to work."

Lou Dold bent over the ledger book, hoping that Jimmy didn't see the grin that had broken over his face. He was only in his mid-twenties himself, and his carousing days were not that far behind him. *Still, assistants shouldn't do that to customers,* he reminded himself.

"Talking of strikers, Jimmy, after we're done here, you wanna' come with me to take some photos? I've got an idea that might make me, us, some money."

"Sure thing, Mr. D.," Jimmy replied instantly, glad that the incident hadn't cost him more than a mild tongue-lashing. "Always glad to help out, you know me."

13

Anna and Sally had convinced themselves it would all be a great adventure even if they didn't really understand why they had to leave their little houses. But after a week, Anna was sick of sleeping under a cart. Finally, when the Andrakises had just about given up hope, they got a tent. The three of them heard the whistle telling the camp the train was stopping but they still didn't believe it was their turn until they saw Tikas smile at them as he came out the headquarters tent. "I was thinking that maybe you didn't like Cretans," Maria said with a smile.

Alberto came over to help them set up the tent and their new Excelsior stove. He had an ulterior motive. "Of course, Alberto, my friend," Spiro teased, "you won't be getting a tent for a few days yet." He paused. "And yeah, there's room for you, so be nice to us, and stop looking like a kicked dog. We know you too well."

Anna had heard the conversation and rebuked her father in no uncertain terms for being so horrible to poor Uncle Alberto.

"You see, Spiro, even your daughter thinks you're a bad man. So you be good to me." It was only when Anna saw the two of them play punching each other, like they did most days, that she realized she'd been silly for thinking her father was angry with his best friend. She looked at the tent, the wooden duckboards for the floor and the stove, and knew she'd be warm tonight.

Spiro and Alberto loaded the material onto a handcart and pulled it back to their plot; even Anna pushed the handcart, her own little contribution to the family effort. "You know, Maria," Alberto said between grunts, "a lot of the families are digging little pits under their tents, for storage and things. You might do that too. Plus, you know, if they shoot at us. It is good to have a place to hide."

"That sounds okay, Alberto, but I still think you men will come to your senses and all this fuss was for nothing."

To Anna, she whispered, "We're dealing with men here, men with guns, and I swear most of them don't have the brains God gave your Kali. But don't tell Papa or Alberto I said that." Mother and daughter giggled to each other.

Back at their plot, they found Sally looking after Kali. Anna ran over to her friend and the two of them sat down and watched her new home go up. Frank, Sally's older brother, came over as well. He kept pulling Sally's hair, but for once she ignored him and continued to watch the activity.

"Mr. Andrakis. Girls are boring. Can I help you instead?"

"Sure, Frank, just do what me and Al tell you, okay?"

"He's a good boy, him," Alberto nodded at Frank. "I see him around the camp, Spiro. He's always tryin' to help someone or other."

Spiro put the three children to work, fetching the large wooden stakes that held the guy ropes down and then holding onto the tent poles while Spiro and Alberto banged the stakes firmly into the prairie sod. They were both using heavy coal hammers, much too big for the puny little stakes, but it was the best they could find. Anna and Sally couldn't stop giggling whenever the men hit a rock, even though Maria kept shushing them. Alberto cursed, as he hit a particularly large boulder and the vibrations shivered his elbow. Frank picked up the heavy hammer and tried to swing it, but only succeeded in falling flat on his backside. Frank's face turned red with anger at the howls of laughter that followed, but he didn't say anything as he tried to retain as much dignity as a ten-year-old boy can.

Elated with having a tent and forgetting just for a moment the misery of the rape, Maria cried out, "Honestly, you two are worse babies than Anna and Sally. I think us three girls could hit 'em harder. What do you think, Sally?"

"Right, wife of mine, let's see you do it." A grin covered Spiro's face.

Maria picked up the hammer and immediately dropped it.

"Hey, you didn't say it was this heavy. But no problem. I can do this."

Alberto put down an armful of guy ropes. "Gotta' see this. Now we get a lesson, Spiro," he said, deadpan.

Maria hitched her skirt up, spat on both her palms like she'd seen her husband do, and picked up the shaft in both hands. She bent over, took a swing, and missed the stake entirely. Unfortunately for Maria, the arc of the swing was more sideways than straight down, and the momentum of the hammerhead took Maria with it. She landed on her side, her face stuck firmly into the remains of an old cow pat, gooey from melted snow. At first everybody was silent, but slowly Maria lost control. First a slight smile creased her lips, then a grin, and finally she was rolling on the ground unable to stop the tears of laughter rolling down her cheeks. Now everybody joined in, especially Anna, Sally and Frank. Spiro and Alberto were doubled up, holding their stomachs. At last, Spiro was able to walk far enough to pick up his wife. He took out a rag and gently wiped the crap off her face. "Oh God, Maria, I swear you are the best thing that ever happened to me. But promise me you'll stay in the kitchen from now on, where you know what you're doing."

"I promise, husband." Anna saw her parents embrace and kiss each other's cheeks, and silently promised herself that one day she would be just like them.

Suddenly, an agonizing pain shot through Maria's pelvis. Another bolt rippled through her. Then another. She involuntarily gasped and hugged her lower abdomen. As quickly as they had come the pains vanished. She looked around but everybody was busy. They had not noticed her.

Maria was frightened. She needed advice from Nora and told Spiro where she was going. He was surprised with all the work ahead of them but figured that she must have a good reason. Maria walked over to her friend's tent, wondering if she had over-reacted for now it was as if the attack had never happened. She was about to turn around when Nora called her to have some tea. The two of them sat outside the tent. Maria was silent, and Nora wondered why her friend had come to visit. But finally, Maria told her.

"Nora, I was helping with the tent and I was stupid and tried to hit the tent pegs. Well, I missed and landed on my face, and I felt, this sounds silly, but I felt something give, as though something had broken inside. And then I had these terrible pains all through my stomach and my legs, everywhere, you know, even down there." Maria was embarrassed to talk so intimately.

"Maria, it could be anything. Look at what you've gone through the past few days alone. You've probably got bad gas, that's all. What else do you think it could be?" She hesitated. "Maria, if there's something else, tell me. You know you can trust me, don't you?"

"Well, could I be pregnant, and something's not right?"

Nora laughed. "Well, only you can answer the first question. Yes, what you felt could be just that. Come on, what's up? There's something else, isn't there?"

"Nora, is it true," Maria forced herself to confront the truth, "if a man attacks you and you didn't have a thrill, a…" Maria searched for the right term, "an orgasm, you can still get pregnant, yes?"

Nora screwed up her face in thought. After a moment, she replied. "I'm no doctor, you know that, but yeah, I think that's right. I'm sorry, love, if a man leaves, you know, stuff in you, then, yeah, you can get pregnant."

Maria's last hope was gone. "Oh, God, Nora. I don't know whose it is then. I don't know, Nora. If it's Spiro's, help me keep it, but if it isn't, well I've been evil, prayed to God to take it away if it was, you know, and now I think He has and I've killed someone and I'm going to hell, and…" Maria's babbling was turning to hysteria.

Nora was harsh. "Stop it right now. You're not making sense.

What are you talking about, girl?"

"Nora," Maria gulped, forcing herself to continue. "Well, remember that day I came over late, when you were sick with the bad water." Nora nodded. "Well." A shudder passed through Maria's body. "Well, on the walk home, you know it was dark when I left, I was attacked. By a man. He…he…" Maria slumped into her chair.

Nora stood up and gently lifted Maria into her arms. "It's alright, Hen, it's alright. I think I know what happened. You did nothing wrong." Maria was sobbing hysterically, and Nora shook her hard. "Listen, Maria. You did nothing wrong. What happens is always God's will. And if you were pregnant and you lost it, then the baby was too good for this world, that's all, whoever's it was. God wanted him right away, so he could keep him safe and happy always. And look you," she added kindly, "it may just be gas. Sit down and finish your tea."

The two of them sat in silence. Maria cleaned her face and after Nora assured her that her eyes were no longer red, Maria stood up to go. "I'm sorry, Nora, for doin' this to you. I'll be okay now, I promise. It felt good to tell someone."

"No problem, my love. Now go back to your husband and your little daughter. Whatever happens, happens. Don't tell nobody about nothing you've told me, especially Spiro. It's our little secret. And, Maria, remember, you know where I live."

Maria smiled back weakly and left for home.

In Maria's absence, Spiro and Alberto had finished putting the tent up, laid the duckboards and then manhandled the heavy cast-iron stove into position under the roof flap. The two of them were now erecting the stovepipe and wrapping it in a sheet of metal where it came out through the roof.

"That should keep it safe from fire, Anna," Alberto explained, as she and Sally watched the two miners hard at work. Finally, the two of them moved in the furniture they had carted from

Berwind.

Maria came back as they were finishing, and she immediately went to work herself, grateful for something to keep her occupied. She unwrapped her precious icons and family photos and placed them on top of the cabinet.

"It's a real home now, my love," Spiro said as he hugged his wife. "We'll be fine. Come on, let's eat."

Maria, sure that the pain would hit her again, tried to act as normally as she could. "Alberto, have some jam," she said, offering him a stoneware jar of strawberry preserve, which he slathered over the rough brown bread. The four of them sat outside, three of them at least enjoying the warm afternoon sun. Putting up the tent had made them hungry and they greedily devoured the little picnic, as Anna called it.

"So tell me, child, why wasn't yesterday's lunch a picnic, too? We ate outside then as well," Spiro asked his daughter. Alberto and Maria looked at her, curious too.

Anna munched slowly on the last of her bread, her eyes hooded as she carefully thought out her answer. Finally, she proclaimed. "Well, Papa, yesterday we had to eat outside. But today we can sit inside or sit outside. We chose outside, so it's a picnic. See, simple." Alberto's first reaction was to laugh but Anna said it with such solemnity that he bit his lip. Spiro and Maria looked at each other, twinkles in their eyes.

"Well, then, Anna," her father with equal solemnity replied. "That makes perfect sense to me. A picnic it is." Anna didn't see the big wink her father gave her mother. Maria tried to respond but it was too difficult, so she just sat there and tried to look as though tiredness had simply got the better of her.

As Maria and Anna cleaned up after lunch, Spiro and Albert sat outside smoking. "Have you heard, Alberto, the companies are gonna' bring in more of that detective agency?"

"Baldwin-Felts? Yeah, I hear. I talk to people in Aguilar and they tell me to expect trouble now, big trouble. They got guns, lots of 'em. And they like to use 'em."

"Tikas tells me that the union's been buying up all the guns in Trinidad, they even sent them down from Denver. Do you know how to shoot?"

Alberto shook his head. "No, but how hard can it be? How about you?"

Spiro scratched his chin. "On Crete every man learns to shoot when he's a boy. We're all *pallikaria* there."

Alberto raised his eyebrows. Spiro explained. "A *pallikari* is a warrior, a man, someone who stands up and fights for his country, his family, himself. And we don't lie down if someone hurts us. We take, what's the word, revenge. Yeah, revenge. No questions asked."

At that Alberto nodded. "In Italy we call it *vendetta,* and it goes on forever. I'm from the city, and you're country, but you an' me, we ain't different." The two of them sat on their hard wooden chairs, smoking silently and looking out across the camp, sharing the same thoughts, the same hopes, the same fears.

They were interrupted by a familiar voice calling Spiro's name. He looked around and saw the diminutive figure of Tikas striding purposefully toward him. Maria stuck her head out of the tent. As much as she admired Tikas for what he had done in Ludlow, she was learning that trouble often followed the union organizer.

"Spiro, Alberto, good to see you. And you, too, Kyria Andrakis. Just came to make sure the tent and everything is okay."

Spiro nodded and thanked him profusely. "By the way," he added, "congratulations." Tikas looked at him quizzically. "I heard that you just got back from Denver and you got your citizenship. So, now you're one of us." Spiro laughed but quickly changed his tune when he saw the look of embarrassment on Tikas' face, a look that quickly turned to irritation. Clearly this was something Tikas wanted to keep quiet, for reasons Spiro could not understand. *Did he feel he was deserting Crete if he became an American,* Spiro wondered. *You'll always be a Greek, Louis,* Spiro wanted to say.

"Spiro." It was Maria. "We're off to take Kali for a walk. We'll be back soon." Spiro nodded and Tikas doffed his hat to her, subtly acknowledging her intuition in realizing he wanted a quiet word alone with her husband. As soon as she had left, Tikas got down to business.

"You know over at Primero," Tikas began, referring to one of the other coal camps. "Well, word is some of the company guards are stopping the families from getting their belongings. We're gonna' go out there tomorrow and check it out, if you're interested. You can come too, Alberto, if you like."

They both nodded and agreed to meet Tikas at the main gate.

The evening was peaceful for the Andrakis family. The sound of a violin drifted across the tent colony, the smells of a hundred different meals hung in the air, and as the night settled in and the lanterns in the tents were turned on, the shadows inside danced across the canvas walls. Spiro chatted outside with friends before he and Alberto went for a drink, and Anna giggled on about her mama and the tent peg. Maria laughed along with her, but as the night drew in, she felt sicker and sicker. It was difficult to tuck Anna in bed, for bending down made the pain worse. It wasn't just a physical nausea either; she knew it was a sickness of her soul as well. She took a dose of pain-killer, Hamlin's Wizard Oil, but it didn't do any good. Maria grimaced when the alcohol hit her throat and wondered why everybody swore by it, since it had never helped her that much. Now, the pain was like razor blades slashing her insides. Careful not to wake Spiro, she got out of bed, an action almost too painful to complete. She threw her coat on, grabbed an old cloth towel hanging on the chair and staggered to the latrine. She didn't need a lantern to find out what was happening. She placed her hands between her thighs and felt warm blood running down her legs. The pain was coming in waves but she was in command of herself enough to cup her hands as a huge expulsion came cascading out. Something instinctive took over Maria. Like an automaton, with no tears or even emotions, she placed the bloody mess into the towel and wrapped it up. She cleaned herself and the latrine as best she could.

Nora's tent was close by. There was no light on, but Maria softly called out her friend's name and the Welshwoman, who must have been awake, immediately was outside the tent. Maria stood there, the enormity of the event finally overwhelming her. She handed Nora the towel, tears rolling down her cheeks.

"Please, Nora, don't say anything. Look after..." Maria hesitated. "Look after it."

Nora nodded, her tears flowing to match her friend's. The Welshwoman stood in the doorway as she saw her friend walk slowly back to her tent, and prayed silently for her soul and that of the child she now held in her hand.

Through the rest of that long night, Maria prayed that the nightmare was ending. She wanted to stay in the bed forever, curled up in a ball, taking refuge from the world like a little child. She kept checking her thighs, hoping for the dryness that would tell her there were no complications, for she knew that miscarriages often made the woman barren, and she wanted to give Spiro at least one more child. She felt Spiro stirring beside her, and knowing he always wanted breakfast as soon as he was up, forced herself out of her cocoon of relative safety into what she could only hope was a semblance of normality.

Making coffee and buttering the bread was almost too much effort, but at least it was a chance to keep her mind elsewhere for a few precious moments. Spiro complained she was taking too long, but she said nothing. Maria kept herself busy, tidying up the tent, waking Anna gently from her sleep, and all the while trying to avoid eye-contact with her husband. They were both grateful to hear Alberto calling for Spiro. He threw on his jacket and went to meet Tikas as planned.

14

At the headquarters tent Spiro and Alberto saw Tikas talking to three men. They were Greeks and Spiro joined in the conversation, leaving Alberto to look at the ground wondering what to do or say.

He finally spoke up. "Mr. Tikas, if it's okay with you, I'll stay here. The Petruccis want help with their stove, it's not blowing right. Petrucci has a bad cold and the wife is real sick. Their other kids are too young to help."

"Yeah, Alberto, no problem. We're just gonna' have a look," Tikas assured him.

The five men piled into Tikas' old sedan and set off. Spiro was in the back seat and as they trundled along the washboard road, he felt something sticking into the bottom of his back. It was the best part of an hour to Primero, so he tried to move it. Although he was packed in tight he managed to squirm around enough to feel what the problem was; he'd grabbed hold of the business end of a double-barreled shotgun. He felt around a bit more until he came across another barrel. Spiro's face drained of color. He knew each side had guns but the coldness of the gun's steel made Spiro realize how easily the strike could turn violent. And as much as he tried to reassure himself that he wouldn't get involved in any shooting, what if the shooting got involved with him? he asked himself over and over again.

After driving through Trinidad they turned west along the Purgatoire River, its waters glistening and silvery in the morning sun. Meadows at the side of the river were full of cattle and they heard birds chirruping in the afternoon air. They followed the narrow road, enjoying the scenery and saying little. The miners first stopped at the Segundo coking ovens, close to Primero. Tikas told them there was a group of miners camped there, but the place looked deserted, so he decided they should look around. Spiro began to feel nervous as the four others picked up carbines from the stash in the back of the car and began to walk through the workings.

As they approached a small bridge over the river, one of the miners laughed menacingly. "Let's give it back to them."

Tikas ordered him to shut up and move on, but the miner ignored him and pulled a stick of dynamite from his jacket, knelt down and placed it against one of the bridge's supporting posts. As he was about to light the fuse, the five heard the thunder of horse's hooves coming down the road towards them. It was Bob Lee, the deputy sheriff in charge of protecting Segundo.

"Goddamn' miners. Fuckin' Greeks; ya'll be the niggers of Europe and now you're fuckin' up my country." His Kentucky drawl hung in the air as he pulled a carbine from his saddle holster and worked the lever to push a round into the chamber. The five miners instinctively ducked for cover.

"Go on, you fuckin' cowa..." His sentence was cut off in midstream by the crash of a shotgun. The miner with the dynamite had fired a blast of buckshot at Lee. At that close a range he couldn't miss, and the full force of the load slammed into Lee's throat throwing him out of his saddle. He lay on the ground, his head at what Spiro thought was an impossible angle, until he realized, as he got closer to the dead body, that most of Lee's neck was missing. Blood still oozed onto his chest, and beyond the corpse Spiro could see gobbets of bloody flesh mixed in with what looked to be part of a bandana. Spiro had seen violent death before; he'd lost count of the sheep and goat necks he'd cut in his life. But he'd never seen a man's life taken away so callously. He slumped to his knees and threw up.

"Christ, man, what you do that for?" Tikas' voice crackled.

"Did you see who it was?" the shooter answered as he climbed out of one of the ovens. "He'd'a' killed us. Besides, he had it coming."

Spiro knew exactly what they were talking about. Lee used his power like a Roman dictator, beating up miners, stealing their money, assaulting their wives, all with impunity.

Tikas looked at the corpse and then slowly turned and stared at the four miners, deep in thought. "You know what I can't figure out, boys? How did he know we'd be here? And..." He paused. "How the hell did he know we were Greeks? Anyway, let's go. Now. Them crows," he said, looking up at the sky and then down at Lee's body, "are gonna' have a feast today, that's for sure." The five of them piled back into the car and roared off down the road as fast as they could.

As they bumped their way back to Ludlow, the murder played over and over in Spiro's mind. He was sure that no one had seen them kill Lee, and in any case he hadn't pulled the trigger. Not reporting the murder was wrong, but, as he grimly told himself, reporting it was even worse. *And in any event,* Spiro repeated to himself, *who would I tell?* He climbed out the car as soon as it slammed to a halt in Ludlow. He wanted to get as far from it as possible, as if the act of distancing himself would detach him from the events of just an hour ago. He did not know what to do, and there was nobody to talk to; he could not confide in Tikas or the other Greeks in case they thought him a coward. Leaving Greece, the trip to America, marriage to Maria, the mines, the accident; he had always felt in control even when he hadn't been. He did not know what to do.

Without any conscious awareness of where he was going, Spiro found himself back at his tent. Maria had been reluctant to have a pit dug under their tent, but after Lee's death, Spiro knew without a doubt that violence was coming to the coalfields. They needed a pit whether Maria liked it or not. He had just finished moving out their small chest-of-drawers when Maria returned with Anna and Kali.

"Spiro, I thought you were going to wait?" Maria complained.

"Well, I'm not. Anyway it's none of your business when I dig a hole or where I dig it."

Spiro was so uncharacteristically sharp that Maria responded in kind. "Don't you dare speak like that in front of Anna. What's up? Tell me what happened. I know you too well."

"Nothing's happened, I just got bored and decided to do this."

But Maria was unconvinced and probed. "Did anything happen when you were off with Tikas?"

Her husband's expression steered her away from further questioning. Maria went back into the tent and fired up the stove, the one object too heavy to move outside. Then she took Anna to get more coal. The little girl hated this job, but at least it meant she and Kali could go for another walk and get away from her father who frightened her in a way she was not used to.

After three hours of work, Spiro finished the pit. It was about three feet deep and covered about half of the floor of their tent. It would take all three of them. Kali, Spiro figured, would have to take her chances. He then replaced the duckboard flooring over the excavation and moved their furniture back inside. He was outside catching his breath when he saw his family walking back to their tent. He looked quizzically at his wife.

"I was at the Hoffmans and then I stopped by Nora's tent, seeing how things were." While Anna had played with Sally and some other children over by the arroyo, Nora had quickly examined Maria and pronounced that things looked good.

Spiro showed Maria his handiwork. "My God, Spiro, now the whole tent smells of earth. It's horrible. And what if it rains? Won't it fill up?"

"For God's sake, woman, leave me alone. You an expert on digging now? I'll dig a trench around the tent tomorrow. You'll be fine then. Any more requests?" His sarcasm was unmistakable. Spiro threw down his spade and stormed off.

Maria looked at her husband's back quickly disappearing into the throng of people around the gate entrance. On top of her own misery, now she had Spiro to contend with. This was not the

Spiro who had protected her at Chania a lifetime ago, the Spiro she had married, the Spiro who had brought them all the way from New York, the Spiro who had looked after them in Berwind with hardly ever a cross word for her or Anna. Something was happening to her husband, and it scared her in ways she could scarcely comprehend.

However, angered as she was by her husband's behavior and depressed by her miscarriage, Maria was forced to turn her attention to another matter as word spread through the camp that a food shipment had just arrived from Denver and was being unloaded at that very moment. It was a whole warehouse of food, courtesy of the union: crates of canned vegetables, jams and preserves, boxes of hard crackers, cans of condensed milk, and even cartons of candies all disgorging from the wagons that had carried them from Ludlow station. She and Anna hurried down to where a large crowd of women had already gathered, eager to see how much food they could get.

Lawson stood on the bandstand and issued orders to a group of miners' wives who, it seemed to Maria, were actually to take charge of the proceedings. As the crowd of women swelled, he ordered quiet and then pulled out a thick wad of papers attached to a clipboard.

"Ladies, there's enough for everybody, so don't worry. This here docket," he held up the clipboard, "has all your families' names on it, and we," he pointed to the women, "this committee here, have assigned how much food each of you gets. We're not making a profit. We sell it for what we bought it for."

Someone yelled out. "Why a committee if you're selling it?"

The mood of the crowd began to sour. The euphoria of the first weeks at Ludlow had worn off as everybody settled in for what was looking to become a long stay. Maria knew that some of the wives were quite capable of helping themselves at the expense of others, but she was comforted when Nora Davis walked out of the tent and took her place with the other committee members. To Maria, it seemed Nora was becoming as indispensable as Tikas.

"Anna, it'll be okay now, Nora won't let us down."

It was Nora, not Lawson, who explained what the committee was going to do. "Ladies," she shouted, her Welsh voice carrying though the thin air, "we want to make sure that everybody gets at least some food. We don't want any of you millionaires out there buying it all up now, do we?" That brought a chuckle from the crowd.

"It'll be like Mr. Lawson said. Each family will have the chance to buy so much food. After that's been bought up, anything left over will be sold. You can buy what you want. But the point is that nobody goes hungry. Okay? It's the fairest way we could think of."

Some women went back to their tents to get what money they had, while others immediately got in line for their allocation. Maria and Anna waited for thirty minutes but finally were able to buy some canned milk, vegetables and bread.

As they walked back with their purchase, Maria explained to Anna that her father could hunt in the hills for them, and he would bring back some rabbit for a stew. "He was a great shot back on Crete, you know, honey, everybody said so. So we won't go hungry." The little girl slipped her hand into her mama's, already anticipating the feast she had been promised.

John Lawson was frustrated and tired from doling out all the food yesterday; some of the women had acted like he was personally preventing them from getting their hands on it. But it was nothing to the fury he now felt. Besides having to deal with the union's distrust of his methods, he also had to face on a daily basis the anarchy bred into the East European miners. He could allow the Italians to go their own way, if for no other reason than they were under the iron hand of Rossi. But to Lawson's way of thinking, the Greeks always seemed just one step short of jumping off the cliff and taking everybody else with them, and to hell with the consequences. Now, here he was again, facing yet another threat to his authority, this time from a gang of armed Greeks, whom he confronted outside the headquarters tent at Ludlow, and who he knew had just traded gunshots with company guards. He wondered if Tikas actually had it in him to control his own countrymen.

"Goddamn' it, don't you get it yet?" Lawson boomed at them in frustration. "You're doing' exactly what they want us to do."

Some of them knew what he was saying but all of them acted as though he was speaking a completely unintelligible language. Their dumb insolence angered him even more. Not knowing what to do next, he was glad to see a battered old car haring down the country road, blaring its horn. It pulled up in front of the group and Tikas jumped out. Lawson, taking out his anger on the Greek, demanded to know where he had been.

"Why, John, what happened? I got a phone call and came here as quick as I could. I've been up at Walsenburg, seeing how they're doing there. It's bad but..."

Lawson interrupted him. "Listen, Tikas, get your boys under control. I dunno' who started it, but there was just a shootout, here, on the tracks, not two hours ago. We've got women and children here, or have you forgotten? Thank God nobody was hurt. It's bad enough they're blowin' up company property, but this is crazy."

Tikas turned to one of the Greeks to ask what had happened. Lawson couldn't understand what they were saying; of all the languages spoken in the mines, Greek to him seemed the worst. He once joked to his wife that it sounded like a machine gun going off, just one long rat-a-tat.

"Okay, John, here's what he said. They were out at Berwind and saw a car full of guards coming down the road. The guards just opened fire on them for no reason. So they shot back. They're pretty sure they saw the two guards who killed Lippiatt.

Anyway, before you know it, there's a bunch of guards on horses riding down and shooting like crazy. Don't know where they came from. Our lot just retreated into Ludlow and that was it. It's over. It's over." Tikas emphasized the last sentence. Lawson wondered who he was trying to convince.

"But," Tikas said, with a lingering tone. "There's something else. You know that water tank by the depot?" Lawson nodded, afraid of what he expected to hear. "They've set up a large gun. This one here," and he pointed to one of the miners, "said it's a fancy big machine gun."

Although no military man, even Lawson knew that the hill on which the water tank stood was high enough to give any gunmen an unrestricted field of fire over the whole area, including the tent colony and the entrance to the Berwind canyon. Now he knew why the miners in front of him had been so willing to fight.

He took Tikas aside. "You know we can't be the first to act. We don't have the firepower. That machine gun is their way of enticing us to fight. But we can't, not yet at any rate. By the by, your fellas didn't have anything to do with Lee's murder, did they?"

Lawson slipped in the last question slyly. Tikas immediately denied any involvement and hoped that his denial was not too quick. Lawson looked at him suspiciously. "I guess I believe you."

Tikas quickly changed the subject. "John, that machine gun scares the shit out of me. Anyways, they fired on us, what are we supposed to do? Just stand there?"

For some reason Lawson marveled at Tikas' use of American slang, but he quickly brought himself back to the discussion. "You know I don't mean that. Hell, I'm the one who's been arguing for more guns."

Tikas began to say something, but stopped as Lawson put his hand to his forehead and rubbed it in exasperation. "Christ, Louis, you know as well as me that this is gonna' turn ugly sooner rather than later. But the more time we have, the more we can get public opinion on our side the better, and that'll get the governor to move in our favor. You do see that, don't you?"

Tikas' face reddened with anger. "But, John, the union's letting Mother Jones stir up the miners, so if they don't want trouble why let her? It don't make sense."

"You tell me what makes any sense around here, and I'll buy you free beer for a year. Hell, two." Lawson added conciliatorily, "Okay, Louis, like you said, nobody got hurt. But for God's sake, keep an eye on them." He glared at the miners to make sure they knew he still didn't trust them. "I'm heading to Walsenburg and then back down to Trinidad. I'll be at the office if you need me. Hopefully, you won't."

Tikas walked back to the headquarters tent. He knew Lawson had a point; if anybody was going to start a shoot out on their side it was going to be his countrymen. He secretly felt pride in that, but it didn't make things any easier for him. *This is America, not Greece, they have the rule of law here.* Tikas couldn't help laughing aloud as the three little words formed in his brain and it drew strange looks from the miners around him. *Rule of Law, Tikas, that's a joke. If you want the rule of law around here, it's going to be at the end of a gun, just like in the old country.*

By the time Tikas had drunk a cup of lukewarm coffee, he had calmed down, allowing him to focus on the mundane organization of looking after twelve hundred miners and their families, his least favorite job. He sat down at the table and began to pore over invoices and supply lists. All the camps needed to stock up on canned goods in case the strike lasted into the winter, which he believed would be the case. He just didn't know how much to store away for the future. The miners were still able to buy fresh vegetables and chicken, and sometimes they got their hands on pigs, sheep and occasionally a slab of beef. Tikas had decided weeks ago to stay ignorant of exactly how they managed this. Plus, many of the miners had taken to hunting whenever and whatever they could, even if it was rabbit and gopher. He had even been offered a roast toad just last week. Tikas smiled at the thought, though at the time he hadn't. As far as he was concerned, the food supply would be the biggest problem for all the tent colonies. He was honest enough to admit that the strike was all beginning to look like a big gamble and he was no longer sure how the dice would fall.

"Mama, Papa, I'm frightened." Anna's shrill voice filled the tent, cutting through the October night air. "What's happening, Mama, I'm frightened." From her bedroll she saw powerful beams of light flashing across the roof and walls. Grotesquely huge black shadows cavorted in front of her; outside, people were screaming.

Even before Anna had finished, Maria was out of bed and holding her daughter in her arms. She turned to look at Spiro but he was already moving through the tent door. As it opened, he thought he saw his first glimpse of hell. People were running around, while others just stood still as though transfixed. Every so often a huge beam of light would sweep the camp, lighting up the figures like it was the Day of Judgment.

Spiro stepped back inside and knelt down by his family. "The bastards have set up a searchlight just outside the camp. I saw them working on something this morning but I couldn't figure out what. It's just a light." He tried to sound reassuring, but he didn't even convince himself. He took Anna in his arms. "Sweet child, there's nothing to worry about. It's just a big light. It can't harm us." Anna tried to wipe her tears but succeeded only in smearing snot over her face. Her mother took a rag and ordered her, gently, to blow her nose. As she did so, Maria looked expectantly at her husband.

"Well, I'd heard a rumor about the lamp, but Lawson and Tikas weren't sure."

"I guess they are now, Spiro," Maria twisted her mouth into a sarcastic smirk. "What's the point of the light, do you know?"

"I can only think they're gonna' do this so we can't sleep, maybe they think it'll wear us down. Look, I'm going outside to see if I can find anything else. Stay here and look after Anna."

But if Spiro thought that all that would happen that night was to be kept awake by a searchlight, he was rudely disproven by the loud staccato of bullets whizzing over his head. Instinctively along with everybody else outside he dropped to the ground. Families jumped into the pits under their tents. Everyone lay still, wondering what to do. After two minutes the machine gun stopped and Spiro, bent double, made it to the headquarters tent where a group of miners were already grabbing carbines and handfuls of ammunition.

"Where's Tikas?" Spiro shouted at them, but they all shrugged their shoulders. Without hesitation, Spiro took command. "Listen, this is what we're going to do." He half expected there to be some dissent, but they all stopped what they were doing and listened. "If Louis was here, he'd tell us to be careful. They want us to go off all crazy and attack them. But we won't, okay. We're gonna' check it out. That's all."

One of the miners, a Mexican whom Spiro didn't know all that well, shouted back in broken English that he didn't care what Spiro thought, they'd scared his family and he was going for them.

Spiro walked up to him and grabbed him by the shirt. "Listen, I know, they scared mine too, but now's not the time. We'll get them, but now's not the time." The Mexican looked sullenly at Spiro and said no more.

At that moment Tikas showed up. Breathlessly, he shouted at them. "Just got back from that machine gun. They're aiming high, just to frighten us, but I left three men with orders to open fire if the gun hits the camp. What's happenin' here?"

Spiro explained what he intended to do.

"Good, Spiro, good idea. But just check it out, no *pallikari* stuff, okay?"

While they were talking, Spiro spied another searchlight a couple of miles to the east, its beam stroking the dark prairie. What that one was for, Spiro couldn't figure out, but for now, he reasoned, they needed to concentrate on the one close by. He told the five miners to follow him, and not to make a sound. He figured that there were about thirty seconds between each pass of the light beam, and in that time he and his group were able to move unseen to behind a parked truck on the other side of the railroad track. From there, the group worked their way west into the hills south of the light. Lying behind a dense patch of scrub oak, they saw what had caused such commotion. The light stood on a crudely prepared platform, so Spiro figured it was there permanently. He could hear but not see the generator that powered it. Ten armed guards were positioned around the pad and clearly were waiting for the miners to rush into their ambush and be annihilated. Spiro looked around at the miner who'd argued with him. The Mexican nodded, as if to acknowledge that if he'd charged in he'd already be dead. Slowly the six miners retreated back the way they had come and re-entered Ludlow.

Lying in their pits, women and children shivered in the dampness and their fear, wondering what would happen next, when the light suddenly went off. The men still in the open blinked, unable to see anything clearly now that they had been pitched back into the darkness. Spiro was frightened. If an attack was coming, this is when it would happen. He was not alone in his fears, and a palpable sense of dread rippled through the camp.

Five minutes went by. Nothing. Another ten minutes. Still nothing. Slowly the night dissipated and thin grey streaks of sky appeared as the sun began to move slowly over the horizon to the east, and the Ludlow camp saw the searchlight in its full ugliness. The guards were now standing up, rifles across their shoulders, contemptuously looking down on the camp below them, as if they were hoping to goad the miners one last time into an attack. But even the hottest of the hotheads at Ludlow knew that would be suicide. The miners stood down and returned to their families to begin another day of fear and despair, laced with an unquenchable hope that the day would bring something better.

That evening, Spiro was sitting outside his tent, trying to shrug off the aching tiredness that permeated his whole body, when he saw Tikas making his way from the headquarters tent. The little man was virtually running and that told Spiro he was not bringing good news.

"Hey, Spiro," Tikas got down to business as soon as he reached the Andrakis' tent. "There's been some trouble. Sounds like a rancher got killed in some crossfire yesterday. The sheriff's blaming us, of course. Do you know anything?"

Spiro was mystified and shook his head, wondering why Tikas thought he would know anything. "Sorry, Louis, I was here all day. Don't know."

"Well, I need to get to the bottom of this. If you hear anything, let me know. This is Lawson's nightmare; it's exactly what the companies want, to turn everybody against us. I wouldn't be surprised if they killed him on purpose, but they'll deny it and how can we prove otherwise? I've got to check this out, maybe get hold of Lawson first..." Spiro realized that Tikas was talking to himself more than to him, and for the first time he saw worry, real worry, crease his face. Tikas was right. *Once civilians started getting killed, it was,* he thought to himself, *what was that American phrase, a whole new ballgame*. Tikas hurried away, barely acknowledging Spiro's farewell.

Tikas had barely vanished from view when Maria came outside, firmly planting a chair in front of Spiro. She sat down. "Spiro, we need to talk. Now."

"Please, I'm tired, Maria. Perhaps tomorrow."

"No, Spiro, now. The way you're acting you might not have a tomorrow."

He knew where this was going, and had expected it ever since he started working for Tikas. His excursion last night had simply given his wife the opportunity she had been looking for.

"Maria. Don't you…"

She never gave him the chance to finish the sentence. "Spiro, if you want to play soldiers and get killed, then you're a fool. But don't you dare leave Anna without a papa. Who'll look after her if you're dead. Who? Tell me."

Anna came out when she heard her name, but Maria immediately sent her back in. She was about to say something, but her mother shushed her. "Come out when I say you can, little girl, and not a moment before. Understand?" Anna's lower lip quivered as though tears would come, but she obeyed.

"Maria, keep your voice down. Everybody can hear, and you've frightened our daughter."

"No, they can't, and even if they do I don't care. And don't you teach me how to look after my daughter. I'm not the one who'll leave her an orphan." Spiro knew this was no ordinary argument. Normally her tempers were flashes of anger, like olive oil splashing on an open fire, gone before he knew it. He had never seen her like this before. "Stay away from Tikas, Spiro. He is trouble. Trouble. Do you understand?" Maria stared at her husband, willing him to look away.

He lowered his eyes and slowly her anger subsided. "Spiro, please, stay away from him. You're married, the other Greeks are single. They don't have a wife or daughter. They've got…"

"Nothing to lose, Maria? Is that what you were going to say? Do you think that family is all that matters? You don't think other things are important, too? Do you think I don't love you and Anna? You don't think all I'm doing is for her and you? Well, Maria, don't you?" Spiro spoke slowly and quietly, as Maria had done. There was a pain and sadness in his voice that only Maria recognized.

"Spiro, I know you love us, I know that. But Spiro, we're not in the old country now. We're here in America, we're Americans. They do things different."

Spiro laughed, a harsh, guttural sound that seemed to come from the depths of his being. "No, Maria, you're wrong. They are all the same. They'll take what they want from us and throw us away when they're done." He paused to let his words sink in. "Maria, never ever forget this. I am Cretan, and I must do this. I have no choice. If you do not understand, then you have truly forgotten where you came from."

The two of them sat in silence as the darkness cloaked Ludlow.

15

Lamont Bowers was cautiously optimistic as he indulged a few moments to look out of his office window and savor a fine autumn afternoon. While he had never accepted the estimates of some of his staff that less than ten percent of the work force had walked out and the strike would collapse in a couple more weeks, he did believe that it would be over much sooner than Welborn and the others expected. *And if we can't get them back to work,* he cynically told himself, *the first Colorado blizzard would have them running as fast as their legs could carry them, begging for their old jobs back.* That, he concluded, would end the strike but more importantly it would set back the damned union cause for years.

Since the strike had been called, Bowers sent regular telegrams and letters to Rockefeller Jr., keeping him apprised of the situation, and now it was time for his latest missive. Bowers went back to his large oak desk, sat down and pulled out a heavy pen from his pocket. The grandfather clock patiently ticking away in the corner told him that he could still get the letter out in the evening mail. His secretary could fill in all the formalities when he retyped it.

Dear Mr. Rockefeller,

I hope that this letter finds you and your family well. I thank you, too, for your kind words regarding my wife, who continues to improve, albeit slowly. As your father has said so often and so wisely, we must keep our faith in the Lord and then all will be well.

Bowers laid his pen down and thought out the letter's details. It had to be realistic enough to convince the Rockefellers that the companies were facing a unified opposition, but optimistic enough to keep their faith in the present course of action. He continued.

Allow me to start with the only pieces of bad news I have to convey. I believe that the vast majority of the miners have now walked out. Some of the small companies have lost all of their work force; fortunately our own facilities are still able to operate, even at a much reduced capacity. Moreover, Ethelbert Stewart, who, as you know, is the representative of the Department of Labor in Washington in the negotiations that Governor Ammons is trying to organize, is not, I am convinced, sympathetic to our interests at all. However, it is my understanding that Stewart is at the end of his tether and will almost certainly disengage himself from further discussions.

I am also pleased to be able to tell you that despite attempted interference by Stewart to halt a grand jury investigation into the illegal activities of the United Mine Workers, specifically regarding the Anti-Trust Act, investigations are continuing, largely due to the indefatigable efforts of Judge J. G. Northcutt in Trinidad.

The company owners and I have made provision to hire more private guards and deputy sheriffs to ensure that the mob does no damage to our property or indeed to the general state of law and order in Colorado. I remain convinced, as I have expressed to you on numerous occasions, that this strike has been stirred up by a small band of anarchist East European agitators.

I am sure that at some time in the near future, the governor will be forced to bring out the National Guard. That will put a severe strain on his budget and at that point he will have to turn to the Denver banks for short-term loans. Of course, he will get them. Because of your efforts they are fully behind us.

I am convinced that Justice will be done in southern Colorado, and the forces of law and order will emerge triumphant.

I thank you and your father for your words of support and encouragement.

Bowers screwed the cap back on his pen and placed it back in his pocket. He read and then reread the draft. He pursed his lips as he read the last sentence over and over again. It did not quite sound right. *Might they think,* he wondered, *that I am not able to manage the crisis by myself?* Finally, he made a decision, took out his pen again and put three heavy lines through the problematic sentence. Once that decision was made, he called for his secretary, handed over the letter with instructions that after typing, it should be in the mail that same evening, and he moved onto other business.

But if Bowers and Rockefeller were sanguine that the strike would soon fizzle out, their confidence was about to be dented as the fire that had been smoldering in southern Colorado grew, finally, into a conflagration.

The strike was entering its fourth week, and Governor Ammons had convinced himself that sending in the National Guard was the only solution to the violence in the coalfields. He just had to convince his own administration. Sitting across the desk from him was Roady Kenehan, the state auditor. They were facing each other like antagonists rather than the colleagues they were supposed to be. Spread on the desk were reams of papers showing how much it would cost the state to mobilize the Guard.

"Roady, I need to get loans off the banks otherwise the state won't have enough money to function, let alone send in the National Guard. I don't mind that you sympathize with the union, but I'm running out of options. The state's fast running out of money. Look at the figures, they're from your own office." He waved his hand across the papers in front of them. "We can get good, low-rate loans off the banks if necessary. They've promised me that, all of them." The governor sounded tired, and having to argue with one of his own cabinet members was an effort he felt he shouldn't have to make.

Kenehan, oblivious to the governor's demeanor, continued to press the same argument he had made for months. "Well, of course, they will, Governor. They're all in Bowers' back pocket. Bowers wants you to take the loans, he probably prays every night that you'll do just that. It'll be one more way he'll be running the show. Governor, if you take the loans, you know what's next. Bowers, Welborn and the others will plead for protection, say that their property is being destroyed by the strikers. They'll box you into a corner, say you have no excuse not to send in the National Guard. Don't you see, Governor, that's exactly what the companies want?"

"I understand everything you've been telling me, not just now but over the last two months. But I don't think I've got a choice." Ammons' voice cracked, almost hoarse from the constant debate and discussions that seemed to have occupied his every waking moment since the union struck.

As he heard those last words, Kenehan inwardly grimaced. He'd become increasingly angry at Ammons' passivity. All through the summer Ammons had sat back and just hoped for the best. Now the strike had been called, he had got worse. Kenehan had been reluctantly forced to admit that the governor, albeit unconsciously, wanted to be driven into corner, so that he didn't have to make a decision but have one forced on him.

Ammons swiveled his chair around so he could avoid Kenehan's stare and gazed out of the window. As he contemplated the ramifications of what his auditor had just told him, he unconsciously placed the flat of his palms together under his nose as though in prayer. Finally he swiveled back.

"I talked with General Chase recently." Kenehan began to say something, but Ammons held his hand up to silence him. "I know what you think of him, the whole capitol knows what you think of him. But I am convinced that Chase is right. At some point, sooner rather than later, unless there's a settlement, we're going to have, I'm going to have to send in the Guard. And for that we need money. And we can't be too picky about where it comes from."

Kenehan changed tack and introduced another argument, one that Ammons had heard many times before. "Governor, and let me be crystal clear, taking such loans would be illegal. An action is either against the law or it's not, regardless of how expedient it might be for you and your administration. And I know this is against the law." Kenehan stopped talking, for he could see that Ammons was losing his patience and was now just as likely to dismiss his arguments out of anger as out of logic.

"Please, Governor." Kenehan took a more conciliatory tone. "Please, just take some time to think of what I've just said. Talk to your legal staff if you don't believe me. Just think about it. And you might think, and I say this with all respect, Governor, of actually going to Trinidad to see firsthand what's happening."

Ammons raised his eyebrows at the suggestion. "Yes, of course, Roady. Thank you. Of course, I'll think about it. Thank you. And the trip is a good idea."

Kenehan stood up and took his overcoat and hat from the stand in the corner. "Thank you, Governor." As the Irishman walked out of the governor's office, he knew he had bought some time, but only a little, and probably not enough.

Ammons continued to sit at his desk, rehashing the conversation. He believed, against all the odds, that good sense would prevail and a settlement could be reached, but he also knew that he was running out of time to make this happen. Every day brought new stories of violence, of gunfights. And now he pulled from his side pocket a telegram from Pueblo, received just an hour ago, that said the Baldwin-Felts company had commissioned a special vehicle to deal with the miners. What exactly that meant he could only guess, but he was sure it would be bad. Governor Elias Ammons was losing control of his own state.

"She's a beauty, sir, a real beauty," Sam King gushed.

Albert Felts beamed back. "Yup, she sure is. You know, Walt, I always believe that if you keep the enemy on their toes, you're one up on them. And this beauty will do just that. Learned that little lesson back East, by the way. Those miners never knew what was comin' at them next."

The object of their admiration stood on the front terrace of the Colorado Fuel and Iron steel works. Felts had bought a large sedan in Denver and then had it shipped it out to Pueblo so he could personally supervise its virtual dismantling and rebuilding. Now all that was left were the original frame and engine. Engineers had installed a thick wooden floor and covered the sides of the automobile with steel plate. They had mounted two medium machine guns and seating for four men, and, as a finishing touch, a searchlight in the front.

"King, I've got to get off at Walsenburg for business, but you know what this baby's for. See how well it works. And report back to me tonight in Trinidad."

King nodded back. He had watched his boss drive the armored car around the goods depot before loading it onto the train and couldn't wait to put it into action.

To King the locomotive seemed to take forever but finally it rolled into Trinidad. As King saw the automobile safely off the flatbed he was joined by Stubbs, still limping from the Lippiatt firefight. The two of them stood in admiration at Felts' handiwork. "Felts says we're to try it out, waddya' think?"

Stubbs smiled in expectation. "I know exactly where, too. Is this thing ready to go?"

King nodded.

"Let's go then."

As they drove north out of town, Stubbs told King that there had been running battles at Forbes tent colony the last few days.

"Well, then, Arthur, my boy," King cracked a broad smile, "it's time we acted for the public good."

The two of them laughed and cranked the sedan into top gear. Forbes was about five miles north of town and it didn't take them long to hear the gunfire. As they got closer they were stopped by another Baldwin-Felts man, who explained that things had got ugly.

"Martin, you know him, right, he's the deputy sheriff around here, well, he tried to get them to give up their guns."

King interrupted. "Damned waste of time, right?"

The detective nodded. "Total waste. Anyhow, shooting's started and now we've got them pinned down in their tents. I think the women and kids are out of the way. Not that I give a damn, one way or another."

"Any dead?" King and Stubbs asked almost simultaneously.

"I think just one, that I know of, but not real sure." For the first time the Baldwin-Felts detective stood back and looked at the vehicle. He whistled in admiration.

Stubbs winked at him. "Come on up, let's share the fun."

Climbing in next to the other two, the detective took the wheel and began a slow drive past the colony. Stubbs and King unlocked the machine guns and began to fire indiscriminately into the tents. The heavy bullets sliced through the canvas like it was not there. The three agents heard the bullets flying off metal stoves and chimneys, the smashing of cups and plates and the cries of terror coming from the men, women and children lying flat on the floors of their tent cellars. Nothing moved except the tents as they were shredded and flapped in the evening wind. After firing over five hundred rounds, the three men stopped to let the guns cool down. They surveyed their handiwork with satisfaction, and as the first miners began to crawl out of the tents to see what had done this to them, they turned the vehicle around and headed back to Trinidad. They left behind a camp totally destroyed, an eighteen-year-old with multiple leg wounds and one dead miner.

Later that night, Felts met with King and Stubbs. After they described the events of that evening at Forbes, the three of them agreed that the vehicle's primary use would be intimidation. Felts nodded, satisfied that the expenditure had been a good investment.

"By the way, boys," Felts called out as an afterthought while the two men were leaving. "I heard something great. It'll crack you up. I talked to the sheriff a while ago. You know what the miners are callin' my little invention?"

King and Stubbs shook their heads.

"This'll kill yer, boys. They're callin' it the death special. How's about that?"

The two men looked at each other and burst out laughing.

"Well, they got that right, boss," King chuckled. And still grinning, the two of them sauntered out of Felts' office onto the street.

Karl Linderfelt, Monte to his friends, felt passionately that the solution to the strike was simple. Lock every goddamned one of them up, and if they resist, shoot them. He had seen it work in the Philippines, where he had been an army lieutenant, and it would work in Colorado, too.

Chase agreed. He had told him exactly that when, right after he had hired Linderfelt as head of the company guards, the general had asked him to serve as his eyes and ears in the coalfields. His latest assignment, to follow Governor Ammons on his tour of the coalfields and report back to Chase, was exactly the sort Linderfelt loved but it had been a colossal waste of time. Mother Jones had organized a demonstration of women and children outside the governor's hotel in Trinidad. In Walsenburg Ammons had met union and company delegations and then immediately left for Denver. Resigned to more boredom, Linderfelt left Walsenburg for Trinidad. A company guard was waiting for him on the platform.

"Sir," he blurted out even before Linderfelt had climbed down off the train. "Sir, things have gone ugly. As far we can tell, some miners and their women harassed a woman – her husband won't join the union – and things blew up from there. The deputy sheriff was forced to open fire, to protect innocents, and anyway three or four miners have been killed. They were all Eastern Europeans, too."

Linderfelt smiled thinly. "This is exactly what happens when you handle those fuckin' wops with kid gloves. They act like they own the place. Goddamn all of 'em."

He said nothing more as he and the guard walked to the car, but was quietly pleased for he knew that this incident was the opportunity Chase had been looking for; one that would make the miners go on a rampage. Ammons would have to send in the National Guard, Chase would find a way to provoke the miners into more violence, and he, Karl Linderfelt, would be right in the thick of the action. He decided to force the issue by immediately moving the company guards onto the offensive. And Ludlow was in his line-of-sight.

The word of the killings spread quickly. Lawson and Tikas were in Ludlow and they both realized the killings could push the confrontation onto a whole new level of violence. Lawson quickly made his decisions. "Louis, job one here is to protect Ludlow, make sure nothing happens. I want you take a bunch of your men north of the camp and stop any train from Walsenburg that you think is carrying guards. Then take the rest and head south. Do the same to the Trinidad trains. And keep an eye on the machine guns on Water Tank Hill."

It was now just before three in the afternoon, and the late October wind was beginning to turn cold. Lawson tied his red union bandana tightly around his neck to keep out the chill, drank cup after cup of coffee, for something to do as much as anything else, and not for the first time pondered the ludicrous situation he found himself in. *Look at yourself, John. Got up like a bandit with a six-shooter and carbine, ready to do what? Fight? Die?* Lawson had never really answered that question, one he had asked himself time without number, mostly because he was afraid to admit that he knew the answer. He saw himself as a reasonable, mild-mannered man who had tried to stay within the bounds of the law, but who had been pushed outside by the simple injustice of the situation. He wished the other union leaders could be as straight-minded as he was. He got angry when union politics got in the way of sound decisions, which happened a lot, even angrier when he himself was accused of playing politics. *Maybe John,* he told himself, *this is where you really belong. Not in a smoky room making deals, but here, with a gun in your hand, a place where everything is black, white and blood red.*

He heard shooting coming from south of Ludlow and five minutes later a runner came scampering into the headquarters tent. "Mr. Lawson, sir, the company guards have set up just south of camp. They say Linderfelt's in charge." Lawson grimaced; he knew the company man was itching for a fight. *Maybe this time,* he thought, *the bastard'll really get it.*

"Anyways, Mr. Lawson, a whole bunch of guards just arrived from Berwind and Tabasco, and Mr. Tikas told me to tell you that we're firing at them, but we're comin' back because there's too many."

Lawson was impressed that Tikas had got a good English speaker to act as their go-between. Lawson found himself remembering something he'd read about the Custer massacre, and how the cavalry screwed themselves because the main runner was an Italian who couldn't speak much English. *Why the hell did I think of that now of all times?* Lawson laughed out loud, and the runner looked at him quizzically. "It's okay, I'm not mad. Tell Tikas to meet me as soon as he gets back."

Families had taken shelter in their pits and the tent colony looked deserted. Tikas joined Lawson in the headquarters tent to plot their next move. All the while the wind increased and the sky turned dark grey, a sign of approaching snow.

"Louis." Lawson looked up to see the wind flapping the tent walls. "If this weather keeps up, we won't be able to do anything after all."

Tikas nodded in agreement. "John, I brought some of our guns back to the camp, and we're ready. But you're right, I think we've seen the worst for now. I don't think Linderfelt will move any closer."

The confrontation fizzled out as the cold October night set in and a snowstorm blew through the canyons, but the next morning it reignited in deadly earnest. Linderfelt had taken advantage of the respite and deployed guards throughout the coalfields to try to protect as much company property as he could. He had set up headquarters at the Ludlow rail station but he had now decided to make a break for Tabasco, where he could take up a better defended position.

Lawson and Tikas were discussing their response when Spiro, who had ignored Maria's pleas not to get involved, walked into the tent. He looked pale but resolute, and Tikas decided to take a chance.

"Spiro, John thinks we need to get some of us over to Tabasco. Are you up to it?"

Spiro nodded.

"Okay, this is what I need you to do. Go with a bunch of our men, I'll tell you who they are, to the hill overlooking the ovens at Tabasco. Take up defensive positions. Stop the guards from settling in if you can. I'm trusting you. Be careful."

Swinging around the Ludlow train depot in the event guardsmen were still there, Spiro and his crew tramped westward up the canyon, towards his old home. He was scared, really scared. This wasn't like Lee's murder, which was over almost before it had started and it was not like the searchlight incident when it was dark and he knew they had good cover. No, this was different. They were in the open, they had guns and in the middle of a battle. For some inexplicable reason he found himself continuously yawning, as if his lungs could not inflate. The miners in his group looked to him for guidance and he hoped he would not let them down.

He arranged the men along the crest of the hill overlooking Tabasco as ordered. An hour of doing nothing, and Spiro wondered if they should back down. Just then one of the men yelled at him to look down the canyon. In the direction of the

Ludlow rail depot, they saw thick black smoke billowing high into the air. He decided to keep on waiting.

"God, it's cold up here," he remarked to his group, as much to allay his own fears as theirs. He felt a cold coming on and had to keep blowing his nose. *Not a very martial image,* he laughed to himself.

"Not much longer now, eh, boss, then things'll heat up," one of the miners whispered to Spiro. It was the first time he'd been called that, and it did not sound right. But the miner was right about the new activity. Down in the canyon he saw signs of movement, guardsmen getting ready to move out. But they were canny and did not present good targets. Spiro and the miners opened fire, pouring ragged volleys into the buildings and at anything that moved. He knew that there was little chance of hitting anybody but it felt good to be able to strike back after months of being on the defensive. He paused to wash his mouth out with some water from a bottle he carried in a bag slung around his neck. As he placed it back he felt a hand rocking his arm.

"Look, boss, there, dya' see 'im, behind the ovens to the right. He's crazy."

Spiro saw a man wearing the distinctive hat of a mine guard caught in the open and apparently unsure of where to run. Spiro worked the rifle bolt and put a bullet in the chamber. But now that the moment was here, Spiro couldn't fire. He had never come close to seriously wounding a man before, let alone killing one. "He's too far away, too far away."

"Shit, I'll get the bastard then," someone else shouted. The striker lifted a Winchester carbine to his shoulder, took careful aim and fired. The shot missed, and the guardsman, realizing he was in somebody's sights, started to scamper for cover. A second shot missed. Thinking that it might be his lucky day, the guard decided to make a run across open ground for the ovens.

Spiro picked up his own rifle. A coldness descended over him;

his universe became constricted to what he could see at the end of his rifle. He aimed carefully, leading the man as he had done years ago on Crete when he had killed rabid dogs attacking his father's sheep. He fired and caught the man full in the chest. Even at that distance, Spiro could see a little crimson bloom erupt and then seep over the man's torso. The guard toppled to the ground. He moved for a brief moment, his heels scraping the dirt at his feet. Finally, after what seemed to Spiro an eternity, the man stopped squirming. He was dead.

Since Spiro had seen Lee gunned down, he had wondered if he would have the nerve to pull the trigger. Secretly he had been afraid that he would be incapable, that he would shame his family of warriors. But as he stared down at the inert figure, Spiro felt nothing but the satisfaction of a job well-done. That he had just ended another man's life, a man he had never met, probably with a family like his, gave him no remorse. He didn't feel the need to justify why this man had died, a man who would perhaps have felt no compunction in killing him. He shouldered his rifle, sniffed at his runny nose, and helped himself to more water.

"Well done, boss," they congratulated him. Now the word sounded right, felt good to him.

Yeah, he was a boss, and they were his men.

Albert Felts was in his Trinidad office when he received Linderfelt's call. He slammed the receiver into its cradle and ran to the rail depot as fast as he could. He saw Sam King on Main and shouted, "Linderfelt needs reinforcements. He's pinned down at Tabasco. We need to get men up there as fast as we can. Look, I'll get our men together, you commandeer a train. Now!"

King ran to the footplate of the nearest train and pointed his gun at the engineer. "You get this train fired up, or I'll shoot you where you stand," he snarled. The engineer's hands were shaking as he took his oil-stained hat off, wiped his brow with an even grimier kerchief.

But in a surprisingly strong voice the engineer shouted "I won't, I won't. You can shoot me, but if you do that, then you'll really be screwed."

The detective was getting sick of these engineers. They were all union sympathizers, and this one was actually refusing to drive the train to Ludlow with the men Linderfelt needed. He cocked his pistol and aimed it at the engineer.

Suddenly, Felts appeared. "Let him go. All we need is to shoot a civilian. Let him go, for Christ's sake. We don't need him anymore. I've found someone who'll drive the goddamned thing."

King waved with his pistol and the engineer gratefully jumped out of the cabin, making sure he exited on the far side. As he ran, rather than walked away from his train, he looked back and saw a new crew jump into the cabin and a swarm of deputies and detectives climb aboard.

Back in Ludlow, the miners knew the guards had left Trinidad but did not know what they intended. Rumors were flying through the tent colonies, unimpeded by truth or common sense: that Ammons had turned out the National Guard; that the U.S. Cavalry were coming; that it was a whole regiment of the Army with orders to deport them back to Europe. The most popular rumor, because it was the worst, had that the President of the United States was about to arrive in Trinidad to negotiate a peace, but the company agents had massive artillery on the train and were going to blow everybody to kingdom come before the man could arrive.

Lawson held a counsel of war with Tikas. He told the Greek that the rumors were crazy with one exception: he believed that the train would steam slowly past Ludlow and rake the tent colony from close range. Tikas replied that he was convinced that the guards would get off the train somewhere south of Ludlow and then fan out to relieve the other agents who were pinned down trying to protect company property. Lawson made a decision that he hoped would deal with both their fears.

"Louis, I want your Greeks to deploy along the rail line between here and Forbes. Stop that train from getting through. I'm taking no chances. I'll stay here with the rest in case the bastards attack the camp."

Tikas nodded. He moved three hundred miners south of the tent colony where they lay in hiding in the hills. Snow was falling and the cold of the ground chilled the miners as they waited in anticipation. Lookouts on the hills signaled the train's approach, the miners checked their weapons were unlocked and loaded, and as it hove into shooting distance all three hundred guns opened up. A sound like hail engulfed the train as hundreds of bullets slammed into its sides, smashing through the windows and ricocheting off the metal with high-pitched zings. The guards threw themselves to the floors of the carriages and scrabbled under the seats for protection.

"Jesus Christ, how many fuckin' guns do they have?" Felts cowered on the footplate. "Get us the fuck out of here," he barked.

The driver didn't need a second invitation, and he slammed the train into reverse. It slowed to a halt and then he shunted it southward as fast as he could. Once out of range, Felts ordered his command off the train and sent individual units to the mines they had been assigned to. He made it to Berwind in the early hours of the morning where he linked up with Linderfelt who had moved his command post further up the canyon away from Tabasco.

Still deployed along the ridge above Tabasco, Spiro and his men, numb with cold, were about to withdraw when he spotted new activity by the coke ovens. The miners opened fire and raked the whole area. As Spiro was reloading, out of the corner of his eye he saw guards making their way up the slope to his west. They were clever, running between folds in the hills, lying low and then moving again as soon as they thought it was safe.

He pointed to a group of miners and told them to stop the guards from taking up positions. If the guards got to where Spiro thought they were headed they would have a clear line of fire onto his men. The miners looked at him dumbly. He was about to repeat the order when he realized they could not understand a word he was saying. He saw the guards were still making progress to the top of the ridge and somehow by gesticulation and a lot of pointing, he got his intentions over to the miners.

I should have sent someone else, he reproached himself, but it was too late, for even before the men had slipped from view, Spiro heard carbine fire and he thought he saw two of them drop to the ground. He didn't know if they were taking cover or had been shot. He ordered the rest of the men back, and they slinked back out of the killing zone. He prayed the two miners were safe but he was not optimistic.

As the fire from the guards increased in intensity, Spiro knew he would have to withdraw. The ragtag collection picked up their rifles and packs and set off in the direction of Ludlow. Their only resistance came from a group of guards going in the opposite direction. Three of them ran away but a fourth stayed around too long. The miners left his body in the snow and continued on down to Ludlow. Spiro's first battle was over.

For Karl Linderfeldt, the reaction of the "fuckin' wops" had been an eye-opener. He had expected them to surrender at the first sight of a real soldier, but here they were still taking the fight to him after twenty-four hours. But he was buoyed by the prospect of a proper fight. Realizing that Chase had to be told of the latest developments and that this was his opportunity to intensify the conflict, he thought about the telegram hard before he allowed it to be sent. He had to convey the threat to civil peace; that this was not just another bunch of crazy foreigners shooting their guns off. His words were terse.

"Rebels at Ludlow say they are going to clean up down here. Situation is critical. We need troops." He looked at the young company agent who served as his assistant. "Yeah, I know. Strong words. But maybe, just maybe, the words, rebels, critical, might put enough fear into Ammons to get him to pull his thumb out of his arse, finally."

The man said nothing, and took the note to the telegraph operator for transmission to Denver.

16

A week after the firefights, calm settled over the coalfields. At union headquarters, the optimism of their successes against the company guards had been replaced by the stark reality that the union was already running out of money. Elias Ammons, knowing that desperation might make the miners reckless, made one last attempt to bring the two sides together. The mine owners were in one of the governor's conference rooms, their bonhomie an indication of the confidence they felt. In a smaller office a subdued Frank Hayes waited impatiently. The two rooms were separated by Ammons' own private office suite.

His voice croaking with exhaustion, the governor spoke to the mine owners. "I have just met Frank Hayes and he believes that they cannot continue. He did not say as much but that is what I think. They will go back to work, I am sure, if the union can meet with you on an equal footing one last time. Just let them save a little face. Please. Gentlemen, if you agree to this I am certain that the union will also drop their demand that you formally recognize them. And this collective misery will be over."

The mine owners were unsympathetic. Welborn responded. "I speak for all my colleagues here and we have to say to you a simple word, and that word is no, sir." The last word dripped with sarcasm but Ammons was past the point of recognizing the insult. "We will not meet with them. Period. Moreover, I must insist that you protect our property. With the National Guard, if that is what it takes."

Ammons slinked out of his own conference room. In his private office, he met a delegation of Denver bankers. They reiterated that they would have money available within a month if the governor wished it, and it would be enough to cover the costs of the National Guard and ensure that the strike ended peacefully. Roady Kenehan, the state auditor, who had stood there silently while the bankers threw Ammons the financial lifeline he desperately needed, finally interceded.

"Gentlemen, I still have the authority in this state to say what is spent by this administration and for what purpose, and I won't play your game. Don't forget that. Get a court order because that's the only way you'll goddamned get me to spend your money on the Guard. I'll give Hayes the bad news." He stormed out of the room.

Ammons tried to explain that Kenehan was a good man prone to Irish excess, but he knew the bankers didn't give a damn what anybody in his administration said. They were in league with the mine owners and they were winning.

Ammons dragged himself back to the mine owners. Welborn started up before the governor could say anything.

"In the interests of a fair settlement to this dispute may we suggest that you write a letter asking us to enforce existing Colorado labor laws as they pertain to the coalmines? I am sure you will agree that a fair resolution to this dispute is simply for all of us to ensure that the current laws are upheld. I can assure you, Governor, that all of us will sign a memorandum of agreement to that effect."

Ammons asked if they could meet that same evening to sign the document. Welborn looked the governor, ostensibly the most powerful man in Colorado, directly in the eyes.

"There's no need for that, Governor, tomorrow will do just fine. We are all rather tired. Good evening."

Ammons was left with an empty room. He was too tired to realize that they had dismissed him, rather than the other way around. At least he could console himself that the strike was over.

But the next day, Welborn and Bowers came to the governor's office and informed him that rehiring any miner who struck was out of the question and that they would be willing to sign a memorandum of agreement only if that provision was included.

Ammons looked at the two of them in disbelief. "But you'll be putting most of the miners out of work permanently."

Welborn shrugged his shoulders. "Be that as it may, Governor. That is what we have decided."

Bowers spoke for the first time. "Governor, you are aware, as I am, that our property is being destroyed. We must insist that the strikers responsible for this destruction never be allowed to step inside our mines again."

Ammons sighed and slumped further in his chair. He knew now that the strike was not only going to continue but going to get worse. *Why should the miners give in if they lose their jobs anyway,* he asked himself. The owners had deliberately withdrawn the last olive branch. They wanted total victory and complete annihilation of the union: nothing more, nothing less. After Welborn and Bowers had left, he summoned his secretary. "John," he whispered, "we need to write up an executive order."

His secretary nodded. He knew its purpose. "Sir, if I may say so, no man could have done more than you to prevent this."

"Thank you, John. There are a few phrases I would like you to include. I've written them down for you."

His secretary took the yellow legal paper. One phrase stood out above all the others: "there is a tumult threatened." His secretary walked into the adjoining office, and instructed the stenographer to type out the gubernatorial order that would declare martial law and direct the National Guard to restore order in southern Colorado. Ammons' secretary took the typescript back to the governor, who added his signature without reading it. He then handed it back with the order that it be distributed to all state-government departments and the press the following day.

Word of Ammons' decision quickly reached the coalfields. In anticipation of Chase's arrival, on November 1st Frank Hayes and John McLennan rushed down to Trinidad, and then drove out to Ludlow to meet Lawson. Hayes handed a telegram to the Scot without even pausing to greet him. Lawson scanned it, then passed it to Tikas who had joined them, but the Greek had trouble with some of the words and Lawson interpreted.

"Louis, Chase is coming with about a thousand men. They're fully equipped, they've even got a hospital staff. He's going to set up two base camps, one in Trinidad, the other in Walsenburg. And I think he's gonna' do one thing immediately; take away our guns." Hayes and McLennan nodded in agreement.

As if on cue, their discussion was interrupted by a miner who stuck his head in the tent and told them they had to see something. Everybody in the camp was staring at a squadron of mounted soldiers, positioned about two hundred yards south of the camp. Two open-topped vehicles emerged from the center of the squadron and drove slowly north. As the cars got closer the four strike leaders realized that they were about to be visited by the great General Chase himself. Three miners, who happened to be practicing on their trumpets for an upcoming concert, struck up 'The Battle Cry of Freedom', as the vehicles drove through the gates. If Chase recognized the irony, he did not show it. The general was a showman, and in full dress uniform he made a great display of surveying the camp before he stepped down and approached the four men.

"Do we kiss his ring?" Hayes wisecracked *sotto voce*. Before anybody could reply, the general surprised everybody by holding out his hand in a public gesture of goodwill.

Initially nonplussed by his action, Hayes and McLennan stepped forward and shook hands. Lawson and Tikas stayed in the background. The general beamed at everybody, even waved at the onlookers who had crept forward.

"I am sorry to have to meet under such circumstances, gentlemen, but you understand we must put an end to this, for all our sakes." His voice was polite, but nobody was fooled by the general's façade. Chase flamboyantly waved for the two officers in the second car to introduce themselves. The four miners cursed inwardly as the first one approached.

"Gentlemen," Chase bellowed, "allow me to introduce Lieutenant Linderfelt. I have just commissioned him into the Colorado National Guard." Linderfelt said nothing. He just smirked at the four miners.

The second officer, however, was more courteous. "Gentlemen, I am Captain Philip Van Cise, in command of Company K. We will be camped over there." He pointed to a field opposite the Ludlow depot. "Many of my men are college boys, they love baseball, perhaps we can get some friendly games against your teams."

The miners did not react, and the stony faces on Chase and Linderfelt suggested that they did not approve of Van Cise's overture. "I am positive that we can resolve this issue peacefully," Van Cise continued, either unaware of or not bothered by his colleagues' reactions. "I am a lawyer by training, and we lawyers love to compromise if at all possible."

Chase spoke one more time. "The camps must turn in their arms. And now, gentlemen, I will leave you in the capable hands of Captain Van Cise. Good day." He turned around and without further ado got back into his car. Linderfelt joined him.

The miners looked at each other, bemused by what to do next, until Van Cise took the initiative. "We do need your guns, you know. It's the direct order of the governor. Look, I'll come back in an hour with a truck to pick them up. Will that work?"

After he had left, Tikas was blunt. "I don't trust him, he's too, what is the word, nice."

"Well, Louis," Lawson responded, "I suppose by the law of averages there's got be at least one decent guardsman. Maybe we just got lucky, eh?"

Tikas hesitated. "We'll see. Anyways, that bastard Linderfelt worries me even more. Now he's an officer. You see how he drove off with Chase, like they're best friends? I don't like that, John, I don't like it."

Hayes interrupted them. "The two of us are heading back to Trinidad. John, stay here and make sure the guns are handed over. And Louis. No trouble. Got it? Let's see how this plays out, okay?"

Tikas nodded in assent. "Let's get the guns, John."

Exactly one hour later, Van Cise reappeared with a truck and four guardsmen. Tikas and Lawson were surprised that he had brought such a small contingent of men for what could be a dangerous confrontation. Lawson pointed to a pile of arms in front of the headquarters tent. A Guard lieutenant started counting them while Van Cise stood silently watching. Miners and their families began to gather.

It did not take the lieutenant long to complete his inventory. "Sir, I counted less than forty, thirty-seven to be exact. And, sir," he hesitated, "they're all pieces of junk; some look like they haven't been fired in years."

Van Cise turned to Lawson and Tikas, saying nothing but raising his eyebrows expectantly. The crowd picked up on the stand-off and began to get restless, murmurs of anger beginning to grow. The four soldiers unshouldered their carbines, but Van Cise waved them down. "Gentlemen, come now, we can do better than that. You must have more, surely." Despite the blandness of his words, the tension mounted.

Out of nowhere came a young boy's voice. "Wait a minute." It sounded nervous. The crowd looked around and saw young Frank Hoffman shrugging off his mother's hold and forcing his way to the front. Very solemnly he pulled a toy gun out of his belt. Cradling the gun in both hands, he knelt down and gravely, as though laying flowers on a coffin, placed the gun on the pile.

He looked at Van Cise. "Sir, I'm sorry, but I forgot about this till now."

The crowd tensed, not knowing how Van Cise would respond. Everybody looked at the captain. Slowly, a half smile formed on his face. Then it became a full smile and finally a huge grin.

"Okay, young man, now I can sleep soundly in my bed. Thank you." The gasp of relief from the crowd was audible. Van Cise turned away towards his car. But as he passed Lawson, he slowed and gave him a cold stare. "I want us to be at peace. There's been enough killings already. But, seriously, I must have those guns. Do you understand?"

A sleety rain dashed against the windows of John D. Rockefeller Jr.'s office. Looking through a small circle he had rubbed in the moisture condensing on the pane, he saw a dull overcast sky that wreathed the tall buildings in a smoky crown of gray. On the streets below, buses, taxicabs and delivery vans flitted along. He smiled with amusement as the business men tried to shrink into their heavy winter coats to keep out the biting wind, vainly fought with their umbrellas or tried simply to keep their hats on.

Rockefeller turned his attention to his father who was sitting in front of the large coal fire trying to stay warm. The senior Rockefeller wanted to know the gist of what was happening in his coalfields, and so without more ado, his son sat down next to him in the other wing-backed leather chair and as his father absent-mindedly poked the coals, he recounted what had happened in the last few months.

"As you know, Father, President Wilson has been putting pressure on Bowers and the others to settle. He thinks that we are the ones at fault, that we're the ones being intransigent."

The older Rockefeller nodded and drew his blanket more tightly around his knees as a particularly strong gust of wind rattled the windows. "I can't say I'm surprised, Junior. The day that man was sworn into office, I knew he was against business. And look at the horrible little men in his administration. They are all for the unions, and to the devil with honest men."

Rockefeller Jr. was surprised by this outburst. Normally his father was objective about his business affairs to the point of coldness. But whether this change in demeanor was due to his father's tacit recognition of the severity of the situation in Colorado or simply that he was losing his iron self-discipline was unclear to him.

The younger man continued. "About three weeks ago, Father, Wilson sent a formal letter of complaint to Welborn and Bowers, regarding our refusal to meet with union leaders. I have here," he said, holding up a thick wad of writing paper, "Bowers' response. In my opinion, and I have told him this already, it is a fair and reasoned response to unnecessary government intervention in a private business matter." Rockefeller omitted the unfounded accusation in the letter that Mother Jones had once been a prostitute and then run a brothel. "I communicated to him that we are with him to the end, even if it means damaging our investment. I am sure you will agree that destroying the union must remain our paramount concern."

His father said nothing, just nodded slowly. His eyes were half-shut and for a moment his son wondered if he had actually heard him. But the old man's eyes suddenly jerked open and his son saw in them all the vitality of a man half his age. "Bowers is a good man. He'll see this through to the end. Right. That was then. Remind me where we stand since Ammons declared martial law."

"Actually, Father, little has changed. Two days ago I received a letter from Ammons, asking me, again, to intercede and settle this strike. I sent him a telegram that same day, telling him no. That we had complete faith in Bowers, Welborn and the others, and we feel confident in continuing to place our trust in their very capable hands. Bowers has told me also that yet another meeting between the union and our people has collapsed. The union is still demanding to be formally recognized as the sole representative of the employees, and they want all the men who walked out to be rehired once the strike is over. They have even held a referendum to that effect. How very democratic of them." Rockefeller afforded himself a smirk as he emphasized the word *democratic.* "Of course, Bowers and Welborn, supported by Osgood and the others, refused their demands.

"I have not yet received anything from Ammons in reply to my own telegram. I didn't expect to. Our sources in Denver tell me that he is a broken man. He has virtually turned over all military decisions to Chase who, as you know, is completely in support of our goals. I believe that the strike will be resolved in our favor very soon."

"I agree, Junior, I agree. I am of the very strong opinion that this strike is caused by a very small group of foreign trouble-makers who do not wish to work but have everything handed to them on a platter. They have no self-respect. That reminds me of when I was a young man on a biking holiday in France."

The younger Rockefeller settled himself comfortably into his chair, to hear, again, one of his father's favorite parables. Fortunately for the younger Rockefeller, no sooner had his father begun then there was a sharp rap on the door and one of his aides entered.

"Sir, this just came." He handed the son a telegram. "It is from Mr. Bowers, sir." Rockefeller nodded at the young man, who immediately withdrew.

"If you will excuse me, Father, I rather think I should read this."

There was silence, save for the ticking of the clock on the mantelpiece and the muted roar of the traffic outside. Rockefeller walked over to the window and perused the latest message from Bowers, while his father sat in the easy chair staring at the fire. The younger Rockefeller put down the telegram on the side table and sat down again next to his father.

"It is good news, very good news, indeed." The younger man allowed himself a broad smile. "Ammons has finally agreed to our bringing in new workers. So, the union has lost all its power to close us down. It surely must now be just a matter of time."

His father nodded. "I agree. It's all over bar the shouting. I always said that the strike was the work of a few diehard reactionaries. The strikebreakers will make it impossible for the union to continue."

17

The day had been just like all the others in Ludlow, now that both sides had settled in for a long encounter: hunger, boredom, shootings and the constant, nagging fear of the unknown. The first meeting with the National Guard, just ten days ago, already seemed an age away, and the camp had settled back into its daily routine. Van Cise had searched the camp for guns but hadn't found many and had left as quickly as he arrived. Maria had not even known he had been there until Spiro told her. There had been some shooting in a canyon, but everyone had become so used to it that nobody paid attention. And they had heard that west of Walsenburg a miner had refused to join the union and was being escorted back to his house under the protection of three company guards and a driver when the car was ambushed. Everyone was killed except the miner. Sheriff Farr had arrested eight miners on suspicion of murder, a suspicion only strengthened when he found a huge cache of rifles in one of their houses.

The camp was settling down for the evening when everyone heard a howling. Immediately thinking the worst, men rushed to their guns, but were relieved to hear it was only Fredo Petrucci shouting that his wife was having a baby and to come quick.

Nora and Maria got to Mary Petrucci's tent at the same time, and Nora immediately told the distraught husband to go to the next tent, boil some water, bring it back and then stay out of the way. Maria smiled, because she'd once asked Nora why the midwives always needed so much hot water and always made the men get it. Nora had pursed her lips and then broken into laughter. "I don't really know," she had replied, "but at least it keeps the poor things occupied while we get on with our business. And Maria, can you stay and help? If you're up to it." Maria nodded.

The Italian woman had been in labor ten hours now, and Nora was getting scared that it was all going wrong. "Don't push until I tell you, honey," Nora gently chided her. Mary was fast losing the strength to do anything at all. "Don't push, honey, I know you want to, but don't. Maria, hold her down."

Maria came around the other side of the patient and held her head and shoulders while another terrible contraction wracked her body. Sweat coursed off the young woman's brows and Maria wiped her face to stop the salt stinging her eyes. Now she looked virtually a corpse as the constant pain took its toll, and she moaned in fear and tiredness. The young woman was at her breaking point.

Slowly her contractions subsided and she was able to relax her body for a few moments of respite. Very gently Nora placed two fingers into the woman's vagina.

"It seems open and I'm sure I can feel the baby's head, Maria, but still." She looked apprehensively at Maria who motioned to one of Petrucci's friends, Patria Valdez, who was due herself in a few months, to stay with her, while the two of them went outside for a breath of fresh air.

"Maria, we really need to get a doctor. The union doc is good, but he can't be everywhere at once, so we'll just have to help the poor girl ourselves."

Maria wiped her hands of her patient's sweat, for Mary was feverish, and asked exactly what the problem was.

"Well, so far as I can see, the baby's the right way up. So, that shouldn't be the problem. I've helped with a lot of babies, you know that, but this one's one of the worst I've ever seen. This is her fourth, so it should have come out real easy. The baby's just too big. We'll just have to work at it. Anyway, whatever happens is gonna' happen soon. Neither of them'll take much more of this."

Now at five in the morning a cold wind was blowing across the camp and the dew was making everything damp and chilly.

Nora stuck her head inside the tent.

"She's still resting, Maria. I think if it doesn't come this time, they're both done for." Maria nodded grimly, for she knew the agony, physical and mental, of delivering a stillborn.

As though reading her mind, Nora took her friend's hands. "I'm sorry, my pet. I should have got somebody else to help, what with all you've just gone through."

Maria shook her head and whispered. "No, really, Nora, I'm good. In fact, I'm surprised it hasn't affected me at all. Maybe God knew it wasn't Spiro's and He took it."

They heard Mary begin to stir and they looked at each other with trepidation as they went back into the tent. The woman was almost spent, but as the contractions began again, miraculously they brought a new fight into her frail body. Mary rose up out of the bed in defiance and firmly gripped Maria's and Patria's hands. She looked at Nora, nodded, said a short prayer, managed a half-smile, and steeled herself.

Nora gently opened up the young woman's legs and bent her knees. What she saw was red and covered with mucus but to Nora it was beautiful; it was the dome of a tiny head just peeking out of the woman's vagina. Nora smiled at Mary.

"Right, my love, now you can push."

She braced herself and pushed like she had never pushed in her life before. Where she got the strength from Maria or Nora never did figure out, but that fragile young thing pushed and pushed. And miraculously, first the head, then the body came sliding out. Nora gratefully took the baby boy in her arms. And as he drew in his first lungfuls of air, he cried out; softly at first, but louder and louder until the whole camp seemed to fill with the sound of new life. Now Nora deftly tied the cord and skillfully snipped it. Then she wiped the baby down, while Mary cried tears of joy. Maria hugged her tenderly because she knew the joy of childbirth. For now, the pain and fear were forgotten, beaten away by the glory of God's creation. Tomorrow would take care of itself. For now at least, life was beautiful.

Fredo burst into the tent, fearful of what he might find. But all he met were huge smiles, and there lying in bed was his wife, exhausted but radiant, and nestled into her, his new son, already trying to feed at his mama's breasts.

Nora smiled. "Everything is fine. He has ten fingers and ten toes. Congratulations."

The Italian impulsively hugged Nora, immediately felt embarrassed and pulled away, and then knelt beside his wife and cried in sheer relief. He crossed himself and then leaned over to look at his brand new son.

"Hello, Franco," he whispered. "I'm your pa." Quietly and unobtrusively the three miners' wives left, for now they were just interlopers in someone else's joy.

Franco's birth, even though it had nearly killed him and his mother was a welcome respite from the boredom of life in the camps. At least for the men, active in the armed struggle, there was a relief from the day-to-day tedium. But for the women, especially with children to help, the daily chores of keeping the tents clean and their meager supply of clothes presentable were hardly overwhelming. Even the constant worry about food for their families took on a sameness that came close to routine.

Two days after Franco's birth, Maria stood outside her tent, wrapped against the early November cold, and watched the camp wake up. It was eight-thirty, an hour after the sun had risen over the horizon. The women were always the first to rise, and already she could see some of them taking the slop bucket to the latrines or getting coal for their stoves. Then, the men appeared, most often signaled by the plumes of blue tobacco smoke as they gratefully drew in their first lungs of nicotine, accompanied immediately by the hacking coughs as they cleared their windpipes of the nightly build-up of phlegm. *A charming beginning,* Maria thought, *to another charming day in charming*

Camp Ludlow.

While Spiro was smoking his first cigarette, Maria grabbed a bucket of kitchen waste, mostly tin cans and broken bottles, walked over to the latrine and dumped them in. The women had found that besides getting rid of garbage, it was a good way to keep the smell of the latrine down by sealing the waste in. That took a whole ten minutes, and as she strolled back to the tent, thoughts of another day of boredom made her think of something different to do. With a pang of guilt she realized that it had been ages since she had visited the Eriksens, but with all that had happened, she consoled herself that she could not be blamed for neglecting her friend. And Ingrid could not come over to Ludlow because her husband still worked for the mine companies and it would have been too risky.

Maria made a decision. Mary Petrucci needed fattening up, and Ingrid Eriksen was just the woman to help.

"Anna, do you know where Papa is?"

The little girl was across the road with some friends and she shouted back that while Maria had been at the latrines, he had gone to the headquarters tent to talk with Tikas. Maria muttered to herself that her husband these days spent more time with him than with her. *Maybe they should be the ones married,* she smiled to herself, but then crossed herself at the thought of such impiety.

"Anna, how about a walk to the Eriksens, eh? Some nice cake, a walk for Kali. Yes?" The little girl grabbed her coat and Kali while her mother left a note for Spiro on the pillow of their bed, and the three of them set off to the ranch.

It was a typical day for the time of year. In the shadows it was downright chilly, but so long as they stayed in the sun, it was pleasant. Maria pointed out the gophers enjoying the warmth, running around or warily guarding the entrances to their underground labyrinths if she and Anna got too close. The sun had thoroughly dried out the roads after the slush of the late September snowstorm, and unlike summer, there was no dust to blow in their eyes.

"I like this time of year the best, Mama, and you know why?" Anna chatted away. "It's because it's like God is saying, I need a new year. So he shuts this one down so he can make another one. Is that silly, Mama? "

Maria looked at her daughter in astonishment. "Well, I never thought of it like that before. I always like spring, because everything is clean and fresh. But fall? Well, at least it's not like winter. Too cold then, little girl, yes?"

Anna nodded sagely, and then ran ahead as Kali pulled her along to check out a particularly smelly cow pat.

Ingrid saw them as they walked through the garden gate, and rushed to the door to greet them. "Here, let me dry my hands first," she said as she rubbed them briskly on her pinafore front before hugging the two of them. "It's been too long, Maria. I was worried about you, but…" she let the rest of the sentence hang in the air.

"I know, Ingrid. And we could have visited you, so I'm to blame as well. I'm just sorry I couldn't work the garden more, like we talked about."

The two adults sat down in front of the stove, while Anna, with Ingrid's urging, helped herself to a piece of candy from the bowl on the kitchen table and then went outside with Kali and began to play on the swing the Eriksens kept for when their grandchildren visited.

"So, tell me you and your family are doing okay. I've heard stories, about the shootings an' all."

Maria nodded. "We're all fine. Even Spiro." Maria wasn't sure why she had added that last phrase. "It's hard on the men, not having work and feeling like they're not looking after their families," she immediately added. "A lot of them are drinking too much. And beating their wives. It's worse than in Berwind, a lot worse. You know, some of the men are drinking the medicines the wives buy, because they can't get beer or whiskey. Not that Spiro does that."

"So, how is that husband of yours?" Ingrid looked hard at Maria. "Peder tells me things about the Greeks, what they're doin'. He says the companies are trying to blame everything on the Greeks, but he thinks they just want you people fightin' among yourselves."

"Ingrid, he's real busy. The accident changed him, and other things too, and now all he wants to do is play soldier. It's like he's looking for a fight." Maria crossed herself.

"Look, Maria, you can tell me to shut up if you want." Maria hastily shook her head at the older woman. "But you know as well as I do," she carried on, "men with guns is just trouble. But I don't suppose he'll listen to you. They never do."

Maria looked away, as though embarrassed to continue the conversation, as though she was being disloyal to her husband. "I don't know what you've heard, but it's not that bad. There's only been a few deaths so far." Ingrid kept her peace. "Still, I agree," Maria continued, "it can get a lot worse. But Ingrid, he thinks he's doin' what's best for me and Anna. I don't know what it's like in your country, but where we come from, this is what the men have always done. And us women can't stop them."

Ingrid frowned. "No, I see that, but it doesn't make it easier on you or Anna, does it?" She brightened up. "Let's have some coffee and see if we can't find something for your little love."

As Ingrid poured out two cups of coffee, Maria had Anna tie up Kali. Ingrid took a large pie from her pantry and cut Anna a huge slice. It was pumpkin pie, one of Anna's favorites. Maria looked longingly at it but didn't want to seem rude. But as soon as Ingrid motioned to her, she nodded vigorously. Anna, in between mouthfuls and sometimes not waiting that long, told Ingrid of what life in the camp was like. Maria was happy to let her daughter chatter on, thinking that it might be good for Anna to talk of Ludlow as though it was now part of her life.

Surprisingly, Anna did not dwell on the bad things. She told

Ingrid of how pretty the stars were at night, how nice it was to be next door to Sally, and how it was fun to have her papa home. "But sometimes he's bored and gets grumpy." She shot a look at her mother as she spoke, but Maria simply smiled back at her daughter. *If grumpy is the worst Anna has seen in her father, then thank God for small blessings,* Maria thought. After Anna had eaten another slice, she asked if she could go outside and play with Kali. Her absence allowed Ingrid to tell Maria some disturbing news.

"You know Peder keeps to himself in the mines, don't you? He doesn't pry into other men's business. But he told me last week that if I ever ran into you, you'd do well to be told."

Maria looked at her friend. She sensed this wasn't going to be good.

"Well, he's been told that they want him to do some maintenance on the water pumps at Berwind. That can only mean one thing he said. They're gonna' go for full production again. And, as Peder figured it, that means the companies'll have to bring in scabs. You know that'll turn things real mean, don't you?"

"But Spiro told me the governor won't let that happen."

"Well, that's as may be, but that's what Peder figures, I'm just tellin' you what he said."

Maria did not want to believe what Ingrid had told her, but deep down she was not surprised. It would make sense for the companies to do this. Maria knew that scabs, the poor men so desperate for work that they'd cross the picket lines, were hated by the miners and their women. But even as she thought these things, Maria didn't get too angry. For what would Spiro do if his only alternative was starvation for his family?

The first shadows of the afternoon were beginning to move across the landscape, and Anna came inside because the shade tree had made it too cold to play outside. It was time to leave, but as she was about to say her goodbyes, she remembered why she had come in the first place. "Goodness me, I can be stupid. I almost forgot. I wanna' buy some greens off you for a young girl who just had a real bad delivery."

Ingrid looked at the little Greek woman, who looked barely old enough to have a ten-year-old child herself, and instantly responded. "Of course, let me get a basket." She came back from the root cellar with a cloth bag full of potatoes, carrots, turnips and a jar of tomatoes.

"That should keep her going for a while."

Anna began to rummage for her change purse but Ingrid placed her hands over Maria's. "Tell her these are from friends. She needs to know we're not all devils."

Maria was glad, for money was scarce and she had secretly hoped that her friend would be as kind as she remembered. She kissed Ingrid on the cheeks and gathered up her things to leave. Ingrid knelt down and gave Anna a hug and kiss too. "Sweetheart, you come to Auntie Ingrid's anytime. And next time we'll have some apple pie. Yes? "

Anna smiled and hugged Ingrid back. Very haltingly, almost embarrassed, the little girl whispered, "I love you."

Ingrid hugged her tighter. "And I love you, too, Anna. Now, you and your ma head back home, and we'll see you soon. Promise?" As Ingrid watched the two of them walk onto the chilly prairie, she wiped back a tear.

Jimmy Dingle, photographer's assistant, was a sucker for a sob story. He knew it, his parents knew it, his employer knew it. But he couldn't resist helping people. He trusted them, and he wanted them to trust him. So when Anna Andrakis came up to him after a photo shoot at Ludlow and asked him for his help, he had to at least hear her out. The two of them had become friends of sorts over the last month. Jimmy liked to show off his cameras to anybody who showed the slightest bit of interest, and Anna, according to his boss Lou Dold, was more than a little smitten with the teenager. She always tried to be there to help him, carrying his equipment or just keeping him company especially if Dold wasn't with him.

"Let me get this straight, Anna," he repeated to the ten-year-old. "You wanna' go to your old house in Berwind and you want me to take you there, so you can get something your ma left behind. I got this right?"

Anna nodded. "Jimmy, I heard Mama tell Papa last night how stupid she was to leave behind her cross. She had it nailed to the wall by the sink, she must have forgot about it when we left. It was her mama's."

Jimmy had heard some crazy requests in his young life, but this was one of the weirdest. "Anna, you do know, don't you, that the place is dangerous? And if we get caught, there'll be hell to pay."

"Jimmy, I know, but you'll figure out a way, won't you? Please, say you will, please?"

"What about your mom and dad, they'd skin me alive if they found out."

"I don't know what that means, Jimmy. Anyway, Mama's going over to the Eriksens, Papa's doin' something with Uncle Al, and I'm supposed to be with Sally. But Sally said that if I like, we'll pretend to go off somewhere to play, and then I, we, can go to our house." Tears began to well in her eyes. Jimmy had never had a little sister, and he was moved by the tale. *Here the little girl is,* he thought, *stuck on the prairie in a tent with winter just about here and all she can think about is getting a cross for her mother.*

"Anna, I'll make you a deal. You tell me where the house is, and I'll go there and try and find your ma's cross. But I don't want you there, okay? And Anna, I can't do it right now, maybe in the next few days, I'll try." Privately, Jimmy wanted time to think this one out. He wasn't convinced that it was safe even to try, what with all the shooting. *Maybe,* he thought, *I'll mention it to her mom.* Anna took a piece of paper that Jimmy ripped out of his notebook and with his pencil she drew what she thought was a map of where her house was. She told him what the house looked like. Jimmy thought it was a fool's errand, and the map was terrible. But her description of the house was a bit more helpful, so maybe he could make it work. But he still had to convince himself.

Jimmy went back to loading the equipment in the car. Then he had some business with a couple of the miners who'd ordered postcards. But all the while, something kept niggling in the back of his head, a little demon buzzing around. He had a bad feeling, and he couldn't put his finger on it.

Finally, for some reason he couldn't fully figure out, he went in search of Sally. He found her playing with Eulala and Mary Valdez. The two sisters were showing Sally their doll's tea set, and all three were engrossed in their game. Anna was nowhere to be seen. Dreading the worst now, Jimmy asked her if she'd seen her friend.

"Jimmy, she said she was going with you. Where is she?"

Jimmy didn't want to alarm the little girl. "Oh, I guess she's around here somewhere. I'll find her." He forced a smile. Now Jimmy began to panic, because he knew exactly where Anna Andrakis was.

Anna had decided that her mama needed that cross right away, and with the fierce logic of a ten-year-old decided she had to go and get it with no more delay. She liked Jimmy and she was sure he'd try, but she didn't know when that would be. *No,* Anna ordered herself, *you've got to go and get it, now.*

Hardly anybody noticed a little girl and a dog walk through the gates, cross the railroad tracks and head off to Berwind. The day was cold, even for late November, with gray clouds scudding low through the sky, but Anna's wool coat kept most of the wind out, and her fast walk kept her warm. So far, she hadn't seen anybody and she began to think it was going to be easy. And Kali seemed to be enjoying the walk as well. The little dog bounced along, glad to be free of the camp for once, with her tongue hanging out as every so often she jumped up and licked her young owner's hands.

Anna and Kali had turned west into the canyon when Anna heard a horse's neigh. Looking around she saw a rider behind her. He looked familiar, but Anna couldn't figure out where she'd seen him. Dave Watson, who was patrolling the area around Ludlow had seen the little girl and her dog leave the camp, and curiosity had got the better of him. He had followed at a safe distance so she would not suspect anything, but when she'd turned around Watson recognized her. He cantered the horse up to Anna, and slung himself off the saddle. As he approached, Anna felt the first stirrings of fear. There was something about the man, the way he looked, the way he smelt even, that made her feel sick to the stomach.

"Don't be afraid, girl," Watson said gently, "I won't harm you. I just wanna' make sure you're okay. Tell me what you're up to."

Anna was not fooled and she began to run away, but he grabbed her wrist, slowly squeezing it tighter and tighter. She screamed involuntarily.

"Mister, you're hurtin' me, let me go, please. You're frightenin' me." Watson tried to force her to the ground and Anna struggled to wrestle free, but he was too strong for her. Kali jumped up at Watson, trying to defend her mistress. Her first lunge missed Watson's arm but the second did not, and her jaws clamped fiercely on Watson' left elbow.

"Christ, get the fuckin' thing off me, will ya? It's breakin' my arm." Watson tried to get Kali off his arm but the dog was too determined. He swung around but only succeeded in lifting the dog off its hind legs. The movement only increased the pain in his elbow. "Fuck this," he screamed. Furious now and hazy with pain, he managed to pull a revolver from his belt, cock the trigger and fire at Kali. The bullet hit the dog at point blank range. Kali dropped to the ground and lay still, blood pumping out the ugly wound. The sound of the bullet reverberated up and down the canyon, and fearful that it might attract attention, Watson, without looking at the two of them further, climbed onto his horse as fast as he could and galloped in the direction of Berwind.

"No, no, no," Anna screamed at the top of her voice, unable to believe what had happened. She fell to the ground and held the dog's head in her lap. Kali's tongue flopped out the side of her mouth as she struggled for air, and she looked up at Anna. Her deep brown eyes misted over, as finally all her movements ceased. The dog, who had been Anna's best friend, who had been her constant companion, was gone. Anna sat there and cried; it was all she could do. She didn't know how long she was there; she wasn't even sure she knew where she was anymore. All she knew was that her lovely little Kali was dead, and all because of her.

A cold wind blew down the canyon, stirring the tops of the grasses and rustling the leaves on the scrub oak, but Anna didn't care. She sat on the cold earth, cradling Kali's head, hoping that the little dog's eyes might flicker, tell her that she was okay, just a little hurt. But there was no movement. The little girl sat with her beloved dog, alone and desolate.

Jimmy had followed his instincts and driven out towards Berwind. As he motored up the road, he hoped against hope that he would not find her and that she was still safe in Ludlow. But even before he reached Tabasco, he saw what he had dreaded.

Anna barely heard the car racing up the track to her. She barely felt the two hands on her shoulders. She barely heard the young man's voice telling her, "We need to get you home." She barely felt Jimmy's arms as he picked her up and laid her gently in the back of his car. As he punched the car into gear, he looked back at Anna. She lay motionless, staring into the back of the seat. There were no tears anymore; they'd all been left on Kali or soaked up by the cold prairie sod.

Jimmy shook his head in anger, whispered compassionately, "Your pa an' me, we'll come back for Kali, I promise."

As Jimmy turned into the gate at Ludlow, he saw Maria and Mrs. Hoffman talking with Sally. Maria looked frantic, Mrs. Hoffman looked furious, and Sally was crying, for she had been found out in a terrible lie. Jimmy immediately blew his horn. Even before the car was stopped, he jumped out. "It's okay, Mrs. A., I've got her, she's fine."

Maria shrieked and ran towards the car. Flinging open the back door she picked her daughter up.

"What happened, my love? Where were you? I was worried sick. Don't do that again, are you hurt?" Maria babbled, her voice oscillating between compassion and anger. Anna said nothing and pressed her face into her mama's chest.

Maria carried Anna home and placed her in bed. She sat on its side and stroked her daughter's hair, every now and then stooping down to kiss her cheeks or her brow.

Jimmy very quietly told her where he'd he found her and why she was out there. "Mrs. A., I feel like I'm to blame. I shoulda' got the cross for her right away, I never thought she'd try an' do it herself."

Maria tried to smile. "It's not your fault. I'm just glad you went up there when you did, Jimmy."

"Mrs. A., I promised Anna, me and her pa would look after Kali. I'd like to keep that promise, so if you don't mind, I'll go back and bury her. Seems the least I can do."

Maria nodded, unable to find words but grateful for this kind young man.

As Jimmy was driving back out along the Berwind road, he passed a truck coming from the direction of Trinidad. It was full of miners, one of whom he recognized as Spiro. Jimmy thought grimly that someone was about to catch hell for what had just happened. He was just glad it wasn't him.

18

The year rolled to a cold and miserable close, and slowly but surely Chase tightened the noose around the strikers, imprisoning leaders without trial and making unexpected shows of force at the different tent camps to look for weapons. Van Cise and the other officers were convinced that all the weapons were cached elsewhere, but so long as Chase kept telling them to search the camps, they had no choice.

In early December, the first major blizzard of the season hit southern Colorado, and both sides were forced into a temporary truce. The sky had darkened steadily throughout the day, the clouds sank lower and lower, and the temperature, as if giving everybody a brief respite before the coming ordeal, rose a few degrees. The miners and their families, hunkered down in their tents, had lived in Colorado long enough to know what was in store for them. The women got in supplies of coal and the men worked on the tents to make sure they were as waterproof as possible. Spiro checked the flaps where the chimney poked through the hole in the roof. He hammered the pegs in securely and tightened the guys, and thanked God for giving him the brains to install a wooden door a month earlier.

"I've done all I can do, Maria," he said as he stood in front of their stove warming his hands. The heat of the tent made his hands itchy as they came back to life and he rubbed them vigorously to get the circulation going again. Now all they could do was wait. "You know Tikas is still in jail? It's been over a week now. Still, at least he won't have to deal with all this."

Maria curled her lip at the mention of his name. "Spiro, you may think he's brilliant, but all the women think he's stupid, bein' taken for a dance by Pearl Jolly." Spiro tried to protest, but Maria continued. "You know he's always at her tent, even eats there. If you ask me..."

Spiro jumped in. "You know nothing, wife. They're friends, that's all."

"Well," she replied smugly, "if you ask me, meals ain't all he's gettin'. I know you think she can do no wrong, just because she's a pretty young thing. I see how she looks at the men, and how they look at her."

Spiro sensed that the conversation was going places he did not want to be; he, too, had looked at her in ways a married man shouldn't.

"Anyways, it's none of our business. How is she?" he asked, pointing at Anna to change the subject. "How is she?" His daughter was curled up in bed, staring blankly at a spot on the tent wall.

"Same as she has been, since…" Maria whispered. "This morning she started to tell me about what happened. She said the man who shot Kali, well, she thought she'd seen him before but she wasn't sure. But then she started to cry and I couldn't let her go on, could I? I tried to get her to drink some Horlicks, you know how much she loves it, but she couldn't even do that."

Spiro hesitated. "Do you think he did anything to her?"

Maria looked at her husband and answered quietly. "No, he didn't, she's untouched. When we first got her back and she was babbling about what happened, all she talked about was the dog. She didn't say anything else. Plus, I'm her mama, I'd know if anything had happened."

Spiro nodded grimly. "I swear if I ever find out who did this, I'll kill him with my bare hands. I swear to God, I'll kill him." He went to smash his fist down hard on the little cabinet, but Maria grabbed his wrist in time.

"Shush, let her rest."

Maria held his hands until he had calmed down. "Spiro, just to make sure, I checked her." She lowered her voice to a whisper. "She's untouched. Okay? Untouched."

The two of them sat on the floor next to Anna's bedroll. Maria stroked Anna's hair and Spiro promised her that when they were back in Berwind she could have another dog.

Anna, facing away from her father, stirred and shook her head. "No, Papa," she was barely audible. "I don't want another dog. All I'll do is get it killed like Kali." Her parents were glad she could not see the tears running down their cheeks.

The snow began falling in earnest just after midnight. Old timers in the ranches nearby remembered the great blizzard thirty years ago. Some said this blizzard was worse. Throughout the night Spiro heard tents rip from the weight of snow, but he was too busy with his own to worry about others. As in the mines, his existence was limited to mindless repetition: clear the roof of snow by pushing it away from the ridge pole; go outside to pull it down onto the ground; drink a quick cup of coffee to make it all bearable.

Maria lay inside with Anna, ready to help Spiro whenever he called, and sighing with relief whenever she heard the dull thud of the snow hitting the ground. As dawn broke, ugly and gray, they were able to assess the damage. The snow was still falling but it was much lighter, and now they could see steam rising from the tent roofs as the heat from the stoves melted the thin layer of snow on top. Spiro started to dig the snow from around the tent walls. It had grown dangerously high during the night, filling the drainage trenches around the tent, creeping up the walls and threatening to collapse them. He hadn't dared clear it out during the night in case his shovel ripped a hole in the canvas. Fortunately, as he remarked to Maria, being a miner had some advantages after all, and he was able to clear a gap around the base of the walls sufficient for him feel that the tent was safe.

By seven that morning, southern Colorado was under two feet of white powder. An exhausted Spiro joined his wife for fresh hot coffee. Maria normally brewed the grounds twice on successive mornings to get their money's worth, even if the coffee on the second day was usually weak. This time she didn't scrimp, and doubled the amount of coffee she normally used. The drink was strong and hot, and Spiro gulped it down gratefully. They sat on their bed wondering what to do next when they heard Sally Hoffman's high-pitched voice outside their tent.

"Mrs. Andrakis," she squeaked. "Can Anna play with us? Frank keeps throwing snowballs at me and I need help." The little girl was bundled up against the cold and the snow. She had a scarf tied tightly around her head, and her mother had wrapped its ends around her neck and tucked them into the top of her coat. Maria told her to come inside. Sally looked over at Anna who had woken up at the sound of her friend's voice.

Maria gently nudged her daughter's shoulder. "Come on, Anna, try to get up, it'll do you good. Anyways, Sally needs help. It's Frank." At first Anna didn't say a word.

"Anna, honest, I need help," Sally added. "He says he's gonna' stop me from goin' back into our tent. He doesn't care how cold I am. Please." Sally had been told by her mother that getting Anna to play would be the best thing to make her forget about Kali, and Sally was determined to do just that.

"Aw, come on, Anna, please, I really need your help."

"Go on, Anna," Spiro chimed in. "You've always said Frank had it comin'. Now's your chance."

Anna at last rolled onto her side so she could see the three of them. Her cheeks were drawn and gray, but for the first time in a week, Maria noted a small spark of life in her eyes.

"Come on, Anna, I really need your help."

The three of them were surprised when Anna slowly got out of bed. She still didn't seem convinced but at least she was moving. Maria hurriedly dressed her in case she changed her mind, and the two children went off in the direction of Sally's tent, with Sally pulling her friend along.

Spiro managed a smile. "She'll be fine, Maria. She's a tough kid. She'll be fine."

Two more feet of snow fell that morning but the storm's

intensity slackened throughout the afternoon, and the inhabitants of the tent camps breathed a sigh of relief as blue slivers began to appear in the sky. But it was a false hope, for by early evening the snow began to fall again. Another three hours passed, of heavy snow, of constant shoveling and incessant checking to make sure the canvas was intact.

Nine o'clock that evening and Spiro shouted excitedly, "Maria, I just saw a star."

Maria, together with Anna who had been buoyed by the snowball fight just as everybody had hoped, stuck their heads out and yes, they agreed, they could see them too. As is so often the case in Colorado, the storm blew itself out quickly. Within the hour there was not a cloud in the sky. But this caused the temperatures to drop. Men doing their last chores before turning in saw their breath turn to crystals before their very eyes and felt their nose hairs stiffen as they drew in the icy air. They twitched their nostrils to keep the passages free of ice. Finally the camps settled down. The last lanterns were turned off and quiet returned. Maria, almost too exhausted to sleep though every fiber of her body screamed for rest, lay in bed. Someone on the far side of the camp was playing a violin, a slow, mournful tune but comforting and reassuring. Slowly she drifted into sleep, with Anna curled up tightly between her and Spiro. At midnight precisely, the guards turned on the searchlights and made sure that nobody got an untroubled sleep for the rest of the night.

Baldwin-Felts was contracted by the coal companies to sign up scabs to work the mines. They quickly set up two recruiting offices in Walsenburg and Trinidad. Linderfelt was at the train depot in Trinidad to watch the first of them sign up. Accountants for each of the companies sat at their desks inside a large heated tent, in front of each of them large ledgers in which they wrote the name of each applicant. Opposite the names the accountants put down their skills, such as they were, and made a quick decision as to what job they could do. Most of the scabs had no experience down the mines, but with the skeleton crews who had never walked out, they would be enough to bump up coal production and put pressure on the unions.

Enrolling took the best part of two hours, but the accountant for the Colorado Fuel and Iron was finally satisfied that he had enough men and nodded to Linderfelt. The lieutenant motioned to the gang of fifty men to move to the waiting trucks. The men were sullen, as though realizing they were doing something wrong but so desperate for money they felt they had no choice.

In Ludlow Maria was talking to Mary Thomas when a woman ran up and told them about the scabs. Mary immediately ordered her to get together as many of the camp women as she could and head out to Berwind. Maria started to walk away, but Mary intercepted her.

"Maria, where you goin', my lovely? We've got to stop them."

"I, I, I," Maria stuttered, "I've got Anna to look to."

"She's okay, she can look after herself just this once. And I've got kids, too. Come on, the scabs are real close."

Maria still hesitated, frightened of what she was getting into. The Welshwoman looked at Maria contemptuously. "Do you think this is someone else's fight? Do you think only your husband should do the dirty work?" Suddenly, the Welshwoman seemed much bigger than her five feet. "Well, do you?" she snarled. Maria blanched. This was not what she wanted to do, but she felt too embarrassed to back down, especially after Pearl Jolly joined them. Reluctantly she nodded her acquiescence, and the three of them headed towards Berwind.

It was unfortunate for the strikebreakers that they came the day after the blizzard. Dozens of women, exhausted by the storm and furious at what they saw as a gross betrayal of their cause, rushed to line the edge of the road leading into the canyon. Maria was not wearing a heavy coat and she shivered, but if it was due to the cold or her fear she did not know. She looked around, seeing children, some as young as five or six. Any place where the ground was bare of snow, women and the older children were picking up rocks, stones and even cow pats to hurl at the scabs.

At last, the trucks appeared. Maria saw stones being thrown at the head of the convoy. Soon all of the trucks were being pelted with everything the women could lay their hands on, the children joining in as though it was a big game. Company guards went through the motions of trying to stop them, but their efforts were half-hearted, as though they just didn't care one way or another. As the first truck passed Maria and Mary, the Welshwoman picked up a huge stone and hurled it at one of the men in the truck, her red hair swinging crazily around her face. The rock missed, but her second was more accurate and it hit the man on his cheek, tearing a bloody gash. The other women were just as accurate, and soon barely anyone in the trucks was unbruised or unbloodied. Mary handed a rock to Maria. She froze, unwilling to join in, but a glare from Mary made her take aim. By chance it hit one of the scabs on the back of the head. The man ducked, holding his head as blood seeped through his fingers.

Suddenly, everything bad that had happened to Maria in those few short months cascaded in front of her, the misery of Berwind, Spiro's accident, the rape, the miscarriage, Anna's attack, Kali's death. A terrible anger gripped her, and she gave into a frenzy of picking up rocks and hurling them at the trucks. After what seemed an eternity but must have been only a little more than a minute, the slow-moving trucks were through the gauntlet. A collective sigh rippled through the crowd and then there was only silence.

"You did well, Maria. They deserved it, you know."

But after her anger had subsided a little, Maria was not so sure. *Yes,* she reasoned, *these men had to be stopped from working the mines, but wouldn't Spiro have done the same for me and Anna if he had to?* Maria walked back to Ludlow, deliberately avoiding the company of the other women. She felt shame for what she had done, but her shame was nothing compared to the anger that raged at the companies that had forced her family into a place they did not deserve.

Once the blizzard had blown through, Colorado took on a picture postcard look. The snow blanketed the slag piles, sparkling in the sun and hiding the ugliness of the mine workings. The tent camps took on a new luster as the accumulated garbage of months disappeared under a pure white covering. Crystals formed in the air, so it looked like people were blowing silver dust out of their mouths. Children turned to snowball fights, trying to forget the hunger pains that increasingly wracked their tummies.

For Lou Dold, it meant the chance to take photographs and sell the postcards for which he was becoming famous throughout the coalfields. Long hours stuck in the small truck cabin as they drove all over the coalfields, setting up photo shoots in the cold had brought Lou Dold and Jimmy Dingle close. Neither of them had siblings and although they would have denied it, they had begun to look on each other as brothers rather than employer and employee, although Jimmy still couldn't bring himself to use Dold's first name. Still, despite their friendship, that did not mean Jimmy always agreed with Lou, and he had no idea why they needed to be making this particular trip at all. The roads were snowpacked, and the truck kept fishtailing despite Lou's best efforts.

"Okay, Jim, I know you think I'm crazy coming out in this weather right after the storm, but there's method to my madness."

Jimmy decided to keep his mouth shut and looked out the frosted window.

"As I see it, the folks in the camps are gonna' look back on this experience in years to come as one of their big adventures. They'll tell their folks about it, right? Well, what better than to have a little memento of the snowstorm that almost killed everybody. So they can show it off."

Jimmy had to admit that it was a good idea from a purely business angle; he just wasn't sure why Lou needed him at this precise point in time. *I mean,* Jimmy reasoned, *I could be back at the studio, clearing the sidewalk, or cleaning up the dark room, that's a lot better use of my time. Or brewing some coffee for when he gets back. But no,* he thought with resignation, *Dold wants my company, so here I have to be.*

"I still don't figure how they can afford them though, Mr. D." It was a fair point, the answer to which Dold himself had taken some time to find.

"I know the photos sound like a luxury, but two things. First, I do believe that the strikers and their families are convinced they're taking part in something historical. It's a real big deal for them. That's why there still out there through all this crap weather. They want proof that they were there, like I said before. Second, I know they don't get a lot of strike pay from the union, but I guess everybody likes to believe they can afford the odd little luxury. You see?"

Dold swung his truck through the gates at Forbes and parked by the headquarters tent. As Jimmy unloaded their equipment, Dold went into the tent and learnt that despite the intensity of the storm nobody had been seriously injured. A few tents had been wrecked but the occupants had been able to bunk up with others until replacements could be delivered.

The two photographers walked through the colony, Jimmy with the heavy camera and tripod slung over his shoulder. The streets were narrowed by the amount of snow the miners had shoveled away from their tents and they had to dodge people constantly.

Dold stopped at a large tent. "I've been here before, Jimmy.

They're good people. There's seven or eight of 'em and they told me to come by next time I was back."

A man in his fifties walked out of the tent as Lou and Jimmy were talking. His gray moustache was flecked brown with nicotine, the bags under his eyes hung loosely.

"Herr Mueller," Dold greeted him. "You remember me, the photographer, Lou Dold, you asked us to call in whenever we were back here."

The miner dipped his head in recognition, but remained mute. Dold was beginning to feel a little unsure. "Er, you know, you said I could come back next time I was here, you know, to take a photograph of you and your family. You wanted me to come back."

The miner looked old beyond his years. "Mr. Dold," he spoke in heavily accented English, "I remember you, of course, forgive me. But this is a bad time. Our daughter has just lost her children. Two of them, twins. Both dead. At birth." Tears welled up in the man's eyes, but he wiped them away and stood there in the cold, dignified and silent.

"I am so sorry, please, extend, please, give my condolences to your family. Say I'm so sorry. Jimmy, let's go." But as Dold moved away, a female voice from inside the tent asked him to stop. A frail old woman came out. She was wearing a black scarf around her head.

"I remember you as well. I was the one who wanted you to come back. My son told you what happened. Yes? We," her voice faltered, "we did want a photo of all of us, as you know, but now…" Her voice trailed off.

Dold doffed his cap as if to leave, but something made him stay a little longer. "Ma'am, I am so sorry, if there's anything I can do?"

The old woman hesitated and then, changing her mind, spoke quietly but forcefully. "Mr. Dold, I want you to take a photograph of our family. I want my children and their children to know what we went through. And I want her," she nodded back to the tent, "I want her to remember where her children were born." She crossed herself, and Dold noticed that she was holding a rosary in her hand.

Dold swallowed the lump in his throat. "Of course."

The old lady stuck her head in the tent and five adults, three men and two women came out. A young boy in canvas overalls also appeared, and the matriarch asked him to get the others from the tents nearby. As Dold waited in the cold, he and Jimmy stamping their feet to stay warm, the rest of the family emerged and the redoubtable old woman took charge of organizing her family's picture, like a general marshaling his troops: fifteen people in all, from herself right down to a babe in arms.

Dold said nothing. He went to his camera and looked into the eyepiece. He was using a Graflex, new on the market. It was a heavy instrument and took a long time to set up, but the results were worth it. The whole family stood still, patiently waiting for the click of the shutter. But right before he started shooting, Dold asked a little girl to move to the center of the group. Her dress was stark white; how it had kept so clean in such conditions he had no idea. Jimmy realized too that the little girl would make the perfect focal point of the photograph.

When they were through, Jimmy dismantled the equipment to move onto their next customer, and Dold walked over to the old lady. Her dignity had moved him and Jimmy beyond what they thought possible. "Frau Mueller. I thank you. I will come back in a week with your photograph. And I would be honored if you would accept it from me as a gift."

The old lady barely smiled, but it was enough to show her deep gratitude. "Thank you, Mr. Dold." She disappeared into the tent.

They were tired and cold from shooting photographs, but Lou Dold and Jimmy Dingle knew they had done something good. As they drove back to Trinidad, Jimmy finally broke the silence.

"Mr. D. You promised that old lady a picture for nothing. And I've seen you do that before. How come?"

Lou smiled indulgently. "I've been doing some reading. It's a new marketing trick they thought up in New York. Basically, I give them free prints at my expense. But they get to know my work, they like it, and, more importantly, they think I'm a good guy. Which I am by the way. So they come back to me, and I make a bit more money. I know it sounds weird, but it works."

Jimmy scratched his head. *Clearly,* he concluded, *there is more to this photography business than meets the eye.* And he stored away that clever little phrase for future use.

"But, Jimmy," Dold interrupted his thoughts. "This time was different. I'm not tryin' to make money off that family. They've had enough crap thrown at them already. A free picture was the least I could do. I hope you believe me, Jimmy. This time I didn't care about the money."

"Mr. D., I know I joke around a lot, but I've got to tell you, something happened back there and I don't know what." Jimmy was pensive and silently gazed through the cab window, trying to search for an answer.

"What do you think happened, Jimmy? Tell me."

"Mr. Dold, I don't know, for God's sake I don't. But that old lady. She was." He stopped, searching for the right word. "She was...classy. She's just lost grandchildren, great grandchildren, and look at her."

Dold said nothing.

"You know, Mr. Dold, people need to know what they're like, you know, what they're goin' through."

Dold just smiled. As much to himself as to his young friend, he whispered, "That's why I'm taking the pictures, Jimmy, that's why I'm taking the pictures."

It was two days before Christmas. That evening, the Andrakis family sat in their little tent. It was cold outside but the stove was powerful enough to keep all of them comfortable so long as they sat close to it. The parents talked of Christmas in Crete. Maria told Anna that on Christmas Day children would walk through the villages, knocking on people's doors and playing Christmas tunes for anybody who would listen. And she told Anna, too, that her mama had always baked the best St Basil's cake in the whole village and when they ate it right after midnight on New Year's Eve, Maria always got the little drachma coin her mama had put in it.

"That meant she got lots of good luck every year, Anna," Spiro chimed in. "And she did." Spiro's eyes twinkled. "How do you think I know, Anna?" The little girl's eyes were wide with expectation. "Well, she married me and she had you." He scooped her up and tickled her, and Anna laughed so hard Maria had to stop Spiro in case she fell off his lap.

Anna and the other children eagerly awaited the special Christmas tree the union had promised for Ludlow, and on Christmas Eve they heard a truck slowly making its way to the center of the camp. Anna rushed out of the tent, barely grabbing the coat her mother flung at her. All the children gathered to watch a tall spindly pine tree unloaded and set into a hole the men had dug the day before. Anna and Spiro and the other parents came over and together watched as a group of miners began stringing lights over the tree.

"Mama, Sally says that Santa Claus will still find us and he'll have presents for us tomorrow. Do you think he will?"

"Well, it depends, Anna. If you've been a good little girl or not. What do you think, Papa?"

Spiro pulled a mock frown. "Well, Mama, remember last June when she spilt the water coming from the well."

"Oh yes, and then there was the time when she got you the wrong tobacco, and you were laid up in bed and couldn't go yourself," Maria joined in.

"And just last week she didn't come home from Sally's when

we told her to. I don't know, Papa."

The two parents looked serious. "I guess we'll just have to see."

Anna's lower lip quivered, and realizing they had gone too far, Spiro picked his daughter up. "Sweetheart, I bet Santa Claus brings you something nice, don't you, Mama?"

Maria nodded. "Come on, let's get you to bed. Remember what we always tell you, the quicker you go to sleep, the quicker tomorrow'll come."

The three of them walked back to the tent, enjoying the mood of festivity building up throughout the camp. Stars twinkled brightly in the clear night and the moon's halo reminded Anna of the icon of the Panagia in their tent. Maria and Spiro put their daughter to bed and then cuddled up, quietly talking about all Anna had gone through but feeling proud of how strong she had been. Suddenly the searchlights came on, right on the stroke of midnight according to Spiro's fob watch. But instantly they went off and Ludlow and the other camps were allowed uninterrupted sleep for one of the few times that month.

Spiro and Maria felt they had been asleep about ten minutes when Anna woke them up by tugging on their shirt sleeves. Bleary-eyed, they begged Anna for five more minutes of sleep, but they knew it was a lost cause. Maria slowly got up and wrapping her overcoat around her she added coal to the stove while Anna climbed into bed and snuggled into her papa's arms. Warmth began to envelop the tent and softly from over by the tree a chorus of carolers began singing. Spiro lay in bed enjoying a first cigarette and coffee, watching Maria ready breakfast.

Anna could stand it no more. "Papa, Mama, please, please, please. Did he come, did he come?" Unlike last night, there was no teasing and Spiro got out of bed and pulled out from under the bed a cardboard box and handed it to Anna. "I don't know how Santa Claus put this here but this must be from him. Happy Christmas." Maria came over and hugged her daughter, who waited patiently, really wanting just to rip the box open.

In her haste she could not undo the string Maria had tied around the box, so Spiro pulled out his knife and slit it. Carefully, ever so carefully, Anna took the lid off and saw the most delicate china children's tea service. A flower was painted on each cup and saucer, and each one was wrapped in tissue paper. There was a miniature teapot, a miniature milk jug and even a miniature sugar bowl.

"We didn't think Santa Claus would find his way here, but he did. Do you like it, my love?" Maria asked.

"Mama, it's beautiful. Papa, Mama." And puffing her chest out, she yelled, joyously and gloriously, "And Merry Christmas." Only Maria and Spiro would ever know that they had pawned two of Maria's treasured picture frames to pay for Anna's present.

"Who's makin' that noise?" Anna heard Alberto's voice. Even before he was through the door, Anna was showing him her Christmas present. "Merry Christmas, everybody." He held Anna in his arms. "Anna, I'm glad Santa brought you this, because this little lady needs a cup of tea," and he pulled from his jacket a small wooden doll that he had bought in Trinidad. "Look, Anna, you can move her arms and legs so she can even sit down for tea, like proper ladies, yes?"

She hugged her Uncle Al tight round his neck, even laughed when he rubbed his bristly chin against her cheek. While the three adults drank coffee, Anna laid the service out on the bed and began to serve tea to her new little friend, Dolly.

At noon the camp gathered at the Christmas tree. Everybody was there, even the African-American families who kept themselves apart from the rest of the camp. The band played Christmas carols and a choir led by Mary Thomas sang along. Sally and Anna were racing around the tree in excitement, playing catch-me with the other children. Everybody looked up as a truck left the headquarters tent and drove over to the tree.

To everybody's surprise, including Spiro's, Tikas jumped out the passenger's seat and climbed into the back of the truck. He lowered the rear flap and took the lid off a huge wooden barrel.

"Children," he cried. "We've presents for you." All the children immediately rushed over and Tikas, a huge smile on his face, handed out bags of nuts and candy and small trinkets.

Now that the children were occupied, Tikas climbed down, suddenly looking at a loss what to do. "What happened?" Spiro asked. "I thought you were in jail."

"They let me out ten days ago, but I've been in Trinidad. Mike is out as well, he's dossin' at the union office. They let us all out. I suppose it's their Christmas present." Louis laughed at his little joke. "Look, Spiro, no business today, okay?"

"No, of course not, Louis. Welcome home and Happy Christmas." The two Greeks embraced and kissed each other on the cheeks.

The rest of the day was peaceful. Most families had been able to scrape together enough money for presents for their children and buy a chicken for a special dinner. Maria invited over Alberto and the four of them played card games until the winter chill bit too deeply and they turned in for the night. Even the companies played their part and left the searchlights off, although Alberto said this was just to give their men a Christmas break and had nothing to do with being nice to the miners.

On New Year's Eve, Spiro ran into Tikas as he was leaving a Trinidad coffee shop.

"Spiro. Got time for another coffee?" Spiro could see that Tikas was tired and nervous.

"That's one thing I've got plenty of, my friend. Come on, I'll let you buy."

They went back into the coffee shop and settled at a table.

Tikas spoke. "You know what happened yesterday, don't you?"

"Louis, I was in Ludlow. Of course I do. I was there. I don't know their names, they'd both worked at Berwind, they had a fight and one of them got killed. You found the guy, handed him over to the sheriff."

"No, I mean last night," Tikas replied impatiently.

Spiro shook his head.

"I was in the depot at Ludlow. And Linderfelt comes in, blames me for hurtin' one of his men's horses or something like that, it was hard to understand. Not a word about me helping the sheriff out. Then he takes me outside and starts beating me over the head with his pistol. Look." Tikas took off his hat to reveal a large mat of dried blood on the left side of his scalp.

"Jesus, Louis, I had no idea."

"I've had worse, though it hurts bad. Another officer pulled him off me. Honest to God, I think he wanted me to hit him so he could shoot me. I was the one who turned the miner in, for God's sake. That Linderfelt is a crazy man." Tikas suddenly relaxed and whispered, "I do not think he likes me, Spiro. Not sure, but I do not think he likes me." Spiro thought he was serious until he saw the twinkle in Tikas's eyes.

"You could be right, Louis, you could be right."

"Anyway, let's drink up and get back to camp. I've got to meet Lawson there. How's that little girl of yours?"

The two of them made their way out of Trinidad, heading north to Ludlow and what they hoped would be a quiet New Year's Eve. It was a bleak and desolate landscape. Skiffs of wind blew across the prairies throwing up whirligigs of snow. They crossed the bridge, driving slowly because the wooden planks were slippery with ice, and then a militia truck pulled out in front of them, blocking their way. Normally it would not have worried them; roadblocks and checkpoints were becoming common since the militia had moved in. But after the confrontation with Linderfelt last night, neither of them was too confident that this was just a routine stop.

Tikas was in the driver's seat and waited for the sergeant to approach him. The car heater wasn't too good but it was better than stepping outside. "Let him catch his death, eh, Spiro, not us."

Saying nothing, the sergeant swung the door of the Ford open and dragged Tikas out by his collar. Spiro tried to get out to help him but found himself looking down the barrels of four carbines. The sergeant ordered both them into the back of the truck. Tikas started to say something but the butt of the sergeant's rifle caught him full in the stomach. He collapsed and it was only with the Spiro's help that he was able to climb up. Tikas expected the truck to turn back to Trinidad and the county jail. But the driver went the opposite way, towards the camps, and a small pang of fear bit into Tikas' guts.

It was difficult for him to talk against the wind as the truck picked up speed, but he managed to get the attention of a private and ask where they were headed. The soldier, who looked in his early twenties, said nothing and turned away from Tikas' stare. *Is he embarrassed, maybe frightened,* Tikas wondered. He passed the time rubbing his stomach. It hurt and he knew there'd be a good bruise there in a couple of hours, but his thoughts were interrupted as the truck slowed down and turned into the militia camp just south of Ludlow. Without stopping at the sentry post, they drove to the far edge of the camp where the militia had constructed a small barbed wire pen that held miners awaiting interrogation or transit to one of the local jails.

Spiro and Tikas were bundled out of the back of the truck and walked over to a pile of shovels and picks where they were joined by the six miners from the holding pen. The sergeant came over to them.

"Well, it's over for you, boys. You know Stubbs's shot dead, clean through the head, and you bastards did it. He was a good man, Stubbs. My friend. And now you're going to pay for it."

Tikas shouted at him, trying to keep the fear out of his voice.

"You know it wasn't us, you've got the guys. Two Italians. That happened over a month ago."

"Shut up, wop," one of the other guards shouted. "You don't have no fuckin' clue. We got all the evidence we need. All of you, every fucking last one of you fuckin' miners killed him. We're starting payback with you lot."

The sergeant glared at the prisoners. "Well, here's how I see it. You're gonna' die, real soon, so if you dig your graves I promise you a decent burial. If you don't, well you'll still be dead, and the coyotes can have a feast. Makes no difference to me."

"For God's sake," shouted one of the miners, "I've got a wife and three kids."

"Oh hell," the sergeant responded, "just to show I'm a good man, here's some paper and pencils. I'll give you five minutes to write a last letter and then start digging. If you want to, that is."

The young trooper who had been in the back of the truck came over to the sergeant and said something, but Spiro and the others couldn't hear anything. The sergeant laughed at the young man, who looked as white-faced as the miners. The private turned around and hurriedly walked away back into the middle of the camp.

Mary, Mother of God, Tikas thought as he saw the young guardsman walk away, *surely they're not gonna' do this.*

One of the miners began to cry, and another wet his pants. Disbelieving, they walked over to the sergeant for the paper and pencils and began to write. Spiro jotted something down for Maria and Anna, but he didn't really know what he wanted to say and quickly gave up after a few sentences. Only Tikas refused to write anything.

After five minutes a guardsman took the papers off the miners. "Okay, get digging."

Each miner was torn with indecision. They knew they could not escape; they were cold and the digging would warm them up. But the faster they finished, the sooner they would die.

They dug slowly, while their guards warmed themselves by a large open fire, acting as though they did not care how long it took them to finish. The two holes were six feet deep and six by six. The miners could not drag out the work any longer. In mortal fear, they put down their shovels and picks. Some knelt and prayed. Others looked murderous, hoping against hope that they would get the chance to take revenge or have their friends do it for them.

The sergeant told the prisoners to stand at the edge of the pits. The wind had picked up and it bit through their clothing; the dying sun was going behind the hills to the west.

"What are you thinking of, Spiro?" Tikas gently probed.

Spiro turned to his friend, tears filling his eyes. He shrugged. "Oh, Crete, my family, my village. Maria and Anna. And you?"

Tikas shook his head.

The clicks of rifle bolts interrupted their thoughts. Tikas saw a line of ten guards with their guns aimed at the miners. At the top of his voice the Cretan shouted, "So, this is it. Be brave, Spiro, you are a Cretan, an Andrakis. Be brave. Let them sing songs about you in years to come. Be brave."

The sergeant raised his arm, and then started laughing, huge ugly laughs that rang around the little compound. The other guards in the firing squad joined in.

"You bastards," Tikas screamed. "Now you laugh at our deaths."

The sergeant stopped laughing and looked them with thunderous contempt in his eyes. "Get the fuck out of here," he bellowed. "You did a real nice job on those trenches, they'll make dandy latrines. See your camp? It's a five minute walk away. Now get outta' here before I change my mind."

The miners needed no second invitation. Some of them ran as quickly as they could. But something neither of them could fully describe made Tikas and Spiro take their time. It wasn't just that they didn't want to show their fear, for it was too late for that.

Still, although they did not saunter, they did their best to walk as though the episode had not happened, as though they were just two friends taking a casual stroll. Even if their indifference was feigned, it gave them the strength to continue, and whether anybody else was impressed, the two Cretans neither knew nor cared.

As they exited the militia camp they finally looked at each other. "If ever I get my hands on that bastard…" Tikas started, but Spiro interrupted him.

"Louis, I swear by all that's holy, he's a dead man. Just give me the chance."

They entered Ludlow and said goodbye to each other. Tikas went to the headquarters tent to get a ride to his car. Spiro made straight for his own tent. He composed himself before he opened the tent door. He walked in and swept little Anna up in his arms.

"How is the most beautiful little girl in the world today?"

Anna giggled, and Maria smiled at her husband. Spiro gently laid Anna down on the bed and walked over to his wife.

"And how is the most beautiful woman?" He held Maria tightly in his arms, kissed her gently on both cheeks and then on her mouth. "It is New Year's Eve. Let us give our thanks to God. Now then, where is this wonderful stew you've been boring us all with?"

He sat down on the bed next to Anna as Maria prepared dinner, and tried to forget the filth of what had happened.

19

Mother Jones despised the authorities for many things, but one thing she did like about them was their complete predictability. So, Jones was completely relaxed, almost smug, when she saw four young guardsmen waiting for her as she stepped down onto the platform station in Trinidad. The corporal didn't look old enough to shave and he was deferential to her, even offering her his hand.

"I am sorry, Mrs. Jones, but under the authority vested in General Chase by Governor Ammons, I am to inform you that you are to be returned immediately to Denver."

"Well, boys," she said, grinning at them, "looks like you and me and are gonna' become good friends. I surely do hope so."

The corporal ushered her into the waiting room. "The Denver train returns in an hour, Ma'am, I think you'll be more comfortable here."

"Thank you, my dear," Jones politely replied.

The guardsmen couldn't help but smile at this demure old lady. Still, regardless of what she looked like and how she acted, they'd been told that they were to get her to Denver, and that is what they would do, come hell or high water.

The train ride to Denver was entirely pleasant. Jeb Stevens flashed Jones a smile and made sure she was comfortable. She pulled out a bag of knitting from her purse and began working on a scarf. Her boys, as she called them to their huge embarrassment, were totally chivalrous, but they did not say a word to her the whole journey; they were under orders to keep conversation to a minimum. Outside the carriage, mile after mile of snow-covered prairie passed by. It was a bucolic scene and all five of them enjoyed it in their own ways. The four young guardsmen thought of a pleasant day in Denver before having to return to the tedium of strike duty, and Mother Jones had the luxury of being able to plot her next move in quiet comfort.

As they pulled into Denver, Jones gently rocked the shoulder of one guardsman. "Here's our stop, boys. Time to wake up from your beauty sleep, young man." The young soldier shook himself, startled by the old woman's nudge, his buddies with huge grins on their faces; he sheepishly turned away from them.

After the train had come to a stop and Jones had collected her belongings, she made a point of shaking the hands of each of the soldiers. "Boys, you've been as good a set of traveling companions as I've ever had, even if you were a bit tongue-tied. Still, this old lady thanks you and wishes you well."

"Er, you're, er, welcome, Ma'am," one of them replied as he doffed his hat. As they watched her wind her way down the platform and out onto the streets, the four of them looked at each other quizzically. The corporal said that she didn't look like the firebrand their own general had called a damnable hell raiser and whose speeches he insisted were full of lies and blasphemies.

Jones stayed a week in Denver at a cheap boarding house that she regularly used. On January 11th, Jones packed her little bag, and set out once more for Union Station. She knew that this time there would be no quick return trip to Denver, for Chase had promised in public that next time she showed up down south she'd be locked up and the key thrown away.

The night train from Denver rolled past Ludlow before the sun had come up. At the last stop before Trinidad she alighted and picked up a union car waiting to take her into town. "Honey, this old girl's famished," she announced to the driver. "I need a breakfast, so how about the Toltec Hotel?"

The middle-aged miner looked at her in disbelief. "Ma'am, that's where the militia eat. They're gonna' arrest you as soon as you step in the door."

She looked back at him blandly. "Oh really? Well, surely those good officers will at least allow an old woman a cup of coffee to warm her weary old bones."

It was then that the driver cottoned on and a grin broke over his face. "Okay, ma'am, it'll be my pleasure to get you set up. My pleasure, yes, indeedee."

In the few minutes it took Jones to sign in at the front desk, the hotel was bubbling with anticipation. She entered the dining room while her bag was carried up to her room and allowed a waitress to escort her to an empty table. She had barely taken her first sip of coffee when she heard cars pulling up sharply outside. Jones continued to sip and pick at some toast while she awaited the inevitable.

However, even she was surprised by whom she saw storming into the room. She had expected a junior officer to arrest her, but it was General Chase himself. The veteran unionist watched him coldly over her cup of coffee as he approached her table. *What a primped up jackass,* she concluded, *just like I thought he would be.* The general was in full cavalry uniform, complete with spurs and a riding crop, which he imperiously slapped on his polished knee-high boots. He strode to her table, and with hands on hips, looked down his nose at the old woman, like a Colossus, or so he hoped, about to take control of his world.

The old woman said nothing, just kept looking back him, her eyes never moving, a steely resolve on her face, body totally still.

"I am General…"

She interrupted him. "I know exactly who you are General Chase, and exactly what you are, too."

"I am General Chase, in sole military command of this area. I have on my person a letter from Governor Ammons ordering me to take whatever action is necessary to maintain the peace and stability of this area."

He went to remove something from his side pocket, but Jones waved him aside. "I have no interest, General, in your little piece of paper. Besides, I suspect even if you didn't have one, you would still arrest me. Because that's what you're here for, isn't it?

I suppose I should just be honored you came yourself."

The whole restaurant was staring at him, waiting for his next move. "Madam, I am not here to debate the legality of my actions. You will accompany these gentlemen immediately." He gestured to the two aides behind him. "I did warn you, Jones, of the consequences of your returning. Now, I have other matters to attend to." He stepped aside to allow Mother Jones to go over to his officers.

She stood up and slowly gathered her coat and purse. As she walked past the general she stopped. In a voice loud enough for everybody to hear, she said, "General, a real officer, a real gentleman, would accord me, an eighty-five-year old woman the courtesy of a title. I am Mother Jones, or if you prefer, Mrs. Jones. Kindly remember that in the future."

Chase was speechless. Very quietly, so nobody else could hear but him, she whispered, "Personally, Chase, I think you're a disgusting bully and a sack of manure. But that's just between the two of us." She immediately moved away to give him no chance to reply.

Chase went bright red. He glanced at his aides to see if they had heard the old woman, but their faces remained immobile, fixed in stone. Trying to muster as much dignity as he could, Chase pulled his coat front down to smooth out the wrinkles and hastily retreated from Jones and his two officers.

Jones' prison cell was a converted private room in a hospital on the east side of town. It had no pictures on the walls, which were painted a light green and which made the room feel colder than it was, and there was an armed guard at the door outside, but to her it looked a lot better than most of the boarding house rooms she'd stayed in over the past few years. She unpacked her small suitcase, which a soldier had retrieved from her room. Jones was wily enough to know that her incarceration might well alter the stalemate that she felt was sapping the miners' will; that was exactly why she had engineered it.

The union was inundated with calls of support when the news of Jones' captivity got out and telegrams from east coast newspapers sought information about the strike. Ed Doyle was quick to capitalize and organized a protest march in Trinidad, and for maximum effect he restricted it to women and children.

On the morning of January 21st, the Ludlow women and children congregated at the camp's front entrance. The Andrakises had argued all the previous evening, Anna desperate to go on the march, Maria as equally adamant against it. Spiro had interceded, finally persuading Maria that the march would stay peaceful since only women and children were involved. Plus, he added, it would do the little girl good to get out of the camp.

They climbed into the back of the truck and found themselves next to Mary Thomas and her two little children. "Well now, girl, I'm glad you're coming along," Mary said with her sing-song voice, smiling. "The more the merrier, that's what I say."

Maria was still nervous but having the Welshwoman next to them made her feel a little safer. The truck bounced its way into town, joining more and more cars and trucks, all of them weaving between lines of people making their way on foot.

Doyle had designated the station as the starting point for the march, but most of the trucks only got as far as the city limits; hundreds of women and children had got to the station ahead of them. As they joined the crowd, Maria and Anna heard impromptu choirs belting out hymns, union songs, the National Anthem. Union banners waved in the stiff breeze, large placards read "Free Mother Jones," "Union Forever," "Doesn't the Governor have a Mother?" Hawkers selling soft drinks, coffee and hot dogs moved through the crowd, their sonorous pitches cutting through the rumblings of hundreds of excited voices. Nobody seemed to be in charge, but without prompting the marchers finally began to move en masse towards the center of town. The bridge over the river groaned complainingly but it held the crowd's weight. Women and children, singing and enjoying what was turning out to be a festive occasion, filled the Trinidad streets.

But when they turned onto the town's main street they saw their way blocked by dozens of mounted guardsmen. Anna could barely see through the adults who towered above her but every so often she caught glimpses of what lay ahead. The horses were lined from one side of Main to the other and they were at least four deep. They looked impossibly huge, with plumes of steam snorting out of their nostrils like the dragons in her picture book at school. Some were bucking and she could see their gigantic, crescent-shaped iron shoes as their powerful legs kicked in the air.

The women slowed down, unsure what to do next. General Chase rode out in front of his command and trotted slowly to the marchers.

"Ladies," he bellowed, "you can go no further. I know why you are here and you will not release Jones from her lawful imprisonment. Go back now."

The women and children continued to advance slowly, determined to stay their course. Maria and Anna stayed right behind Mary, now holding her two small children. Maria did not realize exactly where the Welshwoman was headed until it was too late, for suddenly the little group found itself on the front line of the marchers, right next to General Chase's horse. As Chase turned his horse to go back to his men, he kicked back his right heel to get his horse moving, and his spur caught Anna a glancing blow on the side of her head. The little girl cried out, in surprise rather than pain, and her mother instinctively reached over to help her. Maria's body brushed the flank of the horse and it bucked just enough to unsteady its rider. Chase tried to regain control, but he only made it worse. The horse kicked out and threw Chase onto the ground. As he picked himself up, the women began to laugh and hurl insults.

"Hey, General, not used to something big between your legs?" came one. "Call yourself a horseman?" came another.

Chase's face turned crimson. He remounted his horse and shouted at the top of his voice. "Ride them down. Ride down the women." The officers, twenty yards back with the rest of the troop, looked at each other, uncertain how to react.

"Now," the general cried, and suddenly the troopers broke and with sabers drawn charged down on the crowd. The women and children scattered but there were few places to run. Some hid in alleyways and shops but most of them ran as fast as they could back the way they had come. They were no match for galloping horses and the cavalrymen smashed through them, regrouped and charged and charged again.

Maria and Anna ran too and tucked into a small alley between the shops. Anna saw an American flag ripped out of a child's hands and a large chestnut mare bounce a woman out of the way like she was a feather. One trooper brought the flat of his saber across the back of a girl's head and sent her sprawling. Anna threw up when she saw a woman with one ear hanging down her cheek held on only by a thin sliver of skin, blood pouring onto her shoulder. Right in front of them a woman staggered by, holding out her hands as if in supplication, saber slashes across her arms and hands. The screams of the wounded competed with the commands of the officers as they wheeled around in search of victims. Horses whinnied and snorted, their shoes slapping hard on the pavement. The smell of fresh horse shit and piss permeated the air.

After the third charge Chase ordered his men back to their staging point. Slowly, women and children emerged from the shops and alleyways and began to make their escape. Maria grabbed her daughter's hand and dragged her as fast as she could to keep up with the rest of the retreating crowd. At the junction with Commercial Street, they caught up with Mary and her children, all of them unharmed. The two families hugged each other in relief, but a groan arose from the crowd, and looking back they saw troopers trotting towards them, as if readying themselves to charge again. But this time the cavalrymen dismounted as they got to the demonstrators and started to arrest whomever they could get their hands on.

One trooper made a beeline for a fifteen-year-old girl. She ran away from him but the crowd was too dense and it stopped her escape. He grabbed her and brought the butt of his rifle hard onto her foot. She heard the crack as her bones broke, and she fell to the ground, screaming in agony. The trooper yanked her up by her hair.

"You, you bitch, you laughed at the general."

Mary ran over to the girl and shouted almost hysterically, "We all were. Why are you picking on her?"

The trooper said nothing, but slapped Mary hard across her face. He was joined by two more militiamen. Maria and Anna helped the Welshwoman and the girl up.

The trooper barked out, "Arrest all of them, even the brats."

Maria and Anna, together with Mary, her children and six other women were marched to the jail. A deputy sheriff took custody of them, silently unlocked the cell and motioned for them to go in. He clanged the door shut and left them alone. The cell smelt of stale urine and vomit. There was a small bed and a bucket on the back wall. Mary's two children were too young to know what had happened; they were just grateful to be away from the horses. The adults knew their jailer would not do anything bad to them with so many witnesses. But Anna was caught in that horrible age when she was old enough to be aware of danger but too young to know that it had limits. She burst into tears and shook hysterically.

Only after an hour of rocking by her mother on the hard mattress of the bed was Anna finally able to calm down. As she lay her in her mother's arms, Anna mumbled the simple question on everybody's lips. *"Why? Why did they attack us? Why?"* The women had no answer. Any answer would have sounded trite, for how could they explain grown men on horses mowing down defenseless women and children. They sat in the dark of the cell, Mary's children whimpering with hunger pains, Anna quietly singing nursery rhymes with her mother, and only the steady tick-tock of the wall clock in the hallway to remind them of the passage of time.

A light came on in the office at the end of the hallway. Then the deputy sheriff unlocked the cell door. Standing in the doorway, he shouted, "All of you can go, except you." He pointed at Mary. "You're a troublemaker. We know you're one of the ringleaders, so you're gonna' stay here until the general decides what to do with you."

For the first time that day, Mary showed fear. "What about my children? Keep me if you have to, but let them go back to their Da'. They done nothin' against you."

The deputy sheriff softened. "I'm sorry, I've got my orders. You'll all have to stay. But look, I'll bring some food for you and the kids." The unexpected kindness silenced Mary and she nodded in acquiescence. The deputy herded everybody else out onto the deserted Trinidad street, leaving Mary and her children alone in the cold cell.

The icy wind bit through their clothing but at least Anna and Maria were free. Anna saw Spiro, who had been trying to get in to see his family for the last three hours. She wriggled free of Maria's arms and rushed into his arms. He scooped her up and held her tightly. Maria walked slowly to her husband. She realized that now was not the time to say anything. *Perhaps,* she thought, *there never will be*. Spiro, too, kept silent, just took his wife's hands. But as they climbed into Tikas' car for the drive back to Ludlow, he looked at her plaintively and whispered, "I am sorry. You were right. I am sorry."

Roady Kenehan was through with protocol. He stormed into the governor's office without knocking and slapped down a Denver newspaper.

"See, Governor, there's your great man, Chase, hunting down women and children now."

Ammons barely turned his head to read the headlines. He'd already seen a whole clutch of newspapers, all of them condemning the saber attack and all of them wondering who was in charge, that madman Chase or Ammons.

"Now do you understand, Governor, why I don't want to pay them?"

Ammons had no reply. He was still, just looked out of the window.

Kenehan had concluded weeks ago that the governor had been beaten, by the operators, by Chase, and by the sheer magnitude of events that crushed him down daily. It was as though he had become invisible, and was no longer of any importance in deciding what would happen in the coalfields.

Now Kenehan spoke quietly. "Governor, so far I've delayed payment of the troopers' wages, in the hopes that everybody will come to their senses. But you know I've always released the funds in the end. But from now on I'm not authorizing payments to Chase and his officers anymore. I'm not talking about just delaying their expenses checks. I'm simply not paying them, period. Maybe that'll get through to the bastard." Ammons stirred briefly then slumped back in his chair. "Governor, please, let me explain. Here's the latest expenses statement they sent me. A drinks bill for five hundred dollars, private rooms for officers' friends. You know what that means, don't you. Chase makes four hundred a month, plus he has an expenses check for over one hundred and fifty. Every month. How much moustache wax does the man need? The Guard has one officer for every two men. It's crazy, Governor, crazy. In ten years that damned National Guard has cost the state one and a half million dollars. And guess who's on the authorizing boards all that time. That's right, you got it.

Chase. We've got eleven hundred men down there, and they're going hungry, and they don't have proper winter clothing. Well no more, Governor, no more. It'll be over my dead body before I finance his craziness any more."

"That's all well and good, Roady," Ammons countered, surprising Kenehan with his vitality. "But it's you who's making the common soldier suffer by holding up their pay. I got this letter yesterday from a mother of one of them." He held up a piece of paper. "She told me her son's uniform is in rags, they haven't been paid in months and their food is rationed. Tell me how to answer her."

Kenehan looked his employer straight in the eye, his contempt overriding any semblance of propriety. "Tell her the truth, Governor. Tell her that this was all started by the coal companies. Tell her to get Chase to pay his men instead of wasting it on his fripperies. Tell her that's who she should be blaming. Tell her to complain to him about her son."

"Kenehan," the Governor said, changing the subject. He straightened himself, a half-smile playing on his lips. "You know as well as me we're out of money. And we can't keep borrowing off the banks indefinitely. It has to end sometime. So, I'm ending it now. See this paper here." He waved a paper with the state seal on it. "It begins the withdrawal of the Guard. I'm turning the coalfields back to the local authorities and the companies."

Kenehan was dumbfounded. He had completely misread Ammons' demeanor, thinking that the governor was simply unable to act anymore. The awful, ugly fact dawned on Kenehan that Ammons had completely capitulated. At least having the Guard down in the coalfields, even under Chase, gave the state some sort of leverage. But now the state would be virtually powerless.

"See, Roady, you got your wish after all." Kenehan began to splutter a reply, but Ammons interjected firmly. "It's over, Roady. Now, let me lecture you for a change. The union's just about bankrupt. So are we, and if the companies have to provide protection until the strike collapses, so be it. They will pay for everything. God knows, we can't. You keep telling me that. And you needn't worry about training them, either. General Chase is going to stay on temporarily with a corps of officers. Also, I'm keeping two hundred troopers down there to act as the backbone to the local units."

Kenehan was appalled into silence by the governor's decision to let Chase take command of company men, the very forces that had fomented the crisis and who were gunning, literally in his mind, for its violent end. And he was honest enough to ask himself whether somehow he had indirectly forced Ammons into this decision. All Kenehan could do was shake his head and make for the door.

Despite Kenehan's fears, there was a lull in the violence. The cold froze everybody's minds as well as their bodies, and both sides awaited the spring. But even if the respite was welcome, the miners and their families, Chase and his command, Ammons and his government, Bowers and the company owners, all of them knew it wouldn't last. And as the first hint of spring whispered its way across the prairies, violence erupted once more.

The militia captain pulled his collar high around his neck. "Well, boys, let's get at it. No sense in hangin' around in this weather." The mild weather of just a few days earlier when the operation had been planned had turned nasty again. The March air was like a blade slashing the cavalryman's face, and he could see dark clouds forming to the west. He spurred his horse and with his troop made his way down the track towards Forbes.

A mile from the camp entrance, hidden in a depression, they reined in their horses. The animals were keen to stay on the move and the troopers had to pull hard on them to keep them in check. "Boys," he shouted above the horses, "you need to know why we're here. The general personally told me that this morning Sheriff Grisham arrested a bunch of miners. He said they killed a Negro. They were all from Forbes. He says we need to teach them a lesson."

"Captain," a young voice spoke up. "I heard he was killed when he fell in front of the train. He was blind drunk."

The officer sneered at him. "Listen, college boy, for someone smart, you don't know anything. What the hell are they teachin' you up in Boulder."

The trooper was about to respond but a hand on his arm motioned him to be quiet.

"Grisham says the miners killed him, and that's good enough for me. We're gonna' teach them all a lesson. You don't want to come, that's fine, but you better hope your mommy and daddy can afford a good lawyer, because I bet a dollar to nothing you'll be in irons by the end of the day."

The young man sat still on his saddle, his hands gripping its pommel as if he was willing himself to stay mute.

The captain knew, like Chase, that the evidence against the Forbes miners was non-existent. The train crew had admitted they'd hit the victim, but they hadn't been allowed to speak at the inquest.

On the afternoon of Tuesday, March 10th, 1914 the Colorado militia completed a classic cavalry sweep though the Forbes tent camp, the last ever in a state that had seen many such maneuvers during the Indian Wars of the last century. Without dismounting, the cavalrymen wrapped lariats around the tent poles and pulled them down, scattering the tents and their belongings across the open prairie. As the troop reassembled at the end of their sweep, their job done, the men, women and children who had managed to climb out of the dismantled tents ran for the shelter of a nearby arroyo. An old woman in her seventies sat on the cold ground. Her family clustered around her trying to give her some comfort, trying to get her to move to safety. For the troopers it was a simple cavalry movement, one they had practiced many times, but for the inhabitants of Forbes it was a tragedy. They could only hope that there would be enough room in the tents remaining to shelter all of them until they could figure out what to do.

The captain ordered his men to withdraw, and then he dispatched a messenger to inform Chase that their action had been entirely successful and that they were returning to their barracks.

General Chase was in a good mood. Not only was he winning the battle, he reminded himself, he was winning the war, too, and to celebrate his victory, now so close, he staged a grand military ball in the Cardenas Hotel, in his opinion the finest hotel in Trinidad. The impressive row of colonnades that fringed its front, and the open graveled apron that stretched down to the river meandering gracefully beyond, all spoke of a dignity and calm that he saw in himself. He had ordered a particularly fine new dress uniform for the occasion. His wife thought the gold buttons a little extravagant but to Chase they were a necessary symbol of his importance, and he said as much as they dressed for the occasion.

"My dear," he continued, "I am not surprised that the governor refused to come, but I am a little taken aback that his wife and daughter have accepted."

"Not really, if you think about it." His wife gently pulled up the front of her gown, afraid that her décolletage might be a little too risqué, but she must have been satisfied for she allowed him to fasten a lustrous string of pearls around her neck. The general looked askance at his wife, as she continued with her dressing. "John, it makes perfect sense that he wouldn't come. You know as well as I do that he's diminished in your presence. But his wife and daughter? He knows you'll treat them courteously. It's actually very smart of him. He gets to be present without having to be here himself."

The general harrumphed in grudging agreement and proceeded to put the final touches to his moustache, ensuring that the last stray wisps of hair had been put back in their places. *Yes,* he thought, *this is going to be a grand evening.*

Their car took them to the hotel at seven o'clock sharp, where they were greeted by his officers, like him decked out in their finest uniforms, although some of the jackets, the general had to admit, looked the worse for wear. The ballroom was decorated with the Stars and Stripes, and banners in the nation's colors were draped along the walls. At one end of the room an orchestra softly played Mozart and Bach. The general's aide brought him a glass of white wine with cordial for his wife, while he chatted with his officers. Twenty minutes after they arrived, General and Mrs. Chase were requested to take their places in the greeting line and together they welcomed each of their guests. The Ammons party was first in line, as befitted their status, and Chase was his urbane and charming best.

"Thank you for gracing us with your presence, Mrs. Ammons, and you, too, young lady. May I introduce my wife?" She smiled demurely at her two guests. The four of them chatted for a few moments and only a keen observer would see how the back of the governor's wife would arch every so often.

Karl Linderfelt, feeling out of place in an ill-fitting uniform, stood at the side of the ballroom, sipping a beer with Major Pat Hamrock. He nodded his head in the direction of Chase and his guests. "Can you believe it, eh, Pat? I bet they'd scratch each other's' eyes out if they had their druthers. But no, they're making nice, just like old friends. Look at them, why don't you?"

Pat Hamrock laughed. "Monte, I'd love to hear that conversation." Hamrock had been selected to stay on after the majority of the guard had left because of his military experience. As he had joked with Linderfelt when he found out, it was better than running his saloon in Denver.

The scene was interrupted when a young aide came over to the general, who excused himself and leant low as the young officer whispered in his ear. Linderfelt saw Chase smile and then subtly motion for him to come over. The three of them stood apart from the rest of the party.

"Lieutenant, good news. It appears that our little exercise at Forbes was eminently successful. We have sent those lawless brigands a strong message." The aide asked Chase where the homeless of Forbes would stay. The general stiffened, looked hard at the young man. "It actually is of no concern of mine at all. However, I suppose," and he indulged himself in a small smile, "the prisons can always be opened up."

The soldier opened his mouth as if to reply, but a sharp look from Linderfelt silenced him. "Well, gentlemen," the general continued. "I think it is time to rejoin the ladies and start this ball. What do you say?" The two officers could not agree more.

The next four hours were full of gaiety. The orchestra played delightful airs and melodies, and the officers and their ladies swirled across the dance floor, the officers' buttons glinting in the light from the chandeliers, the ladies' dresses swishing in time to the music. Finally, taps was played and the dancers reluctantly made their way to their rooms or to their cars for the ride into town.

"So, boys, how many of you does it take to keep me here?" Mother Jones laughed good naturedly at the six guards who now watched her round the clock. One of them sat down on the chair next to her bed and tried to explain.

"You know, Mother, it ain't you we're worried about. But what happens if a gang of your cutthroats tries to break you out. That wouldn't be good, would it?"

Mother Jones wasn't so sure about that. She had been cut off from the outside world for almost ten weeks and knew that her presence in jail without trial worked in her and the union's favor.

Still, as she told herself, ten weeks was a bit much.

So she was quietly happy when she received a surprise visit from Horace Hawkins, the union's attorney. The guards moved them into a small waiting room, after Hawkins had demanded client-attorney confidentiality. The lawyer was bundled up against the chill March air and he barely loosened his scarf as he sat at the table opposite her.

"Damn me, but it's cold in here. How the hell do you stand it?" Hawkins's breath was visible, and he rubbed his hands together to keep the circulation going.

"Well, if you look around, you'll see the room isn't heated. This is their little way of saying, 'Welcome Mr. Attorney. Now get lost.'"

Hawkins smiled. "Got it. First off, are they treating you well?"

Jones nodded. "Believe it or not, the boys here have treated me pretty well. But I can tell you that if you're here to get me out, I won't complain."

Hawkins got down to business. "Let me bring you up to date. Forbes has been destroyed by the Guard. Or at least a good portion of it. They went in, pulled all the tents down. Direct orders from Chase."

Jones's face turned red. "I knew that man was insane. First the saber charge, and now this. The middle of March and he's destroying tents, the only things they have to live in. If there's a God, I hope he remembers Mr. John Chase's name. That's for sure."

She was about to continue, but Hawkins interrupted her. "I don't have much time, so here's what we're planning. I heard from the state Supreme Court yesterday. They're going to hear my appeal on Monday." Jones pursed her eyebrows. "Sorry, you really have been out of touch. I've been pushing the governor to let you out, but he keeps deferring to Chase, who says you're a menace to the public good." Jones smiled on hearing the phrase. "Anyway, I petitioned the court to hear your case, that you were imprisoned illegally and that martial law or not, which I personally think can't be enforced here for a number of reasons, Chase cannot detain you indefinitely. I've also included in the petition that all the strikers he's got under lock and key should be released. You know he's got almost thirty of them?" Hawkins paused to catch his breath.

"Thirty, eh, that doesn't surprise me at all. But how come you can visit me at all? Didn't Chase throw a fit?"

"He did at first, Mother, but lately he's had a change of heart. For one thing, any petitioner to the court must have access to his client. Chase had no choice but to let me see you. But, and this is the real reason, I think." The attorney paused. "Our friend, the good General Chase wants you out of prison." Her head jerked up at the statement. Hawkins carried on. "We have, shall we say, friends in the governor's office. Apparently, Chase is terrified that the case will go to the court because that would open up the whole legality of the original martial law edict. He wants to protect his position as long as he can. I'm pretty sure he knows he's on thin ice from a legal standpoint. Anyway, this is how I think it's gonna' play out. I've got no evidence for this, just a gut feeling that they're gonna' let you out this weekend. You've become more trouble for them in prison than out."

Mother Jones slapped her knees and started laughing. "Oh, Mr. Hawkins, do they have a shock in store for them. Just watch me."

At the sound of her laughter, one of the deputies hurried into the room. "Interview's over," he barked peremptorily.

"It's okay, deputy, we're done here," Hawkins responded unemotionally as though it was an entirely routine attorney-client meeting. "Good luck, Mother Jones, you'll be hearing from us."

Hawkins was right. That Sunday evening, while Jones was reading a book, she was interrupted by a sharp rap on her door. At the same time a guard opened it to reveal a tall militia officer.

"I am Lieutenant Jackson. I am here to escort you to Denver. You have ten minutes to pack."

It took Jones less than half that time. She had been expecting this ever since Hawkins's visit, and it was a simple thing to throw her toiletries and hairbrush into the carpet bag along with the few clothes she possessed. So eager were they to see her gone from Trinidad, the lieutenant virtually carried her into the car waiting at the bottom of the hospital steps, its engine revving and its rear door already open. From there it was a quick five-minute drive to the railroad station, where she and the officer boarded the late train to Denver. The lieutenant was not the most talkative of men, and this suited Jones just fine. She had been locked up in a tiny room and she wanted to savor the tastes of freedom, however fleeting they might be.

The ride to Denver was boring, even for a woman who had been locked up for over two months. The lieutenant, whose duty as an officer did not extend to carrying an old lady's bag, flagged down a taxi cab to take them to a hotel a few minutes away. They pulled up in front of the hotel and he leant over Jones and opened the door, motioning for her to get out. Almost before the door had closed behind her the cab had taken off, leaving Jones alone on the sidewalk, and wondering where this bizarre Colorado journey would take her next.

Six days later Mother Jones thought it time to go back to work. As she boarded the train back to Trinidad she saw that Jeb Stevens was working and she greeted him warmly.

"Well hello there, Mother. Off again, are we?" Jeb joked in return. "You know, you're on this train so often, I'll get you a ticket to our Christmas dinner, you know, the one the bosses hold for us workers." He cackled at that and was still laughing as he made his way down the aisle. Jones smiled with him for it was true. She was beginning to lose count of the times she'd made the journey.

As the train clacked its way down south and she passed the

now familiar sights, she reflected on how the conflict had grown bigger and more dangerous every day. Both sides seemed unwilling to compromise; the cavalry charge and then the destruction of Forbes, rather than bringing the men to their senses, had only hardened their positions. The lightheartedness she had shared with Jeb Stevens diminished the nearer the train got to Trinidad, for this time she really didn't know what was in store for her, only that it would be worse than what she had already endured. And despite her bravery in standing up to Chase in the restaurant, she was a little afraid of him, if only because he seemed more than a little insane.

By the time it had cleared Pueblo, the rocking of the train finally eased her into sleep. She dreamed she was playing with her beloved children. They were picnicking on the banks of a crystal clear river. Blue sky and a warm sun basked them and she could hear birds singing. The picnic had made her drowsy and she had to ask her little daughter to stop shaking her arm to come and play. "No, sweetheart, let Mommy sleep, please. Just for a few minutes." But the little girl was insistent and kept pushing. Mother Jones slowly opened her eyes to see a deputy sheriff standing over her.

"Finally, you're awake. Come on, lady, we're in Walsenburg. Guess where we're going." He pulled her up roughly from her seat, while the other passengers looked away in embarrassment.

Jeb Stevens came over. "Sir, she's a lady, treat her like one."

"Mind your own goddamned business, boy, or I'll arrest you as well. You, lady, are under arrest. Now let's get moving."

It was still dark and she guessed it was an hour or two before dawn. The deputy bundled her into a waiting car and took her to the courthouse, an imposing stone structure set in its own grounds. But instead of marching her up the front steps he took her to the side of the building. He led her through an open door and down a steep flight of stairs to the basement. The stairs smelt musty and damp.

At the bottom of the stairs she was met by a round-faced, barrel-chested man. He was wearing a smartly pressed suit that covered a clean white shirt with a starched wing-tip collar. On his jacket pocket was pinned a sheriff's badge. His eyes were cold and gray and he stared unflinching at the old woman in front of him

"I am Sheriff Jefferson Farr and you are my prisoner." As he spoke, his thick moustache bobbed up and down. "I am damned sick of your kind coming to my county and ruining the peace. Now get in there." He pointed over his shoulder at a small room full of old cardboard boxes and filing cabinets. But no bed, Jones immediately noted.

"Make yourself comfortable, woman." He slammed the door shut. Jones heard a bolt being thrown into place and then a key turning. The ceiling fixture in the room had no bulb, and she found herself in complete darkness save for the sliver of light that came under the bottom of the door. She sat on the floor with her back against a wall. Her joints ached from the train ride and the cold concrete added to her pain. Finally, exhaustion overcame her and she drifted into a light sleep, only to be awakened by a rat scurrying across her legs. She tried to kick it away but it was already gone. She felt around the room, trying to find a weapon of some sort. She finally laid her hands on a broken coffee mug. It would have to do.

20

The temperature dipped below freezing just after midnight and an icy wind cut through to the very bones of Paolo Rossi. He and his gang had been hard at work all evening and they were cold, exhausted and thoroughly miserable.

"Scarpelli, grab that end and lift when I tell you."

"Okay, boss," Alberto replied in Italian, "got it."

The two of them carried the last box of carbines out of the back of the hardware store and placed it alongside the others in the truck. For good measure, they threw a thick canvas tarpaulin over the load even though nobody would be able to see through the rear door windows, for it was a moonless night. Alberto and the other Italians jumped in alongside the munitions and waited for Rossi.

The big Italian roughly shook the hand of the store owner who wished them all a good night, nervously looking around to see if they were being watched. Although what he was doing was legal, selling arms to the union was risky, because he knew what the company men might do to him if they found out. And dealing with the tight-lipped Rossi only made the whole transaction that much harder. He breathed a sigh of relief as he slammed the warehouse door closed and heard the truck's engine kick into life and move away down the alley.

They drove out of Trinidad, making for a small abandoned ranch they had used in the past as a temporary storage place.

"If this one gets found, Luigi, we're either being tailed or someone's ratting on us," Rossi confided in his second-in-command. "I wish we could just take the rifles straight to the camps like we used to, but they've got those fuckin' checkpoints up and now they're searching the camps regular."

The Italian nodded in agreement. Three of their caches had been found by the guardsmen in the last two weeks alone, and like his boss he did not know how this was happening. Guns were expensive and the union couldn't afford the losses. "Do you think it's worth carrying on with the strike, Paolo? I mean the Guard's movin' out and the companies are runnin' the show again. And the union's done for." He asked the question Rossi had asked himself many times since he'd first been approached by Tikas.

"I don't know, to be honest. Not many of our guys have joined the union, so that tells me what they think." He paused. "But I'm not sure we have a choice. I couldn't stand by and watch others take the lead, you know? Here's the turn off."

Rossi pointed to a small dirt track that had appeared out of the blackness of the night. It crossed a field and then dipped into a small hollow. Rossi turned the wheel and the truck bumped its way across the frozen prairie. They drove for a couple of hundred yards and then emerged onto another road. But Rossi unexpectedly turned left and drove back into Trinidad.

"Hey, boss, you trying to make us all dizzy?" Luigi smiled at the backtracking Rossi always insisted on. "We're not goin' to the ranch, then?"

"No, somewhere else I found. I know it's a pain, but it's all I could think of to get rid of any tails. Anyway, what else you doing tonight?"

On the edge of town Rossi drove into a small walled enclosure. It looked like it had been a dairy from the row of rusty churns lined up against the wall, but now it was abandoned. Stopping in front of a set of double doors, Rossi jumped out and unlocked the heavy padlock that held the two doors together. He swung them wide open while Luigi jumped into the driver's seat and edged the truck through them into the large barn. Rossi quickly closed the double doors behind them.

"Okay, guys, let's get going, so we can all go to bed." Now that they were here, Rossi felt relieved. *But still, if they lose this load,* he reminded himself, *there'll be hell to pay.*

The crew jumped out of the back of the truck and unloaded the boxes into a corner of the barn. They covered them with the tarpaulin and then strewed some old hay across it. Rossi realized that it wouldn't fool anybody who was seriously looking, but it was the best they could do. Forty minutes later, Rossi and his crew were in the Aguilar bar. He took a slug of grappa and let the fiery liquid burn his throat, trying to convince himself that they couldn't have been followed. But if this cache was found, he admitted to himself, then they had a traitor and that thought was too painful to dwell on.

Two days later, Rossi was back in the bar.

"God damn it, I don't believe it." His voice thundered across room.

Tikas let him rage; it was all he could do.

"I only moved them guns two days ago, and now you're telling me they're gone?"

Tikas nodded. Rossi stood up, looked like he was selecting something to punch out, and Tikas involuntarily drew back behind the table. Rossi kicked out at a chair and sent it ten feet across the floor to crash against the wall opposite. "Shit, fuck." Tikas started to laugh but stifled it quickly.

After five minutes, Rossi calmed down enough to listen. "Hard as it is to admit, Paolo, we have an informer. It won't be the first, you know."

Rossi nodded, unwilling to accept that it might be one of his boys.

"I've been doing some thinking." Tikas sipped his coffee and explained his theory to the big Italian.

"Three of the four caches hit by the militia in the last month were hidden by your gang. Agreed?" Tikas went slowly, his body tense. The Italian stayed silent, his eyes boring into the Greek opposite him. The cigarette smoke drifted slowly out of his nostrils as he nodded for Tikas to continue. "What are their names?" Rossi listed his regular gang, counting out each one on his fingers.

One name made Tikas pause. "This Scarpelli, who is he?

"He's one of yours, he's from Ludlow. Remember? He brought you up here to meet me. He's pretty thick but he works hard." Rossi turned suspicious. "Why?"

Almost too quickly, Tikas replied that he had no particular reason, and that he remembered him now and liked him. Rossi looked hard at Tikas but kept quiet.

"Paolo, I'll get to the bottom of this, I promise you. Lawson wants me to do it, keep you out of it, for now at least. I don't know why. Maybe he just wants to make it look, you know, formal, like it's the union doing a proper investigation. I think that's the right word. Do you agree to give me a week?" The Italian said nothing. The Greek took his hat and walked towards the saloon door. As he was exiting, he heard Rossi.

"I'll leave it with you, Tikas, but only for a week. And if you find out who's snitched and he's Italian, you promise you leave him to me. Understand?"

Tikas spent most of the next day mulling over what he knew. Alberto Scarpelli had known about the trip out to Primero when they'd killed Lee last September. He had begged off coming with them at the last minute. Lee had known they were Greeks before they had opened their mouths. And now Alberto was working with a gang whose shipments were being regularly intercepted. Still, Tikas found it hard to believe that the quiet, helpful Italian was their informer. He needed more proof.

When Tikas learned about what Alberto had been doing, he had debated with himself, agonizingly, for three days whether to tell Spiro. His first reaction had been to spare him the truth, but Spiro was a good man, one of his best, and if he kept him ignorant, Spiro would think he couldn't be trusted. He had to tell Spiro, not that the realization made it any the easier for him. He looked out the saloon window, sipping a beer but hardly tasting it. The wind whipped down Main Street, and only people who had to be outside braved the cold. He saw Spiro crossing the street to get to the bar, the foreboding growing every second that passed. Spiro looked in a sour mood as he sat down next to Tikas and ordered a beer. Waiting to delay the inevitable as long as he could, Tikas asked what was up.

Spiro shrugged his shoulders. "Nothing, I guess. I just tried to buy some candy for Anna, said I'd bring it in next time I was around cos' I forgot my cash. The guy told me no. I shopped there for years and never had a problem. I guess things have changed, eh."

"I know it, my friend. Here's a dollar, Tell Anna her Uncle Louis said Hi." He liked the serious little Andrakis girl. Plus, it might help soften the blow that was coming Spiro's way.

Spiro didn't hesitate. "Thanks, I will. Okay, I'm here, what's goin' on, and why here and not back in the camp?"

Tikas prevaricated. "Well, I was here on business. I wanted to catch you up with things in the union."

"Yeah, so what's new?" Now he was curious.

Tikas turned his eyes from Spiro momentarily, as if he might look back to find Spiro had never been there. But Spiro was still there, pulling on his beer. Tikas took a deep breath. "Spiro, you know the companies have got informers in the union, right? Well, last week company guards got a tip off about a weapons buy Rossi'd just made. They raided our place and we lost it all, guns, ammo, everything."

"Skata," Spiro shouted. "Shit. If I could get my hands on him…"

Tikas interrupted him, spoke quietly. "Spiro, I know who it is."

Spiro looked up from his beer. "Who?"

"Before I tell you, I'm gonna' tell you how I found out. I've got the names of everybody on Rossi's gang. Now, remember when we killed Lee over at Primero? How I was surprised he knew we were Greeks? Well I made a list of the men who knew about the trip." He looked Spiro dead in the eyes. "One man's name comes up on both lists. Do you believe me so far?"

Spiro nodded. "Who is he? I didn't know those guys well. Which one was it?"

"Spiro, it was the man who didn't end up coming with us. The one who stayed behind at Ludlow to help out one of the families. Your friend, Alberto, Alberto Scarpelli."

Spiro choked on his beer, and he began to grin until he realized Tikas was deadly serious. "Don't be stupid, Louis, that's crazy, it's not possible. I know Al, he's a good man. No, you're wrong this time, totally wrong." Spiro tried to stand up, but Tikas, with a surprisingly strong grip, put his hand on Spiro's wrist and forced him back into his seat.

"Sit down and listen. I know. I didn't want to believe it either, so I had him tailed. We've got him talking to Watson three times in the last five days, and once with Farr. And he's made some big wire transfers at the Western Union over the last few months." Tikas held his hand up. "Don't ask me how I know that. I just do. Do you believe me now, Spiro?"

"Tikas, you're sure about this?" he asked one more time.

Tikas nodded. "I'm sorry, Spiro, I truly am. There's something else. I promised I'd find the informer and if I did I'd hand him over to Rossi. I have to keep that promise if we want them to stay with us."

Finally, Spiro looked up in a daze, and asked Tikas if he could be the one to take Alberto to the Italians. Tikas didn't need to ask why. They were both Cretans and Spiro had been betrayed by someone he thought a friend. "You know you can trust me to do this, don't you?" Spiro whispered. Tikas nodded, stood up and walked out of the bar.

Spiro went through the motions of daily life for the next few days as he grappled with what he was about to do. Sometimes the choice was crystal clear, and he would get ready to hand Alberto over to Rossi. But then he questioned whether this Cretan code was outdated, that it was right for his grandfather but not for him in 1914, and doubts overcame him once again. Maria asked him why he was so silent and wouldn't even talk to Anna, but he just told her to leave him alone. It was a small mercy for him that at least he did not see Alberto for the Italian spent most of his time in bed, trying to get over a bad cold.

But Spiro knew he would have to act soon. He arranged to borrow Tikas' car for that evening. Tikas said nothing, just pointed out where he had parked it and walked to the headquarters tent to contact Rossi. Living his worst nightmare, Spiro went over to Alberto's tent. The Italian was lying down under his blanket, smoking, for not even a chest cold would stop the Italian from his favorite pastime.

"Hey, Spiro, good to see you." He coughed. "I am having a cold, don't feel good."

Half of Spiro wanted to use Alberto's illness as an excuse to postpone what he had to do, but the other, stronger half told him to get on with it. Forcing himself to act nonchalant, he asked Alberto if he needed a break from his boredom. Alberto started to get out of bed, but Spiro motioned him down. "Tikas wants me to go over to Aguilar tonight. He lent me his car. Wanna' come? Say about seven?"

Alberto grinned back, but the laugh turned into a retching cough. "It sounds worse than it is. Yeah, I'll go with you. Have a beer, yes?"

That evening, as Spiro maneuvered around the ruts and washboards on the track to Aguilar he kept playing over and over in his head what he would say, and do, when they finally got there. Alberto asked him once why he was so quiet, but Spiro passed it off as a row with Maria, and his friend said no more. They walked into the bar, unusually empty for an evening. Only three old men in their seventies were there, sitting in a corner reading newspapers, and conspicuously minding their own business. Alberto held two fingers up, the two miners sat down and the barman brought over the beers.

All of Spiro's plans to approach Alberto quietly were thrown out of the window now the moment was upon him. He blurted out. "Why, Alberto, why?"

Alberto's sixth sense told him immediately what Spiro was referring to, but at first he tried to brazen it out. "Why what, Spiro?"

Spiro took a pull on his beer and told him what Tikas had found out.

"That's stupid, Spiro, I'd never do that."

"Alberto, don't lie to me. It's too late for that. Just tell me why."

The Italian's body deflated. Very calmly he said, "I needed the money, Spiro. My people are dying of hunger back home and they think I am a big American." He blew hard into a dirty handkerchief and picked something imaginary from the corner of his eye. "At first I say to myself, *Just this once, Alberto.* But it became easier the more I did it, and I know that the money helped. I swear to God, Spiro, I'm sorry." Spiro looked away in case Alberto saw his tears.

Spiro shook his head. "I'm sorry, too. I really am. But Rossi wants to see you. I'm sorry."

It was only when he heard Rossi's name that Alberto realized it truly was over. Tears rolled down the miner's cheeks. Rossi walked in at that moment and came over to their table. Without saying a word, Spiro stood up, leaned over and kissed Alberto gently on the top of his head. And as he walked out of the bar, he said a silent prayer for his friend, because despite what he had done, that was what Alberto would always be.

Spiro did not sleep that night. He thought of his friendship and what they had been through. Alberto had been his pit partner and worked with him in the hell of the mines, had nursed him through his accident, had stood by him and Maria and little Anna through everything, had always given Anna money for candy even when he didn't have much himself. Alberto was his friend. The memories were too painful and he tried to blot them out, but they kept coming back, stronger and more vivid. Had he done the right thing, he questioned himself over and over. He could find no answer. As a watery sun began to work its way over the camp, Spiro finally found a fitful sleep.

Maria sent Anna out to get coal, but she had hardly been gone a minute when she came running back to the tent. "Mama," she whispered, for she knew her papa had had a restless night. "Come quick, there's a man by the main gate. They say he's dead."

Maria ordered her to stay in the tent and hurried over to see what was going on. She came back five minutes later, tears streaking her cheeks. Ignoring her daughter's pleas for answers, she knelt beside Spiro. Gently she nudged his shoulder. Spiro stirred and opened a bleary eye.

"What's up, woman, please, let me sleep for God's sake."

"No, Spiro, listen, it's terrible. There's a man by the gate. He's all beat up. Spiro, it's Alberto. Alberto. He's dead."

Spiro rolled over away from his wife and faced the tent wall. He whispered, "I know. I know." Then his tears flowed uninterrupted: for Alberto, for his family, for himself, for everything in this godforsaken hell he called his life.

21

Lawson's whole body ached with fatigue, and the bone-shaking violence of his car only added to his misery. The drive to Sopris, the small tent colony west of Trinidad, was routine, one he had done many times before to exchange information and supplies. Lawson might almost have felt happy if he hadn't felt so tired, for it was the first decent day in weeks. The prairie grasses were beginning to turn green as the melting snow soaked deep into their roots, the oak leaves up the canyons no longer crackled drily each time the wind caught them, and even the tent camps took on a new luster, as the dew on the worn-out canvas sparkled in the bright April sun.

To keep him company on what would be a boring trip, Lawson had brought along two miners who for different reasons needed a brief escape from Ludlow. Spiro had still not recovered from the murder of his best friend and Lawson needed a fit Spiro, physically and mentally. His other companion was James Fyler, an older man in his mid-forties. Fyler had shown a facility for the minutiae of invoices, bills and receipts, something Tikas detested, and he had become the virtual second-in-command at Ludlow. Keeping Ludlow's accounts in order was a daunting task, and Fyler didn't see much of the outside world, so he'd welcomed Lawson's offer. Spiro, however, had to be virtually kicked out of the tent by Maria when Lawson had dropped by.

Leaving the relative noise and bustle of Trinidad behind, Lawson steered the sedan along an unpaved road towards Sopris. Enjoying the tranquility of the countryside took all their attention and they spoke very little to each other. Fyler started whistling off-key but his two companions did not complain. They were shocked out of their reverie when they turned a corner by a high rock outcropping and saw a large truck blocking their way. Three company guards were sitting straddle-legged on its side and three more were standing by the hood, smoking. All six of them were heavily armed. Lawson got out and told them they were coming through.

"I don't think so," one of them snarled.

"You've got no right, this is a public road. You can't stop us," Fyler shouted from inside the car. He and Spiro got out and joined Lawson.

Three more armed company guards who had been hidden in the truck's bed now stood up. The miners had allowed themselves to be caught in the open. Ordering Spiro and Fyler to get in the car, Lawson slowly walked backwards, fearful in case the guards opened fire, then jumped in the driver's seat and started the engine. He thought the incident was over when one of the guards took his hat off and shouted something at them. Spiro recognized him. It was Watson. He slurred his words and kept winking at the other guards.

"Hey, boys, I hear your girlfriend Scarpelli got it. Sorry about that. He was real helpful. We'll all miss him and his little stories."

Spiro turned a ghostly white. He started to climb out of the rear door, but Fyler, thinking quickly, swung around and pinned his arms down. Fyler was a heavy man and succeeded in stopping Spiro from escaping.

"Reverse the damned thing, get us out now. Do it," he yelled at Lawson, who slammed the sedan into reverse gear and drove backwards as fast as he could. After about fifty yards he swung the car through an open gate, and returning to the road drove as fast as he could away from the guards. Once he knew they weren't being followed, Lawson stopped the car.

"He was your friend, Spiro, I'm sorry. But there's nothing you can do about it. Come on, let's get back to Trinidad. We can hit Sopris another time."

The three of them stopped at a saloon on Main and Lawson made Spiro drink a shot of whiskey. It burnt his throat but it calmed him down.

Fyler spoke first. "Spiro, I know about Alberto, Louis told me. I'm sorry, too. But there was nothing we could do back there. And, you know," Fyler said coldly, all the while staring at him, "some people think he deserved it." Spiro started to rise. Lawson gave Fyler a filthy look and managed to get Spiro to sit down.

"Jim didn't mean anything by it, Spiro. You know that's what some people are saying. Come on, finish your drink and we'll get outta' here."

"I'm okay, Mr. Lawson. But, Fyler, you didn't know Alberto. So keep your mouth closed about him. Okay?"

They left the saloon after an hour and drove into an alleyway by the union office. Lawson and Fyler went upstairs to grab some papers, leaving Spiro alone to smoke a cigarette. He was calming down after Watson's jibes and Fyler's stupid remark. They were right. Alberto had been a fool and had paid the price. He leant back against the car fender, wondering if he wanted another smoke.

"Well, my God, if it ain't my favorite miner. Guess who followed you here. Little old me." Watson stood at the head of the alley. He swayed unsteadily. He put his hand on the butt of his gun and walked towards Spiro. "Hey, Greek, I forgot, I forgot," he stuttered as he let out a huge belch, "I forgot to tell you back there. Your boots were great. But not as good as your missus. She was sweet. Shame I couldn't get your other one either. But at least I got the dog. And who knows, maybe I'll still get lucky." He laughed, hiccupped and began to go for his gun. But the drink slowed him and Spiro grabbed him by the throat and swung him against the wall. Just as his fist was about to crash into Watson's face, Lawson and Fyler grabbed him from behind.

"Thank God. We were just in time, we shouldn't have left him here, real stupid of me. What the hell was I thinkin'?" Lawson's voice boomed.

"Andrakis, there's too many people on the street. Come on, let's go, nobody's seen us." Fyler's voice rasped in his ear. The miner bundled Spiro into the car, while Lawson grabbed Watson and manhandled him to the sidewalk away from Spiro. Watson slumped onto the boards, the effort of standing too much for him. A woman shopper stepped over his splayed out legs and tut-tutted something about drunks.

Back in the car they tried to calm Spiro down.

"Look, Spiro, I don't know what that was all about."

"You're a damned liar, Lawson. You heard everything. You are a fool if you don't."

Lawson had to find some way to make Spiro pause, to give him some doubt if only for a few minutes. "You're right, Spiro. And I'm sorry, God, I'm sorry. But please, Spiro, sleep on this."

"It wasn't your kid he was talkin' about, John. Or your wife." Spiro's voice could hardly be heard, he was speaking so quietly. After a moment he turned to Fyler. "How would you feel, Jim? What would you wanna' do?"

"I'd want to kill him, Spiro, I'd want to kill him."

They rode the rest of the way back to Ludlow in silence, Fyler sitting in the back next to Spiro, just in case. By the time they got to the camp, Spiro had calmed down but in a way that frightened Lawson more than his anger. Lawson walked Spiro to his tent. He didn't know when Spiro would blow, only that he would.

"Spiro, don't do anything without thinking it through first. Promise?"

Spiro reluctantly nodded and walked into his tent.

"What won't you do without thinking it through, Spiro? What's happened?"

"Nothing, wife. Where's Anna?"

"She's with Sally. Why?"

"We have to talk, and I want the truth."

Maria immediately knew what this was about. She was just surprised it had taken Spiro so long to find out. "Did he," Spiro stumbled over the word he couldn't say, "did he, did he, did he rape you?"

Maria put down the dish cloth she was holding. She walked up to her husband and quietly, ever so quietly, said just one word. "Yes."

Spiro's face drained of color. He clutched the tent pole tightly as though he would break it in two. Then, without thinking, he lashed out at his wife, catching her across the cheek with the back of his hand. "Why didn't you tell me, Maria, why? Or did you enjoy it?"

Maria lay on the duckboard floor, more in shock at what he had done than from the actual strength of the blow. "Spiro, I was ashamed, so ashamed. I felt dirty. I couldn't tell you. And I was afraid of what you'd do to him. I was thinking about all of us."

The strength went from Spiro's legs. He fell to his knees and took Maria in his arms.

"Maria," he whispered. "Sweet Jesus, forgive me. Now it makes sense. I thought you had stopped loving me. Didn't want, you know, to make love to me. Maria, forgive me." The two of them sat on the floor and held each other tight, Spiro stroking his wife's hair, Maria's head buried into her husband's chest.

Maria and Spiro stayed together all afternoon, grateful that Anna was happy to play at the Hoffmans. They sat in their tent, keeping warm by the stove, each in their own worlds. Occasionally, Spiro would ask for some detail of the assault, as though piece by piece he was reconstructing the episode. Maria waited for the obvious question, *was she pregnant*? But surprisingly it never came. Perhaps that was just one fact too many for Spiro.

Maria knew her husband would exact revenge for everything Watson had done. She remembered how he had faced down the French sailor all those years ago, a lifetime ago it now seemed. She knew he had been involved in gun battles since he had become one of Tikas' men. And Maria knew too that whatever was to happen could not be stopped, at least not by her. This had to take its course. She, too, was a Cretan.

Spiro knew Lawson was right to get him away from Watson as fast as he could. Otherwise, he would be in prison on a charge of murder. *No, it was better this way,* Spiro told himself. He remembered what the Turks back on Crete said, that revenge is a pie best served cold. Two days after the confrontation with Watson, at seven in the evening, he put his winter coat on and told Maria he'd be back in a couple of hours. Maria started to ask where he was going, but his look told her all she needed to know.

Spiro made straight for the storage tent. He walked in and saw old Joe Perkins who was one of the few who knew where the guns were hidden. Most families had one rifle hidden in their tent pit for emergencies, but the big caches were secreted away from prying militia eyes.

"Hi, Joe, mind if I pick up a handgun for tomorrow?"

Joe looked at the Greek long and hard. "Well, Spiro, that there's a problem. You see, Mr. Lawson told me not to sign you out anything."

Spiro knew better than to argue. *Besides,* he told himself, *there are other ways to skin a cat.* It was one of his favorite American phrases.

Spiro walked over to the baseball field across the road. At the side of the field was a bag of bats. Why nobody had picked them up at the end of the season, Spiro never figured out; he'd seen them himself and had always meant to, but never quite got around to it. Now Spiro was glad that he and the other miners had had other things on their minds. He pulled one out and swung it as though in batting practice. It was the one he used whenever he played. Spiro grimaced at how innocent it had all been, not too many months ago, and how everything had now turned black.

Spiro had worked out the details of his plan that afternoon. As he smoked his cigarettes, he realized that there was a large chink in Watson's armor. When he had stolen Spiro's boots, Watson had been arrogant. He was arrogant when he raped

Maria, he was arrogant when he attacked Anna, he was arrogant when he shot Kali. And Spiro remembered Watson's face just a few days ago as Fyler had held him down in the back of Lawson's car. Watson had the look of someone who yet again had won. It was the look of someone who had yet again put those stupid upstart miners in their place and sent them away with their tails between their legs. Whenever Spiro had seen Watson he had almost always been with other deputies or company guards. But there was one time when Watson might be alone: at night after his work was done. And Spiro knew that Watson was too arrogant to think he was even then in danger.

Spiro did not catch a ride from one of the cars and trucks that regularly ferried men and supplies between Ludlow and Trinidad. Fyler or Tikas, or even Lawson, would have found out and gone after him. It had turned cold and Spiro walked fast to stay warm. After forty-five minutes, he flagged down a farm truck. The driver was taciturn, like most of that rural stock, but nevertheless signaled him to climb on up. Spiro was grateful he didn't ask him why he had a baseball bat at that time of year. The truck rumbled its way to Trinidad, giving Spiro time to think through what he was going to do and prepare himself mentally. He knew that his actions might change his life and those of his family's forever, but he forced himself to believe that he had no choice. What Watson had done to Maria was abominable, but to little Anna? Spiro could find no words. The man, he concluded, was a rabid animal and had to be put down.

Just before they hit the outskirts of Trinidad, Spiro thanked the farmer and jumped down as the old truck slowed to take a sharp curve. He saw the tail lights dwindle into the distance leaving Spiro alone on the prairie. All he really knew about Watson's habits was that he was like the other guards and drank frequently at a saloon just off Main. Spiro walked towards the center of town, taking care to stay on the side streets where the lighting was not so good. It was cloudless and the warmth of the day had long escaped into the night air. Few people were out. He saw the lighted sign of the bar, and positioned himself behind an unlit corner a block away. Now all he could do was wait and hope.

The wind cut through Spiro's coat and his breath billowed from his mouth. *Surely,* he thought, *they can see me. They must think there's a freight train around the corner with all this steam.* He estimated he'd been there about two hours, when he saw the lights of the saloon flicker off and then back on.

Now or never, he thought to himself. He watched two men leave the saloon. They stood on the sidewalk talking, their breath snatched away by the light breeze. One of them lit a cigarette and then they parted ways. Spiro shrank back into the shadows as one of them walked down the street opposite him. Three more, then another two men left the bar. None of them was Watson.

The saloon's lights, including the outside sign, went off and Spiro thought he'd wasted his time. But just as he was about to turn away and go to the union offices for a hot drink and a bed for the night, the bar door opened and another figure walked out into the street. Unbelievably to Spiro, it was Watson, and he was alone. *Stay in control,* Spiro told himself, *stay in control. Think of what he did to Maria and Anna, get angry, but above all, stay in control.*

Watson lit a cigarette and began to walk slowly away from the bar, and away from Spiro. Spiro had no idea where the man was headed and began following him as closely as he dared. Watson halted at a crossroads. It looked as though he might turn right and head to Main, perhaps to Trinidad's red light district, and Spiro's spirits dropped. But Watson decided otherwise because suddenly he swiveled on his feet and began a slow climb to the east side of town. Spiro forced deep breaths into his lungs, the icy air burning his throat, and told himself that although it looked easy, the hard part was just beginning.

There were no street lights; the only illumination was the

reflected light from the town below. Spiro looked around; the street was deserted but for him and Watson. Watson stopped to relight his cigarette, and Spiro without hesitation walked swiftly towards the man. Watson heard the footfall and he turned to see who was coming. Spiro immediately swung his bat and caught Watson on the left forearm. Quickly he swung it again. The bat hit Watson just below his right knee, and he crumpled to the ground. Watson started to cry out but Spiro grabbed a rag from his pocket and stuffed it into Watson's mouth. The guard tried to pull it out but Spiro swung his bat again and cracked the guard's wrist.

Now Watson saw who his attacker was. Spiro stood over him, looking with cold, lifeless eyes at the man who had tried to destroy his family. He brought the bat crashing down on Watson's right arm. They both heard the bone crack. Watson moaned and held his left hand up in supplication.

Spiro spoke just three words. "You know why." Spiro thought he saw Watson nod imperceptibly as he slashed the bat down in a scything swing that caught Watson straight on the top of his brow. The skull crumpled and Watson lay still. There was enough light for Spiro to see a thick red and gray liquid ooze out of the wound.

Spiro looked around, half expecting to be caught and willing to face the consequences. But everything was as it had been just a minute earlier. Spiro walked away from the corpse in complete control of himself. He followed a new path out of town, avoiding the street lights. At the bridge he scrambled down the bank and spent five minutes washing the bat of its grizzly residue. *This is a damned good bat*, he reminded himself. *Be a shame to get rid of it.*

Four hours later, Spiro was back in his tent, wrapped around the warm body of his wife. Maria was not asleep but did not need to ask him where he had been or what he had done. In three days' time it would be Greek Easter Sunday. Spiro fell asleep anticipating the celebration of the resurrection of his Lord and Savior.

Christos Anesti, Alithos Anesti. Christos Anesti, Alithos Anesti. Christos Anesti, Alithos Anesti. Spiro recited the ancient chant to himself, over and again. *I will make a new life for myself and for my family. Christos Anesti, Alithos Anesti.* For the first time in many months, Spiro Andrakis slept deeply and without nightmares.

Part Four
Sunday, April 19th 1914

22

Easter Sunday, and the Greeks in Ludlow rose to a camp already throbbing with the daily activities of life. The fear of the future weighed on them, as it did for everybody, and the beer they had drunk at midnight had been a poor substitute for the raki of their homeland. But even though their festivities had been half-hearted, celebrating Easter had come at a price for some. Spiro, as his wife put it rather unkindly to him that morning, was not a drinking man. His head was throbbing from one, or six according to Maria, too many drinks, but as he had told little Anna as she helped him into his bed, "This is what we do back home, and one day you will celebrate, too."

"Mama," Anna had asked, almost too innocently, "how does being sick celebrate our Savior's resurrection?" Spiro growled and Maria shushed her daughter, not quite hiding the smile on her face.

"Spiro, come with us. You know you love baseball, and it'll take your mind off..." She hesitated and decided not to press the issue of what exactly had happened three nights ago. "Come on, you know your team is playing this morning."

He growled again, Maria shaking her head as she and her daughter left the tent.

Watson's murder barely played on Spiro's mind. The sheriff's office was investigating the death, but the list of potential suspects included virtually every husband in southern Colorado with a pretty wife. His head ached, the coffee tasted sour, and the tobacco smoke burnt his throat, but hearing the applause coming from the baseball diamond he decided that Maria was right and a game was just what the doctor would order. He'd never heard of baseball until he'd come to America, but at Berwind he had achieved a reputation as a hitter, and as he joined his wife and daughter, the captain called to him. "Finally, you show up. Okay, all the bases are loaded. You can step up. Knock this out and we win the game."

Spiro walked to the plate. His team, known as the Meds, was composed of Italian and Greek miners, most of them making up for their lack of skill with a raw enthusiasm for their new country's national pastime. Their opposition was a motley crew of miners from just about every other country in Europe. They were called the Misfits, and they had never been beaten. The diamond was surrounded by a wall of miners and their families, each cheering for their team.

Spiro took in the field. He pulled down the front of his cap and nodded to the umpire. The pitcher was Milan Lazovic, the big miner from Croatia. Spiro had played against the Balkan before. He didn't have much of a curve ball, but he could sling it down fast, probably, Spiro figured, from all the practice he gets on his wife. Spiro knew his best chance was to judge the flight of the ball and let his arm begin to swing just after the ball left the Lazovic's fingers. He had to let the ball do the work, not his arms.

The first ball flew by him like Spiro hadn't even been there. Strike one. *This guy is good,* Spiro told himself, *I need to concentrate. Damn this headache.* He cursed his stupidity of last night. He let the second one come through. It was low. But the third ball was good. It even had a bit of curve to it and it went into the catcher's mitts before Spiro even knew it had been thrown. Strike two. He had one ball left. The pitcher took his time, hoping to unnerve the little Greek in front of him. This time, Spiro knew his only chance was to start swinging before the ball had left the pitcher's hand and hope that it would be too late for the Croatian to change its flight.

The ball came down fast, really fast, but Spiro was ready for it. He caught the ball cleanly and it sailed high into the outfield. At first he thought it was too short and the fielder might catch it, but it flew over the man's outstretched arm and into the field beyond the fence. Spiro began to run as the fielders tried vainly to return the ball. First one, then two, then three batters made it home, and finally Spiro strolled in, for there was no need to run now. The nearest fielder to the ball was still climbing over the barbed-wire to try to fetch it. The Meds had won.

But although the Misfits had been beaten for the first time, Maria noticed that not even the winning players and their families seemed to care. The applause was perfunctory, and she realized that she too could hardly bother to cheer for her husband's victory.

Across the railroad track from the diamond, the militia tents moved gently in the breeze, their walls moving in and out as though alive. Troops milled around outside the tents, waiting for orders. Major Pat Hamrock was riffing through papers in his tent when Linderfelt came in, and helped himself to a mug of coffee.

"You know, Monte," Hamrock spoke without looking up from his desk, "we're pretty thin on the ground now most of our detachment has left. Have you thought of what happens if the union gives one last push to see us off?"

"I wouldn't worry too much about being outmanned, Pat. Two nights ago I signed up close to 150 men. They've formed a special company, Company A. And we've still got most of your company. They'll more than make up for the rest of the Guard going back to Denver."

"Company A. They're mostly mine guards, right? And such like."

Linderfelt nodded.

"So, most of them have no military training, Monte. I mean, do they even have officers, N.C.O.s?"

Linderfelt ignored the question and looked over to Ludlow. Finally, he spoke. "Pat, things are comin' to a head. They won't need training once the shooting starts. They'll know what to do. By the way, you heard Jones got released?"

"Yeah," the major replied. "I heard she's back in Denver, so that's one less thing to worry about, right?"

"Nah, she always thought she was more of a problem than she was. I don't worry about her one way or another. If she comes down here, we'll just lock her up again. Your boys look bored. Why don't you send them over to the game, they can see what's happening. Let them get involved."

Now that the baseball game was over, some of the families made their way to the front entrance of the camp to watch the Greek dancing. The dancers had scrounged enough material to make something approaching their local dresses: some wore the kilt-like *foustanella*, others white shirts, ballooning trousers and red sashes. One of them even had a pair of knee-length, leather boots, which Maria guessed he had brought along with him from Greece and lovingly cared for all those years. She saw instruments from her homeland – a lyra, a laouto, even a bouzouki – and thought nostalgically of her childhood on Crete. The men danced a number of different routines, but they seemed to find it difficult to get into the true spirit. Maria heard them shout the "opas" and clap in time to the music but everyone seemed disinterested, as though they were doing it out of habit, not spontaneity. The crowd clapped along, but they too seemed preoccupied. Not even the smell of the roasting lamb lifted their spirits.

After the dancing was over, some drifted back to the baseball diamond. Maria had promised Anna they would play a quick game with the other women and children. But ten minutes later the two of them were making their way back to their tent.

"Hey," Spiro called to them, as he saw them approaching. "What happened to the game?" He saw Anna's red eyes. "What happened, Maria? Why's she crying?"

Maria tried to bluster that their daughter was upset because she couldn't take a turn at bat right away. But Spiro knew better.

"Come on, wife, what's up?" he persisted.

"Spiro, nothing much, really, there were just a bunch of soldiers and they kept making stupid remarks. Nothing really, I think they were drunk. Anyways, I'm tired. It's okay."

Spiro would not let the matter drop.

"They said they were going to get us all tomorrow, but they were drunk, Spiro, you know what they're like. And that stupid Pearl Jolly tried to pick a fight with them, and Alci Pedragon and Mary Petrucci had to pull her away. She looks for trouble, that girl, I swear she does. Anyway, it's over now."

The incident at the baseball game cast a shadow over the rest of the day. There was not enough roast lamb to go around, and though a couple of dancers put on another display, most of the families wandered away back to their tents.

At four that afternoon, Lou Dold and Jimmy Dingle showed up but nobody was interested in their photographs.

"Mr. Dold, any idea what's goin' on here?" Jimmy scratched his head, perplexed. "You'd think it was a funeral."

Lou nodded his head slowly. "Beats me, Jimmy. Maybe they're just sick of this damned place. Who could blame them? Come on, let's pack up, there's nothing doing here."

The two photographers headed back to Trinidad and saw Louis Tikas walking down the road. His eyes were hooded and his brow was creased, but he still managed the briefest of smiles. The Greek was dressed in a black suit and tie. Jimmy thought he looked like an undertaker and was about to make a joke about it, but he was caught up in the despair that permeated Ludlow and kept his silence. Suddenly, even talking simply took too much effort.

23

Early next morning, Hamrock was busy at his desk, going through a set of daily orders from Chase's office. One in particular stood out. "Sergeant," he rasped, "I need three men. Now." Hamrock reread the message. *Goddam it, more trouble,* he cursed to himself, *and I'm so short of men, it ain't funny.*

The sergeant quickly reappeared with a corporal and two privates.

"Okay, lads, here's what I need you to do. Seems there's a woman complaining her husband is being held captive at Ludlow. I need you to go over there and find out what's what. Tikas the Greek should be there, find him. He's knows everything. And Sergeant, I need you to get a message to Lieutenant Linderfelt. Ask him to move troops to Water Tank Hill and make sure they're ready for action."

Tikas was sitting at a desk with his habitual cup of coffee. A group of miners followed the troopers into the tent to find out what they wanted. The corporal was about to speak when Tikas held up his hand and peremptorily told the miners to leave him and the troopers alone. His face tensed when they relayed Hamrock's message. "I can assure you there's nobody here that doesn't want to be. Look around if you want."

After the three soldiers had left, Fyler and the miners came back in, all of them demanding to know what had happened. More miners tried to jostle into the tent but were forced to stand outside, each of them craning their necks to hear what was being said. Tikas said nothing at first but finally gave them the gist of his meeting with the soldiers. Gradually the mumblings of discontent grew louder, as though a swarm of angry bees had invaded the tent. Finally, a single voice broke out above all the others. Tikas was surprised to hear it was Spiro.

"Louis, I just got here so I maybe don't know what all's gone on, but these guys told me that the guards said we had someone prisoner? And they told me you didn't do nothing, just let them go about their business." Tikas looked hard at his friend. Spiro felt uncomfortable but continued. "Tikas, you and me are friends, I'm behind you, you know that, but these guys are right, we just can't let them in whenever they want."

A miner standing behind Spiro shouted that enough was enough, they should get guns and take them all on. James Fyler immediately walked over to the man and told him to shut the fuck up, Tikas knew what he was doing.

The crowd was beginning to turn ugly when Tikas stood up from the table and motioned for them to be quiet. Waiting until he could be heard, he spoke very softly, so softly that they had to strain to catch his words.

"Boys, I hear you. I'm gonna' see Hamrock right now and tell him what I told his men. But don't you see, if there's gonna' be any shootin', it's them who's got to start it, not us. I've told you this all along. But when it does start, you know I'm with you."

Spiro and the other miners looked at each other, jumping on Tikas's use of the word 'when' not 'if'. As they piled out of the tent, now thick with cigarette smoke, Tikas shouted out to them, his voice cracking with emotion.

"Don't do anything crazy while I'm gone. And if you're gonna' start something, let me get back here at least. Okay? Okay?"

Spiro had never seen his friend so indecisive, as though he knew events were spinning out of control. *And the stupid thing about it,* Spiro told himself, *is that it was all over nothing; just a false rumor about a missing miner, who was probably holed up with his girlfriend even as they spoke.*

Later that morning, Spiro went with Tikas to meet Hamrock and the missing miner's wife at the Ludlow rail depot. Tikas carefully repeated what he had told the three soldiers, but further conversation was cut off by a young officer who excitedly burst in, shouting that the guards had now been deployed along Water

Tank Hill. Spiro was certain that Tikas nodded briefly to Hamrock before he left the tent and started running back towards the water tower. He half-turned in mid-stride. "Spiro, get back to to Ludlow. Get 'em ready for an attack just in case. I'll join you as soon as I can. But I've got to check this out."

The miners in Ludlow had seen the troop movement before the lieutenant had reached Hamrock and had armed themselves. But they were leaderless and did not know what to do. As he ran past the miners to get to his tent, Spiro yelled at them to stay where they were until he got back. He could almost feel the electricity crackling in the cool April air.

He flung open the thin wooden door to their tent.

"Maria, get the girl and hide. I got a feeling this is gonna' be bad," he barked at his wife.

"I don't know where Anna is, I, I think she's at Sally's. I'm not sure."

Spiro hugged his wife. "Well, get Anna and stay here so I know how to find you. Be careful."

Spiro ran back to the miners at the camp entrance. Tikas was nowhere to be seen and the miners looked at him expectantly.

"Look, Tikas is in charge here, I know, but we can't just sit here waiting, and he told me to get you ready. I want you lot," he shouted, pointing to twenty armed miners, "to go north and take up position in the arroyo. And some of you get over by the tracks. Take cover as best you can. Like Tikas said, don't do anything crazy. Just wait. We don't know what's happening yet but I don't like the number of soldiers on Water Tank Hill. It's a lot more than normal."

As they had done many times during the last seven months, two more groups of miners set up firing lines along the south and east sides of the camp. Spiro led the remaining men about a mile to the southeast and had them take up position in a railroad cutting that allowed them to rake Water Tank Hill. He figured this was the most dangerous position of the three he had deployed the men to, and he felt he had to be there for that reason. Spiro had the fit of yawns that always disappeared as soon as the action began. One of the miners nudged him and he saw Tikas running as fast as he could back to Ludlow. To Spiro, there was something vaguely comical in seeing the normally dapper little Greek, still in jacket, shirt and tie, boots laced high to his knees, waving a large red handkerchief in the general direction of the tent colony. But all thoughts of comic relief were quickly driven away when the machine guns began firing at the arroyo to the north of Ludlow and the militia laid down carbine fire on Spiro's command. The strikers needed no orders from anybody and immediately returned fire.

The families in Ludlow, burrowed down in the pits under their tents, heard the shriek of bullets flying above them, interrupted by the deeper rumble of the heavy machine guns. Mary Thomas, stuck in a pit with her children, cursed herself for being so headstrong. She had won the argument with her husband months before that their pit should be shallow to cut down on the dampness. But now she knew he had been right all along. Some of the bullets aimed towards the arroyo were cutting through the flimsy canvas of their tent. Looking up, Mary thought it looked like the tent was made of a lace curtain. One bullet smashed into the stove pipe and ricocheted wildly before careening out though a gash in the roof. She had endured firing on the camp before when the militia had put volleys over the tops of the tents for something to do. But this morning the volleys were heavier and more concentrated than she had ever experienced; and they were hitting the tents, something that had never happened before.

"Kids, come on, we need to leave," she screamed. Waiting for a brief lull in the firing, the family climbed out, as close to the ground as they could get. Mary saw other families doing the same, some because like hers the pits weren't deep enough, others because they just needed to run, anywhere, as long as it was away from the firing. Mary's eyes settled on the pump house fifty meters to her north. Scooping up her children, she ran as fast as she could and crashed through the door. Other families were already there. The wooden shack, she quickly realized, was too small for all of them because most of it was taken up with heavy machinery. Lying on the floor, hoping the ground could swallow them whole, each of the mothers tried to figure where they would go next. Bullets began to rip through the walls, sending up huge splinters of wood. Thomas heard a child's shriek and looking up she saw that a chunk of flying wood had sliced into the arm of a six-year-old girl. For the first time, Mary realized that the families were not alone. Curled up in the corner was a bald man in his sixties, looking calm in spite of the mayhem all around. Their eyes met and both tried to smile.

"My name's Low, I'm charge of this place," the man replied to her raised eyebrows. "This is a death trap, lady, we all need to get out of here."

Mary nodded in agreement. "I think your best bet," he continued, "is to make for the well. It's real deep and made of concrete. You should be fine there. And it's not far away. I'm heading for my shack."

The thought of going outside appalled the Welshwoman; at least the pump house gave her an allusion of safety. But just then a bullet crashed through the window, sending slivers of glass everywhere.

"He's right," she cried to the others, "we've gotta' get out of here."

Making sure her kids were ready, Mary opened the door, took a deep breath and raced to the well, her children bouncing along in her arms. She didn't look behind. *If the others want to come with me,* she told herself, *good, but it's their funeral if they don't.*

The family got to the edge of the well and rolled themselves in. It was not full to the brim as the spring run-off hadn't yet started in earnest. The drop to the surface was long and they hit the water hard. There was a thin coating of algae on top and Mary spluttered as she took in a mouthful. As soon as she came back to the surface, she looked around and grabbed her children, keeping them together as they made their way over to a concrete platform on the well wall. They climbed up onto the platform and although her children were still waist-deep in water they were at least out of the line of fire. In family groups or singly, more and more women and children jumped into the well.

Many families, especially those closest to the militia, stayed in their pits, unwilling to face the heavy firing. The Pedragon family's pit was in the southwest corner of Ludlow. It was six feet deep and eight feet long with an entrance hole only three feet in diameter, and Pedragon had reinforced the pit with timbers. There his wife Alcarita and their two children, together with Fedelina Costa, well along in her pregnancy, and her young son and daughter took shelter, completely safe from the firing overhead; they could hear the bullets zipping over them, but their mothers kept hushing them and reminding them their papas would be home soon.

Late in the morning, they heard someone shouting for them. Alcarita looked gingerly over the top of the entrance hole and saw the face of Patria Valdez. Crowding around her were her four children, the youngest of whom had been born in the camp a few months earlier. "Our pit is in a bad way, Alci. It's too shallow and the kids are frightened. Can I come in?"

Alci looked around, reluctant to make her pit even more cramped, but the look on the children's faces left her no choice. Patria had brought a small bag of bread with her, and she shared it with the children old enough to eat solid food.

Patria said, "There's a bunch of women and children in the well. There's some in the ditch to the north, but the men have got us defended good, so I think we're okay if we stay here."

Alcarita nodded in agreement. "It's gotta' end soon. They don't have enough bullets to keep this up." She adjusted her position in the damp earth as one of her children snuggled deep into her thigh. "We'll be okay. We'll just stay here until the men get us."

Maria ran to the Hoffmans' tent. "Thank God, you're here, Anna. Come on, let's go." She pulled her daughter up from the pit and rushed her back to their tent. She yelled back at the Hoffmans. "Spiro says it's bad; stay in your hole, don't move, and pray to God."

"Anna, help me." Maria burst through the tent door and began to tear open the duckboards over their pit. "Grab that water and bread." Anna dithered, but her mother was in no mood for kindness.

"Now, little girl," she screamed at the ten-year-old who hastily passed the water and food to her mother before jumping in. The two of them crouched in the bottom of the pit, like they had done a dozen times before. The smell was the same, damp and musty, and tinged with the odor of unwashed human bodies, and the canvas on the walls was beginning to rot, but they were safe, at least for the moment. The bullets kept smashing bits of crockery and picture frames and the shards rained down on top of them. Maria protected Anna from the flying fragments with her own body, and Maria knew their situation would soon become intolerable.

"Mama, why can't we leave? I'm frightened." Anna's whimpers were getting to Maria, but she had promised Spiro they would stay where they were. "Mama, I'm thirsty and the water's gone." Maria was angry at herself for not stocking up the pit with more water, but realized there was nothing she could do about that now.

"Papa will be back soon. He'll come and get us." She tried to sound convincing but knew she wasn't.

A machine-gun bullet smashed into one of the tent poles. It began to bend and then with a loud snap broke in two. Half of the tent collapsed in on itself, blocking the entrance to their pit. Anna screamed and Maria hugged her as close as she could. The two of them lay in the near total darkness, rocking each other and screaming in fear as bullet after bullet slashed through the canvas.

Maria could not believe she might have dozed but it was as though she was awaking from a deep sleep. "Maria, are you there?" The voice was faint. "Maria, for God's sake, let me know if you're there." Now the voice was louder. She heard movement overhead and realized that somebody was trying to pull the tent away from the entrance to the pit. "Maria, it's me, Pearl. Pearl Jolly. Are you there?"

Maria jolted herself into action. "Pearl, it's me, Maria, and I've got Anna."

Pearl's voice was brusque. "Come on, let's get you out."

Maria could not hear the machine guns and for one beautiful moment thought the fighting was over. But an ugly burst of fire in the distance ended her fantasy.

"Maria, I don't know why they stopped, but they have. Come on, let's get out of here. Hand me Anna. Now."

Suddenly light streamed into the pit as Pearl pulled away the last of the tent to reveal a clear blue sky. She wore a nurse's uniform and a bright red cross adorned both her sleeves and the white bib of her apron. Maria looked around. Many of the tents were like hers, either fully or partly collapsed, and all of them, so far as she could see, were shredded by gunfire.

"Maria, listen to me." Pearl's voice was hard. "We're gonna' make for the well. It's safe there, but we've got to hurry, in case they start again. Anna, you've gotta' run like you never ran in your life. Pretend Frank's after you, eh?"

Anna gulped and nodded.

"Come on now. Run."

The three of them took off as fast and as low as they could. A machine gun began firing and Maria saw bullets whipping up the earth. Anna and Maria flung themselves into the well, not caring who they knocked over. Maria immediately turned around to the lip of the well and saw Pearl about ten yards out, running like the Hounds of Hell were after her.

"No!" Maria screamed at the top of her voice. Maria saw Pearl go down in a cloud of dust. She tried to leap over the lip but someone pulled her back.

Pearl lay still, but suddenly she jumped up, hobbled the last few yards and rolled over into the well. Maria hugged her. "I thought you were…"

Pearl interrupted her, laughing with relief. "I thought I was too. I thought they'd hit my foot, but look." She took off her right shoe to show everybody that its heel had been shot off by a bullet. "I swear to God, I'll be sending a receipt for damages to our General Chase. Now, I've got more work to do."

As she got ready to scramble over the lip of the rim, Maria grabbed her arm. "Pearl, I don't know how to say it. I, I. Thank you, and God bless you."

Pearl smiled back. "It's my job. I'm the camp nurse, you see." She caressed Maria's cheek briefly then leant over and kissed Anna on the head. "Don't worry, I'll be back. See ya'." And she was gone.

"I guess we all got her wrong, didn't we?" Maria turned towards the voice and saw Mary Thomas.

"I don't know what to say, Mary. She is so brave, and I was a crying baby."

"I wouldn't worry much. We're all different. You did just fine. Hey," Mary changed the subject, "at least we're safe here, right, pet?"

"I just wish I knew Spiro was alright. I saw him an hour ago. I guess he's with the rest of the men."

"Well, I know it sounds hard, but there's nothing we can do about that. And my man's off too, so I guess we're all in the same boat, or well!"

Relief began to wash over Maria, as her stomach muscles loosened and the adrenalin slowed in her veins. She started to giggle.

"Hey, Mary Thomas, wanna' hear something funny? Spiro, you know what he said? He said be careful. Can you believe that? Be careful. Men…always saying the, what's the word, the obvious."

"That's nothing, mine said the same thing, oh and *keep your head down*. Like I was gonna' do anything else. Oh, and here's somethin' else. You know when we got out of jail after the march, right?" Maria nodded. "Well, the big lummox picks me and the kids up and the first thing he says is, 'Have you thought about what's to eat tonight?'" Mary began to laugh hysterically and Maria joined in, and soon the two of them were in gales of laughter at the stupidity of men in general and husbands in particular. Their children looked on in astonishment as the two women wiped the tears from their eyes.

Shouting to make themselves heard over the firing, Linderfelt and Hamrock plotted their next moves.

"Pat, we need to get those bastards out of the railroad cut." He pointed to where Spiro and his men were deployed. "We should send out two platoons. Get one to work their way to the cutting. I want the miners pushed back to the camp. Put the other to stopping miners from leaving Ludlow. And I'm gonna' take a platoon and work my way north. As I see it, if we fire on the tents, it'll draw them back to defend the camp. And that's exactly where we want them. We need to get them into as small a killing field as possible."

Hamrock knew that a lieutenant was telling a major what to do. But Hamrock had served in the Indian Wars and knew the strategy made sense, and Linderfelt knew the lay of the land much better than he did, anyway. Hamrock gave his command their field orders and the men moved out.

Linderfelt established his men west of Ludlow with orders to pin everybody down who moved and ran back to the militia tents where Hamrock had just received word from Chase, in Denver, that they were to hold their position.

"The general assured me we've got help on its way. Plus more ammo."

Linderfelt grunted his satisfaction. "Pat, this time we've got them, you know that don't you. This is the big one, the one we've been waiting for. You know, he's only an eye doctor but that Chase sure as hell knows what he's doing. We'll finish it off today for good. I know it."

Hamrock didn't reply. The phrase 'killing field' kept repeating itself in his mind. He had been around the block, as he told himself, he knew about killing, even if it was only useless Indians, but there were women and children down in Ludlow. To Hamrock, Linderfelt sounded like he was bloodlusted, willing to push the conflict way beyond what was needed to win the day. He remembered a young lieutenant at Wounded Knee back in 1890, when the cavalry had finished off the Sioux. He had kept firing his Hotchkiss Gun long after every Indian was dead. There was a look on the young's man face that was ecstatic, sexual even. He now saw that same look on Linderfelt and he inwardly shuddered.

"How many men are we getting? Do you know?" Linderfelt's question brought Hamrock back to the present.

"Probably close to a hundred, maybe more. A lot of 'em are mine guards."

Linderfelt looked at the major and whispered smugly, "So, they'll know what to do." An ugly smile passed over the lieutenant's face but was quickly gone.

So far, Spiro and his men had not seen any real action. The machine guns were concentrating on the camp, and the militia fire aimed at Spiro and his men from Water Tank Hill was intended only to keep their heads down. He could see the camp from his position but the distance was too great to identify individuals. He told himself that Maria was a sensible woman and had taken Anna to safety, but the sight of tents being shredded and collapsing did not make him confident.

He snapped out his thoughts when he saw two groups of soldiers moving towards him. They were not well-trained men, he realized, for they didn't use the undulating prairie as cover for their movements. The miners opened fire. It was over in seconds. Spiro saw guardsmen fall from the withering volley. He told his men to cease fire, and in the lull the soldiers began to take their wounded into cover in a small hollow.

"Finally," Spiro shouted to the man next to him, "they're usin' the ground properly." One of the machine guns on Water Tank Hill swiveled towards them. "We're goin' to get it now, boys," Spiro yelled. Unable to poke their heads above the cut as the machine gun systematically traversed the ridge, all they could do was lay low as soil and grass exploded above their heads.

"No good, boss, can't fire from here," one of his men cried out in frustration. They all looked at Spiro, wondering what to do.

Spiro nodded. "Okay, we've done all we can do here, let's head back. Make for the Black Hills. Tikas told me that'd be our fallback position."

His men began to run down the slope away from the firing. He got up to follow them but carelessly, stupidly, he moved too near to the lip of the cutting. A machine gun bullet struck a pebble and ricocheted into Spiro's right arm.

"Christ almighty, fuckin' son of a whore, I've been hit." He slithered down the bank, bright red blood flowing down his arm.

One of his men ran back and ripped away his shirt. "Don't worry, boss, I've done this before. It looks worse than it is, what with you pumped up an' all. The bullet didn't go in you. I'm pretty sure it just sliced you open, okay?"

Spiro's arm was burning like it was full of hot iron. The miner pulled a small bottle of whiskey out of his pocket, took a slug, gave one to Spiro and poured the rest of the bottle over the wound, Spiro screaming that it was worse than the actual wound.

"Stop your bawlin'," the miner yelled. "I've seen worse on my kid's knees." He clamped a rag over the wound and expertly tied it tight with a piece of cord. The whole operation took just over a minute. "You'll be okay now, Spiro. Honest. But you'll need to get it wrapped up proper soon." Spiro grimaced as the whiskey continued to burn into the cut, but thanked him just the same.

Spiro and his men made it back to the Black Hills. Looking over the battlefield he saw that most of the militia fire was still being directed towards the tents and that fighting had opened up again along the railroad tracks. He met with Tikas as soon as he had guzzled down some brackish water and got his wound cleaned. Tikas was brusque, asking about his wound as though he did not really care.

"Louis, I think we've got more men but I don't know how long we can last."

"I agree. The militia is definitely sending in more men from Trinidad and Walsenburg. Lawson's gonna' try to round up more of ours, but they'll still outgun us. He's out here, you know. I saw him about thirty minutes ago. He's scared, like we all are, but he told me we've got no choice now but to hang on and hope we can get enough men together. I think he's off to Trinidad for more help."

"What do you think, my friend?" Spiro looked hard at Tikas who seemed uncertain how to answer.

Finally, very softly, he replied. "Lawson's right, we can't stop now. My hope is that the two sides figure out nobody can win, and we call a truce. I want that to happen. Spiro, have you seen what they're doin' to Ludlow?"

As soon as the words came out, Tikas winced. "I'm sorry, Spiro. Maria and Anna are okay. I know it. They're tough women, those two, especially the little one." He grinned at Spiro but it was forced, and Spiro knew it. A shiver of fear ran through his body. Not for the first time Spiro asked himself what the hell he was doing in the middle of nowhere fighting other Americans like they were the Turks.

Tikas knew that the sides were evenly matched; about two hundred men each. But even his untrained mind recognized that his enemy had all the advantages of military leadership, heavier weapons and a better ammunition supply. Plus, and in his eyes it was the biggest problem facing the miners, the militia controlled the high ground of Water Tank Hill. He desperately needed to talk to Lawson about the promised reinforcements. Through his field glasses he could see that the soldiers, inexplicably, had still not cut down the telephone line from the headquarters tent. He reasoned that they would spot that error sooner rather than later. Skirting the eastern edge of the camp, keeping low and hiding in the natural prairie dips as much as he could, he then bolted hard. He rushed into the tent, saw Joe hiding in a pit, grabbed the phone and lay on the ground. He was amazed that he got through to Lawson as quickly as he did. But running the gauntlet had been pointless. Lawson did not have good news. His only advice was to hang on and he'd try to get them help. He'd sent Livoda and others out to round up volunteers. Tikas made his way back to the arroyo, swinging well to the east to avoid the volley fire as much as he could.

"We should be safe, Maria, the firin' ain't so bad. Are you ready for this?"

Maria looked at Mary Thomas, terrified for what she was about to do. "Anna, you stay with Nora. Do what she tells you, my love."

Nora Davis put her arm around Anna's shoulders. "Don't worry, Anna, it's real safe. Your mum will be fine."

Anna was not convinced and told her mama exactly that, but

Maria had decided that she had been passive too long. All around her people were being heroes, her husband included. It was time for her to get involved.

"Okay, let's go." Mary took a deep breath, climbed out of the well and ran towards the boxcar, followed closely by Maria. The abandoned rolling stock was the pumpman's home, and Low had shouted to the women in the well that he had food for them if they could get to it. The thirty yards seemed an eternity, but the two women made it safely and gratefully barged through the door. Low started filling an old burlap sack with vegetables, fruit and a few loaves of bread.

"I've got more if you can risk another run. And here's a couple of jugs of water. You'll need this more than the food."

Mary started to thank him, but as if in embarrassment the old man shrugged and turned away. "Get away, woman. Anyways, what am I supposed to do? Watch children go hungry?"

Maria picked up the jugs while Mary cradled the sack in her arms, trying to find the right position for it. Impulsively, Mary put the sack down and walked over to Low. She kissed him gently on both cheeks. "I'll never forget his. And tonight I say a prayer for you."

The pumpman's cheeks flushed red. Gruffly he said, "You ladies be careful, now." Then more softly, "And I am praying for you and your families, too."

Imagining a lull in the firing, they waited until the pumpman opened the door and then they retraced their steps. Maria saw a line of bullets flicking up dust as they traced their way towards her and for one ghastly minute she thought they would reach her, but they abruptly stopped and she and Mary gratefully dove back into the well.

"Nora, you're good at this. Hand this stuff out," Mary ordered her. "Maria, you up for one more trip? I am. Let's get some food over to the arroyo. I bet they're as hungry as us." Mary's voice rang with confidence and Maria nodded.

Making their way safely to the boxcar they greedily drank down a cup of water.

"You'd better have this, too," he said and handed the two women a bottle of whiskey.

Maria shook her head, but Mary slugged it down, telling him that rotgut never tasted so good. She laughed as the liquid helped calm her nerves. As Mary sipped on another whiskey, Maria risked a look out of the window that Low had cut into the side of the car, trying to work out their best route to get to the arroyo. To the south she could see the tents being slowly and systematically shredded. Occasionally a woman made a run for it, but the bullets would begin to trace a line to her and she would scurry back to where she had started.

"Dear God. No!" Maria yelled involuntarily. Mary and Low joined her at the window and saw a man running straight across the camp towards the arroyo. The bullets were catching up with him. "I know him, it's Charlie Costa. He must think his wife and kids are in the arroyo."

Costa was a young man, barely in his thirties, and he ran quickly, zigzagging to avoid the bullets. "Do it, son, do it. You can make it," Low cried as if his words might put added power into the miner's legs.

"He's going to make it," Mary cried exultantly, for Charlie was now only a couple of yards from the lip of the arroyo and safety. But as the words came out of her mouth, his whole body arched as a bullet caught him in the middle of the back. The impact threw him into the arroyo and he slithered obscenely to the bottom, pushing up a wall of earth and stones as he descended. A miner ran over to him. He was barely alive. The miner cradled Charlie in his arms as his blood coursed out of the wound. Charlie looked up and mumbled "Union Forever." Then his eyes went blank and the miner gently laid the body on the ground and covered his face with his coat, not knowing what else to do.

"Dear God, no, go back," Maria shouted with all the strength she could muster, for haring across the killing field was another miner.

John Bartolotti had been put in the southern firing line by Spiro. All day he had stayed at his post, firing at the militia trying to work their way down the railroad lines. Now it was afternoon.

He turned to his partner. "I've gotta' go, I'm no good here, worrying about them. But I'll be back. Okay?"

Bartolotti took a deep breath and made a mad dash for the headquarters tent, the nearest one, feeling that every militia barrel in southern Colorado was aimed just at him. The miner jumped through the tent flap and dove for cover in the pit dug in the corner. Catching his breath he saw he was not alone.

"Hi, Joe, hot day, eh?" he joked to the old miner in charge of Ludlow's supplies.

"I've seen worse, Johnny boy, I've seen worse, though for the life of me I can't remember when."

They sat there for a few minutes, mesmerized, as a particularly heavy volley of fire shredded most of the north and south walls of the tent. Then the two of them heard the fire switch elsewhere, and Bartolotti asked if Joe knew whether the women and children were safe.

"All, I know," Joe replied, "is that I haven't seen no one leave. Anyways, you'd have seen them from where you were, right?"

Bartoloti nodded. "Of course, I guess I'm not thinking."

"That's okay, no problem. Maybe they're under your tent." Joe smiled and the calmness of the older man helped Bartolotti.

"I did hear, John, that a bunch of 'em are in the well, you know the one over by the pump station. That's about the safest place in the whole camp."

Guessing what the miner was thinking, Joe chastised him. "John, don't be a fool. It's too dangerous out there, you know that."

"Joe, it's my family, I need to know."

"John," Joe's voice took on an edge, "if they're alive, they're alive, and if they're not, well, there's nothing you can do about it."

"But it's not your family we're talking about here, is it?" Bartolotti's voice was angrier than he intended. Softer, he added, "I'll be fine. I'm not crazy."

Bartolotti stood up and ran out, making first for his own tent. It was still standing and he dove in through the door flaps. He scrabbled over to the pit, but it was empty. The well was less than a minute's fast run and he decided to make a straight line for it. As he ran, the world closed in on him. The bullets flying around him sounded dull, not like the sharp cracks he had got used to. As he saw the well getting closer and closer, the world formed a tunnel wide enough just for him. Nothing else existed. He heard his breath as he snatched at the thin Colorado air. He heard himself wheezing as a long winter in the camp caught up with his forty-five years. He tasted the bitter almond in his mouth as the adrenaline pumped through his veins. And then he tasted the salt of the blood rising up from his punctured lungs as four bullets slammed into his body. The miner crashed to the ground. His body twitched for a few seconds and then it was still.

Mary collapsed to the floor of the boxcar. "I can't take this no more, I hate it, I hate them. He had a wife and two kids. What'll they do now? What'll they do now? What'll any of us do now?"

The pumpman took her in his arms and rocked her like a baby as she cried out her anger and misery until no more tears were left. Maria slumped down against the wall, and cried with her friend and prayed that the killing would stop before they all were dead.

The women and children in the well were miserable, up to their knees in icy water, hungry and unable to see what was going on around them. But at least they could breathe fresh air. Many of the miners and their families had not escaped the tents and now they had been trapped in their pits for six hours. They were losing their sanity as their whole world was confined to what they could hear but not see; tents shredded, stoves, beds, even coffee pots ringing as the bullets blasted them, crockery smashed, a lifetime of savings, a lifetime of family memories, all gone as the pitiless bullets ricocheted above their heads.

The Hoffmans were at least all together. William, the head of the family, had no rifle in his tent when the firing started and did not join the other miners at the firing lines. They had not eaten or drunk anything since breakfast. Hoffman never kept food in his tent pit, and the younger children were crying as hunger gripped their stomachs. Fear produced a constant craving for the water that was long gone. William realized that they needed to get something inside them fast.

He looked at his wife. "No, Bill, it's not safe," she replied. "We'll have to stay here."

"Look at the kids. They're all scared shitless. They can't go much longer. And we all need food and drink. Let's wait for a break and make for the supply tent. I can't believe they'd fire on women and children."

His wife pursed her lips but said nothing. She, too, was tempted by the thought of food and drink, even if it might only be bread and water, and anything had to be better than skulking in this hole. She finally nodded in agreement.

Suddenly, for reasons Hoffman could not figure out, the volley fire stopped and all they could hear were the machine guns to the north. "Stay here so I can make sure."

"Dad." It was Frank. "I just looked under the tent wall and it looks clear. I mean, I don't see nothin' gettin' shot up. I think it's safe."

William looked at his wife and they nodded to each other.

Elsie picked up her two youngest children. "Sally, you stay with Daddy. And leave your dolly behind, we'll get her later, I promise. We're gonna' get away from here. We'll be safe then."

Frank crawled over to her. "Hey, sis," he said gently. "It's okay. Dad an' me, we'll look after you. Trust me? And we'll come back and get Greta." Tears and snot ran down the little girl's face, streaking the dust on her cheeks.

"When I say run, run!" William shouted.

Cautiously the family edged out of the tent. Frank looked back at Sally and smiled. "Hey, sis, I'm gonna' get you the biggest cup of water you ever had. Sounds good, huh?"

"Now. Run!" The family sprang up, led by Frank. But the little boy had taken only three paces, when his body was whipped around. A large splash of something red swirled around his head. He crumpled to the ground.

"Frank, are you hurt?" his mother cried.

"Keep the kids back," William yelled at his wife. Crawling toward Frank, he saw that the back of his head was missing. Skin and hair flopped over where the skull had once been and he could see his son's brain, livid gray and shiny.

His mother tried to run over to them, but the bullets were still traversing the open prairie and William crawled back quickly and pulled his wife down. "We can't do nothing. He's gone, God rest his soul. Don't let the kids see him. Get them back in the pit. I'll look after him."

Elsie lay on the prairie sod, paralyzed with the knowledge that her son Frank, the joker of the family, the helper of anybody in the camp who needed him, the little boy who wanted nothing more than to be a man, was gone. She heard Sally asking if he was alright. She shook her head. The bullets began striking the earth around her and finally she moved the rest of her family back to the safety of their pit.

William lay next to his son's body, shock preventing him from recognizing the full enormity of what had happened. He took a rag from his pocket and rubbed some of the blood off Frank's face. He tried to spit on the rag but his mouth was dry. Finally, as bullets traced their way closer and closer to him, he kissed his son's cheek, lay the handkerchief across the face, untouched and serenely young, and crawled back to join his family.

24

Dusk crept across Ludlow.

"You look tired, Pat."

"Monte, I am. Dead Tired. All I want is a warm bed and a good slug or two of whiskey. Don't even know how many men I've lost. God knows how many miners are dead." He shrugged as he was past caring.

"Well, Pat, if we can keep up the machine gun fire into the tents, it'll soon be over. Look, I've still got that kid and his platoon firing into Ludlow. I'm gonna' go and meet up with them, see how they're doin'. Are you okay, stayin' here and mannin' the phone line?"

"No problem. You know, in the last hour their return fire is a lot less. I think you're right, it'll all soon be over."

Linderfelt joined the young lieutenant and ordered him to keep suppressing fire on the tents and across the open land between the colony and the arroyo. He also ordered a small group to try to outflank the arroyo from the west. The young officer looked at him questioningly.

"Sir, I think we've won. They hardly return our fire."

On any other day, Linderfelt would have told the young man to shut his mouth but certain victory had made him magnanimous. "Son, ever heard of a pincer movement? If we trap them in the arroyo, we'll have the lot of them. Then we can all go home."

As directed, the group of soldiers crouched low and moved north before swinging to the west. But Tikas had spotted them.

"Spiro, take five men and keep an eye on that group. Hold your fire until they're real close. Then you know what to do."

Spiro looked at the group of miners; different nationalities, different ages. At a small bend in the gully Spiro arranged his men along the top so that they were facing west. The troopers were cocky. They kept below the line of the railroad tracks as much as they could but they were coming too quickly to be careful, and as they came into range, Spiro and his men opened fire. The exchange was brief. Two of the attackers went down and the rest of the soldiers retreated.

"Well done, boys," Spiro shouted exultantly. "Come on, let's head back. I'm gonna' check with Tikas. See what he wants us to do next."

He found Tikas laying on the edge of the arroyo, looking north towards the camp.

"We got them, there's..."

But Tikas held his hand up in interruption. "Look," he said, and he pointed to the tents. "By the gate, look," he repeated to Spiro's questioning gaze.

Now Spiro saw it, too. The tents in the southwest corner of Ludlow were on fire.

"Jesus, Louis, you think there's people in them?"

"How the hell do I know but yeah, I'd think there are. Right now, there's nothing we can do for them."

Private Fred Johnson was a drifter, but he had finally found regular employment as a rifleman in Company A. Positioned with three other troopers at the south end of Ludlow, he saw smoke coming from a tent.

"Must have been the bullets set something on fire. See that drum over there? Betcha' it's full of oil. Wanna help it along?"

"Fred, there's women and children out there. Come on, knock it off," one of them shouted back at him.

"Listen shithead, I heard the lieutenant say we should smoke 'em out. Hey, we're just followin' orders."

A boy in his late teens lying on his back, rolled over and made to get up. "I'll check with the sergeant."

Johnson angrily pulled him back down. "Like hell you will. I'm in charge here and I say what goes. But if you're chicken, get the hell outta' here. We don't need you."

Johnson and the two others crawled forward towards the oil drum. The machine gun fire had ceased, and the militia along the west side of Ludlow could see what they were doing. No officer stopped them. The three entered what looked to be a deserted camp. Two of the tents in the southwest corner were on fire, and the soldiers took brooms that were standing up against the remains of the supply tent, dipped them in oil, set them on fire and ran them up and down the walls of the other tents, starting with the line that formed the southern edge of the colony. The canvas was old and dried out by the incessant prairie winds and the line of tents quickly went up in flames as the evening breeze blew blazing canvas from tent to tent. More troopers joined Johnson. Some grabbed pieces of dry brush that had been stacked for kindling; others took newspapers and threw them into the tents themselves. Thick black smoke began to wrap the colony like a death shroud.

Through the crackling of the flames the troopers could hear the panicked cries of the women and children as they tried to escape the infernos blazing all around. Some troopers helped women and children to safety. One young trooper tried to pull back one of the men from setting fire to another tent, but he was pushed down and kicked hard as the frenzy of hate possessed the militia. And as miners tried to climb out of the arroyo to help heavy rifle fire from the railroad tracks drove them back them down.

Alci Pedragon, Fedelina Costa and Patria Valdez were certain their husbands would be back for them. But now that the sun was setting below the hills and darkness creeping rapidly across the tent colony, they felt the first pangs of real doubt. And still the firing was intense. All they could do was wait and drift in and out of sleep.

"Thank God, finally." Pedragon woke the others. "I can hear a woman's voice. That's gotta' be good, right?" Looking up they saw the face of Mary Petrucci looking down at them. She had her three children with her, the youngest, Franco, not yet six months old and clasped tight to his mother's breast.

Alci stood up stiffly. "Help me get out, Mary, I feel a hundred years old."

Mary did not move. "No, you don't understand. You've gotta' stay where you are. Troopers are coming into the camp. They're setting the tents on fire." Without invitation, she virtually threw her three children into the pit, quickly followed by herself.

"What the, watch my stomach, can't you see I'm…" but Fedelina Costa was cut off by the Italian woman's plea.

"The kids are beat, they can't take it. You've got to let me stay. Goddamn it. Let me in. Where else do I go, they already set fire to my tent." The woman was only in her early twenties, but had reached the end of her strength, both physical and mental.

"Well, I see as how we've got no choice, have we?" Pedragon said curtly.

"Lord, look at us," Fedelina joked. "Four women and a bunch of kids in a pit the size of a latrine. Mary, are you sure they fired your tent? I mean, it wasn't an accident."

"Jesus, I don't know. My tent caught on fire, we barely got out, and troopers are everywhere. So, what do you think? I hate those bastards." She snuggled into her three children to give them what little comfort she could.

The Pedragon tent went up in flames. The women and children heard a loud whoosh as the canvas above them was engulfed. They tried to get out of the pit, but the burning canvas and tent poles collapsed, covering the entrance hole and forcing them back. Thick smoke bellowed into the pit, the children terrified as they clung to their mothers. Everybody was coughing and tears poured from their eyes as the smoke blinded them. Alcarita burned her hands and arms as she tried to push the burning mass away from the hole. Mary Petrucci joined in but her sleeve caught on fire. The women and children yelled as hard as they could, but all of them were retching, and their screams could not be heard. Costa and Valdez ripped their skirts to serve as masks for the children to help them breathe, but that just seemed to scare them even more. The smoke poured in, clogging their lungs and burning their eyes. A cabinet, set on a chest of drawers in the tent, toppled down in flames over the pit. Gradually the cries for help became weaker and then altogether ceased. First the children and then their mothers collapsed, and soon there was only silence.

The darkness of night was now almost complete, and only the flames from the burning tents illuminated Ludlow. A train steamed by on its way to Trinidad. The engineer saw tents exploding like pine trees in a forest fire, paper and clothing tossing in the thermals and dancing twenty feet into the evening sky. Troopers moved through the tent colony even as other soldiers fired across the dead ground south of the arroyo. The engineer decided to bring the train to a dead halt immediately west of Ludlow, blocking the line of fire of the troopers and giving some protection to the women and children trying to make it to the arroyo.

"Move this train now. That's an order." The engineer looked down from his platform at a sergeant wielding a gun at him.

"There's women and children there, you're killin' 'em, so fuck you."

"Move the train. Now." The sergeant cocked his carbine and pointed it straight at the engineer. Reluctantly, the engineer moved the train on. It had been stopped only ten minutes but it was enough time for many of the families hiding in their tent pits to make it to the arroyo.

The women and children in the well also made it to safety. Maria and Anna slid into the arroyo, scarcely able to believe that the drenched nightmare was over. Maria hugged Anna but the little girl struggled free.

"Mama, I think I see Papa. Over there. Look." The little girl pointed to a clump of armed men thirty yards away lying down on the arroyo lip. It was almost dark, but Maria could recognize the profile of her husband illuminated by a lantern at the bottom of the arroyo.

She heard someone shout his name. It took Maria a moment to realize it was her own voice. At first Spiro did not hear. But finally one of his men turned around and pointed out the two of them to him. Spiro ran the distance faster than he thought possible. Ignoring the constant throbbing pain in his arm, he slid down the slope of the arroyo, and jumped into his family's arms. The three of them said nothing, just held each other tight, Anna kissing his face and burrowing herself deep into her father, Maria embracing the two of them, never wanting to let them go.

"I thought I'd lost you," Spiro finally choked out. "I looked for you but I didn't see you come in. I thought..." but Maria gently placed two fingers over his mouth.

"Ssshhh, you didn't. We're here."

"What happened, where were you?"

But Maria just shook her head. "Time for that later, time for that later." She sank wearily onto the arroyo slope. "Spiro, your arm!" she screamed, seeing for the first time the blood-stained bandage poking out from under his shirt sleeve.

"It's nothing, no really, it's nothing. I'm fine. It just aches."

Maria stood up to get fresh linen, but Spiro pulled her down. "Maria, the best medicine for me right now is you two."

"Papa, I'm thirsty," Anna cried weakly.

"Of course, my child, I'll be back." Spiro was glad to do the mundane tasks of life again. He returned with a canteen of water and an open can of mixed fruit in syrup. He cradled Anna's face gently in his hands and kissed the top of her head. "Get this down you. You, too, Maria." He looked at his wife, sadness filling his eyes. "It's over, my love. They've won. Come, look."

Fatigue washed over Maria but she managed to climb to the

top of the arroyo with Spiro and as she looked out over what had been their home, she knew he was right. Thick black smoke still hung over the field, unmoved by the evening breeze. The only things standing were the remains of cast-iron beds and stoves, each surrounded by burnt debris, all that remained of a family's possessions. The smell of charred canvas, clothing and gasoline wafted across to the arroyo. They heard an explosion and everybody in the arroyo cowered, but it was only cans of fuel igniting.

Now there was no firing, and calm descended over the battlefield. Although some tents still smoldered, the troopers were now busy with stealing what objects the fires hadn't destroyed. James Fyler's wife tried to stop the militia ransacking the remains of her tent, but she was pushed away roughly. A few troopers tried to stop the looters, but they were in the minority and they soon left the field, too embarrassed to survey or even acknowledge what they had done.

Spiro and Maria were about to slip down to the arroyo bottom, when they saw a horrific sight. Walking slowly from their tent were the Hoffmans, led by William. In his arms he carried the body of his dead son. Mrs. Hoffman, Sally and the other children followed behind as in a funeral cortege. They did not hurry. Erect and dignified they walked slowly to the arroyo. At its edge, William handed his daughter to one of the miner's wives. Still holding Frank's body, he sat down. Only then did the tears begin to flow down his cheeks.

Maria and Anna went over to them to give what little comfort they could. William cradled Frank's body, holding it tight as though he might force life back into it yet. Over the boy's head, to give him some dignity, his mother had carefully placed a towel she had scavenged from one of the tents. Her children lay around her, frightened, confused, in shock. Sally half-opened her eyes when she heard Anna's voice and as her friend sat down next to her, she curled into her body. Only the occasional shudder told

Anna her friend was still alive.

"What'll you do?"

William and his wife looked at Maria, uncomprehending. "I suppose, well, we can't work here anymore, so, I suppose, I don't know…" William's voice trailed off listlessly.

"No, I mean now," Maria persisted. "Let me help you with…" she hesitated, searching for the right words. "Let me help you look after Frank."

William stared at Maria, as though not knowing what she was talking about, but his wife stirred. Her words were toneless. "Maria, no, Anna and Spiro need you. We're going to Trinidad. Take the train back. Frank needs to rest." Then unexpectedly her body shuddered and she let out an inhuman cry of agony that silenced everybody in the arroyo. Maria held her friend tight, as the shock wore off, to be replaced with the dreadful, crystal clear knowledge that little Frank, their innocent little boy, was gone.

The family stood up and began the walk to Ludlow. Anna's tear-blotched eyes followed Sally as she disappeared into the evening gloom, aware, though not knowing why, that she would never see her friend again. William and his family followed the railroad track, now littered with spent cartridges and upturned ammunition cases. A few hats and tunics lay abandoned, moving slightly in time to the evening breeze coming in off the foothills. They watched the troopers ransacking the tent colony, carrying lanterns from tent to tent in case they had missed anything. They heard them laughing, boasting of what they had done and how easily the miners had run. The Hoffmans smelt the burnt canvas, still imagining all too vividly that frightful moment when Frank had fallen down so suddenly that his brothers and sisters thought at first he was joking around, like he always did. William's shoulder was sticky with his son's blood, which had soaked through the thin towel covering his head. His mother kept her hand on her son's body as she walked, unwilling to let him go. Sally and the others followed behind, too tired to speak.

As the Hoffmans got closer to the depot, a group of soldiers confronted them. They waved half-empty beer and whiskey bottles at them menacingly. "Still wanna' fight us?" one of them yelled into William's face. "Fuckin' go back where you belong."

The Hoffmans stood there, bereft of all fight, of all resistance. Linderfelt came out of a nearby store and shone his flashlight over them. "Where ya' think you're goin'?" he snarled.

William finally stirred himself. "You killed my boy. We're takin' the train to Trinidad. For God's sake, if not for me, show some pity for his poor mother."

Linderfelt stood his ground, unwilling to let them move but unsure what to do with them. "No train tonight, you'll have to wait till tomorrow and not here either."

Mrs. Hoffman walked up to the militia lieutenant. "You killed my boy, an innocent little boy. What did he ever do to you? You're a coward, a filthy coward who hides behind the law. We're goin' to that depot, and if you wanna' stop us, you'll have to kill us. Though that'd be a relief after today."

His men's eyes bore into Linderfelt. He started to say something, but the woman was too much for him, and he held his tongue. Finally, quietly, he told them all to get going. "I'm a Christian, you can wait in the depot till tomorrow's train."

The miners and their families did not know what to do. They no longer had homes and they feared the militia would open fire again soon. Some of the miners who had fought with Spiro looked at him, but he was spent. The enemy had won, and so all that was left for him to do was care for Maria and Anna. He shook his head at the miners.

"I don't know. I guess we just wait and see what happens."

They saw Tikas hurrying across the prairie towards them. He stood on the arroyo lip while the remaining miners and their families clustered around. He cut a disheveled appearance. His tie was loose, and his dust-covered cheeks were smeared with tears. In a low voice, he told everybody that they needed to move east to find shelter in the Black Hills. Lawson was coming up from Trinidad, he said, listen to him. Do as he tells you. And finally, his voice cracking with emotion, he summoned his last remaining strength and yelled, "Boys, we're not done yet. Union forever." There was no response from the miners. Reluctantly at first, but then more quickly as they realized that the arroyo might not be safe, the families started the walk east.

"What's gonna' happen to you, Louis?" Spiro gently questioned his friend. He had never seen Tikas so low, never thought that such a brave man would ever cry.

"Spiro, I'm goin' back to Ludlow. Something real bad happened in one of the tents, over by the track." Spiro began to ask for more information but Tikas cut him short. "Don't tell anyone, I'll find out more, but from what I hear, and it's rumor, two women and ten kids. All dead. Look, don't tell anybody. No need worryin' them. They've had enough today. Spiro, go to your family, they need you now more than ever. I'll catch up with you."

Tikas watched the last of the families slowly wend their way to the Black Hills. He was alone, unsure what to do next. All he knew for certain was that the militia was not done; if not tonight, but certainly tomorrow, the fighting would again erupt. He needed to rest. He lay down on the slope of the arroyo and let his thoughts wander inconclusively. Should they surrender, or get a temporary cease-fire to allow the families to look after themselves? Should they take the fight to the militia tomorrow? A new day might bring new hope. At the very least, he concluded, he needed to talk to Lawson who he prayed was in Trinidad waiting for him to phone. But how could he do that, he asked himself, because the telephone line had gone up in smoke along with the headquarters tent. Tikas needed to move, get warm, find a phone, but his body ached. It felt so luxuriantly good just to stretch out and smoke a cigarette uninterrupted by anything that required him to make a decision. He lay there for ten, fifteen, thirty minutes, he was not sure, for time had blessedly ceased to exist.

He was woken up by a triumphant shout and three troopers jumped on him from the lip of the arroyo. One of them lifted him up by the scruff of the neck and punched him hard in the stomach. Another kicked him in the shoulder.

"Go tell the lieutenant who we've got. It's Louis. Louis the Greek. We've got the bastard."

While the private ran on ahead, the other two troopers frogmarched Tikas down the railroad track and threw him to the ground. He rolled over and as he raised himself to his knees, he saw Karl Linderfelt standing in front of him. Fear bit into the Greek's stomach. Behind Linderfelt were two miners, James Fyler and a young man whom he did not recognize. Fyler's face was badly bruised and there was a deep gash on his forehead. He nodded to Tikas, even tried a smile, but it was too much and he looked away as though embarrassed to find the two of them in this situation. The other miner was young, in his early twenties. His youth had allowed him to take the beating a little more easily than Fyler, but still his nose dripped blood and he had to support his right arm, which hung uselessly to his side as though it had been broken.

"Mr. Tikas," the young miner was almost crying, "I'm Rubino, Frank Rubino. Please help me." His words ripped through Tikas, but the Greek knew the fight for them at least was over. He looked at the young man and tried to say something, but he could find no words of comfort.

The soldiers pressed in on the three miners.

"Let's string the bastards up. I've got rope. Come on, let's do it," one of them cackled, and another threw a rope over the cross trees of a nearby telegraph pole.

Linderfelt told them to shut up and get back to their duties.

"Sergeant Cullen, you and your men. Take the prisoners over there." He pointed to an unlit area behind a stationary goods wagon.

Tikas had no illusions as what was going to happen to them, and the stark realization liberated him. "Linderfelt," Tikas said, straightening himself, uncowed. He stared at the lieutenant. "Kill us in cold blood like you did those women and children in the tent and I swear to God you'll never have peace on this earth again. And when you die, I'll be waiting for you. I swear to God, I'll be waiting for you. You're a coward, Linderfelt, a coward." Tikas had lost all fear. Silently, he sang songs from his homeland, and he knew now that people would speak of him down the ages, he knew now that his name would never be forgotten. From the beaten husk of the American immigrant there emerged the soul of a Cretan warrior. He was ready to die.

It was the second time in as many hours that someone had called Linderfelt a coward. He tossed his Springfield rifle around so he was holding its barrel and he swung the butt at Tikas' head. The wood cracked with the force of the blow, and Tikas went down. Blood poured out of the scalp wound and over his face, its salt burning his eyes. Dazed, he tried to stand up but slipped as his legs gave under him. He tried again to stand, the blood blurring his vision. His back was to Linderfelt. Three shots rang out, reverberating in the thin Colorado air. One hit Tikas below the shoulder blade and a second smashed into his backbone. The two bullets exploded out of the front of his body. The third round lodged in his ribs. He coughed, as though trying to clear his throat. A large gobbet of thick blood erupted out of his mouth and then the body slumped and moved no more.

Frank Rubino turned to Fyler, his eyes wide open, his face pale and drawn. Fyler took the young man's hand and whispered a prayer for both of them. A single revolver bullet hit James Fyler in the middle of his forehead. Two rifle shots blew out Frank Rubino's chest.

Linderfelt looked at Cullen and his men. "Damned foreigners, if they only hadn't tried to escape. Still they had it coming, I guess. Come on, nothing for us here."

25

A day after the destruction. Stoves and bed frames stood skeletally stark against the washed-out green of the prairie. Wisps of smoke curled up from the tents, a burnt smell clinging to everything. A few troopers walked through the camp, some trolling for undiscovered loot, but most simply looking around, in shock at what they saw. Ludlow was shunned and unhallowed ground.

Lawson scanned the remains of the camp through his field glasses, and saw the bodies of Tikas, Fyler and Rubino exactly where they had been gunned down. He had played over and over in his mind whether it could all have been averted had he taken some other course of action. Now he shook himself from his depression, realizing that this was not his doing; this was the work of the men he had fought against all his life. He walked slowly back to the Black Hills, forming his next move.

"Look at what they've done," he shouted to the gathered families. "Men and women dead, innocent children slaughtered. For what? So they could keep their profits. Look at your homes. All gone in a flash, up in smoke. But the owners will sleep pretty tonight, won't they?" A roar of approval arose. "They'll still have a roof over their heads, they'll still have fancy linen on their beds, their children won't be cold and starving." He paused. "I say it's not over yet. We've got the guns and by God, we've got the men."

Lawson wiped his brow with a red bandana, about to continue, but without further prodding, the men broke up into small bands and moved off in different directions as though each one knew where best to hit back at the companies that had done this to them. Lawson tried to stop them to find out at least where they were going, but their anger was too great, and in any event he knew he would learn their destinations soon enough. Lawson was alone except for the women, the children and a small group of wounded men.

"No, Spiro, don't be stupid, it's over for you." Maria's voice was commanding.

"Woman, it's none of your business. I'm going with them."

"Spiro, of course it's my business. Don't be stupid. I have never defied you in my life, but if you go, don't expect us to be here. I'll take Anna and you'll never see us again. I, we, cannot do this anymore."

Spiro stepped forward as though he was going to grab hold of her, but the movement brought him up short as a bolt of pain shot through his arm. It had stiffened during the night as he lay on the cold ground.

"My God, Spiro, you can't even lift it. You couldn't shoot if you wanted to." He glared at her, but she continued defiantly. "Spiro, don't you think you owe Anna something? You've done enough for the damned union."

"Papa." It was Anna. "Papa, please don't go. Please don't get killed. Please, I lost Kali, not you too. Papa, I don't want to do this anymore. Mama, I want to go away, anywhere, Mama, anywhere but here." She paused then continued, her voice quivering. "Papa, this place is bad. It's like Hell the teacher talks about in Sunday school. There's fire and people screaming. Please, Papa."

Something in his daughter's voice stopped him. It wasn't just what she said. Stupidly, he realized, he had never really given much thought to what Anna might think, the risks he'd taken for months and the danger he'd put her and Maria in.

But his pride would not let him back down completely. "I'll do as you ask. For now. But once I get my arm back, I won't sit here like a woman."

Maria spoke softly. "I've heard the bodies are still there, in the pit. Those babies and children, untended and unblessed. " She crossed herself and prayed for them. Spiro said nothing. "What do we do now, Spiro?" She slipped her arm under his as they sat on the slope of the hill.

A familiar voice answered her. "You all come with me. Now." Looking up, Maria saw Ingrid Eriksen standing not five yards away, hands placed on her hips. Anna immediately ran over and buried herself in Ingrid's pinny, hugging the woman as though she might never let go. Maria and Spiro stared at her, speechless. "And I don't want any arguments." She directed this at Spiro. "Look, Spiro, you can get your arm fixed proper. Come on, take help for once." Ingrid gently disentangled herself from Anna, walked over to Spiro and kneeling down wrapped her arm around him to help him to his feet. He did not stop her.

The four of them walked across the prairie to a small flat-bed truck. Peder was in the driver's seat, a pipe stoically wedged between his teeth. He nodded to Spiro, smiled at Anna and Maria and then stepped out of the cab to help Spiro into the back of the truck. Spiro was nervous, for he associated Peder with the company, an enemy despite his wife's friendship with Maria. But there was something about Peder's demeanor that allayed his unease and he thanked the man sincerely.

The ride back to the Eriksen's farm took enough time for Anna to eat a large slice of cake that Ingrid had brought along. She and her parents slurped down water as though it was the finest champagne.

Thirty minutes later, the five of them sat at the Eriksen's kitchen table. Maria and Spiro nursed large cups of strong coffee, while Anna devoured glass after glass of milk and slice after slice of cake. Maria asked how they had found them, and Ingrid nodded at Peder.

"He asked around, some guards told him that your people were in the Black Hills, some were over at one of the ranches, and others had just disappeared. So, we just drove around and, well, here we all are." Maria didn't know how to thank her and kept her silence. But her eyes told Ingrid everything.

"Now you're here, I'll get the stove goin'. I've got some nice stew, Anna, how does that sound?"

Anna helped Maria stir the pot as Ingrid removed the rough field dressing on Spiro's arm. Peder poured him a stiff brandy. "Down in one, Spiro, it's medicine." Spiro did as he was told, the sharp fruitiness of the liquor so different to the harsh tastelessness of the raki he remembered from all those years ago.

Ingrid washed his wound, trying her best not to break the main scab but needing to wash away the encrusted blood to see the full extent of the damage. She worked quickly and quietly, speaking only to tell Maria to serve the stew if it was hot enough. Finally, Ingrid was satisfied and reassured Spiro that no damage had been done, so far as she could tell, to the bone or muscle.

"Thanks, Ingrid, I..."

But the woman shut him off gently. "Spiro, no thanks. We're neighbors, it's what we do." Spiro nodded and turned gratefully to the hot stew Maria had placed in front of him.

Ingrid and Peder saw their three guests beginning to wilt as the stew filled their stomachs and they basked in the warmth and safety of the ranch house. Anna laid her head on her folded arms and began to snore. Spiro and Maria slumped ever lower in their chairs, trying to fight sleep.

"You're all dead beat. What am I thinking of?" Ingrid led the three of them, Anna cradled in her father's good arm, into a spare room where she had made a bed for them.

"Now I've put out some clothes for tomorrow. Anna can have one of the girls' dresses. Lord knows why I kept them all these years. And Maria, I've left you one of mine. Oh, and a nightie as well. Spiro, I'm afraid Peder's shirt and trousers might be a bit big, but it's all we've got I'm afraid. Tomorrow we'll fire up the boiler and you can all take a bath. Don't get me wrong, but I think you could all do with one." Ingrid's face creased into a sad smile.

They were too tired to speak their thanks, but Maria kissed her friend on the cheek. Almost before Ingrid was out of the room, the three of them were asleep on the bed.

It was dark when Maria awoke. Bad dreams: of guns, and

killing, of her rape, of Anna hurt and crying. She lay there in the dark, wondering if it was all over. On her left, Spiro was snoring, as he always did, but he looked restful. Anna, on Maria's other side, away from her father in case she knocked his arm, was asleep. Her sleep was troubled, too. Occasionally she would stir and mutter something incomprehensible before settling back. Maria prayed that what her little girl had seen the past forty-eight hours would not stay with her for the rest of her life. Closing her eyes, Maria fell back to a troubled sleep.

Bright sun streamed through the crack in the curtains, hitting Spiro directly in his eyes. He rolled over, cursing as his weight came down on his bandaged arm. He looked at it; no blood had seeped, a good thing. Maria and Anna still slept. They needed as much sleep as they could find, he knew, and carefully, so as not to disturb either of them, he rolled out of bed.

Leaving his boots where he had kicked them off the night before, he quickly threw on his trousers and flipped his suspenders over his shirt. He walked out into a kitchen redolent with fresh coffee and grinned sheepishly at Peder and Ingrid, both of them sitting at the table. "Guess, I needed that. What time is it?"

Peder answered. "Eleven-thirty. That must be a record in this house, even when the kids were teenagers, eh?" He tried to make a joke of it but it was forced and the three of them looked at each other uncomfortably. Ingrid pushed a cup of coffee into Spiro's hands.

Peder frowned and then spoke. "Spiro, I've got news about the strike. I don't know if you wanna' hear this just now." Spiro gave no response, so Peder continued. "Okay, there's a rumor Chase is coming down from Denver with more troops."

Spiro grimaced, though whether it was at the news or his wound, Peder wasn't sure.

"But," he looked hard at Spiro, "and this is good news, I think. There's a pretty strong rumor going around that the

President's sending federal troops in. They'll take over and Chase won't have any power at all. He'll be finished. Finally." Peder pulled on his pipe, letting the smoke settle deep into his lungs. "You know, I wasn't for the strike at first, in fact I thought you people were wrong. But, after what happened, especially to those poor women and kids in the pit, I can see why you did it." He hesitated. "I just thought you should know that, Spiro." The miner nodded back and smiled briefly, and then both turned their heads away, as though embarrassed.

That evening, although the April air was already chilly, Spiro and Maria sat outside on the porch. Anna was inside, helping Ingrid clean up after dinner. So far, Maria was encouraged by her daughter, who seemed not to be outwardly upset by what had happened. The couple talked about what they should do next. Spiro said that he wanted to stick around, not to help out with the fighting because he knew his wound needed time to heal, but because he believed the union would still win, and they could all move back to Berwind and to a better life.

"Spiro, it sounds good, but you know it'll never work for us here. Too many bad memories for Anna, for me as well. Think of what happened to our friends, to little Frank. And to you, too." Tears began to well up, and she wiped them away with her blouse. "And Spiro, God knows, you're not getting younger. First your knee and now the arm, how long do you think you could stay down the mines anyway?"

Spiro did not answer, just looked away across the darkening prairie. Maria pressed home her argument. "I don't think the union'll win. And even if it does, do you think the companies will let you back? They know you're one of the leaders. You're, what's the word you use, blacklisted. Yes?"

"So what do we do, Maria? You know this was the first real job I had, even if it was lousy. What did I do before? In New York, I dug railroad tunnels. Then I worked the docks. We were hungry all the time, Maria. It was no better than Crete. At least there we were with our own."

"Even if we wanted to, we couldn't get back to Crete. We've got no money. Anyway, Spiro, we all left Crete because we had to. It's no better there now, you know that, surely?" She cradled her husband's cheek in her palms. "Spiro, we've lost everything, everything. Did you see our tent? Totally destroyed. And everything in it. We've got to stay in America. We have no choice. Just not here, okay. You do see that, don't you?"

"I know, wife, it's just that I feel like I'm runnin' away." Spiro paused, his brows furrowed, as though trying to form the right words. "Maria, Anna was right. You know, what she said yesterday. I guess we go someplace else. You remember my talk with Anna ages ago, on our porch. I told her we'd take her to California. Well, I guess that's what we'll have to do. We'll just have to figure a way to get the money. And I guess my pride will just have to get over it." He smiled then at his wife, and she kissed him gently on the mouth. Spiro took Maria into his arms. "I've been no good for you and Anna. But I promise I'll make it right."

Maria felt his tears on her cheeks, tasted their saltiness as she kissed him again, this time more passionately. "Don't say a word, my love. You're a good man. We're together, we're alive and we have little Anna. Our life can be good again, I promise."

The two of them held each other tight as the Colorado night swallowed their shadows.

Lou Dold drove his car through the gates at Ludlow, swarming with Red Cross volunteers, sheriffs' deputies and a few miners and their families trying to salvage what they could. He pointed to burnt-out tents by the gate.

"That's where they found the bodies, Jimmy. They were all suffocated. Only two of them got out. One of the women was just wandering around that field over there. The youngest was only three months old, Jimmy, a little girl. What the hell did she do to anyone?"

They stopped outside the burnt-out shell of the headquarters tent. A middle-aged woman with a large red cross on her sleeve looked to be in charge. Dold told her who they were, what they wanted to do.

"I guess there's no harm, everybody knows what happened." She went back to studying what appeared to be a long list, though of what Dold could not make out.

"Jimmy, grab the equipment. Let's walk about a bit, see what's what."

Jimmy Dingle surveyed the devastation. "Mr. D., I know it was burnt down, it's all over Trinidad, but I didn't think everything had gone. I mean isn't that where the Andrakises' tent was. You remember, don't you, the kid with the dog that got killed." Dold saw tears glistening in the boy's eyes. "Look at it. There's nothing left, just the bedstead and the stove. They were nice people, I liked the little girl, she was real keen to help me."

"I think she had a thing for you, Jimmy." Dold tried to smile but it was too difficult.

"Where was the Greek killed?" Like all young men, Jimmy had a macabre fascination with the dead, but nevertheless he was glad when his boss pointed out where the bodies had been found and he could see nothing.

"They moved them yesterday, Jimmy. Last night. That's three days they were left lying there. Jimmy, we're just gonna' tell the truth with these pictures, okay? I mean, no poses or anything like that. Just take the photos."

Jimmy agreed. "It wouldn't seem right to do nothing else, would it, Mr. D.?" Almost as an afterthought, Jimmy turned to Lou. "If my dad had to let you bring me here, does that mean it's not safe?" Jimmy looked around, as though half-expecting the firing to start up again.

"Well, I did ask his permission, but we're okay, Jimmy. He just didn't want you to see anything…" he struggled for the right word, "anything unsettling. Anyway, the Red Cross is here, so it must be okay. Did you know the union and the troops have made a truce, and President Wilson's sending in troops to keep the peace? We're okay, Jimmy," Lou repeated to assure the young man.

As they walked through the field, Dold continued. "Jimmy, from what I can gather, after the massacre, there were hundreds of miners who went crazy. They attacked company guards and at one mine, not sure where, they trapped forty company men and their families. There was even a rumor that they'd blown them up. And, Jimmy, remember that woman, Mother Jones, you know the one Chase locked up, well, she's back in Denver and she's got huge crowds picketing the state capitol. It's all crazy, Jimmy, all crazy."

But the words washed over Jimmy as he looked around him. Here in Ludlow, it seemed so serenely sad that a peace had settled over the place. For here, at least, the struggle was over.

The two of them walked through the burnt tents, stepping over broken furniture and smashed crockery, suitcases and boxes ripped open by the looters. Jimmy tried to imagine what it must have been like, bullets flying, women and children screaming and the crackling of the dry canvas as the tents went up in smoke. He thought of that little girl, Anna, what she must have been thinking, how scared she must have been, what a terrible hand life had dealt her.

Jimmy's thoughts were interrupted. "We're here, Jimmy." Dold pointed to a large hole under a burnt out tent.

"Is this it, Mr. Dold?" Jimmy was reluctant to go any further.

The older man nodded. "They took the bodies away. There's nothing to be afraid of."

At that moment, a militia man popped his head out of the pit, startling both Jimmy and Lou. Even Dold laughed uneasily. Jimmy didn't like that black hole, with the stench of burning. He thought he could even smell dead bodies. Dold asked the trooper to hold his arm up and touch the roof of the pit while he took a photograph. Jimmy said, "I didn't think it was so big, Mr. D. How many died there again?"

"Ten kids, two women. Come on, let's go. I need a drink. So do you. And, Jim, don't you think it's time you called me Lou?"

"Anything you say, Mr…Lou."

"Mr. Rockefeller, it could have been a lot worse." Bowers had been summoned back to New York and sat uncomfortably across the table from John Rockefeller Junior. The silent presence of Senior, in an arm chair by the unlit fireplace, only made his trepidation more acute.

"But still, women and children were killed, Mr. Bowers. It did not have to end like this."

"I know, sir, but as we always maintained from the start of this conflict, there was always the risk that the union hotheads would explode, and that's exactly what they did." Bowers was concerned, and a little irritated, that the Rockefellers seemed to be holding him responsible. He did not bring up Senior's insistence all through the strike that the profits keep flowing and the union should be broken. He had done both of these things, but apparently it was not enough.

The younger Rockefeller threw down a wad of newspapers. "Look at the headlines. All of them blaming us for what happened. You would think we personally had pulled the triggers and set the tents on fire."

The room was silent except for the clock ticking away in the corner.

"Sir," Bowers finally spoke. "It was not our fault. There were two sides with guns on that field, the miners and the National Guard. The Court of Inquiry will determine who was at fault, and I am quite confident that the forces of law and order will be completely exonerated. Yes, it is tragic that women and children died, but, sir, we did not start this conflict. The union did, and they must bear the shame for what transpired."

"I am sure you are right," Rockefeller Sr. said. Bowers breathed a little more easily. "I suppose this whole mess has left us all feeling a little, shall we say, vulnerable. And as you say, the Court of Inquiry will decide who was at fault, and in all conscience I cannot say any blame can be laid at our feet. But still." Senior's voice was quiet but forceful. "There is the little matter of those newspapers. Both of you know as well as I do that bad publicity, even when it is unfair, can kill an enterprise as quickly as poor management or shoddy products. Gentlemen, I think this is our real problem. Any ideas?"

Bowers shook his head, but Junior nodded vigorously.

"As it so happens, Father, I have an idea. And it stems from our philanthropic work. I have been working with a number of young men in advertising who think that our work with charities can be used to offset the negative publicity from the strike. They say it will not happen overnight, but it can be done. I think we should do this. By the way, they call themselves public relations experts. It's a new term but rather apt, wouldn't you say?"

Senior snorted but said nothing.

Bowers decided it was time to leave but he could hardly do so without permission. "Gentlemen, I intend to head back to Colorado as soon as I can. It is important that we bring the coalfields to full capacity as quickly as possible. Welborn and the others are already hiring new workers, none of them known to be strikers, and he estimates that we should achieve full capacity in two weeks. So, all in all, I think that the unrest will in the long run cost the company very little. In fact, now that the union is broken I do not see why our profits should not increase dramatically. And what time does not quickly erase of current public perceptions, I have every confidence that Mr. Rockefeller's public relations strategy will."

As if in response to Bowers' prompting, the junior Rockefeller wished him a pleasant and safe journey westward. "And do please give our regards to your wife."

Bowers smiled courteously and left the two men, confident that he still had their trust and that the crisis had been settled completely and irrevocably in their favor.

On the 27th April, seven days after the massacre and two days after the other victims had been laid to rest, the union buried Louis Tikas. Spiro and three other Greeks, armed with Winchester rifles they had sneaked into the funeral parlor the night before, guarded his casket. The union had paid for a priest to come down from Denver, and now the five men offered prayers that Tikas' soul, and theirs, might find mercy. *At last,* Spiro thought, *Louis looked at peace, his face smooth and untroubled.*

The priest began Psalm 119, and the words "Blessed are those whose way is blameless, who walk in the law of the Lord," rang in Spiro's ears. He was no longer in Colorado; he was on Crete, listening to the village priest incant over his grandfather's body.

As the service drew to its close, the priest anointed the corpse with earth and oil: "The earth is the Lord's, and the fullness thereof; the world and all that dwell in it. You are dust and to dust you shall return."

Tears rolled down Spiro's cheeks. All the deaths, the destruction of everything he and the other families had owned. *For what,* he asked himself. *For nothing. I have failed.* The ache in his wounded arm was nothing to that in his heart as he tried to find some crumb of comfort in what he had put his family through.

Spiro walked out into the drab April day expecting to see Anna and Maria waiting for him, but he could not see where they were, for standing in the street were thousands of men, women and children, of all nationalities.

Tikas' countrymen fell into two lines behind the funeral bier, the black plumes on the horses' bridles fluttering in the breeze. The cortege moved off, and the crowd followed, all silent save for the shuffling of their feet and the clopping of hooves. The procession made its way down Main Street towards the cemetery on the outskirts of the town. Men and women on the streets stopped what they were doing; men doffed their caps.

At the cemetery Spiro finally spotted Maria and Anna and he joined them, melting into the crowd as if he craved once more the anonymity that the last seven months had denied him. Maria placed her arm around her husband for she had seen the tear-stained cheeks. Anna said nothing, just held tight to her mother and father as the priest stood over the coffin and asked that all the earthly sins of Ilias Spantidakis be forgiven and that his soul be granted eternal rest. The three of them stood together as they watched the casket lowered into the ground. Together with the other mourners, they chanted "May your memory be eternal."

Outside the cemetery Peder and Ingrid waited for them. "Time to go," Peder gently spoke, and the five friends climbed into the Eriksens' automobile. The drive to the rail station was mercifully brief, for all of them, even Peder, were dreading this moment.

"Peder," Spiro said, looking at the Norwegian. "I thank you with all my heart for what you have done for us. Not just the money to get us to Denver but for…"

Peder brusquely told him not to worry and turned away in case Spiro saw his tears.

The train's whistle sounded, and the porter yelled "All aboard." Ingrid, Maria and Anna hugged one final time, all three sobbing uncontrollably. They let go of each other, and handing Maria a large packet of food for the journey, Ingrid hurried away, Peder holding her tightly as her body convulsed with sadness.

The three of them settled into the hard bench seats, and the train pulled away from Trinidad. Spiro prayed they would never see that town again, prayed he would never have to work a coalmine again, and prayed above all things that Anna, their little gift from God, would never again know the misery he had put her through.

Anna, her nose pressed against the window was excited to be on a train, off to their new adventure in California, with her beloved mama and papa. They were safe and they were together. But as the train pulled its way slowly across the prairies, sadness engulfed her. She saw one last time the canyon where her Kali had died, she saw one last time the field at Ludlow where she had lived in a tent and played with Sally, and she saw one last time the well where she and her mama had sheltered while the bad men fired guns at them. She turned from the window to see her mother and father staring blankly at the remains of the tents.

"Mama, Papa, let's go home. I don't know where it is, just let's go home." The little girl snuggled into her parents and the gentle rocking of the train lulled her to sleep.

Epilogue

Riverdale, California

Six months after her trip to the Ludlow Memorial, Anna Papadopoulos passed away. In accordance with her wishes, she was buried in the Greek Orthodox Cemetery in Riverdale, California, next to her beloved husband of forty-two years, Dimitri.

Two weeks after the funeral, Nik, their son, visited the lawyers to clear the will. Besides the normal residue of a full life, the stocks, the bonds and savings accounts that had to be transferred into his name, there was at the bottom of all the legal papers, as Anna had promised her granddaughter, a nondescript cardboard box, the sort that holds typing paper. The box was sealed with scotch tape and on its lid was attached an envelope with the name "Maria Papadopoulos."

Nik took it home and waited until Maria arrived from school. He gave her the package. Maria removed the envelope and carefully opened the box. It contained a handwritten manuscript, written with a fountain pen. The handwriting was so familiar. How many times had she seen that beautiful old-fashioned script on birthday cards, Christmas cards, name day cards? She turned to the first full page of writing.

It began, "The shotgun blasts rolled through the valley. The men lowered their guns and looked at each other expectantly. In the distance they heard the chapel bell toll midnight, and then all the villagers in unison shouted *"Christos Anesti"*, Christ is Risen. *"Alithos Anesti,"* Truly He is Risen."

She opened the envelope and removed the letter inside. Again, she marveled at the beautiful handwriting. Maria read her grandmother's final words to her, and the tears welled up. The young girl burrowed into her father, and at last, after she had no more tears to shed, she looked up at her father and read the letter out to him.

My darling granddaughter, Maria:

My early life was hard as you surely know. But it all changed when I met Granpa, the light of my life. And then the Good Lord gave me your father, a son to be proud of.

But nothing has matched the blessedness of you, my dear child. From the first moment I saw those beautiful brown eyes, so like my mother's, I knew that God had given all of us a special priceless gift. You have grown into a beautiful young woman, and I am sorry that I can now see you only from Heaven. But rest assured that Granpa and I will watch over you for the rest of your life.

Maria, remember our visit to Ludlow and how I told you what happened? Well, this is the story of what I went through.

For years I was angry at what they did to me and my family and all those other innocent souls. I wanted to hurt people like they'd hurt me. But as I grew older, I realized that it wouldn't change anything, and it would just poison me, and that would be one more soul they had destroyed.

I will never forget what they did, and I hope you, my darling granddaughter, will not either. But I have found forgiveness in my heart, and that perhaps is the best revenge.

Maria, our precious Gift from God, walk safely through life under His all-embracing love.

Your loving Grandma

Author's Note

I have tried to be as historically accurate as possible, but for the sake of the narrative I have invented many episodes and conflated real with fictional characters. I also altered the sequence of events when I thought it necessary. To paraphrase Zoe Oldenbourg (*Heirs to the Kingdom*, 1971), even if it is not history, I am reasonably sure that what I have written is pretty close to the truth.

A few words about dialog. I have not attempted to represent how the miners at Ludlow would have spoken. For most of the miners, English was their second language, and rather than risk stereotyping their particular patterns of speech I decided to write their words in modern English. I would rather be accused of being inaccurate than condescending…or worse.

A grammarian will also note that I have simplified the case endings for Greek masculine proper nouns like Spiro so that the nominative has the same ending as the vocative and accusative.

For ten days after the massacre there was virtual civil war as John Lawson launched guerilla-style attacks against company guards and mine property. The tide of public opinion rapidly turned against the companies and the state government. Some militia units ignored orders to move south and railroad crews refused to carry troops. By April 30th the situation had become so dire that Governor Ammons was forced to appeal to President Wilson for federal troops. It was their presence alone that brought the violence to an end.

As word of the massacre spread Pearl Jolly, Mary Petrucci and Mary Thomas toured the country (they even met with the president), and donations poured into the union. But they were not enough, and by December the union was bankrupt and was forced to end the strike that same month. Some strikers and their families stayed at Ludlow until early 1915 and others were rehired, but many miners were blacklisted and either stayed unemployed or moved out of the state.

Over four hundred miners were indicted on various charges. Of these, 332, including John Lawson, were indicted for murder. The legal proceedings lasted until 1920 but most of the cases never came to trial and the others were eventually dismissed at the urging of the Rockefellers who wanted an end to the bad publicity. No company man was brought to trial. Ten militia officers and fifteen enlisted men were court-martialed but none of them was convicted of any offense. Lieutenant Karl Linderfelt was found guilty of assaulting Louis Tikas, but not of his murder. Although the Colorado National Guard was completely discredited, General John Chase managed to retain his command until he was forced to resign in 1916.

The US Commission on Industrial Relations initiated hearings on the strike at the end of 1914. Led by its anti-Rockefeller chairman, Francis Walsh, the commission succeeded in vilifying the Rockefellers. At the hearings Walsh angrily confronted John D. Rockefeller Jr. with a photograph of the body of Frank Snyder (the fictional Frank Hoffman) laid out in the undertaker's office, the back of the boy's head horribly distorted. In response to the horrible publicity, the Rockefellers established a public relations office (the first in the world) to rehabilitate itself in the eyes of the American public and also initiated reforms in the coalfields such as improved working conditions and the formation of a company union.

Mother Jones met Rockefeller Jr. in New York and persuaded him to tour his coalfields (she continued her union activism through the 1920s, passing away in 1930.) But strikes and sporadic violence continued in the coalfields for many more years, and it was only the New Deal reforms of the 1930s that brought some degree of harmony.

On a personal note, my wife's paternal grandfather, Charles Edward Gudger, was killed in the Twin Branch Mine, West

Virginia in 1928. The mine was owned by Henry Ford who threatened closure if the miners joined the union. Mr. Gudger's widow, Rosie, was paid a monthly pension of thirty dollars on which she raised six children.

In 1918 the UMWA bought the forty-acre site at Ludlow and erected a stone memorial that still stands. Mike Livoda is buried in the memorial compound, his headstone just inside the north fence. The coalminers of southern Colorado remained in the UMWA until the last mine closed in 1996. Local 9856 in Trinidad is still active and every year it organizes a commemoration of the Ludlow Massacre. Ludlow is sacred ground, a testimony to the continuing struggle for human rights and workplace dignity. And still today mines throughout the world, whether it is coal or other minerals that are sought, are places where profit regularly trumps the safety of the men who work them.

The Greeks at Ludlow had left their homeland because of one of those quirks of fate that can turn a man's world on its head. A fungus had attacked the vines in France and, to compensate, traders turned to Greece to the extent that a very large proportion of the Greek economy depended on grape production. But when the French industry recovered, Greek produce was no longer needed and the country fell into a massive economic depression. Tikas, Spiro and Maria were just three of the thousands of Greeks who were forced to emigrate.

Tikas's village is still pretty much as it was when he left all those years ago. Sitting on the porch of his house where his father served coffee was one of the most moving and poignant experiences of my life.

The fictional Andrakis family quickly took on a life of its own and often I found myself writing simply to find out what was going to happen to them. Maria, Spiro and little Anna became my very dear friends, and it is comforting to drive through Spiro's and Maria's villages and know that after all their travails the three of them, as Anna had hoped, finally came safely home.

Recommended Reading

The first two books are indispensable for anybody interested in the Colorado Coalfield War.

The Great Coalfield War. George S. McGovern and Leonard F. Guttridge. The definitive account of the events leading up to Ludlow and its aftermath. Scholarly but highly readable.

Buried Unsung. Louis Tikas and the Ludlow Massacre. Zeese Papanikolas. A beautifully lyrical account of Louis Tikas and his part in the coalfield wars, written by a master storyteller.

Legacy of the Ludlow Massacre. A Chapter in American Industrial Relations. Howard M. Gitelman. An incisive analysis of the massacre and its impact on the course of American industrial relations.

The Archaeology of Class War. The Colorado Coalfield Strike of 1913-1914. Edited by Karin Larkin and Randall H. McGuire. The comprehensive synopsis of the archaeological excavations conducted at Ludlow and Berwind by the "Ludlow Collective."

The Archaeology of Collective Action. Dean J. Saitta. An evaluation of the archaeological investigations at Ludlow seen through the prism of how archaeology can affect our understanding of our present.

Acknowledgments

The Western Crete Writers Group, founded by Bob Zablok, encouraged me as I entered the thicket of writing a novel. I am grateful to Marie and Brian Smith, Heather Morison and Cheryl Romanek, all of whom looked at various drafts and offered improvements that I willingly accepted. Special gratitude is owed to Murray Morison who was always willing to carefully critique anything I sent to him. I am honored to call Murray a colleague but I am even more honored to call him my friend.

Brady Vredenburg edited the first complete draft of the novel and with his keen eye considerably tightened up syntax, dialog and "flow." He also patiently answered questions about writing that only a first-time novelist asks. My son, Adam assured me I was on the right track and also checked my medical facts.

I was a member of the "Ludlow Collective" that excavated the archaeological sites of Ludlow and Berwind. The project was inspirational for all involved as we realized the potential that archaeology has for revealing truths about the past that are often overlooked. In particular I would like to recognize with grateful thanks my principal colleagues in the collective: Dean Saitta, Randy McGuire, Mark Walker, Paul Reckner and Margaret Wood.

Thanks to Anesti Stais, Angeliki Soumala and Nick Mavrotheris for advising me on the minutiae of Cretan culture, and to Zeese Papanikolas whose book on Louis Tikas inspired me and who gently corrected some of my more egregious wanderings from historical reality.

I extend my thanks to Autumn Barlow and the rest of the staff at John Hunt Publishing. Balsam Wood drew the map of southern Colorado. Thank you. Thanks also to the Denver Public Library for permission to reproduce one of their historic photographs.

Finally, Donna, my wife. How she has put up with me as I wrote academic books and articles and then a historical novel is beyond me. But she does, I am delighted to say. She sustained me whenever I thought of giving up, either chiding me or encouraging me as necessary. This book is as much hers as mine.

TOP HAT BOOKS

Historical fiction that lives.

We publish fiction that captures the contrasts, the achievements, the optimism and the radicalism of ordinary and extraordinary times across the world.

We're open to all time periods and we strive to go beyond the narrow, foggy slums of Victorian London. Where are the tales of the people of fifteenth century Australasia? The stories of eighth century India? The voices from Africa, Arabia, cities and forests, deserts and towns? Our books thrill, excite, delight and inspire.

The genres will be broad but clear. Whether we're publishing romance, thrillers, crime, or something else entirely, the unifying themes are timescale and enthusiasm. These books will be a celebration of the chaotic power of the human spirit in difficult times. The reader, when they finish, will snap the book closed with a satisfied smile.